AF251885

PLEDGED

Louise Grace White

www.louisewhitebooks.com

Copyright © 2015 by Louise G White.

All rights reserved. No part of this publication may be reproduced, distributed or transmitted in any form or by any means, including photo copying, recording, or other electronic or mechanical methods, without the prior written permission of the publisher, except in the case of brief quotations embodied in critical reviews and certain other noncommer- cial uses permitted by copyright law. For permission requests, address to the publisher on the contacts page at the address below.

www.louisewhitebooks.com

Publisher's Note: This is a work of fiction. Names, characters, places, and incidents are a product of the author's imagination. Locales and public names are sometimes used for atmospheric purposes. Any resemblance to actual people, living or dead, or to businesses, companies, events, institutions, or locales is completely coincidental.
Pledged/ Louise G White. -- 1st ed. ISBN :
0993081767
ISBN-13: 978-0-9930817-6-7

For my wonderful sisters
Karen
Lorna
& Deborah

ALSO BY LOUISE G. WHITE

THE GATEWAY SERIES

THE CALLING (BOOK 1)

CHASING THE DEMON (BOOK 2)

PROLOGUE

"Close your eyes, Note. I'm only going to observe while you check on each member of the team." Until now, the Kistatus had been practising his new power with a mix of excitement and trepidation. He always felt a little foolish when he worked with Sean. The high mage was ancient, with a set of skills and experiences that would put any magic user to shame.

Raised on another realm under the constraints of his father, Hecaton, Note was used to dealing with powerful individuals. Despite their ages, the high magic users maintained the appearance of youth. There, though, the similarity ended. Whilst Sean worked for Earth's Protectorate, a benevolent and sacred organisation, Hecaton's position, High Mage of Skean, led him to wield his control over Note's people with brutal abandon.

The young Kistatus felt ill equipped to deal with the power that his father had painfully forced upon him during their last encounter. The reasons behind the action were as yet unclear but Note had used the extra clout to strike during a period of Hecaton's weakness. In a moment of recklessness –Morgan referred to it as genius – Note had brought his chief's stolen mate, Amanda, and their two children through the gateways and returned them to Earth.

Currently installed in a secure Protectorate facility, Amanda suffered the long process of withdrawal from her chief. Note's actions had not exactly been borne from the need to rescue the woman as much as for the bargaining chip she represented. Note's own mate, Carolyn – and he *still* chose to think of her as such – happened to be Amanda's daughter, cursed with the same breeder traits and so valuable to the demon realms. Chiefs and high mages would procure such individuals by any means, even stealing them from other lands and from their current mates, as had occurred on a number of occasions with Amanda.

When Carolyn's mother and older brother, Edward, had been taken by Hecaton to the Skean realm, it had left Carolyn on Earth with a mission to restore her family. The process led to her becoming a destroyer, a mythical gateway-chosen being who travelled the portals, rescuing humans and killing demons without the complications of higher thinking or being hindered by mercy.

As was typical for "un*anchored*" destroyers – there were less than a handful throughout the world – she had been mentally unhinged until quite unexpectedly anchoring to Note. That was the point when Note considered his life to have truly begun.

It had been a long and frustrating year as, shortly after their anchoring and subsequent *claiming* – his breath caught at the memory – Carolyn had been lost on a mission to the Lilim realm, along with Sean's apprentice, Mario. As she was altered and reconditioned to suit the chief's whim, Mario had been ground down and beaten into submission. Somehow the pair had come together and established a truce of sorts with the chief.

Carolyn was due to remain on Empustat for a total of twenty-one days, after which she could return to Earth, *if she chose*. That was where Note struggled, and hence his decision to recapture Carolyn's mother.

Note's new talents meant he could access the members of the Protectorate team with relative ease. Mario and Ethan were currently inaccessible on the blocked realm of Empustat with Carolyn. Using high magic, Note had got through to her on occasion and Hecaton had – so kindly – reactivated their *claiming bond*. Shortly thereafter, the connection had been shut down on Carolyn's side. The frustration and anger abated somewhat and Note learned to be grateful for the small mercy he'd had.

The Protectorate had let him off lightly for his unofficial rescue of Amanda and he had sworn to keep the information from Carolyn until the end of the twenty one days grace. After that, further measures would be sanctioned. It wasn't nearly good enough.

Note closed his eyes and thought first of the most challenging members of the team to locate: Mow, Jonah and Rak – all recruited from demon realms, as he had been. The Mow and Rakshasas had been renamed in accordance with Protectorate rules against naming by race. Rak was amended to Rake, by virtue of the fact he looked nothing like one and that he simply wouldn't answer to any of the other names they'd tried. Mow had become Mace due to his charmingly lethal ability to spit acid at opponents.

Note's own abilities were equally charming, with a bite that could injure, kill or *claim*. The team definitely pushed the boundaries with the demons' naming but Note had yet to hear of their displeasure. Having been raised by the Agency, Jonah was one of two hybrids created in their labs and now lived under Protectorate care. His unique talents proved invaluable, allowing access to be gained to Empustat. Ordinarily, travelling through a tear rather than by means of a proper gateway would slice up any being who tried to enter that way.

Note's mind brushed against Morgan's, a delightful sensation of blessed liquid warmth, languor and–

Hey! She scolded through the link just as Note realised he'd disturbed her bath.

Sorry – it's practise. She threw a virtual sponge at his back as he retreated with a grimace. Consequently, his form thrummed with the urge to find a body of water – *any* body of water – and indulge the joys of his reptilian, fully Kistatus self. Both he and Carolyn shared a love of water. He wondered if she had a list similar to his, and whether hers incorporated less selfish items than his current fantasy of their swimming the Scottish lochs together.

Note opened one eye to find Sean watching him and so set his thoughts of Carolyn carefully aside. He could recommence this self-torture later. "Bet Morgan wouldn't have agreed to this if she'd known the threat to her privacy."

"Wrong," said Sean evenly, a half smile softening his stern features for a moment. "She likes it. They all do."

Note doubted *that* but moved swiftly on his mental journey to find Sam in a city supermarket, choosing vegetables to put in his trolley.

Oh, hello there, Note. Thankfully, the older caretaker hadn't spoken aloud. Sometimes, much to his embarrassment, he did exactly that when Note contacted him in a public place. Note's Kistatus heart warmed with the exchange. He felt an odd mix of protective sorrow about the enforcer who had lost part of his mind during a Lilim attack almost twenty years before. *You're getting good at this*, Sam was saying. *What do you think about haggis tonight?*

Note quickly shielded his true feelings, which was not as easy as it seemed. *Sounds fine to me. Remember to pick up the veggie variety for Morgan and Sean.* Neither enforcer was vegetarian, but they preferred it to the real deal. It was a small concession to allow Sam his haggis.

No worries, I'll get it at the deli. Note noticed two giant cartons of eggs in Sam's trolley and the former enforcer chuckled through the link. *Do you think I'd forget about your snack food, boy? Eggs for you, chocolate for Jonah and Ethan's…* Sam's thoughts had clearly clouded. Note knew it was a familiar frustration for Sam, that he'd now be wondering why he couldn't keep up with the present?

Hey, it's fine, Sam. He'll be back soon, assured Note, *and he's going to be glad you thought of him.*

Sam's frustration appeared to diminish. *That's right, Lad. I'll see you back at the flat.*

"Mmm, haggis night," came Sean's wry assessment.

Note didn't bother opening his eyes again, hoping his tone would be convincing. "No, you're not going to find some urgent job to keep you safe from dinner, Sean. You said the vegetarian stuff was fine."

"It's the smell of it I dislike, I don't need to–" The Englishman expelled a long suffering sigh. "I had a moment of weakness when I thought to protect his feelings and have been paying for it ever since. You should remember that, Note. No good deed goes unpunished."

"Preaching to the converted."

"Quite. Now, where were we?"

Jonah's face formed in Note's mind. Neither Jonah nor Rake had bonded to the team as fully as the others but the Rakshasas was much more open to these exercises.

Focus. Sean was right, thought Note as he fought the easy slide into

Mace's mind and concentrated fully on Jonah. In particular, he envisioned the wide Faery eyes, slightly narrowed – as they tended to be whilst viewing the Kistatus. *Just a little push*, guided Sean. *They're in a more secure location.* That made sense. Note clenched his teeth and gave the required mental shove.

A feeling of glee and superiority – Jonah's – filled him as he trained with Mace in the basement of a Protectorate safe house. The emotions fled to be replaced by a measure of resentment, and Note, having accomplished his goal, acknowledged the hybrid before dipping into the Mow's consciousness.

The basement had been kept deliberately dark for the enforcers' exercises. Jonah's black leathery wings erupted from his back and he dived over the larger demon to land behind him. Mace was quick to spin and make a grab for Jonah, but not fast enough. He hadn't activated his restraint charm in time, and so watched in frustration as the hybrid dissolved in his grasp, shadowy particles streaming around the Mow to appear whole again, off to one side.

Sorry, I put you off. In the background Note heard Sean comment about the importance of attention during training scenarios. Not helpful. The big guy was working up a serious sweat with his efforts.

I wish that was it, returned Mace miserably – and hopefully ignorant of Sean's input – *I just can't seem to coordinate a grab and restraint for this slippery little devil.*

Protectorate enforcers trained hard to gain expertise in as many methods of combat as they could handle. Mace's acid spit would certainly deal with Jonah's attack but it was wise to develop skills other than the predictable.

I'd better be going. You'll get it, assured Note. *Remember, you've got the most challenging partner ever. If you manage a restraint with Jonah, then no-one else should be a problem.*

Yeah, we'll see, Note. Best of luck with your own training. He could feel Mace's humour through the link, as much as to say Note had got the raw deal.

Want to swap?

Mace chuckled and Note had his answer when the big demon turned to beckon forward the haughtily posed Faery.

Mel next, and he found her effortlessly. With Rake beside her, she was watching the latest Disney movie, humming softly to the music. *Jonah's going to be upset you're watching this without him.* It was no secret that the *otherworlders* loved watching television, with a special emphasis on animation and fantasy. Rake nodded to Mel, recognising the visitor. Mel's eyes flashed Kistatus gold for an instant and the former Rakshasas soldier smiled at the trick. She was quick to tease Note.

Hey, hot boy. Who said you could use me to show off.

You *did.*

I did, didn't I? Her good humour sparkled through their link.

And you need to stop calling me that.

But it's true, sweet Notechis – kiss, kiss. You are a very hot *boy.* Rake rolled his eyes, as though knowing Note would be receiving an unfiltered earful from the outgoing mage. Note recognised she was hyped up on caffeine, sugar or … or something. Was he being too harsh? She deserved to enjoy her down time. The sing song mental voice continued to chime with a slightly edited, *Don't'cha wish your girlfriend was* hot *like me—*

You're giving me a headache. As he left her to return to the film, he couldn't help the unwilling grin that lifted the corners of his mouth. His eyelashes fluttered open, and he returned to the room with Sean. The dark mage was back-lit by the glow from the hallway, giving an impression of menace that no longer existed where Note was concerned.

"You shouldn't encourage her."

"That *was* me not encouraging her."

It was Sean's reasoning that the powers that be had given the team a great gift, one they had a duty to explore. Mel simply liked to push the boundaries as much as possible. Magic users could share each other's thoughts in a variety of ways, generally physical contact being required, but their Powers sanctioned link needed so little effort that Note had to agree with Sean.

Note's first session with him had revealed the enormity of the price the powerful mage had paid for supporting the demon. Though the team was strengthened, Sean had weakened. The mage was still wreathed in light and dark magic, but where relative stillness prevailed before, the energy now churned and danced to Sean's awakened emotions. He suffered from the obligation he'd made to the Kistatus, and Note repaid in the only way he could.

He stood in front of the mage and gave a long blink. After his brush with Hecaton, Note had gained the icy blue of his father's eyes: a visible indication of the power he could hold in his human form. Whilst useful for blending in with humans, the new colour freaked him out a little, and he preferred, where possible, to return to the luminous gold of his native race.

Bright eyed, he stretched his arms out and Sean placed his cool hands in Note's. *Rather embarrassing if the others were to walk in on us now.* Note smiled thinly. Sean couldn't hide his discomfort well enough to trick him. The mage disliked being in a position of comparative weakness and *having* to take power from Note, but both knew that their new arrangement benefited from it.

The transfer itself would last only minutes, but it was always intense. Sean was adept at concealing most of his thoughts and emotions but occasionally something would leak through. Disturbingly, the last time had showed Note a candlelit mausoleum and a raven haired beauty – Note had not asked.

The familiar rise of white hot energy spiralled to the surface within him. Sean's hands warmed for an instant before resuming their corpse like chill, and there was an uncomfortable moment as Note pressed his magic towards his friend. It reared back, repelled by the foreign magic user and Note grimaced.

If any of the powerful mages were repellent, it was Hecaton, the mage who had brought them to this point. Even as Note tried to deny the magic, he felt the sting of its betrayal as Sean communicated with the power, coaxing and bending it somehow to change shape. Note realised in that moment that Sean was not only removing Hecaton's stain – his signature – from it, but Note's as well. When had *that* happened?

I give this freely.

Sean acknowledged the alteration of their energy sharing and continued to prepare the surplus whilst it was still attached to Note. The Kistatus exhaled as the power shift occurred, the excess magic no longer recognising him and the balance reorganised to Sean's advantage. Note welcomed the equalisation of the energy diffusing smoothly away from him.

Ah, much better, they agreed in unison.

Note felt the need to explain. "I'm sorry, Sean. I don't understand what's changed, but that's become more difficult."

The older mage frowned. "I know. Your father's power is not being recognised as foreign to *you* anymore."

"It's becoming a part of me."

"I'm afraid so." The mage looked well, his dark eyes gleaming. He was energised as expected, but his expression showed concern.

"But, I don't want it."

"Sometimes the magic chooses you, my boy, and there is nothing you can do … other than safely share whilst it's possible." Note heard the uncertainty. The magic was changing? What would happen if Sean could no longer siphon the excess? "You will grow to accommodate it," the mage continued, as if Note had spoken his fears aloud.

"Would you become cold again if given the choice?" Sean's midnight eyes held secrets that the Kistatus had no desire to learn, but in that unguarded moment, his response rang true.

"I mustn't mourn what I willingly relinquish."

The mage retrieved his duster length jacket from behind the door. As he slipped it on, it billowed slightly with the breeze that always seemed to accompany his presence.

You've lost weight. Sean looked surprised and annoyed, whether by the observation or the continued link, Note couldn't be sure.

He didn't think Sean meant him to hear his aggrieved response, but Note nearly laughed aloud. Poor Sean. Like Hecaton, he had been used to using magic to sustain his physical appearance. His illusion of eating – along with other functions – would need to become reality… and just in time for the dreaded haggis night.

CHAPTER 1

Ethan

The early evening sun was making its slow descent, bathing them all in a warm red-gold glow. The country retreat had been a novelty at first but nearly two weeks had passed and Ethan was going stir crazy. "Who lives like this, man," he grumbled to Mario.

"Apparently *we* do until the chief sends us home." The boy raised a glass of champagne to his lips in salute and returned to his novel, here where the company rested under the partial shade of a garden canopy. Their active day had been cut prematurely short by an envoy from the fortress, seeking the chief's counsel.

"I don't know why we had to come back with him," muttered Ethan. "Things were finally getting interesting." He perched before Mario, and the Lilim closed over his book and set it aside on the patio table.

"Just because they let you loose with the bow, Ethan." Mario smirked at the reddening of the mage's face. "They were testing you to see if you'd be stupid enough to turn on them." Ethan would be lying to say that the thought hadn't crossed his own mind, but he was loath to put Carolyn, now sitting with her dog a little way off, in any further danger. The girl had complete faith in the chief honouring his promise to allow them to leave at the allotted time. "Anyway," continued Mario, softly, "this isn't the worst."

Admittedly, that was part of what bugged Ethan most. He'd witnessed first-hand, as had Mario, how prisoners were treated in the realm. The special handling they received now was thanks to Carolyn and the fact that her father wanted to keep her happy. After the activities of the day, they were supposed to be enjoying drinks before Arthur joined them for dinner at the lodge.

Carolyn had discarded her serviceable day clothes and had donned a formal blue frock. It made him smile that although she conceded to the chief's whim in the manner of dress code, her hair had been brushed free from its braid and lay in silken waves over her shoulders. The sun brought out a fiery hue that shimmered with the slightest movement.

Abandoning the upholstered wrought iron furniture, she chose instead to sit on a patch of flattened grass. With her dress pooled around her, she looked like something from a Victorian romance novel – not that Ethan had experience of such – her bare feet peeking out from under the frothy blue material. Her toes were clenched in the grass, clearly enjoying a deliberate uptake of earth power.

Ethan joined them regularly for practise and credited Carolyn as a swift study rather than throw tribute at Mario for his teaching skills. It was not entirely one way, however, for only this morning she'd taught Mario how to change partially, taking advantage of the enhanced sight in his then animal-mage form. He'd been able to catch the movement of a tiny beetle on a blade of grass from a distance of a hundred yards. That Mario was a hawk to Ethan's seagull was a disappointment in itself. Arthur's neutering of Ethan's abilities was the first in his long list of complaints.

An attendant stepped out from the building to refill their glasses and Mario waved him away. Carolyn's drink was practically untouched at her side. The smiling Lolilim had set beside her a silver tray, cut in a flower design, upon which to rest her glass.

Wresting his eyes from the vision in blue, they came upon Mario's sly smile and Ethan felt the distinct urge to wipe it from his face. He didn't have time for the boy's snide comments. It wasn't often that the chief left them all together, and he'd be damned if he didn't make the best of it.

Ethan had already scouted around the building. He knew that the men at the rear of the property were practising manoeuvres and were primary backup to the four discreetly watchful guards that had been spaced out at the front of the lodge. There had been no chance to check beyond the first ring of "protection" for he'd been stopped by a good natured reminder to stay within sight.

Empustat seemed to be one of the more agreeable realms, very similar to Earth. He'd worked out the differences between the native Lilim and Lolilim. The guards and servants were predominantly Lolilim and appeared to be human with no discernible magical ability. They were generally nice enough whereas the Lilim were supercilious freaks like Mario.

"Where did Arthur say he was going?"

Mario's pretty boy brows rose marginally, as though he could tell where Ethan's thoughts had gone. "He didn't say exactly. 'An old friend'?"

The look on Arthur's face hadn't seemed commensurate with seeing an old friend. Ethan couldn't quite work it out, but the chief had worn the look of someone about to indulge in pursuits best not shared with innocent company. Ethan knew that expression, he'd seen it on enough faces – witnessed it too often on his own – to surmise that the chief was up to any good. "Why don't you sneak a peek with your spidey senses?"

Mario rose quickly, scuffing his boots across the flagstone that bordered the grass. "Just because *you* can't, doesn't mean *I* should," he said as he moved away.

Grinning at the irritated response, Ethan stretched his legs out, bracing one against the leg of Mario's abandoned chair. That the boy had sought higher ground was a small victory. It didn't matter that he'd got his wish to grow up; he was still a little shit with the same offensive tendencies on the inside. "What if it's something to do with us, or with *her*," and Ethan motioned to Carolyn who was harmlessly plucking flowers from the grass, and making … a daisy chain of all things.

So, his world was seriously skewed. He couldn't bear to watch her. It was easier to focus on Mario.

"He would know if I spied on him," said the exasperated Lilim. "For God's sake, man. He cultivates that kindly, aristocratic look *especially* for her."

"You both get that I can hear you, right?" Carolyn seemed unconcerned as she continued in her charming but somehow surreal task. That was another thing that bothered him: their destroyer wasn't acting as she should. She was more like a Disney princess right now, and not even the modern kick-ass version he could stomach. Why then was his heart in his mouth every time she looked his way?

"Hey, no secrets from our girl," he placated. Damn, but her hearing was better than his.

"Which of you would like this?" Getting to her feet, she seemed to glide towards them amidst a whisper of silk, strands of her hair lifting behind her. Oh, but she was beautiful, her pale features having plumped out a little in her time in Empustat, holding the glow of health and well-being she'd lacked back at home. Perhaps she did fit in here. Could she live in both worlds? *Shut. Up.*

Ethan knew that Arthur, despite his assurances, wanted Carolyn here, and God help Ethan, but looking at her now, this was exactly where she belonged. It was almost comical when he remembered the offending article she carried. The blooms had grown fatter than seemed possible, thrumming with the earth magic she exuded, and both he and Mario halted her simultaneously, their hands held up.

Carolyn shook her head and glanced at the dog that had padded silently behind her. It was perhaps a stretch to call it a dog. The massive hound had been adopted by her after their showdown with her father. The beast had gone from a snarling vicious killer to "old faithful" under Carolyn's oblivious power. He whined and sank to the ground, huge paws raised to cover his face. Carolyn laughed, the sweet chime causing the guards in the distance to step forward.

"Oh, well. I suppose I'll just have to leave it here for the bunnies to eat." With a wry smile, she dropped the flowers on the table beside Ethan and spun on her heel. Only a few steps and the mage found himself standing right in front of her. With his magic under wraps, he was surprised that his speed had remained. Ethan coiled the daisy chain with surprisingly gentle hands, and with a mocking ceremonial bow, placed the flowers on her head.

"I grew up with girls," he said, shrugging off the question in her blue eyes. It had the desired effect and she smiled her thanks. "Can't have your good work go to waste."

"Oh, pul-ease," said Mario, the instant she was out of sight. "Man, you have got it bad." Ethan rolled his shoulders, feeling his will fully return . Hell, if she asked in private, then he'd wear the damned daisy chain and let her whip him with sunflower stalks if she wished.

Ah, had he really just thought that? Even the hound seemed to offer him a reproachful look before it followed Carolyn into the lodge. Ethan lifted her discarded glass and watched the play of bubbles as they streamed to the top. Not his drink of choice but it would do. He drained the glass's contents before returning to Mario's knowing smirk.

"However good she looks, she's still a shell, and it's partly her own doing," said Mario, barely above a whisper.

"She has her memories." That she chose not to embrace those of Note was a bonus. "I thought you'd been helping her sort out the connections." To his credit, the Lilim met the accusation head on.

"Arthur doesn't encourage *certain* connections. I don't know, exactly, but I think her link to Note is directly related to her destroyer capabilities."

Ethan felt his ire rise. "How can you blame her when *you're* the puppet?" He angled towards the house so the guards wouldn't see his anger. Two remaining, he noted absently. He'd seen Mario working on the claiming tattoo she so willingly offered up. That meant something – damn it! He knew it was more than taking the pain of separation; she was sacrificing her feelings for Note.

"We are all puppets." The Lilim had gone still, his breath caught before he released it in a long and ragged sigh. Ethan outright refused to pity him. "She doesn't want to fight the connections. They're all in place now, including the attraction she has for you. The only thing that's missing is what makes her *ours*."

Ethan swallowed the bile that rose to his throat. Back home, her connection with Note had been hard to accept; for it to be part of her destroyer role was a blow. "You think I've been sitting on my thumbs?" Mario accused. "I've watched you with her. You don't fit the criteria to bring her back. We're at an impasse where you and I represent her Earth life, and while she denies Note and consequently *us*, we seriously can't compete."

Mario bent to lift the silver tray from where Carolyn had been sitting. It picked up sparkles where the sun caught it. "We can't bring Note here," he continued belligerently. "We agreed to abide by Arthur's rules, and even if Note *were* here, how do we know that Carolyn would allow her feelings to attach to her memories. As it is, she focuses on what she remembers of her dependency on a demon and fails to understand their full connection. Hell, we don't really know how it happened."

His dark eyes found Ethan's in the failing light. "You botched your attempts to anchor her, but with Note it simply came about." The talk of Note served only to sour Ethan's mood further. "Of course, there's another reason for her to reject him. I've seen how her mind works." Ethan couldn't head off the wild look of expectancy that crossed his features, and Mario returned it with a sly smile. "It's the thought that he's simply acting in a way dictated by the bond."

Ethan knew for a fact that her thoughts on Note weren't right. The Kistatus never lost hope. "He'd made a new life as an enforcer so he could—" Understanding dawned and Ethan caught himself. Mario's satisfied expression showed that he understood. Ethan had been about to say that Note had proven to be true, that he'd become worthy. Shit, this wasn't good. Where the hell was Sean with his words of calm logic when he needed them? The guards had closed in fractionally, Ethan noted. His lips pressed together in an unhappy resolve.

"What about her tattoo; I've seen you working on it. Why don't you stop messing with that and we'll see what happens."

"I can't." The frustration behind his words revealed more than Ethan would have liked, but it made sense. High blood Lilim like Arthur couldn't afford to lose their daughters to what they considered inferior races. Despite the chief's recent cordiality towards Ethan, he was still a bloody Nazi.

"And you expect her to fight," Ethan said.

"You don't get it." Mario shook his head and turned away from the mage to watch the lodge. "She's terrified of that connection. I can only imagine how Note feels about this if what you think is true."

Ethan rubbed the hint of stubble on his jaw. If Carolyn regained her complicated link with Note, she would get back to normal and Ethan would be forgotten. There *had* to be another way. Sean had once entertained the possibility of the anchoring having been split between Note and himself, and hence the overpowering attraction that Ethan felt for Carolyn. He could remember how bad it had been for him when she'd first joined the Protectorate. That burning obsession, though, *had* reduced.

Was he arrogant enough to believe he had gained better control, or was the attraction lessened because, even a world apart, their destroyer still belonged to Note?

Arthur

The air thickened, constricting Arthur's chest, as the wards of the retreat recognised him. The seer had already known he was coming; she did this merely to cause him discomfort. He felt the substance of another – the mystics – reality materialise. He had grown out of the habit of taking a sentry with him. The guards being a superstitious lot, they were best left at their stations with quiet tongues whilst he stopped at Alyssa's plane of existence.

Throughout the realm, Arthur was in full control of those who entered and exited Empustat. Having barred gateway access after Carolyn's arrival, someone had seen fit to create a tear that led between the realms. He could confidently assume that its human creator had been shredded, for the feature remained unused by all except the Faery hybrids and their foolish friends.

Arthur had ensured that Carolyn remained in his realm and planned to lose no sleep if her companions disappeared through the tear. Had he not been so stretched, it would have been wiser to have repaired it. He was loath to do so, though, considering the immense amount of energy required for such a task, one best completed by using the creator's own blood. Its continued existence at least served to illustrate the trust he placed in his daughter and her friends.

Arthur's revived interest in the seer stemmed mainly from her arcane ability to access the realms. He had varied and interesting memories of Alyssa. A rarely gifted Lilim, and despite her value, one who had been feared and often ridiculed, though never within her hearing. At some point she had negotiated the acquisition of her quaint cottage from Arthur's uncle who had, quite frankly, been happy to oblige, and so keep the strange and powerful seer away from the demands of her people.

Though court life had become tame in the past decades, Arthur knew that Alyssa would not give up her sanctum and return. In her virtually untraceable ability to communicate through and with others from the realms, she had proven invaluable in keeping the actions of the Kistatus pest under control. It *was* cause for embarrassment, though, that Arthur's former mate and their daughter had succumbed to the uncertain charms of the Skean king and the son of their high mage, respectively.

Helping to mute Carolyn's bond with an entirely unsuitable mate, Mario was trusted by Arthur to be nothing more than a useful tool, but one to be wielded with care. The young Lilim seemed to have Carolyn's best interests at heart, as did Arthur; the chief merely needed the time to prove it to her. The next few days would be crucial to his plan, and Alyssa, whatever her idiosyncrasies, could be trusted.

Arthur's breath puffed out in a white mist before him and he paused in his descent to the forest clearing. The shape of the cottage appeared before him as he solidified his presence within the mystic's reality. The semi-transparent structure grew more solid until he could make out the rose bushes twisting up past the lintel of its rustic door. The scent of the blooms now stirred fond memories.

"My Chief," came the voice of a maroon-clad guardian. Stepping into view from the side of the cottage, he executed a small bow. "Welcome."

"Thank you, Ustav," Arthur replied.

The chief could sympathise with Alyssa's requirement for solitude but it was a waste of perfectly good guardians to watch over her, ones whose deployment to such a no-man's-land meant for them only a quiet, uneventful and unchallenging life. Four time served, rotating shifts reported on their limited interaction with the seer. Alyssa's current guardians had been with her a long time, though, and so Arthur suspected she sweetened the deal for them somehow. Requests for transfers had become rare.

The solitude, he thought, had to bring about undesirable effects, something of which he'd encountered on his previous visits to disturb her. The cottage door creaked open and he stepped over the threshold to meet one of Alyssa's most disturbing expressions.

"Why must you take that form?" He had not learned to keep quiet when the seer irritated him like this. She was *not* Amanda. He knew it, but the sight of her image, whilst it mocked him, drew him in. His resistance was minimal when she appeared this way. Alyssa posed demurely while his eyes devoured her. The mystic could always torment him so, taking pleasure in his conflicting emotions. It was easy to have his own convictions once out of her sight but the information she accessed was not the only thing that kept him returning.

"Wonders will never cease," the seer breathed. "I am honoured by your visit."

Arthur removed his jacket to reveal dark formalwear over a pristine white shirt. "Would you do me the favour of returning to your true self?"

"True self indeed. You are not so keen on truth, my liege." She waved a finger in possible admonishment: all was not always clear with Alyssa. "Your daughter is perhaps the only one in your kingdom who is true, and yet you choose to keep her soul shackled."

"You're being overly dramatic, Alyssa." He half turned, quite unable to remove her from his line of sight. "How can I listen to you when I am distracted by this?" He was not ready to lose the vision of Amanda, slighting his paternal abilities as she was, but he needed to move on quickly.

Whilst wearing Amanda's face, she seemed to exhibit a corresponding wish to protect his daughter, but by means that differed from *his* own plan. It caused him a grief he didn't want to feel, not when he was so close to assuring the continuance of his reign through Carolyn.

"Why would I be me," said the seer, now seductive, "when this is so much more interesting and, if I may say, quite pertinent to your current situation." Alyssa fussed for a moment with the lace that only partially covered her cleavage; Arthur had to remind himself that the true Amanda would never wear such an article. Damn the woman!

"How I enjoy the responses this face and body elicit." She ran her hands suggestively from breast to hip. In the years that Arthur had visited, he'd had no trouble distinguishing honest behaviours from those designed to confuse or titillate. Alyssa's lips curved in a half- smile, her green eyes filled with knowledge, with a hint of something dark that he could never reconcile with the memory of Amanda.

"You wish to visit your lost love, my liege? You protected her for nearly fifteen years on foreign soil and she repaid you by running off with the first chief who beckoned."

"That was not what happened," Arthur snapped, and Alyssa shrank back as he placed his hands either side of her head. Through the years, the seer's skill in portraying Amanda had grown. He'd seen how Alyssa had been quick to rectify any physical differences from the original. The way her hair felt under Arthur's palms had been one of the first amendments. "I grow tired of these childish games." It was a relief but also a penance to watch Amanda's face become Alyssa's. The hair between his hands melted to a lesser, finer texture that lacked the lustre and spring that had been uniquely Amanda's.

"Of course," she croaked. The knowledge that she had overstepped the boundaries clearly flickered into being. Arthur could only hope her lucidity prevailed a while longer. "Please forgive me; it's been a while since I've spoken with a being in the actual flesh. These guardians you send are of little satisfaction. And then you venture into *my* realm with your massive … aura." Her eyes glinted in sudden humour. "That, and your bloody single-mindedness. You must pardon that I get carried away at times."

"I need to know if you have news for me."

"So imprecise, my liege." The brunette batted her dark eyelashes and Arthur shrugged indifference. Sometimes such an open question could have remarkable results. Not today.

"Amanda's wellbeing?" Arthur prompted.

"I cannot penetrate the protector's shields."

"They can't keep her so tightly wrapped for ever," murmured the chief. "We must ready ourselves for when the time comes."

"My people are in place," Alyssa purred and tapped the side of her nose.

"I can find friends everywhere in my mind." Her fingers slid up to her temples, a sadly manic smile playing on her lips, "but I can't touch them like this." She took Arthur's hand in demonstration and he sighed.

"You could return to the fortress with me. Your old rooms are unoccupied."

"Could I wear any face I wanted?"

"No," he said, and then lifted his chin to the air. "Were you baking?" A rich warm scent teased his nostrils.

Something flickered in Alyssa's face. "I knew you were coming, so I had the guardian fetch ingredients at the changeover. Come through," she said, leading the way from the illusion of a cosy lounge into one of a bright country kitchen. Arthur's mouth watered in Pavlovian response to cakes sitting on a baking tray. "What do you seek from me?"

"We both know the answer."

"My liege, you need to ask the correct question if you have hope of receiving the answers you seek." Arthur drew his gaze from the over stacked cooling tray. The room too closely mirrored the kitchen he'd "seen" Amanda use during her fifteen *free* years on Earth.

The chief watched the mystic slide a few of the cakes on to a plate. "I think she knew you were responsible." Her eyes darted to a dish of icing that she proceeded to stir then drizzle over her creations. "For protecting her, I mean." Arthur was intrigued by Alyssa's observation. He leaned forward, hopeful of more. "I misjudged," Alyssa said, wiping a drop of icing from her finger with a towel. "This will take a while to set."

Arthur frowned, to which the woman tipped her head to one side. "Ah, yes: Amanda. Well, she may not have known *how* you managed it, but I believe she knew."

It was pleasant for Arthur to hear affirmation – of sorts – from Alyssa. "Perhaps," he said, and set an enquiring brow before choosing a cake from the plate. Taking a small bite, he only now remembered how good her creations tasted. "You should send this recipe to the fortress."

A knowing smile slid across her features. "Where do you think I got it in the first place? though I expect you've changed the staff since I last attended." Alyssa uncorked a bottle and poured him a glass of the honeyed dessert wine she favoured.

"Thank you." He remained standing and drew a large draft while Alyssa sat down at the table, both hands curled under her chin. "My sources confirm that she is safe with the Protector."

It was an effort to distance his thoughts enough to ask, "What about her most recent claiming?"

"*That* will take a little longer to wear off, my liege. If he dies, of course, then the process would be hastened. You should have struck before the Kistatus made his move."

"I promised." Even to Arthur's ears, the words seemed hollow.

"Better the consequences of a broken promise. The lady would have understood."

"Had you given more information, seer, I could have acted before that beast stole her from under me."

"Under you?" Jumping to stand before the sink, the mystic's hair shook free as she scoffed, "Not under or *over* you for nearly eighteen years." She sneaked a glance behind her, her voice dropping to a fervent murmur. "I urged you so many times to take back what was yours. All the years you *watched*. How much time did she need to *find* herself?" Alyssa turned to face him, her hand gripping the draining board behind her. The seer's gift appeared to be warring with her own thoughts.

"All the time she needed," answered Arthur coolly. It was almost amusing that she could stand up to him as though as an equal.

"And where did it get you?" Alyssa's cheeks reddened. "You *allowed* the Kistatus chief to take what you would not claim in the name of true love. I am a crazy old mystic but even *I* see where you went wrong."

Arthur didn't rise to the bait as he might once have done. "I have learned my lesson."

Alyssa's voice wavered slightly, and the chief knew that this was usually the time when her gift took proper hold. There was nothing other than the slight paling of her irises to give this away. "The little one is not a pawn…"

Arthur was before her in a heartbeat. Alyssa's small shoulders trembled in his hands as he urged her to carry on. "You still attempt to tame that which cannot be tamed," she breathed. "A strategy that fails and will continue to fail throughout the realms. It was unsuccessful with Amanda, but you try too hard with the young one. Although you do seem to learn as you go along, adapting areas to suit, it is not enough; it can *never* be enough. Carolyn has a calling that you do not understand. The undeveloped Kistatus is necessary to her but you would *rob* her of that connection and foster relationships that can only do her harm."

Alyssa shook her head and blinked vaguely at Arthur. "The latter part is not so clear."

Arthur didn't *like* what he'd heard, but he could still plan for the possible outcomes. "Go on," he pressed softly and Alyssa groaned.

"You would do better to facilitate her plans. Denying her the Kistatus will force her into his arms."

Arthur's face darkened. He quashed the "Like mother, like daughter" phrase that came to mind. He couldn't allow such negative emotions to cloud his mind. Neither had been in control of their "breeder" status.

Carolyn admittedly had the "destroyer" role, which protected her somewhat, but what good was such protection when she faced death every day as an anchored destroyer. At least, while she had been unanchored, her feral nature had kept her safe. His daughter was unaware of the extent of her vulnerability whilst under Protectorate "control". He forced himself on to his next concern.

"And what of the young Earth seer?"

Alyssa's irises flickered, and she smiled maddeningly at the change of subject. The chief had found it interesting that the child seer on Earth had come into his own ability after Carolyn had rescued him from trade. Notwithstanding the fact that seers' gifts would often manifest after an ordeal, Arthur was intrigued with the possibility that Carolyn had somehow helped create the phenomenon.

"He is curious about his predecessor, but that is unimportant," Alyssa continued. "I can only use him as a conduit to others of ability, and I must always remember to do so during moments of inaction."

That was good, thought Arthur. In days gone by, seers would be burned at the stake, exorcized or lobotomised as the manifestation of their gift could take various worrisome forms. The Earth realm was generally civilised enough nowadays, but unfortunate treatments or accidents could still befall the mystics of all the kingdoms.

"Your household is in flux, but something will happen soon to change all that."

"Riddles, dear Alyssa. I sometimes wonder why I keep you alive." He drew her closer, tightening his grip as though he could squeeze more revelations from her.

"Me neither," she said, now breathless. "You could solve most of your problems by reopening the gateway access to your realm, though."

Alyssa's ability was clearly coming to its conclusion. In the circle of his arms, she closed her eyes briefly but then opened them to reveal irises that were almost pure white.

"What do you really wish to 'see', my liege?" He released her from his grip but the seer pressed forward and grabbed him with unnatural strength. "Use me as you will, but first – a gift." She paused, at which Arthur felt a chill crawl over his chest. "How about a memory," Alyssa suggested. Her hold lessened, but he didn't want to stop her nearly enough to pull away. "I think you'll like this one best."

The clarity of the vision was breath-taking, whisking him off to a time when he had been complete. Amanda's face was now above him, looking down upon him with those witch green eyes that needed no Lilim guile to entrance. *No! He couldn't let the seer warp that memory.*

Forcibly, Arthur detached himself from her sweet poison. The feelings she'd pulled from him reminded him of what he'd felt the enforcer direct at Carolyn. That was a relationship he was already trying to exploit. As unsuitable as the boy was, Arthur was not averse to encouraging the attachment. At the end of the twenty-one days, should he remain, the problem could be solved. The young mage liked archery, Arthur had learned, and accidents did tend to happen to thrill seekers, the kind the chief had recognised Ethan to be. Mario was not the perfect choice for his daughter but he would do. Their children would be strong, beautiful and pure undiluted Lilim, thanks to Carolyn's breeder status.

Fingers traced the length of his neck and jaw before dipping lower. The seer was certainly persistent as the sweet scent of Amanda's hair surrounded him and Arthur lost himself for a moment in the memory, breathing her in. A loose curl tickled his nose, and he brushed it away. The image of her physically hurt him as he reached for her, as he brought her lips to his own in a scorching venture of exploration.

The weight of reality crashed in upon him and he opened his eyes to the seer's liquid darkness.

"Such love – such passion will exist for you once again, but you must first send your daughter home. *She is Earth bound*, but it's up to you whether she returns."

"I can't risk it."

"You can and will. The only way to keep any part of her is to let her go."

Exactly the same advice he'd received about Amanda and much good had it done. "I cannot."

"Then she is lost to the realm. Perhaps not this week, or even this year, but lose her you will."

"You are wrong. You are not yourself. This gift..." The seer took his hand and placed it against her face. He allowed a trickle of his own power to fuel her appearance, but on *his* own terms. He closed his eyes, unable to bear watching it any longer, cursing his weakness and wondering how often they had danced to this familiar tune.

"I am who you need me to be." Arthur's breath caught as his eyelids fluttered open to the beautiful illusion now filling his vision. He deserved a treat, to lose his senses for a time, for a short while at least within that which he had so sorely lost.

CHAPTER 2

Carolyn

The scent of leather and soap alerted Carolyn to Ethan's closeness at her side. "So the little shit likes his new teaching position," he was saying. Carolyn cringed, hoping Mario hadn't caught the insult.

"He's not deaf, you idiot," she hissed, wondering if the boys' quarrelling would stop when they returned to the fortress. She especially didn't like the way Ethan spoke to Mario, though she was well aware that the Lilim had provocation down to a fine art. Either alone would be fine but their differences were magnified by the enforced proximity of their situation. Perhaps Arthur believed that three weeks with the enforcers and she'd be happy to kick them back home without her.

She was being unfair. Spending daylight hours in the great outdoors and their evenings in front of roaring wood fires in the hunting lodge, the days had bled beautifully into each other. Other than wearying of her role as peacemaker, she had enjoyed the company of the two very different males. Perhaps she should make them strip to the waist and have it out with each other before one of them blew a gasket.

The mental image made her smile. As good as Mario would look without his top, the thought of Ethan sent her pulse racing and brought a wash of heat to her cheeks.

Going back to the fortress would mean an end to the lack of restrictions they currently enjoyed. The impending change had all three on edge. Arthur had allowed them a lot of "freedom", taking care not to monopolise Carolyn's time as he could have done. He had trusted her to maintain her part of their bargain, and she was appreciative of his generosity.

It was a pity the boys couldn't see the positive in her father. She had caught them whispering and plotting more than once, and though annoying, it was preferable to the open animosity they each displayed for the other. In Arthur they'd found a common foe. If she hadn't worried so much about them, Carolyn would have been angrier. As it was, she had to force herself to remember the things for which the chief was capable and adjust her tolerance levels accordingly.

The river bubbled noisily, and she hoped the Lilim was too engrossed in his rock collecting to bother with Ethan. Mario looked up from the water's edge, the dappled effect of the light through the trees lending an otherworldly influence to his beautiful, though currently grim expression. His eyes glinted from where he stood on the riverbank.

"He's certainly something," said the mage, producing that large artificial smile that always alerted Mario.

"I'll tell you what he is, you big bag of…" but there was no word Carolyn could reasonably use. "Crap," she finally plumped for, evoking a surprised blink from Ethan. "He is my friend, without whom I would still be under Peter's thrall and planning an autumn wedding."

Ethan had the grace to redden but clearly felt some sort of righteousness in his treatment of Mario. "He's getting a kick out of being able to use magic when—"

"You can't," Carolyn interrupted, frustration raising the pitch of her voice. "Yes, for the hundredth time I know, Ethan, and I'm sorry, but Arthur thinks you're a significant threat, otherwise he would let you practise as much magic as you damned well please."

"Well, when you put it like that," and with those words the tension drained. He dropped a playful wink, and she was unable to curb her answering smile.

Carolyn couldn't let him off *that* lightly. "You are an arse."

"Couldn't agree more, pretty lady," the Lilim said, having crept up on them. *Point to Mario.*

"How can you stand this," said Ethan, and Carolyn's eyes widened.

"I just have to accept that you don't get along well."

"Not that. This!" and Ethan gestured expansively. "Our being here until Arthur finds a way to dispose of us."

"My father is a man of his word," she snapped.

"So am I, but if I saw a threat to someone I loved, my word or not, I would get rid of it."

"I don't know what you mean," she said, adding an irritable tone to her voice, hoping he'd take the hint and let it rest.

"He sees us as a threat, Carolyn. We're playing this stupid game and we all know it's not going to end well."

"It will all work out fine, Ethan. Why must you be so negative?"

"I have work, a job to do, and I can't do it while we're languishing here."

Mario rubbed the stones in his hands, debris falling at his feet to disappear into the muddy ground. "You might be *languishing* but we're working."

"I can still … work. I know more of the theory than you, anyway."

Mario raised a brow, seemingly happy to have Ethan on the defensive. A smug smile ruined his handsome face. "I doubt that."

"Just test me when I have the magic back and we'll see."

Mario stepped into his space. "You'd like that wouldn't you. I'm not a kid you can bully any more."

"I *never* bullied you." Neither male backed off so Carolyn stepped between them, forcing the boys apart, a hand on each of their chests. "This is a bit childish even for you two. If you're not careful, you'll bring the guards over."

Ethan's eyes followed her prompt, scanning behind them before meeting her gaze with a disturbing intensity. "I swear, Carolyn, he just drags it out of me."

"Mmm, right. And you're the innocent one in this?" and her voice dropped. "Please don't do anything stupid, you don't want to give Arthur a reason." Ethan seemed surprised at the acknowledgement that they were in danger. Silence followed, Ethan recovering first.

"Is that a threat?" He snatched a stem from a nearby shrub and began to strip the leaves from it. Carolyn realised he probably just needed something to do with his hands but the gesture was oddly intimidating.

"No, damn it. You know very well what it is. A warning. A simple 'play it safe' notice, if you like. Keep your heads down and we'll all get out of this."

"You're a bloody daddy's girl, Carolyn. You shouldn't forget what's happened to you because of that man."

"Don't start, Ethan."

"You think he trusts you?" He tossed the stripped stem into the mud and Carolyn felt almost ill. He took her arms in his hands while Mario tried to intervene.

"That's done it. Here they come," muttered the Lilim as the guards closed in.

"I'm not going to hurt her, you idiots, back off."

Carolyn caught one of the sentry's eyes. "You heard the man. Back the hell off."

Neither looked happy, but they did stop their advance at Carolyn's assurance, a few metres away. The whisper of an unsheathing sword served only to heighten the tension. They wouldn't dare strike an unarmed man. Ethan made a light scoffing sound – he'd heard the blade being drawn too?

– and leaned in to murmur in her ear. Carolyn's traitorous pulse leapt, and she shuddered with anticipation. The shame of enjoying this *way* too much lit through her , but then he spoke and ruined it all.

"If Arthur trusts you, Carolyn, why are the gateways still barred?"

Hecaton

Hecaton had traced the boy to being inside the barracks. From a distance, he surveyed the first product of Lucas and Amanda's union. Edward cleaned and polished his short sword with practised efficiency.

In human form, as ever, he was large, standing almost a foot taller than Hecaton. Despite being sun-bleached, his tresses were still several shades darker than his mother's. The style, shorn at the back, was kept long on top. He shared the same vanity as his father in regard to his human appearance.

Hecaton thought it frivolous; his own white-blond hair was uncut and trailed down his back. Edward's uniform, like all guards' apparel, was designed to accommodate the change to Kistatus, but the boy had yet to embrace his heritage. It made him weak.

Hecaton speculated that Lucas's son would be among the most impressive of their race if he ever chose to accept his abilities. As it was, Edward had proven to be stubborn, but at least he'd gained skills in combat that were remarkable enough for the others to overlook his refusal of their native standards. Only two of the king's guards – whilst in Kistatus form – could best the boy.

"Not training with the men today?" Hecaton said. Edward raised his green eyes from beneath the unfortunate swath of hair that almost covered them. His expression was one of anger and confrontation. Hecaton crushed the swelling desire to put him firmly in his place. He had to know that an unarmed high mage was far more dangerous than many an entire army, yet still he surveyed Hecaton with something close to loathing.

"How do we get them back?" Edward grunted. Hecaton understood the animosity but not the bright hint of something else entirely that shone from Edward's young face.

"We wait."

Edward sheathed his blade with a ferocity that should have cleaved through the leather binding. "For what, Hecaton? It's been nearly two weeks. Do we wait for Notechis to come back and finish the job he started?"

Edward's eyes widened in fear as Hecaton's irises flashed gold. "I spoke out of turn," he hastily added, tilting his head with all the arrogance of youth. "It was meant to serve as an apology."

Hecaton could discern no such thing. He stepped closer to Edward, looking up into his face. The boy was trying to hide his fear and failing. The high mage said nothing as he watched a trickle of sweat gather and bead at Edward's temple. An unfortunately tragic response, he thought. Most Kistatus who changed regularly lost their ability to sweat. Edward was rather different as he'd spent his entire life as a human.

"I am Lucas's Man." Hecaton's words held soft menace. "You forget yourself. Your blood does not assure you this kingdom."

The boy stepped back sharply, as though Hecaton had hit him. "I don't want the blasted kingdom. I just want my place in it." He slid onto a bench, clearly uncaring of the high mage's superiority. Lucas wouldn't have backed down so readily and the fact only cemented Hecaton's view that Edward was *never* going to replace his father.

The boy wanted his *place*. It was absurd. "What place would that be if your father dies?"

Edward flinched before straightening, his hand caressing the hilt of the blade resting at his side. Hecaton could see the thoughts aligning. He thought himself to be a warrior, and among the ranks on the Skean he *was* a force to be reckoned with.

The boy lived as a regular guard most of the time but took advantage of certain benefits, enjoying luxuries many of his friends were denied. Edward would never attract a suitable mate with his sick adherence to his human form but it had to hurt him at times, especially when his companions used the springs and waterways that were admittedly in short supply throughout the realm.

Even if Edward were lucky enough to find a breeder, the magic would deny him unless he showed some mettle and took Lucas's place as chief. With grim satisfaction, Hecaton knew that *that* was not about to happen anytime soon.

"If you send me through the gateway to Earth, I can find my mother and bring her home." Hecaton looked away as Edward continued, emboldened. "Hell, the authorities will probably *take* me to her right away. All we'll need is an opening for her to do her mojo and get us home."

Did the boy think he himself hadn't considered the possibilities? The castle seer had loudly proclaimed that Amanda's blood would once again return to Skean, but Hecaton had seen through the wording to what Lucas could not see. Her blood could mean that she herself would reappear, but it could also apply to any of her offspring, including Carolyn, though not Kistatus, for she was a breeder, and her interest in the high mage's own son had merit.

"The *mojo* you refer to will be kept at bay in an Earth prison," to which Edward sucked in an angry breath as Hecaton watched him pale before saying, "I don't think your mother would be happy to find you incarcerated and of no help to either her or our chief. Amanda would take comfort in knowing you remain here."

"But I'm not *doing* anything."

"Your presence in the castle is enough," and Hecaton turned on his heel, effectively dismissing the young prince. "For now." It was time for a meeting with *his own* son.

Edward

It was as though everyone in Skean castle could sense Edward's ill humour since he'd spoken with Hecaton. The high mage couldn't hide his disdain and Edward suspected he knew much more about Amanda's whereabouts than he let on.

Thinking the south wing of the castle to be warmer than usual, he made his way down to the springs beneath. The perceived temperature change might be due to the anger that now roiled within him. Hecaton had been absent when the chief needed him most, but Edward struggled with his own festering guilt. He had allowed Notechis and his bleeding heart Protectorate band to overpower and raid the castle. He half-growled at the direction of his thoughts. Perhaps the high mage was right to think him worthless.

A serving girl brushed past him on the narrow steps. Head covered and bowed, she carried a pitcher of water. "Stop," he said.

"M…my lord?" she stammered, and Edward was reassured. The girl didn't even raise her eyes as she turned, showing him the top of her covered head.

"Never mind." Irritable, he couldn't understand what bothered him. Harassing the servants? He continued down the steps, realising that she hadn't moved. Still hearing nothing as he reached the foot of the stairs, he turned to address her. He knew he'd become paranoid these past days. The Protector had taken what he wanted from them and now Edward was seeing spies in half-witted serving girls.

"Be about your duties," he began, but then thought the girl could be useful. It was late and he would be unlikely to find service beneath the castle. "You can fetch some wine and bring it to me in the springs." The slight figure above mumbled in accord and Edward grumbled as he opened the door to the steam laden cavern below.

He found the night watchman scrubbing down an antechamber. Edward could still smell its day's use, either that or it was the sweat streaming from its lone human night worker. A look of sufferance crossed the man's face as he noticed his visitor. If it had been within his power, Edward was sure the man would have chased him out and suggested he return during normal hours.

"Good evening, Sir," the attendant said, draping a cleaning rag over his sweat soaked vest. "Nice to have you back so soon, my lord." His surly expression contradicted this statement and Edward was almost disappointed that he'd enlisted the serving girl's help. The human needed a dressing down but Edward had more pressing things on his mind.

The attendant's brows rose when Edward advised that he wouldn't need his services and to let the server in when she returned with his wine. A knowing and rather envious smirk replaced the man's expression and Edward did nothing to correct his assumption.

Timid serving wenches were not on his "to do" list tonight, or ever. There were altogether too many fawning, attractive and willing participants to be found within the castle if he felt so inclined.

The water caressed his body when Edward lowered himself into it. Something had altered, though. His gaze swept about his surroundings, coming to rest on a gilded ledge on the opposite side of the pool.

That was it, he realised, startled at how different the springs looked without the massive amounts of vapour billowing up the walls. Ordinarily, steam obscured everything, lending a surreal quality to the bathing experience. Now he could even make out the detail on the barrier that encased the castle springs. There was no-one around, so why did he now feel so exposed?

"Your wine, Sir," came a masculine voice from behind him. The serving girl had either been sent away or had elected to drop off his order with the attendant.

He dismissed the human and tried to remember what he knew of the springs. Not an academic, he hadn't studied the realm, preferring to learn whilst "on the job".

As far as Edward was aware, the castle and its grounds were maintained by magic. It would naturally be bolstered by Hecaton presence as high mage but the real power lay with the chief. It had always been Lucas's.

Edward refused to think about his father being unable to recover. He *had* been bitten during Amanda's abduction, but only a stronger Kistatus could kill from a single bite. That Lucas was so ill was testament not only to Note's strength but also to the chief's suffering at the loss of his mate. It was only to be expected that Lucas would struggle with the potent combination.

The lack of power in the springs continued to bother him. If he'd brought some agreeable company, he could have forgotten his troubles for a while. Too tired to get up and find the attendant, Edward decided he would send for one of Cassandra's girls when the man returned to check on him.

CHAPTER 3

Sean

A single lamp cast diffuse light into the room. Using Protectorate funds, the team regularly leased properties in an effort to blend into the community as well as for other reasons.

This particular property overlooked the river Clyde in Glasgow city centre. It was near their secure base beneath the watercourse, so the enforcers had the benefit of a little autonomy whilst being available for quick calls to action.

Sean preferred the darkness, but living with the others encouraged him to conform to their – and increasingly his – idea of normal.

Though he didn't spend all his time with the team, he checked on their whereabouts three times a day. After his session with Note, he had needed to gather his thoughts by doing one of the things that gave him peace.

He'd whiled away a few productive hours under the Clyde with his passion for potions. Almost every ingredient lay at his fingertips, the stock kept replenished of the more exotic items by Sean and a handful of others who were so inclined.

If he'd taken his new leadership role more seriously, he would have asked Rake or Mel to accompany him. Though large, built like a mountain, and more suited to combat, the Rakshasas had shown an interest in the skill. Mel, he suspected was simply interested in anything that could be of advantage out in the field.

Sean didn't feel any more than the smallest twinge of guilt for failing to share his knowledge. The potion preparation had allowed him some respite from the team.

He had been trying to source a rare ingredient on the internet. Having come across nothing but new-age sites and charlatans, he needed to delve deeper.

Ethan, as a child of the modern age, was better at recognising keywords and symbols related to authentic activity. For that reason alone, Sean was reluctant to trust up-to-date methods, but they had their uses. With his whisky in one hand, he tapped with single digits, beginning to close the sites he had visited.

"You may show yourself," said Sean.

"Hell, Sean. I've been practising with this one for a while now," Morgan's voice said to him from a space in the air before him.

"I wasn't only talking to *you*, my dear." Sean's lip twitched as he paused to tap the table lamp at his side.

In the community setting, he'd tried to make use of non-magical means wherever possible. Though he'd done more than simply blend in with the team lately, the effects of their gateway-sanctioned bond had been sufficiently muted with Note's help. Why the powers that be should show their favour by restoring Sean's humanity was a mystery that still lay completely beyond him.

A hazy patch appeared beside Morgan who now stood before the open doorway, talisman mark five or six – Sean couldn't be sure – dangling from a cord in her hand. They had filled their time effectively whilst waiting on Carolyn's return and Sean had been impressed with their distraction tactics for Note.

Morgan's expression soured slightly when Jonah came into view a few feet beside her. "Not fair," she murmured, "I can't compete with that." Jonah offered a small conciliatory smile.

"It's not skill," the Shadow-Faery volunteered. "My abilities work differently. Invisibility is not a natural state for you to achieve." Despite his words, the young demon couldn't hide his smugness at being able to accomplish what the magic users could not so easily undertake.

His cap of dandelion fluff hair had been shorn recently to a tight haze which gleamed unnaturally pale in the gloom. Extra wide Faery eyes betrayed part of his heritage and the other half showed in his ability to transform to shadow. Sean was interested in both the genetic and magical effort that had brought about Jonah's existence.

"Of course," said Sean precisely, "without your added concealment charm, a competent magic user could detect you in your shadow form as well."

Jonah frowned slightly at the reminder, his gaze straying down to examine the braided design on his wrist. There was no doubt he liked the added power it provided, but his consternation came from the fact he needed the assistance it gave, or that he owed Sean and the team for his freedom – such as it was.

Sean and Note had fashioned the new charms to appear similar to the claiming tattoo worn by Carolyn and the Kistatus. It seemed fitting somehow. The design incorporated an array of easily used enchantments – that could survive form changing – without the need for their primitive, blood activated predecessors. There was an added advantage that Sean and Note could instantly "call" any or all members of the team to action with no need to rely on the response to their "gateway" devices.

During trials, they had discovered that the tattoos worked well through most of the gateways. A little tweaking and Sean was hopeful of the effects lasting through all the realms. Once home, the situation with the remaining enforcers would be quickly remedied.

"You did well, Morgan." Sean allowed some praise to enter his tone and the girl's long spiky tendrils of bright red hair bobbed charmingly. *Stop it.* "The abilities that are innate in Jonah and the destroyer require a lot more effort from us. We need to work on an additional soundproof spell to remove the noise."

Most mages had the ability to deflect attention and avoid casual regard. Courtesy of their missing destroyer's talents, he and Morgan had taken it a step further. They had isolated components from Carolyn, using cells from her toothbrush, to create a talisman that rendered the operator invisible to even the most advanced magic user.

"Noise?" Morgan regarded the half empty glass beside Sean before lifting it to her nose with a grimace. She set it back down and turned her witch eyes on him.

"Your breathing, my dear."

A small self-mocking sound erupted, and she stretched her arms out on the coffee table before him. Sean could detect the faintest trace of perfume, or maybe it was the hairspray she used to create her gravity defying, impossible hair style.

"Most people don't have your enhanced senses."

"Some do."

"Not a lot of you running around, thankfully." Sean watched her expression as she surveyed him more closely – a little too closely – concern etched on her pretty features. Her mouth opened before snapping shut, and Sean realised she wasn't going to speak her mind while Jonah was in the room.

Perhaps Sean had swallowed more whisky than he ought; he had almost forgotten the hybrid was present. Morgan chose instead to sit beside him, plumping a cushion on her lap. She made no effort to conceal her interest on the remaining websites he'd been visiting.

"Fossils?" she murmured, a quick smile revealing a flash of teeth. "Potions stuff, then–"

"You called?" Jonah's chiming voice interrupted.

"Patience, Jonah." A being of few words, the Faery demon said little except when it came to his rather strange relationship with Melanie. Sean was amused by Morgan's astuteness. It would be nice if she took an interest in learning the craft. Perhaps in a year or two he would broach the subject with her.

Jonah would know the reason for his call; it hadn't changed over the past fortnight. The creation of a tear into Empustat was an injustice the Protectorate should address, but until then, they would continue to ferry information – and other necessities – back and forth.

With Jonah's limited team bond, he was a bit more of a danger than Sean would have liked. However, with the agreed constraints imposed on the being, Sean remained confident they could use him carefully until more permanent arrangements came about.

"I've been thinking," began Morgan, slowly.

"I hope it didn't hurt, my dear." Sean closed the lid of the laptop, looking up to catch the warning spark in her eyes.

"Watch it, buddy. Those good looks only get you so far with me."

She thought him good-looking? Her teasing tone reminded him of days long gone. Did Morgan even realise she had been treating him differently since the team bonding. Her tone sobered.

"I've been thinking about Carolyn's brother and whether we should have brought him back."

Sean drained the last of his whisky. The boy could certainly be a problem but his actions had spoken clearly. "From what I understand, you didn't get the choice. He would have killed the three of you if you hadn't taken the castle by surprise."

Her green eyes blinked and Sean had the impression he shouldn't be studying her so thoroughly. "Right," she said, "but what if he's been brainwashed and that's why he's so against us."

"Yes, there will be elements of that." Sean's gaze flicked to Jonah who had stepped forward with sudden interest.

"I too was brainwashed, and for *many* years I accepted that the Agency was my family. *I* got over it." Sean almost smiled at Jonah's fervency. The really young ones always thought they knew it all until life experience showed them otherwise.

"Yes, but the Agency didn't treat you as a favoured son with rights and privileges, Jonah. They used you." Sean spotted Morgan's wince at his tone and he tried to soften it. "Edward is being used too, but it's with his full cooperation and understanding. He wasn't a child when he was taken. I can understand his actions, up to a point."

"We can all appreciate the difficulties," said Morgan, her eyes shifting to encompass the Faery. Jonah frowned, clearly in thought. "But his mother..?" She let the sentence hang, and Sean's lips twisted in acknowledgement. There was no doubt that Amanda had suffered in ways none of the enforcers could comprehend.

"It's all about perception, my dear. Amanda would have been kept *happy* by the claim Lucas put on her."

"But it's so—"

"Superficial? Primitive?"

"Not just that," said the pretty mage. "The claim would have tricked her into believing a lie."

"Not exactly," said Sean. "The ancient practise of claiming has served the realms well. Some societies would have collapsed without it."

In response to her horrified look, his lip quirked. He could well remember a time when women were mere chattels and many of them content to propagate the practice. Certain cultures even now frowned upon educating their females in fear of the consequences. He raised his hand in placation. "But, yes, my dear. I see what you mean."

***

It wasn't much later when Sean returned to his room in the underground facility nearby. He rubbed his fingers along the back of his neck. Physical hindrances were getting to be a pest.

As he dropped the minor spell he wore, the mirror reflected an image barely distinguishable from the one before. He could see that his normally white flesh held a tinge, the faintest glow of being suffused with life. The whisky wouldn't have helped.

A spot of blue light appeared from a fixture behind him, dropping in a stream of sparkles where Victor now took a loose shape. Multifaceted eyes glimmered, and Sean frowned, wondering – not for the first time – if he could find another way for the spirit to find form.

"You look well, Victor," said Sean into the mirror and was rewarded by a hearty chuckle from the magical being.

"Self-praise is no praise at all," Victor said, inadvertently reminding Sean that he *could* very well have tried to achieve a better job with him. "I wish I could say the same for you but I see how it is."

"Yes, you do. I'm afraid I don't have any news for you, my friend, but hopefully all will run to plan with our destroyer's return." Victor's magic pulsed brightly in anticipation. A spirit of sorts, he was not unlike the being that had bonded to Carolyn prior to her incarceration.

Victor controlled the use of enchantment throughout the Protectorate facilities and ran on energy and magic given freely from others. Sadi, however, had been without form for too long before latching onto Carolyn. The parasite had thrived on the destroyer's existence in return for bolstering her weaknesses. Carolyn would undoubtedly be better off now, but it had served a purpose before it died.

Victor streamed back into the electrics through the light switch and Sean sighed. The entity didn't grudge the team their community time, but he *had* to miss them and likely for more than their energy levels. Sean resolved to throw the destroyer a celebration on her return that would keep Victor glowing like the sun until Christmas.

As he settled for the evening, he went through the usual routines to slow his processes and enable him to sleep.

It had been a hundred years since he had felt the warmth of blood rushing through his veins, and he now had reason to bemoan *it*, as well as the rabid mortal thoughts that fired along his synapses. His retirement plans foiled, it was now uncomfortable to speculate on the future but it was likely that his "gift" would continue to produce undesirable results.

The Protectorate team had grown to include three sanctioned demons, or four if the destroyer's Anchor was considered the first – and Sean did include him.

Carolyn had also brought about their involvement with the demon underground population on Earth through her connection with Abitaz, a Motus. Better known as Taz, the demon ran a series of establishments throughout the UK and Ireland.

Though Taz himself was unremarkable, there were a few of his associates who deserved further investigation. Certain demons came via gateways and were chosen for Protectorate use, others did not. Taz's organisation collected these latter misfits and helped them find a place in the community.

Though aware of the network, Sean hadn't realised the scale of it. The Protectorate kept tabs on the community which mostly policed itself, but until recently, he'd thought of them as damaged and frightened asylum seekers of sorts, and therefore unworthy of closer inspection.

The situation called into question the old magic of the gateways that recognised some as "pure hearts" – gateway-sanctioned – and others as not.

Sean knew for a fact that the demons Taz harboured were not evil, and had witnessed the self-sacrifice of their Tracer, Siren. A special case, granted, the sultry demon had been lured and recruited for Agency purposes. Whilst maintaining her Agency position, she had apparently found and supported Taz's group.

Note was another of a similar ilk, though gateway-sanctioned he performed beyond expectations, continually placing himself at risk to further the goals of others. Sean couldn't fathom Hecaton's plan in gifting his son such a massive infusion of power. It did, however, increase the boy's protection many times over.

The timing was too convenient as well. Note had been an unwilling receptacle – he certainly didn't think of it as a gift – and there was the uncomfortable fact that Hecaton had failed to intercede on behalf of his chief when Note had broken Amanda out of Skean.

So much could happen in such a short time. The powerful mage wouldn't sleep easy until Ethan was back and Carolyn's fate secured, or as safe as they could manage.

What would the young leader make of Sean's progress with the team — his spirit and flesh binding to the enforcers?

Eventually, Sean stretched out on his bed, fingers laced around the back of his head. Absolute darkness used to bring him some sort of peace. Not now.

He hoped Ethan was faring well with the destroyer. His lips tilted in the darkness as he wished for the irascible mage's return with a fervency that surprised even him.

CHAPTER 4

Miranda

Miranda occupied one of the largest offices in the Agency complex and disliked visitors over whom she had little control. As a valuable Investor, Croft was one such individual.

She rearranged a few things on the oak furniture, pausing for a moment before a photograph she'd framed and set on top of a display cabinet. It was the one personal item she allowed in her work place. Having accumulated many books and awards through the years, her assistant had presented them nicely in the space provided.

Casting a glance at the man sitting at *her* desk, and on *her* chair, she knew what was about to happen on the laptop's screen.

Croft peered at the footage before him. Sharp black eyes didn't blink behind his rimless spectacles. The sound was muted, the Investor listening on a headset. Miranda poured him another glass of water from the jug on the desk and watched his hand close around the drink with a perceptible tremor.

She didn't have to watch his face to know what he was thinking, but she studied him nevertheless with a growing sense of satisfaction.

"I need a list of all witnesses." His awe didn't reflect in his tone but Miranda understood his business-like act better than anyone.

"Agents Wentworth and Ferdinand." The names tripped easily from her tongue. Activities at the Agency London site were under tight control, but she'd taken certain liberties, leaving little to chance. Had she carried out the testing at the Glasgow facility, Croft would have been suspicious enough to forgo the opportunity he ought to be seeking.

"Ferdinand?" Miranda was surprised only by his taking this long to mention the other female in the footage of the control room.

"Judy Ferdinand. Magic user, former Protectorate."

"Ah, yes, of course." His eyes widened to show the whites, or rather the decaying yellow around the irises. "Skills and knowledge?"

"Protectorate wiped, but she retains sufficient abilities to be of value to us."

Croft had paused the recording. He made an odd noise in response to Miranda's description and proceeded to tap the screen where another figure was frozen at the station before an open gateway. "This one?"

"Veloces," she stated mildly. Croft pressed the key to resume, and sure enough, the demon's lean frame came into clearer focus when the gateway light extinguished.

This was the second time they'd watched the recording and, as expected, the questions kept coming. Miranda caught the precise instant when Croft made the connection and she had to work hard at keeping her face straight.

"The one who—"

"The killer?" Her eyes widened innocently and Croft waited for her to continue. "No, we haven't been able to trace him yet."

The missing Veloces had been stripped of his tags for execution. An interesting night, and billed as an event, the demon had been entered into an Agency fight from which he shouldn't have surfaced, never mind put on a spectacular show for the paying guests.

No-one had been more surprised than she when the supposedly weaker demon – a successful clone – had slain their prized champion and escaped without trace.

Miranda took a breath and brought positive thoughts to mind. In exchange for sacrificing the clone in his stead, the demon in her care had offered to pledge his service. It was a first in Agency history and she hadn't shared it with the organisation. As far as all were concerned, Miranda had merely taken charge of the remaining, innocent Veloces.

Having missed the last cycle, the pledge would take place in two weeks' time under optimised conditions that she had yet to arrange. Had she known that both demons were equally lethal, she may have played it differently.

Miranda's charge had taken the name Loci, and had played the part of the meeker brother beautifully.

"I missed the fight," said Croft with no real regret. He would no doubt have bet on the champion and lost a lot of money. "You really can't trace the killer?"

"They're stripped of markers before they hit the arena," she directed in a way that suggested he should keep better informed. Miranda didn't have to like anything about the Investor but it was becoming increasingly difficult for her to hide her true feelings towards him.

The chances of finding the missing Veloces were about the same as retrieving their shadow demon which had been appropriated by the Protectorate. Eventually, Miranda planned to keep total control of their useful acquisitions through pledges, but for now, she couldn't risk detracting from her primary goals.

Croft's eyes flicked to the screen before his gaze rested again on the live version of Miranda in the room. He *had* to be excited about her accomplishment and she was certain of where his thought processes would lead. He surprised her by returning to the matter of the demon. "Does this Veloces have a similar skill set to his brother?"

"No, he's docile, but still quite useful." Her choice of word was deliberate: Judy as "valuable" but Loci, "useful". Without Croft to play to, she would have cast them both as merely "useful". Value implied something that shouldn't exist for her with these beings.

On screen, the Veloces sealed up the gateway, and the camera focused on the agent who had returned from his short visit. Though present at the time, Miranda had dissected every detail since. The agent's entire form had suddenly snapped backwards before folding in on itself.

"Pull him up!" Real-time Miranda mouthed. On-screen, her agents appeared, and between them, they rolled the subject up by the shoulders to face the camera.

The change had already begun, his form, though practically unconscious, had visibly filled out, grey hair melted to a vibrant dark, and the face? If Miranda hadn't been present, she wouldn't have believed the sight. Old Bob in modern times would be considered a hottie as evidenced by Judy's captured expression.

Croft's hand reached up to pull on one of his rather ugly ear lobes. "We need to carry out more tests to check the permanence of the effects – and whether we can make modifications."

Yes, why offer the full deal if they could break down the properties to manageable and more profitable chunks. If she hadn't disliked him so much, she would have applauded his thinking. "This does look promising."

Promising? Miranda lowered her head briefly to hide her annoyance. Let him downplay the massive leap forward she'd made. She could be patient when the situation demanded.

"I am obligated to share discoveries of this magnitude and naturally I thought of you first." She baulked at her simpering, "I expect guidance on how to proceed."

He gave her a cringe worthy appraisal, and his eyes narrowed. "*You* haven't been tempted?"

"With Wells nearing retirement, he seemed to be the perfect guinea-pig."

"Yes, good choice," murmured Croft. His gaze returned to the compulsive viewing before him. It would shortly detail a sequence of tests conducted at regular intervals: motor, cognitive and sensory exams, as well as more invasive testing for which the subject had been anaesthetised.

"I thought you'd want to share the news with the others at our next meet." Miranda kept her voice level. "Even with the strictest of controls, it *will* get out." She knew Croft would know well enough that each of the Investors, like him, would have their spies at the Agency, ferreting out snippets here and there, but Miranda was certain Croft had known nothing before she'd called him in to the project, and therefore it stood to reason that no-one of importance would yet know.

"This warrants intensive testing at the beta site."

Miranda offered a tight lipped smile. "Already begun."

"Same team?" She watched him rub his eyes and blink several times. Did he think she was born yesterday, that she would involve *everyone* in such a sensitive venture? Miranda swallowed down her negative energy.

"Of course," she said tightly, aware that her offence leaked into her body language. Croft didn't seem fazed.

"Right, I don't have to remind you that secrecy is very important at this point."

Miranda clenched and released her fists. He would be leaving soon and she could then relax. No, wait, she couldn't. Sonia had scheduled her for a business lunch – a nuisance, yes, but she wouldn't allow the client to keep her indefinitely.

Croft was still speaking but Miranda edged a little towards the door, and the Investor unconsciously rose from Miranda's seat. "What I'll need is full reports – on a flash drive will do – directly to me from you." His eyes lifted heavenwards, expression slackening. "I don't mind if you send the ex-Protectorate girl." No surprises there. He'd get more than he bargained for with Judy. "Also," he continued high-handedly, "I want you to compile an abbreviated version – no technical jargon – and schedule me for processing day after tomorrow."

He tore a page from the notepad on Miranda's desk and scribbled an address, writing on the flat of his hand; the man was beyond cautious.

Miranda feigned surprise as she pocketed the note. "That's very soon. Are you sure it wouldn't be wiser to wait a little longer."

"No," he stated firmly. "If this gets out, the board will lock it down hard – which they should," he added quickly, "but I think they'll respond better if one in the hierarchy has been through the process already."

Miranda kept an expression on her face that hopefully conveyed that his request was not unreasonable. Inside, she rejoiced.

CHAPTER 5

Ethan

The door creaked and Ethan's heart almost stopped.

A figure emerged from the wedge of dim light, moving slowly and deliberately towards him in the darkness. Ethan forced his body to remain still and his breathing constant.

He had expected the cowards to try something like this. The guards were going to kill him as he slept and tell some lie that Carolyn would swallow with the support of her charismatic chief. Rage surfacing, he felt the intruder close in.

Ethan swung his legs out of bed and cast a circle whilst lunging away from the figure. He felt the air move at his side, followed by a clatter and a groan.

Sidling along the wall, he blinked furiously, trying to adapt to the dim light. All was silent, and Ethan thought perhaps his circle had worked, though it shed no glow with which to be sure.

He fumbled for the switch beside the door. Damn. He remembered the lodge was not serviced by such frivolities as a Lilim equivalent of electricity.

"Circle" he said again, invoking both protection and light as he now stared at Carolyn, sprawled out on the floor by the bed. Ethan watched with guilt and annoyance as she curled forward to reach beneath her trouser leg, rubbing the milky skin beneath as she looked about the room.

"It's so small," she said, and Ethan choked back a laugh. That was the last thing he'd expected to hear from a girl in his bedroom.

Perhaps sensing his improved humour, she scowled. "You should've asked for a better room."

"Trust me; it's an improvement on some I've had." There was no need to remind her of the shed where Peter had kept him. The Lilim didn't go easy on interlopers.

"I shouldn't have snuck up on you, enforcer." She turned him her vibrant cobalt eyes in reproach. Sounding a little more formal than he'd come to expect, he wasn't about to pick her up on it. She was in his room, for God's sake. He never thought she would actually seek him out like this. His mouth dried up and his voice, when he released it, came out gruff.

"I thought you were at the fortress." His brain continued to struggle with the sight of Carolyn beside his bed and the thoughts of what he *should* be asking her. "Is everything okay?"

She was wearing day wear, as if planning to go riding or climbing, the glow of his circle reflecting as a soft sheen from her skin. Hair loose, he enjoyed this mix of the feminine with the serviceable, though in his humble opinion she was still wearing far too much to be really comfortable in his room.

He put a hand out to help her up, and she took it.

Mistake! The circle swallowed them and he was suddenly embraced by her sweet summer fragrance. His skin seemed to come alive as she rose into his own personal space. Her exhaled breath fanned his bare chest.

Right. He was only in his underwear. Somehow he couldn't manage a smart comment about it as he realised her eyes hadn't left his face. Her expression was unreadable. He should move – no – *she* should move back from him.

He flashed back to the memory of their river encounter, to their every interaction thereafter, limited as each had been. What had he missed? Did it matter? There would never be another moment like this.

Everything had been building up to their being right here, right now. So far, Ethan had been careful to keep his distance, hadn't he? Any resolve he'd had now simply vanished, replaced by the promise of fulfilling a need they must surely both share.

There was something he should remember about that, but, dear God, she was right in front of him and rationality was only making his head ache. The instant her gaze dropped to his lips, there was no further thought and he launched his best attack.

It was as though he were drowning, spiralling ever deeper into the experience. Her soft lips collided with his and yielded. His teeth scraped against his lips as she returned his kiss with a fervour that matched his own. Every part of his body she touched lit up under the inferior glow of his circle. Their heartbeats pounded in his ears and his hands found the soft curves beneath her shirt. She murmured a complaint as their mouths parted.

It would take just a moment to remove the clothes that separated… His breathing was now uneven, a sense of urgency filling him so strongly he thought he might die if they couldn't be flesh against flesh—

Ethan hit the floor with a thud and crashed back to reality. The room was dark, cool and undeniably empty. Had it been a dream? Would it have been too much to have hoped to play it out to its conclusion?

That's just sad, my friend. Ethan could almost hear Sean's admonishment.

There was absolutely no chance of returning to sleep now so Ethan made his way to the facilities where he scrubbed away the last remnants of slumber and lust.

The slope of the roof of the lodge was shallow enough for the mage to perch upon. He felt the blanketing force of Arthur's power enforcing his limits. Had it eased up a bit perhaps since Carolyn's departure?

Arthur's measures had been pointless really. Compared to the Lilim chief and his guards, Ethan's skills were of little real consequence, even at full strength, but, like Carolyn had said, it meant something that the chief hadn't let his powers continue. The few, useless abilities that remained had only been allowed by Arthur as a "good faith" gesture.

Good faith, his arse, thought Ethan irritably, having learned by painful lesson that transfiguration hadn't been one of the talents left him. Sheer bloody pride stopped him from seeking Arthur out to beg the return of *that* one skill.

He was due back at the fortress later that day and believed the constraints there would make those he now felt here seem like nothing more than a simple grounding, rather than the gross infringement of his liberties they really were.

Unworthy of proper guard, Ethan was able to move freely throughout the hunting lodge. He knew of course that if he stepped outside the guards would be upon him, but the roof was blessedly free of their presence.

Similar to the twilight on the realm, dawn here was a lengthy affair, and Ethan tried to allow its calming and positive effects to filter through into his being. It had been tough at the lodge, with Carolyn being so close yet so distant.

Now fully awake, Ethan remembered his decision to back off from their destroyer. Had it been his choice? Given the heated, curious, and yes, admittedly guilty looks she had passed him over the past days — and sadly, he recalled each one in detail — Ethan was fairly certain he could live without her attachment to Note being sorted out. Despite the advantages — and it was hard to overlook these — it was just another reason for Carolyn to stay under her father's roof, and Ethan couldn't be having that.

While absent from the Earth shenanigans, Sean would be leading their merry little band of enforcers. With Ethan's history of rash decisions, his friend was sure to impress the powers that be with skills that stemmed from the powerful mage's level head and sound logic.

Ethan remained for some time on the gravelly sloping roof, his legs akimbo on a wide protruding rafter end. The hairs then prickled on the back of his neck, and his gaze moved to the gravel strewn ditch beside him.

"About time," he muttered, and watched as the stones stirred themselves and shifted to a face resembling that of the Faery hybrid. Although able to move through the tear, making a recognisable form was clearly tricky for Jonah under the blanket of Arthur's magic.

The face partially fashioned, Ethan watched in fascination as the gravel mouth opened and a lump appeared within it. The pseudo eyes seemed to plead with him to do something, and Ethan had to fight down his surge of disgust before reaching into the wide shape of a mouth. Urgh! His fingers closed over a hard, familiar object and he withdrew it in his hand.

The gravel face appeared to soften. "Thank you," it said, without the attractive Faery tones that were particular to the race, the sound being created only by the movement of the stones. Ethan watched a gravelly eyebrow rise. "That was a most uncomfortable mode of transport," Jonah said. "You need to take it now."

"Don't be ridiculous," snapped Ethan, now irritated that the stray puppy they'd adopted thought he could tell him what to do. To be fair, though, he knew the Faery was only following instructions and so Ethan's tone softened slightly. "Of course I'll drink it, but you should get the hell away before one of the guards decides to investigate why the idiot up here is talking to himself."

"If he knows you at all, he'll think nothing of it." The gravel face now laughed at him. Ethan just got all the breaks.

"You've been spending too much time with Sean and Mel," he retorted, deadpan, and felt a little satisfaction that it seemed to have found its mark. Jonah's gritty face scrunched up noisily for a moment before evening out again. "I have information, and Sean said to watch you take the potion before telling you."

"She's not even here," hissed Ethan. "If I've been fine for the past two weeks, I'm sure I can keep it going until I get back to the fortress today."

The enchantments had relaxed with Carolyn's absence from the lodge. Jonah had only managed to access him once since their agreement with Arthur, and it had been on the furthest reaches of his wards some days before, while they'd been climbing the hills that bordered the chief's private land.

Jonah's appearance in the scrub had entertained the three of them, though Carolyn had been uneasy about the contact, not that she didn't have reason. Jonah's counterpart, Ella of the Agency, had once tried to take Carolyn through the tear between the realms.

"Sean warned me you might resist."

Damn the mage. Ethan flashed back to his dream of Carolyn. He couldn't be sure – didn't *want* to be sure about the dream's validity. It had been *too* real. Too *vivid*. If he was being truly honest, could he deny the trace of magic he'd sensed that was neither his nor Carolyn's. He was perfectly placed for the Lilim to exploit.

Ethan glared at Jonah's image while he wiped the bottle on his shirt. It was a small dark bubble of a thing, in the style Sean used for his most complex potions. Ethan knew he *had* to take it and so strengthened his resolve.

"I'm giving trust here." The words were meant for Sean, and he twisted the black stopper from the bottle. The scent of magic rushed up his nostrils.

His thoughts shifted to Carolyn's kiss on the riverbank, on the occasion when she'd found him. *That* had been reality — sort of; the dream had not. Ethan downed the contents, finding it remarkable only in its bitterness that collided with the sweetness of his memories of Carolyn. Sean had further modified the potion from last year's efforts when Ethan had been slugging the stuff down like an adolescent would cheap beer.

"What?" Ethan replaced the stopper in the bottle as Jonah's face twitched weirdly in the dirt.

"I was expecting more opposition, that's all."

Ethan flexed his arms and curled them around his legs. He listened with all the focus he could muster as Jonah brought him news of the team.

Note

Note stared at his father, incredulous.

"I'm just trying to get this straight. You want me to come through the gateway to Skean and *fix* your oasis." He was very aware of Mel, seated on the other side of the scrying pool. Rudimentary, to say the least, the pool consisted of nothing more than an old ceramic mixing bowl, half filled with water, atop the city flat's coffee table.

They'd chosen this safe house deliberately. Had they opted for a Protectorate facility, the procedure for scrying another realm, whilst risky at best, could have had disastrous results.

Note had consented to Mel's presence on the condition she stayed out of sight. The mage was tough but her feelings about Hecaton were clear. Twirling a lock of wild, ebony hair, she had shrugged in apparent indifference. Note trusted his senses rather than his eyes.

"I am simply surprised you want to see me so soon after—" but was now unsure of the best way to finish. Hecaton continued to stare at some point Note couldn't see, somewhere at the edge of the ruined oasis in which his father stood.

"And that is partly why I need you, Notechis." Note cringed inwardly at the use of his full name — a name he associated with his prior-to-anchoring self. Hecaton's eyes glinted with something too close to humour for Note's liking.

"But your energy *is* replenishing." Note wasn't sure whether it was a good or a bad thing to have his father strong again.

"It is a slow process. As you know, my timing was perhaps not the best." Note couldn't help but feel a little compassion mixed in with the complicated emotions he felt towards his father. The high mage showed more regard for his sanctuary than for anything else in the realm. He had still drawn upon it to use against Note. Surely his father had to resent being pushed to do *that*.

"You have my word that you will return unharmed to the human realm." Note didn't have to imagine the disgust with which the word "human" had been uttered.

The remains of Hecaton's oasis beckoned to him. He could clearly hear water lapping at the high mage's feet. Note imagined he could smell vegetation at the water's edge, as though it was right next to him rather than a world away.

His concentration snapped back into focus when Hecaton added, "You may bring a friend if you wish, and I will extend to them the same courtesy."

Mmm, of course he knew that Mel was with him. "Terms?"

Older than dirt, the high mage looked as young as his son. His lips drew into the semblance of a smile. "I believe it a fair return for having allowed your previous visit to Skean."

Note felt the familiar anger with his father surge once more. *Allowed?* A human would not agree he'd been allowed. Note had after all been faced with an angry chief and his immediate guards to dispatch. Had his father attended, Note believed the result would have been hugely different and far bloodier. It was disconcerting that Hecaton still knew how to exploit Note's weaknesses.

"One hour prior to sunset tomorrow, in the corner of the world you currently occupy."

Note blindly talked over his urge to agree. "We have to speak to Sean," he said definitively as Hecaton's image disappeared in a wash of bubbles. Mel got up from her position on the floor and threw a tea towel over the bowl.

"Cancello," he muttered, securing the end of the call. Note didn't miss the uptight specificity of his father, not at all.

"I want to go with–" A gust of air behind her made Mel jump and Sean appeared.

"You finally answered Hecaton." Sean motioned towards the covered bowl, but Note couldn't discern any reprimand in the mage's tone. He noticed abstractly that Sean never spoke of Hecaton as being Note's father. The enforcer thought this was deliberate, somehow reinforcing the weakness of the blood tie that so clearly existed.

Note sank back into his chair and Mel perched on the end of the sofa, her scowl deepening as Sean stepped further into the room. The mage examined the city view from the window.

"What do you want to do about it? We can reinforce the wards and tap other sources to keep his calls for you at bay, for a while longer at least."

Examining Sean in profile, Note sighed. It was a tempting thought, but there was a solution to their problem, though it was admittedly a short term one. No-one could argue that Hecaton's calling was Note's fault, and that the gentle pull of his father threatened to increase to a level where the team would struggle. With Ethan away, the enforcers already felt the strain on their resources.

"I should go alone."

Mel's eyes became like saucers. "Hell, no, Note. Are you crazy? You can't go back there. The chief won't be caught unawares twice."

The Kistatus met her anxious glare, his gold irises flickering to an icy cold for an instant. If she noticed, she didn't say anything. Defeating his chief hadn't been the challenge he'd expected; one bite from Note and Lucas had fallen. In the conspicuous absence of his high mage, and fuelled with Hecaton's power, Note, Morgan and Mace had incapacitated the remaining guards, returning to Earth with Amanda plus two.

The toddler had been cute, reminding Note more of Carolyn than her mother. Reactivation of Amanda's breeder status had returned her physical appearance to that of an eighteen-year-old, and her resemblance to Carolyn had become disturbingly akin to the one Note shared with Hecaton.

Of course Hecaton was evil and Note wanted only to be free of him. Amanda was merely a slave to her own claiming.

"You still owe East," Mel said; as if he needed reminding of his *other* unfinished business in Skean. Note glanced at Sean who remained unmoving and apparently unconcerned at the window. It was uncanny how Mel knew the direction of his thoughts and Note smiled at her. His vision blurred for a moment before he realised what was happening.

Jonah's shape took form between Mel and himself. Predictably, the shadow Faery cast a glare towards Note that bordered on the hostile.

The Kistatus wasn't at all perturbed; he understood how protective the hybrid was about Mel. Somehow, the feeling didn't give its usual measure of relief. Mel's infatuation with Note – as he chose to see it – had dimmed since their return from Skean, and it was clear to all that something was happening between Jonah and Mel.

Mel slid around the shadow-Faery, barely acknowledging his arrival, and looked expectantly at Note.

"I don't forget," he said simply, and his foot that carried East's mark tingled in agreement. "Hecaton will grab me the instant I cross into Skean."

"I don't believe he'll harm you," said Sean, only now turning to speak to him directly.

"What makes you think that?" Note said, his expression more a grimace than a smile. "Because he let me beat the Chief and take off with his family?"

Mel's voice dropped uncharacteristically; she obviously hadn't forgiven him for keeping her out of *that* adventure. "No. Family's different. You *rescued* Carolyn's people, and deep down Amanda knows that. Hecaton seemed… I don't know. I *want* to tell you to stay back from him but I didn't get the sense he was lying." She looked to Sean for agreement but the mage seemed to be waiting on Note's reaction.

"My father does nothing good, Mel. *You* know that. He's got an agenda, and I'm not–" Note struggled uncomfortably with his thoughts. Not what? Not smart enough, not competent, not *strong* enough to best him?

"Melanie is right," Sean offered. "I … I witnessed your exchange and Hecaton spoke the truth."

Mel looked momentarily pleased before her expression darkened. Sean met her accusatory glare where a lesser man would have withered and died before it. Note smothered a laugh. Sean was perfectly capable of appearing before them with minimal fuss. The fact he deliberately provoked Mel by appearing behind her unexpectedly was certainly only for the mage's own amusement.

Jonah took a position beside Mel, mirroring her stance. She elbowed him, and he thrust out his arms. "I can't help it," his voice chimed melodically.

"It's no wonder," said Sean. "Though it may put an end to the entertainment, I'll teach you how to control those basic emotions that cause those like Jonah to leap to your aid and attract attention."

"What, you mean he's not really in love with me?" She had clearly meant it as a joke, but it had evidently fallen flat, for Jonah stomped off to the kitchen.

Mel shrugged before returning to the matter of Hecaton. "He's going to keep pulling until you talk to him, be it face to face or … or–" Note didn't like the look on his friend's face, as though an insight had struck her and she was about to offer a ridiculous suggestion he may very well accept. "See, Note, no-one hates the guy as much as I do, but if you don't answer his summons, he could do something drastic."

Yes, thought Note. Articulation of the thoughts he shared had cemented his decision. Sean remained quiet. He'd offered what he could and Note was grateful for that much. Hecaton could eventually cut through to him while Note slept or was otherwise weakened, and he had to minimise the risk by returning while he had at least the illusion of choice.

"I'll go alone," he reiterated, and Mel's groan clearly showed her frustration.

"You don't need to do that, you idiot. I've seen his worst. I'll come with you." Note couldn't even pretend annoyance at the slur. She had most definitely not witnessed Hecaton's worst, but the high mage *had* already played with her and so she wouldn't have the same appeal as a new face.

Mel's reaction was only another sign that she cared too much about him. The pretty mage was oblivious to the Faery, now returned from the kitchen. Jonah folded his arms across his chest and stood as still as a statue, watching Mel with his fixed, wide-eyed stare.

Note tried not to frown. Between Mel's single-mindedness and Jonah's clear annoyance, he didn't know which troubled him the most.

"I will speak to the precators," Sean said, "as I imagine that they will want to assist with a controlled pass. The gateway cannot be unsealed while we have the heirs to the realm in our care."

That was one way to put it. Amanda wouldn't consider anyone to be "caring" for her, livid as she was about her forcible removal from Skean. Without her mate, the presence of her two young children kept her scarcely civilised as she suffered withdrawal from the claim and the control of the Skean chief. "Choose Morgan, Mace or Mel to accompany you," Sean said. Mel smirked, as though she'd seen the acceptance in Note already.

The Kistatus was glad Sean hadn't suggested any of the *specialists* that existed in the other teams. As great as they were, he couldn't imagine any of their members faring well with his father.

The UK and Ireland were better staffed than the others, being the areas that possessed an unusually high number of gateway focus points from which to travel to the demon realms. Note had worked with almost all the Earth teams at one time or another during the last year and never once regretted being sucked into the cause. Working in opposition to Earth's Agency, they were dedicated in their mission to rescue humans, and lately demons from the realms.

Bound as he was to mages and demons in Carolyn's home realm, Note's position was unique. Whilst debating the merits of visiting his father, Note knew he hadn't entered this life for the altruistic aims that permeated the Protectorate's doctrine of peace and balance; he had done it for Carolyn, and for her alone.

The promise of her return was the thing he focussed on with an intensity that bordered on insanity. They had never become lovers in the traditional sense of the word, but he wondered with a lover's intensity what she was doing at this very moment as he counted off the minutes to her return.

CHAPTER 6

Carolyn

"**B**rute's gone rabid, milady." The groundsman grappled for the harness secured around the hound's head. "*Ruined,*" he spat. "He should be put down for everyone's safety."

Mario seemed merely amused by Carolyn's horror. The small man had appeared from nowhere as their carriage drew up to the fortress, so it was no wonder the beast had reacted badly. She had half a mind to let the groundsman struggle with him. But no, a castle guard, seeing the disturbance, drew his sword on approach. Mario, for once, was being unusually quiet, and he shrugged indifferently as she threw him a look. Carolyn leapt to retrieve the leash the groundsman had lost, causing him to splutter.

"M…milady?"

She drew herself up to her full height. "Don't 'milady' me. You watched him come out of the carriage. Do you think he would have been allowed to ride all this way with us if he'd been rabid?" Tether in hand, she waved off both the groundsman and the impassive Lilim guard while Mario looked on with a moderately surprised expression.

"This hound has been with me day and night for the last two weeks at the lodge, with my father's approval, I might add. I return home and suddenly you think you can take my dog because he treats you as a threat?"

"But, milady. You misunderstand. That's not—"

"It doesn't matter. You really want to take him?" Carolyn held the leash to both the groundsman and the guard. They ducked their heads, neither willing to embrace the inferred reprisals.

"Milady," demurred the guard while the groundsman made an

incomprehensible mumble.

"I thought not."

Mario caught up with her as she strolled to the entrance steps. "Well played," he acknowledged. "You don't really think of this as home, do you?"

Carolyn stopped to stare at him. He looked genuinely curious, and she considered for a moment. Yes, she loved Empustat; there was no question about it: the temperate climate, the forests, sea and land were all beautiful and magical. That she got to enjoy it with her father and her friends was wonderful.

How did she feel about the fortress, though? Everything within the walls was quaint and lovely, a city well protected. At the centre of the chief's extensive grounds, she could sense the added layers of protection which seemed unnecessary, almost cloying.

The whole effect was, however, impressive and otherworldly. Carolyn couldn't remember her exact words but knew what Mario meant. Home wasn't supposed to be simply where you happened to be for any length of time.

"No," she said eventually. "I know where my home is." The hound whined softly at her side and Carolyn dropped her hand to rest on its large head. Mario didn't press the point, for which she was grateful.

"Sure you want to take it into the house?" His brows drew together as the dog returned the Lilim's stare. Calling the chief's residence a house was an understatement. It was a mansion, with a magically crafted link to the outer fortress walls. She had been unable to understand the mechanics, though, despite Mario having tried to explain; Carolyn merely accepted it.

The dog nudged her hip as if to remind her. "Did you see those guys; they were going to hurt him." Carolyn didn't want the poor thing *disappearing* without a trace.

"I did, but–"

"There's no way I'm going to leave him outside, Mario. I don't trust them *not* to do something."

The Lilim chuckled. "The threat of your father is enough to keep them away." He folded his arms across his body, adopting an arrogant pose she was sure would have suited him better had he still looked like a teenager. It had to be hard for him to adapt.

"Maybe… I'm not taking the risk."

"At the start of this, I bet you didn't think you'd be stuck with the beast."

Carolyn's mood cracked, and she brought her head down to the hound's level, burying her hands into his furry neck. Mario rolled his eyes as she looked up, a smile lighting her features.

Was the Lilim going to be consistently weirded out by the hound? The beast had defended Carolyn, Ethan and Mario on the riverbank when they'd saved Ethan, and Carolyn couldn't imagine being without him now.

Admittedly, not a lot had happened since she'd rehashed her deal with Arthur that night. One of the boys had said it was like being on holiday and she supposed that was exactly how it appeared.

Thoughts sticking with Ethan, she felt it a shame they couldn't have travelled in the same coach. They'd been delayed for hours with a broken wheel and, though Mario was good company, she missed Ethan's challenging presence.

"I'm reeking of horses already, Mario," she said ruefully, and stood to examine the grime on her clothes. "And anyway, it's nice having him around. He's not like the other dogs."

"You can say that again." Mario had stepped up beside her, his voice a whisper in her ear. If she had been susceptible to his charms, she would have melted right there.

"Okay—" Carolyn snickered mischievously. This version of Mario possessed definite grown up appeal, but *he* really hadn't changed much at all. "He's not like – Ow!"

The Lilim's elbow in her ribs was only to be expected, but the big hound grumbled and wedged his large frame between them, trying to force them apart.

"Oh, good boy," praised Carolyn as Mario pulled a long-suffering face.

"She's going to get fed up with you soon," he teased, and Carolyn shook her head automatically before realising he was laughing at her gullibility. It was only natural she be protective of the hound. Arthur had been remarkably silent about the shift in the animal's loyalties. It was, after all, the actions of his best men, Peter and Patrick, that had led to Carolyn having her own personal guard dog.

Little had been seen of the two ranking guards whilst at the lodge. They'd lost privileges such as being around her father constantly.

By Carolyn's reckoning, it wasn't nearly enough reparation. Having thwarted Peter's romantic designs and following Ethan's epic failed mission to find her, Peter had released Ethan from custody, to be hunted down like a common criminal. Worse than that, she remembered, those hounds weren't supposed to do anything other than rip the mage to shreds at the end of the hunt. Carolyn wasn't altogether sure about her father's lack of involvement, but it did her no good to think on it.

Mario had clearly guessed the direction of her thoughts. "I wouldn't think too much about the two P's," he muttered. "I'm sure your father has worse in store for them now we're back at the fortress." Carolyn suppressed a shiver, equal parts anticipation and revulsion.

Arthur could be harsh. "You don't think—" The thought of Peter's punishment didn't trouble her *too* much, but she didn't want him to die for it.

"Rehabilitated, I'm sure. Pure born Lilim don't exactly grow on trees around here." Otherwise their fates would be very different, Carolyn realised. Mario returned his attention to the hound. "He's a decent guard dog, I'll grant him that, but if you're going to keep him around, at least name him something other than 'Boy', and let me have him bathed." There was no reason to refuse, but the animal flinched at the mention of a bath.

"Mario's right, Boy – Beni." With a smirk, she used the name that had been occasionally popping into her mind. Was it a mistake, or had she already bonded with him. Fingers still in the deep ruff of his neck, she knew the answer. Failing to name him for so long had been futile. "Tell you what," she said decisively, "I'll go for *my* bath and come fetch you when I'm clean again."

She stood up and offered Mario the corded leash. Taking it, he answered suavely, "Only for you, pretty lady."

"You are simply too kind, Mario," she said, mimicking his over the top style and fluttering her eyelashes to his amusement. "Whatever did I do to deserve you?"

As she entered the building, she swivelled to watch him struggling to restrain the hound. Clearly toying with him, Carolyn new the beast could easily pull Mario off his feet.

"Beni – really?" he chided irritably, "as in benivolens, Latin for 'friend', Mutt. God spare me from sentimental females." Carolyn caught his eye as he turned, his teeth flashing before he resumed his one way conversation with Beni. "You plan to live up to that name?"

Carolyn practically skipped up to her room. Was it wrong for her to feel so … so joyful after everything that had happened? Mario and Ethan were safe and her father was to send her away in just over a week. Her stomach gave an odd little lurch at the thought. Her concept of home definitely needed more scrutiny, but she wasn't really up to it yet.

"Morning, Milady." The maid turned from tying up the curtains in Carolyn's chamber. Fragrant steam billowed in from the bathroom, carrying the enticing scent of sweet herbs and flowers. Carolyn returned the greeting and started to strip. "Milady Lena asked me to let her know when you got back in."

Carolyn froze for a moment. Yes, of course, Lena would certainly want to catch up with her. The Lilim hadn't stuck around for long at the lodge, and Carolyn realised she had missed the quiet company of her father's pretty consort.

"That's all right, Katie. I'll find her when I finish up here."

"Very good, Milady." Katie dropped into a little curtsey, Carolyn merely nodding her acknowledgement. Perhaps she should be worried about becoming all too tolerant of such deferential treatment, but the bargain with

Father had brought their relationship to a more acceptable balance of power, and damn it all if it wasn't such a nice feeling.

Trust, however, was something else entirely. She would see what she could do about the gateway issue but didn't look forward to her father's response. It was easier to wait it out, regardless of Ethan's thoughts on the matter.

The bath was a delight. A simple waterfall lever gave access to warm water pumped from fire heated tanks beneath the fortress. With the bath's outflow cut off, it had filled to the brim. Carolyn eased from its iridescent polished surround into its watery silence, savouring the warmth and energy that seeped into her. She spun slowly, her hair wrapping around her in a light embrace.

Her thoughts returned to her current situation. Following their capture, they had been lied to, reconditioned, and in Mario's case, tortured and humiliated. After discovering her talent for shifting forms, Carolyn had happened upon him, half-starved and slightly mad but still retaining his self-assuredness and spirit.

Mario had helped her when nothing had made sense, and by it she had begun to fight back against her restrictions. A beautiful Lilim, as they all were, there was so much more to him than his looks or his magic – and he certainly could use *that*.

As well as tutoring her, Mario had preserved her sanity. A fine example was Note's claiming tattoo she bore, the effects of which were kept entirely under control due to her friend. Fifteen years of pubescence had been brought to an end by her father's hand. Of course, it had been him who had cursed Mario to begin with.

The young Lilim was doubtlessly reporting back to the chief. She could only hope he wasn't reporting on Ethan too. Her father hadn't restored Mario out of the kindness of his heart, of course, but Mario *was* her confidante and she needed him to do whatever was necessary to maintain her status. If he were free, then Carolyn would no longer have her friend *and* teacher. His new matured state was slowly registering with her but mostly all she saw when she looked at him was the boy she'd met during his incarceration.

Common sense told her to detest her manipulating father, and she had to admit she *disliked* the fact he'd influenced her, but she couldn't quite manage to hate *him*.

Part of her dilemma was that he accepted her for what she was *now*, with all her freaky non-Lilim skills as well as her Lilim talents. The Lilim had the ability to "surf" the minds of others, and it was a nasty, invasive trick, but she had used it twice in this realm. Carolyn had used it with her father, and, having been inside his mind, could now almost understand what had driven him. He cared about her, of that there was no doubt, and it would be wise to focus on that simple truth rather than the unorthodox methods he'd used in enforcing her care.

Carolyn didn't need reminding of the fact that he had robbed her of her past; he had, after all, reinstated all she had lost. Surprisingly, the chief had known all along that she had for a time been rediscovering her abilities … and yet, he'd allowed it. He hadn't been repulsed by her talents, and so she had earned a certain amount of his respect. Or rather, earned enough that he wouldn't match her with a perfect Lilim to continue his line in her "breeder" capacity.

Carolyn shuddered at the thought. Discovering *this* plan had somehow been worse than discovering she was a warrior – the mythical destroyer – in her home realm.

She knew her anchor, Note, had saved her from a feral existence, bringing a whole new set of problems with it.

Hmm. A surprised stream of bubbles escaped her lips as she recognised her cowardice in regard to Note. Should she be worried that it didn't sit too badly at all? Was she being fair to anyone in her life? Now that Mario had attached her emotional connections to everyone else, she baulked at the thought of attaching them to Note.

The connection to her family was stressful. The fact she couldn't be with her mother and Eddie caused a dull ache that Carolyn couldn't bear to focus on for long.

She wasn't confident enough to try accessing her link to Note. There had been times on Earth when she had been quite monstrous in her "passion" for the Kistatus. Once back with the others, she would find a way to reach her family and find a decent method of dealing with her anchor.

Carolyn reluctantly emerged from the water and wrapped a fluffy towel around herself. She was interested to see if her wardrobe had been updated in her absence. Alongside the impractical dresses, she happily examined the small range of serviceable clothing she preferred, opting for navy trousers in the softest leather, matched with a pretty blue top. Though her choices had improved somewhat, she could only find matching soft pumps for her feet. They would never do if she managed to get some riding in later today. She was keen to be reacquainted with Zelda. The horse should have healed from her injury by now.

Carolyn was slipping on a pair of short grey boots when her gaze rested on her box of hair accessories. Opening it on the dresser, she withdrew a pretty item that she recognised from her life before the fortress. *Morgan* was the name that came to mind and Carolyn's smile became a frown as she twirled the gilded piece in her hand. A faint tinge of magic surrounded it.

"Referro," she muttered, and felt the changes ripple over the accessory.

It became a plain long-bladed screwdriver. She squeezed and released the rather obscure item. It didn't fit into this life of hers now – but at one time she had relied on it – loved it? Raising it to her nose, there was a faintly discernibly metallic scent that came not from the blade but, she suspected, the blood with which it had come into contact.

Previously, she knew the piece had been a ceremonial knife – a witch's athame, but *this* was the form she'd accepted and used to good effect in answering her gateway *calls*, first alone and latterly with the Protectorate team of which she, Ethan and Mario were a part.

Carolyn, half-smiling, recalled the spirit of the team. It had felt wonderful to share in something so powerful – almost blessed. Her heart sank at the sudden feeling of failure. Had that sense of purpose been lost to her for ever?

Hearing a whine from outside her door, she was glad of the distraction. Carolyn didn't want to dwell on thoughts that caused her pain. Crossing the polished wood floor, she wasn't surprised to see Beni, a bedraggled Mario in tow. Her mood lifted at the sight of them and she bent to pet the still dry and undeniably filthy animal.

Casting a look behind her, she came to a swift decision. "The bath is non-negotiable, Beni. I'm putting you in *mine* before it drains away."

"Good luck with that," returned Mario, ungraciously, but he followed Carolyn through to the bathroom and watched as the big animal responded to her coaxing. Dropping her hand into the remaining water, she shut off the outflow. "You're going to smell like a girl now," the Lilim said as they watched the hound splash around in the suds.

"Ouch!" The exclamation followed a clattering sound that came from Carolyn's bedroom.

Mario's eyes locked on hers. What was Lena doing in her room – uninvited? They went in to find the Lilim shaking her hand in the air. Unlike Carolyn, Lena seemed to be born for sweet dresses and contrived hair do's. Her sleek tresses shimmered as she spun towards them.

"Lena, what are you–" Carolyn saw the screwdriver, now rolling on the floor, and bent to retrieve it.

"No, don't tou–" Her vehemence sapped when Carolyn held out the item, innocently resting in her hand. "I was curious, and when I tried to touch it, it burned me." Lena's curiosity had clearly returned for she now peered intensely at it.

"I am so sorry," Carolyn said, scowling at Mario who had curled a lip at the consort's outburst.

"No, no." Lena took a deep breath and offered a sheepish smile. "It's my own stupid fault. There's such strange goings on, I should have known better than to touch things that belong to you or *him*." When her gaze slid beyond the doorway, it was clear she was referring to Arthur. Carolyn hardly deserved the kind of agitation her father elicited, or anything close to it, but she thought she understood what Lena had meant by it.

Cordially, Mario raised his hand and stepped before Lena. "If you would allow me, my lady?" Carolyn felt she could breathe easier with Mario back on proper form. Lena placed her fingers tentatively over his, Carolyn unsurprised by the trust he could foster in someone like Lena.

"Sana carne," he whispered, and a violet glow encompassed Lena's hand before soaking into the now healed flesh.

"Thank you." She flexed her fingers, and with a watery smile, turned to Carolyn. "I wanted to see how you were?"

"I'm fine, Lena. Really."

Lena's features tightened in earnest. "I never wished to keep anything from you," she exclaimed, wrapping her arms across her body. "You must believe that!"

"I do." A little overwhelmed by the woman's vehemence, Carolyn knew *she'd* be forgiven if the situation had been reversed.

"You have nothing to be sorry for, Lena." Carolyn pocketed the screwdriver. "I know it was all my father's doing." Carolyn chose to ignore Mario's cocked eyebrow.

Lena sighed, the relief softening her features. "You are an angel." No, not even close, Carolyn thought, but it was nice to hear the compliment. "I want to tell you that I never agreed with Arthur's actions. You deserved so much better." Her nose crinkled adorably. It was easy to see why Arthur had chosen the Lilim as his consort.

Mario's expression, as he stood behind Lena, was perplexing. *Don't trust her*, he broadcast, and Carolyn rolled her eyes heavenwards. Given what she knew of Mario, she couldn't completely have faith in *him*, but Lena had only ever been straightforward – mostly – in her dealings with Carolyn.

Was the dog the only one who didn't have his own best interests at heart?

Lena did concern her slightly, though. The woman owed total loyalty to Arthur, and therefore shouldn't be discussing him with Carolyn. But what had she said really? That she didn't agree with his methods? Well, neither did Carolyn. Surely disagreement was allowed between any couple, regardless of their standing.

Mario was being overly cautious, but it wouldn't hurt to take his advice. Besides, Carolyn *agreed* with Lena, she *had* deserved much better treatment, but her father had only been doing what he thought – in his own rather warped way – was best for her.

Carolyn could only thank Lena for the support and her promise to chat further later. The Lilim left in a rustle of skirts and assurances to help with her – soon to be expanding – jewellery collection.

With a sigh, Carolyn closed the door and leaned back against its frame, crossing her arms before her. The light room seemed to brighten further in the silence that now filled it. "Odd?"

Mario shrugged, and then the concern on his face melted to amusement as he tilted his chin towards the bathroom. "Let's get Beni. He's being remarkably quiet in there."

Carolyn rubbed the hound down with a towel as Mario showed her how to finish drying him using a touch of air magic. Surprisingly, Beni allowed her to practise on him with what seemed like bored acceptance.

"Oh, you're lovely now, boy," she said playfully, "but Mario's right. You smell girly." The beast chuffed lightly before circling to place his great head beside her. She scratched behind his ears obligingly. "Don't mean to insult your masculinity," she soothed, "but I am glad you're clean."

Katie entered with a trolley a while after Beni's bath. Giving the hound a wide berth, she unloaded the contents onto the breakfasting table. "I thought you'd be hungry, Milady. You missed tea downstairs."

"Oh, I didn't realise the time," said Carolyn, casting an inquisitive look at Mario.

Large-eyed affected innocence was her reward. "What? You expect me to keep you right, your highness? I've not exactly been keeping note of the routines around here." Carolyn scowled at Katie's horrified expression as she scurried from the room.

"You must know that the servants report everything," she scolded. "You should at least pretend to fit the mould." Somehow, she just couldn't control the iciness in her voice. It was so easy to forget that Mario had only recently become subject to the formal routines she kept, but she knew he *knew* he had to be careful.

"Which mould would that be, pretty lady." The "pretty lady" part was devoid of its usual charm. "The one where I bow and scrape and act as if I'm glad to be here?"

Carolyn looked on, speechless at the outburst. She wasn't used to this from him. What had happened? *You like it here*, her brain supplied. *He's a prisoner.*

"No, I-" What could she say? "Damn it, Mario, I'm not sure what I mean now." Her eyes prickled with warmth. Was she being selfish and shallow? Manipulative?

"I do know what you mean, Carolyn. That's the point." His hand slapped against the wall behind her. "The lodge was simply to lull you ... *us* into a false sense of security." His tone had gone from mocking *her* to being self-derisory.

Carolyn couldn't keep up with him, but weirdly she felt more alive than ever. A tear escaped her eyes, and she brushed it away. "Look around you, Carolyn, what girl doesn't dream of being a princess. At least here you're with your own kind; you haven't to worry about being snatched away by the Agency, or by the Rakshasas wanting you as a broodmare. Maybe *you* should stay."

"*I* should stay!" Was he really saying that he and Ethan should leave her with her father, under the care of the Lilim. Once aired, what had seemed like an attractive proposition waiting at the back of her mind had suddenly lost its appeal.

Mario stopped in front of her, visibly deflating. He looked torn and emotional in a way Carolyn hadn't witnessed before. Crazy and irrational, yes, but not this.

"I'm sorry," he said eventually. "I'm partly if not fully responsible for our situation. I'll play the game, of course I will, but you have to remember that Ethan's right." His gaze roved the elaborate and beautiful surroundings and Carolyn's followed suit, trying to see as he saw. "You referred to here as 'home', and maybe it is … but Ethan and I … we're just biding our time until we get back to Earth." The last words were spiked with an edge of desperation.

"You don't think he'll let us go." It came out as an accusation rather than the question she'd intended. Mario wasn't lying, she *was* too comfortable and only moments before had been sad at the thought of leaving her life in Empustat.

"But he promised." The words sounded weak even to *her* ears.

"Right," Mario said, his lip curling at one side, "so we all keep our promises. We don't influence and *help* people come to an alternative decision that they end up believing to be their own."

Carolyn bristled at the thought. "Maybe I'm a bit naïve, but really, Mario. I haven't had life experience that's in any way comparable to yours but *that* won't happen to me. I won't *let* it."

Mario shook his head, as though she was incapable of understanding, and stopped to smooth a lock of hair that had fallen in front of his eyes. "Whatever you choose, I'm there for you." Then under his breath: "I may not have a choice, but I'm telling you now that if you decide that this is what you want, then to hell with the Protectorate and the team, I'll stay. Maybe if I teach you enough, I can keep you from losing yourself."

Carolyn's mouth dropped open. He was willing to give up his goals to keep her happy? She didn't want to explore how much of that loyalty was true and how much Arthur's influence.

He had worked hard to give her a decent grounding in magic, and had suffered so much because of her. She was doing him an injustice by leaning on him.

But who else was there for her? Her father? Ethan? *No.* She took the screwdriver out of her pocket and set it on the table before her. More questions surged in her mind, begging to be asked, but Mario cut her off. "Show's not over yet," he said obscurely.

"And what about Ethan?" She felt as though she'd poured all her vulnerability into those few words.

If Mario noticed, he didn't let on. "Not my favourite subject, but yes. Nothing will keep him from returning home."

Not even me. Carolyn quashed the thought, affronted that it had emerged at all. She didn't belong to Ethan, or to anyone. She wasn't an abandoned love-sick little girl. She felt something for the mage, but it couldn't be love. Having experienced the effects of the emotion, it wasn't pretty, changing her from a tough unanchored destroyer to a needy snivelling wretch.

But Note *had* enabled her to function as a human again. She had regained her conscience and begun to function within a team, using her abilities and training to be a better warrior.

It would be easy to forget the negative parts that distinctly outweighed the positive. She'd taken Note from *his* world to live a life with strangers, and tried to protect and control him by selfish manipulation, and by pushing the boundaries of their bond.

Note wasn't like Arthur or other chiefs and high mages who *took* everything. Even after her disappearance, and probably out of some warped sense of duty, he had reached her in Empustat and helped to mend the damage Arthur had inflicted. But no more, she was done with using him.

The Kistatus would be better off if she never set foot in her home realm again. How could she take the chance of accepting her link to Note when she may never be able to function as an individual again.

She had begun to enjoy being the Carolyn she now was, but Mario's words gave her pause for thought. Her existence here was indeed a beautiful, flawed and incomplete dream where she would have no chance of reaching her potential, but she could be *happy* and the Lilim would keep her safe. Why were *both* choices becoming equally repellent?

"You are quite delightful when you're thinking," Mario said as he joined her at the table. Carolyn was grateful for the lighter banter but remained wary of what lay beneath. "Penny for them?"

"Probably not worth that much." She poured tea from a silver pot, Beni watching her every move from where his head rested on her lap. The hound didn't budge as she absently swiped crumbs from his coat.

"It's a shame you and Ethan don't get on," she ventured.

Mario sprayed tea as he laughed and Carolyn threw him a napkin to clean up. "Compared to back home, we get along famously – but at the lodge, that was all the better for Arthur to work on us, my dear."

Carolyn didn't flinch at the news. She *had* noticed the difference in the air on their arrival. And what of Ethan, they'd hardly spent any time alone to explore what existed between them.

Her father, Mario or one of the guards had always been close by, and at night she had barely undressed before falling into the deepest of sleeps. *Now*, she wondered at that. Their fun-filled pursuits *could* have accounted for the exhaustion, but it hadn't been the reason. The new knowledge hurt.

Arthur could still keep them compliant, but it would be more of a stretch for him at the fortress. "I don't really get on with anyone," Mario continued in mock dejection, seemingly in ignorance of her own revelations. "Why do you think I was with Sean?"

"That's not true," she said abruptly. Was he trying to make Carolyn doubt everyone and everything? Her hand rested on the screwdriver on the table.

"May I?" Carolyn passed it to Mario without thought and he watched her expression with what seemed like disappointment that it had been so easily relinquished. What did he expect? It was only a thing.

As he twirled the item in his hand, it sluggishly changed from screwdriver to hair rod a couple of times. "Lena used up the enchantment by touching it," he observed. "Morgan must have added something to the decorative charm."

His voice dropped, Carolyn having to lean forward to catch his words. "We should do a little work on your destroyer skills. *This–*" He tapped the tool in his palm for emphasis. "This *chose* you, or vice versa, for a reason. Sure, you can change just about any item you need to suit your purpose, but *this* is special and particular to *you*."

He passed it back to Carolyn, and she resolutely said nothing about the spent silvery band and tiny stone that had suddenly adorned Mario's little finger. "About Ethan?" she prompted. Mario frustrated her by taking a huge bite of his sandwich which he then munched on rapturously before saying, "It wouldn't all go to hell without Ethan, but yes, it'll be hard for him to stay this final week. He hates the magical constraints more than anything, especially with the Lilim guards watching his every move." He gave her a moment as she digested the fact. "As you've seen with our training sessions, Arthur didn't mute *our* powers. If Ethan was going to escape, he would do it before returning to the fortress. If he gets a chance, he will probably take it."

Mario was not trying to spare her feelings, and she resented the odd twist of his mouth that hinted at him laughing at her. "Why are you smiling like that?"

"I'm not," but then he shook his head. "If your bond with Note hadn't been tampered with, you'd be a different girl." He easily met her glare. Carolyn didn't appreciate the reminder that her feelings had been messed up, but she remained adamant that the anchoring and claiming had skewed them to begin with. "Think about it," Mario continued unashamedly. "It's not just that Ethan can be a bit of a dick at times."

"Yes," Carolyn huffed, realising she could never stay annoyed with either of the boys for long. "This coming from the angelic Mario."

He lowered his brows and waggled them suggestively. "Got it in one, pretty lady."

CHAPTER 7

Sean

The warehouse kitchen was not a favourite location for the team but Sam's ruddy face beamed as he chopped a large turnip on the scarred counter top. Jonah was perched on the table's edge, looking deceptively fragile with his knees drawn up to his chin.

"Mel likes a man who can cook," said the Faery, presumably by way of explanation. He lifted his huge eyes to Sean's, and the mage accepted Sam's warning thunk of the vegetable knife on the counter.

"I suspect most women could be swayed by the like," Sean replied vaguely and was rewarded by Sam's wide smile. "Chocolate works too, but she would have to fight *you* for that I expect."

Sean held back a moment on his request as Jonah's expression changed from smug to moderately alarmed. Mel was training with the others in the basement, accessible from the kitchen, and it was interesting to see Sam was not above a little manipulation to gain help with his chores.

"Mel's not 'most women'," mused the Faery.

"You're with her at meal times," Sam boomed. "It's the way to a woman's heart, my boy." He slid the vegetables to one side with the edge of his big knife. "One day we'll bake a huge chocolate cake with a heap of frosting that even *you* wouldn't manage on your own."

Jonah's eyes lit at the prospect. Sam's desserts were popular. "I'll need a medium pot for these," Sam said and Jonah obediently slid off the counter to fetch one from the cupboard while Sam picked up a bag of potatoes from the floor. He poured them on to the work surface while Jonah unhurriedly scooped the prepared vegetables into the pot.

"I'm sorry, Sam," Sean eventually said, "but would you mind if I borrow your helper? It shouldn't take too long."

"No problem," said Sam. "Speedy's coming over and I'm about to stop and make sandwiches for the team. I expect they'll be famished by now." He indicated the basement door, left ajar and through which jubilant hoots and shouts rose to their hearing.

What *were* they up to? Sean thought, strongly suspecting that Jonah was helping Sam in preference to sharing Mel with the others.

"You know how they get when they're training." Sean did – mostly. The amount of food they could consume was quite revolting. Sam bestowed a big, lopsided smile on Jonah. "The job comes first. The boy should manage this okay, next time."

"It's Jonah." The hybrid frowned. "I wanted–" but he faltered at the sight of Sean's raised eyebrow. "I … I'll just grab a pack."

"No need," said Sean, encouraged that the petulance hadn't developed. The quirks were undoubtedly from the boy's Faery side but he was gaining some control. A messenger type satchel appeared across Jonah's body. A minor adjustment left room for unobstructed wing release if required. "You shouldn't need the supplies, but best to look professional when we're assisting another group."

"Which one?" asked Sam, showing a rare glimmer of interest.

"We're going to Morocco for this call."

"Right you are, then. Don't let me hold you up." Sam offered an alarming wave, the knife still being in hand, as Sean took Jonah's offered arm.

They began their trip through the Earth network of gateways until reaching the final one from which they would access the Tangier base.

Sean congratulated himself on his choice of enforcer. Jonah didn't suffer the disorientation that some of the others struggled with. Mel had once vomited on his shoes after such a journey and he wasn't keen to repeat the experience. Before Sean's change and current Protectorate restrictions, he would have accessed the realm directly from Scotland, and traversed the smaller land by magical as well as more technical means.

Limits aside, there was no sense in depleting the stores that Note had so graciously shared when the procedural routes sufficed.

"Shit." Jonah fumbled as a sword began to form in his hand, and Sean made a mental note to discuss the team's use of language. The Faery was too quick to pick up bad habits and couldn't always discern their appropriate usage.

"Better safe than sorry," he said, answering the unspoken question.

The sunlight was almost blinding as they emerged into the Rask realm, and Sean set a protection circle with a one word invocation to cover them both.

The scene before him was disappointingly well under control. Of five men, two were circled in the same fashion as he and Jonah. Sean surmised that the circled enforcer was new to the job. He bowed slightly in acknowledgement of the late arrivals. It was mildly disheartening to see the increasingly common practice of binding the victim while the team took care of business.

The two Rakshasas they had been fighting were almost secure, the three un-circled enforcers in the process of fastening the last rope around the second large demon. On completion, a shimmer of magic halted their struggles. With the mountainous creature roped to the ground, Sean was reminded of the Lilliputians' antics in Gulliver's Travels.

Sean dropped his circle. "Primitive, Faisal, but effective." He approached him, Jonah as close as a shadow at his back. "It appears you have no need of our assistance."

"It is nice to be commended," returned Faisal, pausing only to wipe sweat from his brow. He clasped Sean in an embrace, and Sean returned it with a pat on the exuberant enforcer's shoulder. Once released from the bear hug, Sean welcomed the air returning to his lungs. There was no-one else who would greet him with such fierceness. "Protectorate rules state we must investigate the claims that this male is making."

The enforcer pointed an accusing finger towards the human circled with Faisal's new man. "He says he has papers."

"That's—" Sean racked his brains. "It's quite preposterous," he muttered. Yes, he'd been very busy lately but surely he would know of people travelling under sanction. Or perhaps he was giving himself too much credit. He already knew that the precators didn't always share, which was contrary to expectations.

"I'm inclined to agree," Faisal said, his eyes resting on Jonah, unable to disguise his curiosity. "We didn't want to bring him back without a formal check."

"Unfortunately, I can't do it here." Sean thought the circled male looked annoyed, but he mellowed slightly when the mage continued persuasively, "If all is in order, I'll personally escort you into the Rask stronghold. Our forces have expended considerable effort, and it would be advisable you cooperate in this small way." His tone left no room for quibbles, however pleasantly the news was delivered.

"I was never in danger," muttered the man – mage, amended Sean as the enforcer at his side dropped his eyes and the circle dissolved. This allowed Sean to read the signatures of Faisal's new man and the lesser magic user who cast an envious glance at his young captor.

Sean could discern the traveller had no special skills, probably on a par with Agency type workers. "My name is Graeme McCann," said the mage imperiously, "and I assure you there's been some mistake here." His eyes shifted from the restrained Rakshasas to the satisfied if work weary enforcers. "What should I do about my guards in the meantime?"

The tiniest waver in the mage's voice betrayed fear rather than exasperation and Sean was intrigued. Why would any magic user choose to be in the demon realms if not traditionally traded or – as was common – a demon groupie of some sort? The latter would seem to be a stretch, whatever the mage's story, but one could never tell.

Though neither Rakshasas could move, their eyes rested covetously on their soon to be escaping prey.

It was hard to imagine that these were Rake's people. The realm's high mage, Roland, had shipped the dissident to work and die in the Mow mines.

A traditional warrior race, the people were not known for great intellect, but they held huge respect for magic and users of the craft. Roland had undoubtedly rid the land of any competition for his title. It was a pity, thought Sean. There was strength in numbers when it came to magical pursuits, and much could be done to improve the lives of the realm's natives. Not that it was any of Sean's concern. Led by their chief and high mage, as was the norm in many realms, the populace would honour and keep to the wishes of their masters at all costs.

"Once we're through the gateway, the guards will shake loose from their restraints and should await your return. They're not going to go back to Roland empty handed if they can help it."

Faisal gave a snort, his grin brief. "It's been a while since I've dealt with the Rakshasas high mage," he nudged Sean lightly. "I heard that you've not been so lucky."

Sean merely nodded. The enforcers would know that Mel and Rake had been the product of their last encounters in the lands of Rask and Sedert, respectively. They had been swiped from under the noses of their captors without the face-off that would have been expected during high mage disputes.

Faisal continued his curious appraisal of Jonah as the party left through the gateway. "Quieter than Mario, this one," he said by way of introduction, the skin at the corners of his eyes crinkling in speculation. Jonah squirmed uncomfortably under the scrutiny and Faisal chuckled with a depth that seemed to come from his boots.

Sean had no doubt the black-skinned enforcer could guess the demon's origin with a decent chance of accuracy. There was no point in depriving Faisal of his fun but Sean would have to apologise to the boy later.

The enforcer beamed and offered his hand to Jonah. The surprised hybrid was summarily spun like a dancer as Faisal went on, "Tell me, friend, where *do* you keep your wings in this garment?"

*N*ote

"Bloody hell, Note, you did it. You did it."

They'd been practising changing into each other's animal-mage forms and Note was exhausted. On the training room mats, Mel was on all fours, facing him as he struggled with the very last of his transformation. As he willed the return to his human shape, the headstrong girl positively glowed with satisfaction.

It was a source of pride as this was *her* skill they were practising. Before Jonah had become a fixture in their lives, she would have jumped all over him. As it was, Note was glad of her restraint. She had witnessed up close and personal how difficult the task had been for him.

Mace high-fived the Kistatus as he stretched up from the mat, and it was as though everyone held their breaths while Note fished in his pocket and retrieved the gateway device they'd been using for practise. Having started with six of the inactivated older models, they were now down to three. The others hadn't had the same difficulty, managing to keep their clothes and weapons as they transfigured back to their Earth selves.

From her cross-legged position behind Mel, Morgan awarded him a wink and a grin as she recorded the new results into her personal device. The bright haired witch had been invaluable with helping him control the magic. He was finally getting to practise all the spells she'd painstakingly taught him when his power had only been latent.

The support of the team and their belief in him had borne fruit in the most unexpected ways. He couldn't forget that Hecaton's involvement had hastened the process – Morgan's guess. She hadn't been present when the high mage had "gifted" him and he was fairly sure that she didn't comprehend the sheer volume of power he carried.

"Phone *and* clothes," she said directly to him. "That's a huge improvement."

"You think?" Mel interjected, skimming her eyes over Note's body. She crossed the hall and tossed him a t-shirt from the rapidly decreasing pile on the table. He caught it and quickly pulled the fabric over his head.

"Still only the lower half," he said, more pride than disappointment in his voice. This had been his first real success. Practising the skills of the others had been frustrating, but good fun.

"Where do the missing things go?"

"Shadow realm." Mel didn't miss a beat and everyone stared at her.

"Where Jonah's—" Morgan's voice held a tinge of fear and Mace slid up to her side, resting a big hand on her shoulders.

"Oh no," Mel suddenly seemed to catch on to what they were thinking. Clever as the girl was, her thought processes couldn't always be followed logically. "Jonah's DNA originates from somewhere different," she explained. "I meant that I think the lost things end up on the Mystics' plane. We can't travel there but bits of us are picked up by the seers. In your case, Note, quite literally."

"You're sure about this," said Morgan.

"Hell, no," huffed Mel. "I'm no scholar. Note knows that better than anyone. It's just a reasonable assumption."

"This could be bad," Morgan said, accepting Mace's hand to get up from the mats. "If I'd thought, I wouldn't have suggested practising with the old gateway devices."

"Mmm, like the seers have any need of those." Prompted by the silence, Mel threw up her hands. "I disabled them."

Morgan seemed only moderately reassured. "I'll have to ask if Sean can recover them."

"If you really, truly have to," said Mel, her sudden meekness causing Morgan to relax slightly.

"It'll be fine. Note's just so close to getting this transfiguration perfect. It's trickier for him as he's changing back to human, having to bypass the natural choice of his true form." Note hadn't thought about it that way but he had to agree that the transformation would have been easier in his Kistatus body. If he'd used that method, he wouldn't have been inadvertently dropping his clothes into the seers' realm.

Working with "humans", it had always seemed practical and good manners to spend most of the time in his gateway chosen self. *Nothing to do with Carolyn's love of the form, of course.*

Mel's eyes sparked with unexpected mischief. "I wish we could practise more on this and maybe go for a walk about town?"

"Yes, I'll get a couple of leashes and maybe those cute studded collars." Mace scratched behind Note's human ear. "Doesn't feel the same without fur, does it?" Note batted the hand away, acutely aware of the cat like motion.

"I don't think you put cats on leads," he said.

Mel snorted with laughter, falling back onto her elbows on the mat. "Did you see the big-assed cat that Mace turned into? We could take *him* walkies without being laughed at."

"Yes," agreed Morgan, shaking her hair to scoop it into a ponytail, "but they'd be calling the zoo rather than pet rescue if he was spotted anywhere."

"Thanks," said Mace, in genuine pride. The demon had been favoured by Hecaton during his first visit with Note to the realm. Instead of his Mow appearance taking the gateway chosen form of a seriously overweight, though selected male, Hecaton had replaced Mace's given physique, using the mass to fashion a secure shape which looked uncannily like that of a young Dolph Lundgren.

Most certainly, this was due to the Rocky movie they'd watched the night before the escapade – the image plucked from Mace's rather envious recollections. Best of all, the form had survived rigorous testing from the

Protectorate forces.

Other demons who travelled were not always so fortunate. If not "chosen", their true forms tended to remain the same, often stripped of weapons capabilities. If they were lucky, and taken in by the underground network, a competent magic user would create a *veneer* which enabled them to blend into the human world.

"Then we'll need to work on the charms so we don't get spotted."

Note hated to be the one to dampen their spirits but they couldn't afford to get too excited about their new games. "We must remember that it's because of this link between us that we can use each other's gifts." They eyed each other like guilty children. Sean wasn't keen for them to explore talents they may not be able to keep.

"Imagine if Jonah had joined us fully," said Mel.

Note's chest constricted. Without a filter, she invariably spoke her mind and Note knew that she was thinking of Jonah's interests, but he winced at the reminder that he couldn't fetch Carolyn through the tear. Both Jonah and Rake, though proper team members, hadn't been involved in the intimate binding the enforcers had been caught in. Sean had been the first to pledge, sacrificing most where the others had only gained from their close five-way arrangement.

Note's stomach rumbled loudly and broke the awkward silence. Morgan looked up from her phone to laugh at him.

"Go check on Speedy and Sam for food."

Morgan was right, his gut was cramping with hunger brought on by the physical demands of training.

Speedy had arrived not long after Sean and Jonah's departure and Note was happy that Sam got along with the Veloces so well. Note had tuned into the kitchen conversation as he climbed the stairs, hoping for a hint as to when they could eat.

"They're a noisy bunch," the demon said, sounding like a grumbling older brother. The clink of ice followed, prompting a need in Note to down an entire pitcher of water … or whatever Sam had prepared.

"That they are, boy." Note could visualise the easy sympathetic smile that Sam had for Speedy. More rattling and scuffing ensued as Note approached the top of the stairs from the basement.

"Let's get these down to them. I swear the energy they expend should be bottled and sold."

Sam chuckled at his own joke and Note emerged into the kitchen as Speedy added, "If it were possible, Miranda Levy would have done that already."

The mention of the Agency head caused Note to freeze, Speedy's narrow face lengthening further as he saw his new friend's reaction.

Note had only experienced a fraction of the horrors that Speedy had survived, but the Veloces had been unaware of Note's brief but memorable dealings with Miranda Levy.

Not long after he had anchored to Carolyn, the Agency had taken them to The Block in Glasgow where Carolyn and he had been tortured and experimented upon. With the assistance of Ethan's team, they had escaped and been kept under protection.

Note summoned a smile, hoping it conveyed to Speedy that there was nothing to worry about. The Veloces offered a hesitant response. The demon usually avoided chatting about his life at the Agency. Maybe the time had come for him to exorcize his demons, though Note was out of his depth where Veloces's issues were concerned.

He reached for a nicely loaded tray beside Sam. "Need help, guys?"

Witnessing the odd exchange, Sam sighed and set his giant plate of sandwiches down. "Speedy," he said, "I'm sorry you had to go through that. I know the Agency fight was bad enough. God knows, with what the lads told us–"

"No worries, Sam." Good-naturedly, he clapped the caretaker on the back. "I'm lucky to be alive. It's just the moving on with the future part that's giving me trouble."

"Early days yet. You'll find your place, lad."

"If I was on the run and sleeping in doorways, I'd still be better off," assured Speedy. Note felt like he was intruding as he stood, poised with Sam's tray in his hands.

"You had to leave your brother, though."

"We're quite different," said Speedy, sounding wistful, his features tight.

Note thought it significant that both Speedy and Jonah were unlike their Agency counterparts. Jonah was fully accepted into the team for the abilities he possessed but he was no more trustworthy than the Veloces who had shown incredible skills but maintained a distance from their tight group. Mel assured Jonah's interest whereas Speedy didn't wish to join the Protectorate. Note couldn't blame him.

Speedy had issues with organisations, and it was understandable. The Veloces had emerged from an exploitative and barbaric system that had ultimately forced him to take the life of a fellow demon for no other reason than the entertainment of a bloodthirsty crowd.

The activation of the group tattoo was a welcome distraction and Mel appeared at his side, followed by the others, all grabbing baps dripping lettuce and mayonnaise. Sam was quick to stop Rake and Mace from pocketing a couple of extras. "Only takes a second to wrap them," he grumbled whilst popping open a new pack of napkins.

"Something's happening at the London base," Mel told them, her face a curious mix of intrigue and annoyance.

***

On route to the city Protectorate facility, Note had learned that it was situated beneath the gardens at St Paul's cathedral.

The site was well concealed from humans and had apparently existed before the cathedral's post fire of London rebuilding programme. Morgan had a real passion for the gardens here, but her horticultural history lesson had to be curtailed when they entered a conference room in the base.

In the controlled access area, they were greeted by Sean's frowning countenance and Jonah's frustrated pacing. Concerned glances were shared as the team spread out. A strange magic user occupied a chair at a large table, an array of paperwork set out before him.

Note sealed the gateway and quickly put out his hand to support Mel. "Thanks," she grumbled. "This should be getting easier." The grey cast to Mel's deceptively sweet face, coupled with her wobbly frame, meant she was taking longer than usual to adjust to their current mode of transport.

Note slid out one of the chairs, the legs screeching over the polished concrete floor. With a wince, she landed gratefully on it before leaning back slightly from the young magic user now opposite her.

Note nodded to Jonah's soft enquiry and the hybrid moved to join her. Rake took Jonah's vacated position at the other side of the stranger. He slid in to the seat beside the mage who huffed in annoyance.

It was a surprise to learn that Sean and Jonah had taken charge of an irate magic user who claimed to have authorisation to work in Rask.

"Team, this gentleman is Graeme McCann." The strange mage's face tightened in disapproval, presumably at his details being given without reciprocity. Sean drew their attention to the papers on the desk. "I thought this would be best shared, as we may see more of these 'licensed' humans within the realms."

"This is what I'm saying," said McCann, who tried to lean forward but was thwarted by Rake whose large arm slid in front of him. "I have a right," he blustered, but Rake simply waited for McCann to relax back into his chair. Keeping quiet, the big demon crossed his arms and Note cast an amused glance at him. Even seated, the Rakshasas was still seriously intimidating.

"It was only a matter of time," said Mel, stretching forward in her chair to look at each of them. The slight annoyance in her tone was overshadowed by an understanding. Having been brought up in close contact with otherworlders, and travelling the gateways with her trader grandfather, the girl was well placed to understand the realm laws.

"The precators have confirmed that this is legitimate and we must allow passage of individuals who carry these," Sean told them, pointing at a piece of paper on the desk. "Once his term is up, he will return to Earth by the usual means."

"I don't like it," said Morgan, snatching up the paper. "This would be easy to copy."

"The seal's not." Mel reached over to smooth a finger over the magical mark at the top of the page.

"O.W.E. – Otherworldly Work Experience!" Note thought that if Morgan's hair wasn't already standing on end, then the shock would have done the job for her. "You have got to be kidding."

"Unfortunately not, my dear," Sean assured her, evenly. "It is believed that this document, issued to Mr McCann and those similarly afflicted, will reduce our work load and bring about a better understanding between the peoples of the realms."

Note understood that, whether Sean was in agreement or not, he planned to accept the processes.

"So bureaucracy takes a closer hold on our ancient organisation? This sucks," said Morgan.

"Much as I dislike your choice of language, I must agree." The grim expressions that surrounded him made it all too clear that every one of them was suspicious of this turn of events.

"What exactly will he be doing for the Rakshasas?" said Morgan, and all eyes turned to the licensed mage, his face reddening under the scrutiny.

"I am a lawyer, recently graduated in Law and Business."

"So what do *we* get in return?" said Mel, focussing intently on him. "What do *you* get?"

"I'm being funded by an outside source – a private individual, to lend my services and learn everything I can from this magnificent race of beings."

Rake aside, Note couldn't think of a worse people to study. Carolyn had described her experiences with the high mage Roland and the Rakshasas. Then there was poor Mel whose grandfather had tried to trade her to their chief. Mel's face had contorted at the thought and Note took her hand under the table and tightened his grip on it. She produced a grim smile, returning his squeeze almost painfully.

"So, I'm allowed to go then?" said the stranger, and Sean waved a finger toward Note.

"Would you like to do the honours or shall I?"

"Crap, Note." Morgan seemed as impressed as she was horrified. "You can do mind wipe as well." Note could hear the unsaid "Oops" as McCann attempted to gather a repulsion spell.

"There's no need for that." Morgan stilled the mage's efforts with a simple "Silencio".

A black haze had collected under McCann's hands and the table beneath them shuddered.

"Omitto." Mel's angry spell chilled the air and smothered the effects of McCann's preparation. "That wasn't even a clean spell," she muttered in disgust. "He was going to—"

"He's panicked. That's all," said Note, watching as Sean gathered McCann's haze of black to himself. *No need for waste.*

"Why can't we just wipe him and send him home. He's not about to become a better person after his time with Roland."

"Didn't you hear? He's obviously being paid good money to lend his services." At Morgan's disgusted expression, Sean looked at her and added, "Don't judge, my dear. No-one knows what brought him to this point."

"Other than greed," spat Mel. "I've dealt with guys like him before and seen enough to know that this O.W.E. business is going to be really bad for the realms."

Note couldn't disagree.

CHAPTER 8

Sean

"What makes you think we'll be better received today?"

Sean had brought the ladies directly to Glasgow from the London base. He didn't have an immediate reply to Morgan's question. Amanda had thrown him out twice already from her rooms at the facility, and he could do without further drama.

The Protectorate were reluctant to use measures more forceful than the minimum required. Achieving that sort of balance was an art, the process supported by having Amanda take care of her children at the Scottish base.

"I live in hope," he muttered.

"Since when?" said Morgan, adopting the same tone, and Sean's eyes held hers for a moment. They both knew the answer to that.

Security was of necessity as strict under the Clyde as it was in London, and the powerful mage appreciated the use of such measures as they passed the final check on Amanda's floor.

Mel muttered at his other side as they approached Amanda's rooms.

"Neath river and earth, the breeder finds rest,
Old ties fail as blood wins the test."

Sean didn't miss a beat.

"In painful demise should the demon roar,
From Earth's dark prison, her spirit will soar."

Morgan cocked an eyebrow and looked at Mel with new appreciation in her vivid green eyes.

"What?" said Mel. "You think I don't read up too?"

"Not at all," answered Sean, "but I expect you to return valuable books when you're done with rifling through them."

"Oh, but I di–" Mel's footsteps stopped, realising her mistake. Sean's lip inched up at one side as Mel's expression twisted in agitation.

"You didn't, so I can only infer that Note is the culprit." Sean's accusation held no weight, though Mel's discomfort was obvious.

Morgan shot him a look, clearly aware that Sean knew all of his facts beforehand. "It's a good thing to be reading up on this," she directed at Mel, "regardless of who keeps you company, but that particular book was written over three hundred years ago."

"Until recently it was merely inferred that death would free the breeder from the curse, but I do wonder." He was sure that underground facilities hadn't existed when the text had been inscribed but the Protectorate forces had made use of caves and tunnels in days gone by.

"I guess it's really valuable."

Ah, the book. Sean sighed. Mel couldn't do "repentant" well at all, even when she tried. They found the door to Amanda's room guarded. Sean recognised the Frenchman watching them approach. There was a distinct twinkle in the enforcer's eye. "Private sale in the right quarters would fetch a price of millions," the man said.

"Bonjour, Pierre, I see you still listen to conversations that are not intended for your ears."

"I do find ways to relieve the monotony." Pierre had risen from a rather uncomfortable looking folding chair, a wide smile transforming his lean face. He grasped Sean's right forearm, his free hand reaching over the other enforcer's shoulder in the traditional warrior's embrace.

Sean watched Mel's reaction as Pierre's gaze moved to linger on her curves. He could have predicted that the black haired beauty would capture the enforcer's interest.

Used to such attention, and apparently unimpressed, Mel was still musing about the book. "I would never have thought. Why don't we get them copied?"

Morgan answered casually, "I expect it would increase the chances of leaking information to the Agency. As it is, you can't just tuck any of those books into a pocket and read it on the bus."

"Quite so," said Sean. Hiding his amusement, he watched Morgan stiffen as Pierre tugged her into a modified embrace; the addition of a kiss to her cheeks making her blush. She acquiesced gracefully whilst introducing Mel.

"I have not had the pleasure," he purred, offering her the same clinch Morgan had endured. He held her for a longer time, though, and if Sean wasn't mistaken, sniffed her hair. So many of the older enforcers had no concept of personal space.

Mel stepped back stiffly, eyes wide. Sean thought Pierre to be lucky Mel hadn't aimed a well-placed knee in his groin. "Um, hi," she mumbled.

Pierre laughed, his expression distinctly at odds with his youthful appearance. Sean recalled helping celebrate his ninetieth birthday. Longevity was rare and celebrated amongst enforcers. Each mission into the realms was one from which they may never return.

"I've heard much about you, Melanie. Welcome to our community."

Sean really wanted to get their visit underway but he couldn't deny Pierre a little respite in his important though boring work detail.

"I've been here a year, already."

"Pft, that is nothing, mon cheri, but I do hope the Protectorate has treated you well." Sean saw Mel's expression flicker. She was not used to dealing with those like Pierre, and though not *like* Sean, the mage was coated in strong magic that repelled almost as well as it drew other magic users.

"It's been … fine," Mel returned cautiously, and Pierre smiled.

"Allow me to offer my services if at any time you feel overwhelmed by the rigours of your position." The gleam in the Frenchman's eyes held a definite promise for their young mage.

With overdone flirtatiousness, she shot back, "Thanks so much, Pierre, but I do enjoy my … rigours. I'll be sure to keep your *generous* offer in mind, though." Sean choked back a laugh at Mel's "like for like" approach to the lecherous mage. Pierre reacted a fraction later than expected.

"I await your call with bated breath."

Morgan snorted in her efforts to keep it together. "Mel's a match for you," she said to the hopeful mage, "but she's taken."

Pierre looked suitably devastated but a devious grin played on his lips.

Sean was almost sad to end the banter, but it was definitely time to do it before Morgan ruptured something in her pains to keep a straight face.

"The lady is expecting us?"

"Of course." Pierre resumed his previous role with a sigh. "If you would allow me?" With exaggerated motions, he rapped lightly on the door before opening it fully into the room.

Amanda's voice rose impatiently from within. "I have no idea why you keep up the pretence of social niceties, Pierre. You fool no-one."

"Yes, Madame," Pierre said as he sealed the breach behind the guests. He propped his back against the door frame, allowing the visitors to introduce themselves.

The air smelled faintly of antiseptic and other less agreeable odours.

As Sean moved forward, flanked by Mel and Morgan, Amanda stood with her back to them, working over a clear, hospital acquired bassinette on the far side of the room. A door was open to reveal an en suite bathroom.

The bedroom was closed off and Sean sensed the sleeping presence of a third occupant. That was good. Toddlers were loud, curious, showed no restraint, and knew no barriers – his attention slid briefly to Mel who shrugged her *"What?"*. He was glad she couldn't see the parallel in his thoughts.

Small improvements had been carried out to make Amanda's unit more homely. An oversized sofa and two comfy chairs had replaced the institutional originals. Currently displaying a mobile country scene, a large flat screen television had been secured to the wall, and off to the side, fresh cut flowers in a bright arrangement sat on the centre of a mid-sized dining table beyond which a compact kitchen area could be seen.

From Sean's vantage point, the area looked well stocked with the addition of an extra-large refrigerator, microwave oven and a – still in its box – coffee maker. Excess baby products, breakfast cereal and such-like were stacked high on top of the limited cupboards.

Sean wondered if the informal modifications had been due to Amanda or the efforts of Protectorate staff. He was guessing the latter as the woman's first priority would be to return to Skean and join her mate.

She didn't turn to greet them, but it was clear her manner hadn't improved since last he'd seen her. Sean could tell she was fighting her anger though her distrust would remain for a while yet. Her struggle could be observed in the tightness of her posture and the deep breaths she was using to relax.

Unhurriedly, Amanda bagged and binned a soiled nappy. While she washed her hands in the en suite basin, her eyes slid over Sean and his unusually quiet companions. He allowed the happy gurgles of the baby in the bassinette to break the frosty atmosphere.

Sean could read every emotion that crossed the lovely face that was so like the destroyer's. Amanda's dominating feature was her witch green eyes that held a wealth of knowledge and hardship that was difficult to reconcile to the facade.

Having escaped her "breeder" status for a brief fifteen years, she'd managed to raise Carolyn and her brother on Earth. One day soon, when he could be sure of a truthful – he'd settle for a civil – response, he would ask how she had accomplished it.

The woman proceeded to cocoon the baby in a light blanket before cradling him gently in her arms. Her tension drained markedly as she changed position to pat the bundle. Air erupted from the tiny thing's mouth at her shoulder, bringing with it a dribble of milky spit.

Morgan appeared to be captivated as Amanda wiped the baby's face whilst praising him for his accomplishment.

Mel seemed more wary than Sean would have expected, but the young mage had a lot of experience with otherworldly beings – she sensed the danger in Amanda. The vision of maternal bliss and its effects were deceptive. Amanda was not some sweet innocent mother they'd rescued from the gateways. She was strong and magically gifted in her own right.

Currently mated to the Chief of Skean, she wouldn't think twice about disposing of everyone before ripping a route through the realms to get back to Lucas.

The children were the key to keeping her civilised. Note's decision to use Carolyn's small siblings to force Amanda's compliance couldn't be faulted.

"I *asked* to see Notechis," said Amanda smoothly, laying the baby down in the bassinette. She wore the standard Protectorate garb, the curls of her strawberry blond hair having begun to escape from the messy bun at the back of her head.

"I don't think that is a good idea, Amanda. As yet, you have given us no cause to trust you." Her bright eyes narrowed and Sean could see that her struggle wasn't abating. Focusing on him, it was as though she "saw" something and with it an unnerving smile blazed across her face.

"I am still myself," she declared, relaxing her stance a little. It is only a show, Sean reminded himself. Any opening – any weakness, and she'd take it. Was it possible that she would leave her children in Protectorate hands?

The effects of separation from her mate, regardless of the organisation's methods, would be in their zenith by now. They were counting on her maternal instincts to be stronger than the mating bond as was right, proper, and evidenced by her history, but no-one could discount the primal properties of her link to Lucas. "I know what I should be feeling and what I *do* feel. The emotions for my mate are not real, but the sentiment has usurped all else."

"I understand," said Sean, simply, and Amanda's eyes flashed with annoyance.

"You offer platitudes. You who have never loved can't begin to…"

The shrill assertion petered away. The stoic exterior hadn't lasted long and Sean almost felt sorry for her.

"I can't… I can't do this." She smoothed a stray curl that had somehow blown across her face. With a deep breath, she continued: "If I can't speak to Notechis, then bring me Sam."

The air rushed out of Mel, Sean's warning glance coming too late. Amanda noticed and blinked in confusion before setting her lips in a thin line. "Dead? Of course he is. Longevity applies better to some than others." Her eyes settled meaningfully on Sean.

Mel shifted uncomfortably on her toes while Amanda braced her hands against the back of the sofa between them.

"When Notechis drew me out, he thought he was saving me, and that he and my daughter have this … this connection, but when he hurt my mate, I could only think and act in a way to eliminate the threat to my chief."

Her brow creased. "No. That's not right, Lucas is not…" Her hands clenched and released at her side as she visibly fought the effects of the bond. "He was, however, my first love." A soft scoffing noise erupted from Amanda as she caught Mel's sympathetic gaze.

"No, young lady. You do not feel sorry for me. Lucas used me," and she tapped her temple. "I know it here. First Lucas, then…" but she only groaned in frustration. "And back to Lucas *again*." Her hand covered her heart. "This part didn't get the memo. This part needs to catch up. That's all. I'll get over this, and I'll concede to the Protectorate reins on me."

"You have no choice in that," said Sean coolly. "We are using you to aid Carolyn's return."

"Don't think for a minute that I don't want to see my daughter. I do, I do." Amanda circled the couch towards them, her eyes narrowing at the sight of Pierre's deceptively relaxed stance. Sean got the impression of a lioness pacing her cage. One second … one fraction of a second without due care and any handler would be a bloody mess.

Sean was glad that only the most seasoned enforcers had been charged with her maintenance. "I also know that my daughter is safer now, exactly where she is, as opposed to running through the realms, risking life and limb as your precious destroyer."

It was a hard truth that Sean couldn't deny. Why was he not steering the conversation in the proper direction? Part of him wanted to hear her rambling thoughts, considerations that closely resembled the ones that fired through his own brain: messy, chaotic.

"She's held captive," said Morgan firmly. It was with consideration that the enforcer regarded Amanda but her eyes clearly conveyed that she couldn't understand the point.

"And you're not?" returned Amanda with a sneer. "You could just leave and go about your business as a normal person anytime you like?"

Morgan's face contorted slightly. Amanda had hit a nerve. Chewing her lip, the young mage wisely opted to remain silent.

"I thought not."

"It's different for us," snapped Mel, and Amanda tapped her chin as though seeing her for the first time. Chagrined, the girl ducked her head.

Amanda was too easily exposing their weaknesses. "We *chose* this," continued Mel, more evenly. "Carolyn *chose* this."

"Of course you did – fools. Exchanging forms of bondage."

"But you want Carolyn back, right?" Amanda turned to what had sounded almost like a plea from Morgan, and closed her eyes momentarily.

"I feel her loss too."

Sean wondered exactly who Amanda was trying to convince with her assertions. She seemed to be fighting her holds exceptionally well, but they needed a little more time and a lot more magic to free the woman from her mate's claim.

"Why shouldn't we let Note talk to her," said Mel, clearly uncomfortable. "Of all of us, he's the one most likely to understand what she's going through."

Sean sighed, but he didn't miss the gleam in Amanda's eyes at her small victory. No doubt, the lady would prefer Morgan's assistance but she would take help from any source. Mel was right about Note's position, but the Kistatus wasn't thinking properly in his current state, and Amanda was smart enough to manipulate him.

Also, there was the fact that Note had seriously injured the chief – an act that should not have been possible. By regular laws, it carried the ultimate penalty, which Note's own father should have been bound to enforce. In many ways it would have been better if Note had killed the chief outright.

"It's early in your recovery, Amanda," Sean reminded her.

"It doesn't feel like it," she muttered. "When can I see him?"

"Not in the immediate future."

"You see no need to humour me. I like that." Her expression, though, contradicted her words. Head held high, she made her way to the kitchen area and began to fill the sink with water. Sean needed no further clue to know he'd been dismissed.

Edward

It had been a muted affair without Lucas's larger-than-life presence among the men. One day each week, the chief celebrated a meal with the guards and a few of his chosen. The language would deteriorate throughout the evening, and Lucas would leave the revellers to continue in their well-earned recreation.

The court had its own musicians, artists and magic users who could put on a decent show. The entertainment had been good tonight but the weight of their failing chief's mood had cast a cloud over the proceedings.

It wasn't often that Edward thought of his previous life but occasionally he missed the trappings. Not that he'd ever trade back. He was nothing special there, and *something* here. It wasn't even that he was the chief's son. That meant zilch … well almost zilch to him, but it assured him of retaining his well respected position.

The stone bench on which he sat felt oddly comfortable, and he breathed in the scent of night blooming flowers. Edward had moved out to the courtyard, half-filled goblet in hand, to get some fresh air and to keep away from all the well-wishers. Voices intruded from nearby and he groaned inwardly before he caught his breath. The melodious and calm voice of a woman contrasted sharply with the harsh sibilant speech he recognised as Cassandra's.

Cassandra was always a welcome sight in the castle. Her mate was long dead, but between the pair of them and their connections throughout the realms, the Kistatus could access all sorts of things for the right price.

As the two figures moved closer, he saw that Cassandra had a female in a half embrace. The protrusions of one upper limb draped over her shoulder and around her waist. The girl walked tall, lacking the subservient demeanour Edward was accustomed to seeing in Cassandra's girls. Neither saw him as, curious, he remained still in the shadows.

With her face half-lit, he thought he recognised her as one of a new batch, brought to the castle the previous month. "I thought help was needed in the classrooms," the girl was saying. "This whole mix-up is not my fault." Cass seemed to take the girl's irritability in her stride. They clearly had a relationship that bordered on friendship for Cass's good humour continued.

The girl indicated the recreation hall from where sounds of laughter and merriment could be heard. "I'll not go in to entertain that rabble. I don't belong there. Put me on the domestic rota or something."

"We tried that," Cassandra said smoothly, unwinding from her. "You lassted lesss than a week and they filled your place. I checked. I know you're not one of mine but acquissitions put you here."

Edward's stomach tightened with the reminder of an old wound. He was always discomfited by the mention of that department. He didn't want reminding of the other girl who had also suffered through acquisitions. The female mumbled under her breath and Cassandra turned, momentarily blocking Edward's view. "You haven't even spent time with the others."

"Whores and entertainers, Cassandra, and really–" The girl put her hands up in placation. "I'm not belittling them, they're a great bunch and fulfil a demand, but they *want* to be here. *I* don't, and they can't understand it. My mere presence upsets them so that's why I stay out of the way."

"The time has passed for that, Rhona. You must find a way to earn your keep before the next cycle."

Edward smiled at Cassandra's half-hearted ultimatum. Could he stir himself to talk to Hecaton on her behalf? The girl was nothing to him; mildly interesting, but nothing special. *Not like Sarah.* He berated himself for even thinking her name. The bitch set him up for a monumental fall. *Shut up!*

"I know I'm just a resource but they put me in the wrong section. I didn't agree to this. I have papers."

"Unfortunately, OWE's don't mean a thing here, not without Hecaton's approval. He didn't recognise yours and so perhaps it's besst that he didn't give you to one of our magess."

"It's because those gorillas caught me before I reached him to clear it, isn't it?"

"Could be," said Cassandra wryly. "What good is a magic user who can't avoid a drunken band of roguess."

"I came here to learn, damn it."

"And learn you did. Don't trusst so quickly." Cassandra sighed, clearly troubled. "It happens more often than you would think, little human. Acquire new skillss by all means but speak to Jesssie first."

Jessie was familiar to Edward as one of the castle favourites. Not only was she easy on the eye, the girl could sing, dance and her private sessions were booked for cycles in advance. Was Cass suggesting that *she* hadn't always been happy to be in the realm?

"But it's so unfair," the girl said.

"Life rarely is, Rhona."

"The mages don't scare me," she said so softly Edward had to strain to hear. "It's the party animals I don't want to be around." Edward's interest spiked. The girl was a complete novice. Would it be such a chore for him to do Cassandra a favour and break her in – gently of course?

"It's been a month already," Cassandra said. "If I don't start hearing good reports, I'm letting you go. In the interim, I'll make enquiries to see if I can trade you to someone in the outlands, someone who needs to train a witch, but chances are they'll be a lot less understanding than me." With a rustle of her dress, she turned and made her way through the door to join the revellers within.

"I'd really appreciate that," the girl called, but Cassandra had already disappeared into the noisy hall. Rhona's shoulders slumped and she began to move away.

"I couldn't help but overhear."

The girl turned to peer at him. Edward stepped out from the shadows so he could be seen. She didn't appear startled, and he had the sudden, uneasy thought she had been waiting for him. Her eyes lifted to meet his and all thoughts of what he was about to say vanished from his mind.

It wasn't fear or any discernible emotion he'd caught from her, despite her predicament and her fairly amicable exchange with Cassandra. It wasn't the disdain or mockery that showed in the quick curl of her lip. It was that, beauty aside – and God, she was stunning, the expression on her face was mildly inquisitive, far from eager. He couldn't remember when anyone had looked at him like that. Perhaps back on Earth when he'd been a nobody?

All at once he felt disturbed, intrigued, and excited. Taking advantage of his lack of speech, she dropped her eyes and showed him the top of her head. "I'm very sorry, my lord, but I have work to do," and with that, she turned to leave.

He was on her before she'd made a single step and let her turn quickly in the circle of his arms. "What the hell, Eddie, get off." His lips swooped down to catch hers. Her mouth was warm and yielded perfectly beneath his own as she stilled in his grasp. He broke the kiss with a sigh. "You might not need to be one of Cass's girls if you play your cards right."

Her hand came up in a wide arc to strike him on the cheek. He took it, smiling. She hadn't, though, objected to the kiss. This had to be something else entirely. Was she ashamed of her response?

"I never liked Richard Gere, or that bloody film," she sniped, and Edward relaxed a little. She had originated on Earth, as he'd suspected.

"You're right," he said, hands still firmly on her waist, her warmth leaching into him. "I should've asked first."

"You should have." He bent to kiss her again, and she placed her hand in front of her lips. Edward leaned back, no longer smiling. "What the hell's the matter with you," she now said. Her look of disgust was clearly faked, but she'd asked a good question. He wasn't usually given to acting impulsively with women but this one brought something out in him that he was keen to explore.

"You must have heard what I said to Cassandra, so forgive me if I find your lack of respect a bit insulting." Respect? No more than a slave, yet the girl spoke as if she were the queen. Interesting.

"I can make your life easier, Rhona." He liked the way her name sounded on his lips.

"Don't flatter yourself," she whispered, "and let me go, you Neanderthal."

Neanderthal?

She moved beyond his reach; he struggled to put his thoughts together. "There's a bunch of people in there," and she angled her chin in the direction of the recreation room. "They actually *want* you to be with them, so go practise your charms on them." She took a step back, increasing the space between them. "Touch me again and I'll use your own bloody sword on you."

His fingers reaching to the tingling cheek she'd struck, he shook his head. "I could report you for this."

"Like you're going to tell anyone that your seduction skills suck. All the best with that." She backed up again and actually smirked at him. "I'll not say anything if you don't," she said, her look of disgust making him want to strike out.

"Hey, what you doing out here," Krisp called from the doorway and Rhona used the distraction to flee, her steps light and fast. Edward felt foolish when his friend arrived at his side and he'd been left staring after nothing.

"What?" he answered acrimoniously. "You miss me, in there?"

"Well," said Krisp, his broad face breaking into a lewd grin. "The company is definitely more agreeable. Everyone's asking for you. That's all." Edward started in his direction and the young Kistatus danced in front of him, to block his way. "No, no, if it's too much for you, I'm sure I can keep them all happy in your stead."

Edward's angst dissipated. "Hey, what would I do without you?" Krisp's arm went companionably around Edward's shoulders and he belched loudly in his ear. "Lovely, that's just lovely, man."

He laughed, waving away Krisp's rancid ale-laced breath. Thoughts of Rhona vanished when two of Cassandra's girls welcomed them inside. *They didn't choose to be with either for their damned social skills.*

CHAPTER 9

Siren

Siren always slept lightly, but she groaned at the mental tip tap of Taz's man, John. Being a Tracer had recently become a full time occupation. Where were all these demons coming from? It wasn't her job to quiz her marks for details but three in less than a week was rare.

One of Miranda's arms was draped across her and Siren's eyes widened to see that the woman was still wearing her ring. Miranda *always* took it off when she was sleeping with Siren but for some reason she hadn't bothered tonight. Siren knew what the item did, though her lover had never discussed it with her.

The protective gem in the setting was a potent magical artefact, imbuing power to the user, able to repel attack and influence, both physical and mental. Such an object had its downside too. It was hard to feel anything when a powerful artefact held you in its grip. Was Miranda tiring of her that she didn't want to feel?

The thoughts rose and were quickly quashed. Siren couldn't forget that she was mere property to Miranda. It was foolish to expect a trust that the Agency head was incapable of giving. *I can't come,* she communicated to John. *Miranda's wearing the ring.*

Couldn't you slip it off her finger?

No. If only it were that easy.

She could feel John's exasperation turning to thoughts of chopping her hand off. Not helpful.

I'll get back to you.

Miranda's breathing was deep and even in Siren's ear. She tried to emulate it and relax. Who would John send to help her? The seconds ticked by and then a wash of magic blanketed the room. It felt nothing like the magic of the usual mages. This was complex and multi-dimensional. Catching a gleam of black eyes in the shadows, she nearly shrieked in alarm.

The mage was silently assessing them… No, realised Siren, he was considering Miranda. The setting of her stone cracked open and the gem flew into the upturned palm of the mage. The dark mage, of course: Sean. She'd heard about him from Miranda who sometimes used his services. Characters from the underground network spoke of him too, but the organisation being as it was, their claims were often exaggerated. It seemed the stories were less inflated than she'd thought.

Siren twisted the enchanted cap on her upper right molar and the enchantment washed over her as the spell activated. This astral projection charm gave the illusion that she remained in bed while her true self eased away from Miranda. It wasn't perfect, but if the woman tried to wake her, Siren would be pulled back to her body. Siren had only once had to leave a job uncompleted.

Though probably unnecessary, she raised a finger to her lips to ensure Sean stayed quiet. Regular surveillance didn't extend to Miranda's bedroom, but it was unwise to take anything for granted.

"No-one can detect us." His teeth gleamed white in the dark. *Predator?* She shook off the unbidden thought. He was here to help her but he couldn't just walk off with Miranda's stone, no matter how glad Siren would be to see the last of it.

"Okay, thank you, but you can't take that with you."

The stone spun slowly in his palm. *Show off.* "I can't?"

"No." Siren found it a struggle to keep her tone respectful. The first time this mage comes to assist, he threatens to put an end to her job. Of all the self-important– What was wrong with her?

This was new, that's all. She should be glad he wasn't charmed by her Siren skills and trying to say all the right things to her, but he'd unearthed a real fear: that she would one day lose her usefulness to Taz and the others who relied on her. Meeting Sean's eyes, she thought it better to explain. "Miranda will know I had something to do with this if the ring goes missing now."

The dark mage leaned closer, freaking her out a little with the intensity of his black eyes that searched hers with no sign of lust. *Kindred?* Again, she shook off her musings and tried to listen to him.

"Firstly, I believe your situation is already compromised, and furthermore, it might be *her* ring, but this stone does not belong to her."

Siren shrugged. It wasn't as if Miranda shied away from acquiring anything she wanted. The artefact was important to her, and Siren guessed that if it came down to choice, the ring would rank higher than Siren. "She's had it for a while."

If the mage knew who it belonged to, he wasn't going to tell her. Why was she even discussing it? This magic user was less human than most and would be more able than Miranda to do what he wished, so why did she get the feeling he was actually listening to what she – a mere minion – had to say.

"What would you have me do? Lodge a report with the local constabulary?"

Siren's eyes widened. The mage was trying to get a rise out of her and it was unnerving. "Well, no, of course not. Anyway, we've not met. I'm Siren."

"A pleasure to meet you formally, my dear." The mage clearly had the advantage. He took her hand, Siren experiencing the effects of his magic much stronger now.

Do not wake until we return. Siren felt the direction of the spell rather than the words targeted at Miranda. She tried to tug away from Sean, to reach her closet, but the mage shook his head and placed her fingers in the crook of his arm. She was almost naked, the cool air attesting to it as a breeze swirled around her. Was he going to make her attend a gateway in her baby-doll nightie?

In an instant, they were transported out of the building. "Thanks," said Siren as she felt clothing wrap her body from head to foot. They had appeared in the basement of her apartment block. No surveillance. Good.

"Don't thank me. This is a onetime assist, I believe. Continue as normal and I'll follow." Siren shivered despite her clothes and hailed John who was waiting nervously for her contact.

Had me worried for a while there. You okay with the dark mage? he replied.

Yes, fine, John. He's going to accompany me. Go ahead.

John passed her the information which Siren soon digested. Her Tracer magic surged and a picture formed in her head of where the traveller had arrived. *Kelvingrove Park, John.* She heard the reluctant humour in his answer. It was where *he* had emerged into Earth several years previously.

"Do you have a visual?" asked Sean, a bit too casually. If Siren didn't know better, she'd think the superior male was looking forward to their little adventure.

"It doesn't work exactly like that," she said, again enjoying that he could look at her easily – as a person. "But yes, I'll be drawn right to where the alien energy signature is strongest."

"Danger?"

"I get no strong sense from this one, though I have the power to send them back if they're incompatible with us."

"And how often would that situation occur."

Siren grimaced; the figures were admittedly a bit sad. "About eighty percent need to be declined." Sean nodded, giving her no clue if that was what he'd expected. It was strange to think that the calls *he* attended would have a greater percentage of gateway sanctioned travellers. Siren was more likely to deal with fellow misfits. It would be interesting to compare notes. Siren suspected that Sean was an authority when it came to gateway knowledge.

"You should reconsider your situation with the Agency," the mage said, returning to what he'd earlier intimated. Siren couldn't give up her place beside Miranda even if she could find another way, though Taz had already been twitchy for months regarding her position with the organisation. Siren was in an excellent spot for spying and reporting her findings back to Taz and the others. Their operation was small but significant.

"No, we need to get going with this." Sean, she knew, had much more direct access when pursuing his freelance activities. Miranda called him in for emergencies, for which services he was paid handsomely by the Agency, and would obviously then return to the Protectorate with valuable information.

An uncomfortable thought struck her: when Sean had said *she* was compromised, was he suggesting that *he* was compromised. Siren's knowledge of him *could* be exploited in the future, she supposed.

Her situation was complicated, having gained a position of trust which was incomparable to anyone else's, Protectorate or underground – as far as she knew. Catching the quizzical look on Sean's face, she scolded herself for overthinking. She tilted her head back and tapped in to follow the Trace. The feeling was slightly different this time, somehow bypassing the usual stomach lurch, feeling now only the familiar drawing sensation of her tracing talent. A cool wind surrounded them as she emerged with Sean into the Glasgow park.

True to his word, the mage had followed easily, and she suspected his presence had contributed to the easy transition. Taking a deep breath of night air, Siren became fully aware of the blanketing spell that extended from Sean to cover them. His use of magic seemed integral to him. They moved forward as one, footfalls soft as they angled closer to a pale shape at the edge of a duck pond.

"I don't see the gateway," she murmured, her gaze flicking up to meet Sean's black eyes. "I take it—"

"Yes, I can open a gateway if required."

Siren felt pretty much like an amateur in Sean's presence. "Good," and she smiled widely.

The Mow had flattened over the surface of the water. "He's drinking," said Siren, unnecessarily. As she pondered how best to deal with the thirsty demon, a young man burst out from the shadows, another figure in tow. "I tell you, something came out of a big circle right over there."

The other male laughed nastily. "Ooh, the aliens are coming to get us…

You wish." His tone was offensive rather than the teasing of a friend. "I know exactly what you dragged me out here for." He grabbed the younger man roughly, twisted his arm and pushed him face first into a tree, his bulk obscuring Siren's view of the smaller figure.

Her expression froze and Sean glided forward towards the two men, the younger of whom had started to sniffle. Siren felt the blanketing spell extend and pop, placing a secrecy lid on the area as they approached.

Sean softly uttered something that broke the pair of newcomers apart, but the hairs on the back of Siren's neck rose and she turned to see the Mow sliding back to the bank. She was about to warn Sean when she saw his hand was now raised behind him. *Wait for me*, she heard him think and a silver shimmer coated the demon, freezing it as it came to rest on the edge of the pond.

"You saw nothing of interest here," Sean intoned at the intruders, and Siren settled slightly, recognising that this was exactly how Taz's magic users would have dealt with the situation.

She was now free to note the lower class street clothes worn by the younger male, his sharp and wary look of hard lessons learned laced with desperation. The other was sullen featured and wore expensive looking black shirt and trousers, the gleam of a wedding band on his finger. This was clearly an illicit liaison.

The younger man's situation chimed with her own, and she wrapped her arms around her stomach in anguish. The boy's eyes widened when they wandered from Sean to her, really *seeing* her. Her empathic nature would surely kill her one day.

Sean's words cut the air like a knife, his eyes glittering silver in the moonlight, and Siren felt the edge of his wrath. "You," and his gaze narrowed on the older male. "Let the pain you inflict on others be visited upon yourself," and the man winced before his arm contorted painfully behind his back and his knees hit the earth at their feet.

"You broke my fucking arm," he hissed.

Sean coldly smiled. "Nothing but the feeling of such."

The street boy seemed to shake himself free of his shock. "Um, thanks, man. Anytime you want—" Sean raised a finger and confusion filled the boy's face. He held a hand to his head, shook it a few times then raced off into the night.

"As for you," Sean directed at the older man, and a yelp rose from the man's now quivering lips as he warily grasped his arm closer, pain and fear coursing through his features. "Take my lesson and be off with your life," and the man shot to his feet as though dragged up by invisible arms. At Sean's raised finger, he too shook his head but then soon stumbled into a run, racing away into the darkness.

Siren *felt* the depth of the sigh that escaped Sean's lips. He stiffened as his focus returned to her, as if for an instant he'd forgotten her. "No-one else will trouble us." At her shocked look, he softly told her, "I understand you've been stretched lately. You can't be expected to continue this mission much longer."

Siren bit her lip. "I can't stop yet, enforcer."

"Sean."

"Right, Sean." Weirdly, she didn't feel at all awkward using his name, and appreciated what seemed to be his genuine concern. "I'm the one in this position, Sean, and I would get out if I thought it had come to that, but it hasn't. Miranda has something important coming up, something you'll want to know about. I just need some more time."

"Perhaps your wish to expose her plan has clouded your judgement."

Siren felt the need to cross her fingers behind her back when she assured him, "Taz is fine with this." A barely perceptible frown crossed Sean's handsome face, suggesting he'd heard the lie. "Miranda's close to modifying the gateway access, allowing agents to gain the perks currently only enjoyed by enforcers."

Sean stared deep into her eyes. "The ring your mistress wears prevents you from tracing, and from leaving her side without notice. She clearly doesn't trust you." Siren's cheeks flamed at his reading of her situation.

"She's not my … my mistress," she said, wondering in which context he'd used the term. "She's my mark."

"A mark who believes herself to be your mistress."

Siren let out a small breath. "Maybe, but I don't know if it's as simple as that. She's very protective of me."

"You are her prize, Siren, but she will only incarcerate you at best, and at worst, sell you off or eliminate you if she thinks you threaten her plans."

Sean might have sounded old-fashioned but Siren knew he was right. "Yes, I know."

Sean glanced over at the frozen Mow. "But what of this one?"

Siren was glad to get back to her job, and, holding up her hands as if in supplication, she sang to the Mow. The language was sweet and familiar, but altered somehow by the presence of the mage at her side. Siren felt Sean follow the rhythmic weave of her magic as it embraced the demon. The words became more than just a melodic hum and the demon weaved its gelatinous mass towards them, slithering ever closer.

She looked to Sean with a gentle nod of her head and he sketched a figure in the air, creating a gateway which swelled open before him. The Mow seemed oblivious to anything but Siren's song. A ripple from the gateway detached itself and wound its way around her once before doing the same to the mow. When it faded from sight, and Siren felt the power of the gateway pulse with living energy, she changed her song. No longer gentle and coaxing, it was now strident and urgent. The Mow slid towards the gateway, all four of his eyes trained on the enchantress. He paused only long enough to lift his tentacles over the edge of the opening, and, with a thick glugging sound, was swallowed by the gateway.

"Very well done, my dear," said Sean. "You hardly needed me at all." With a simple finger jab into the air, he sealed the gateway.

Sean

It troubled Sean that he was irritated by his encounter with Siren. Although "irritated" was perhaps not the right word, but it would suffice. He didn't want to consider the hurt he'd done the "innocent" human, where turning a blind eye would have been more prudent. Not a fan of bullies, he had to admit that Siren's approval had been oddly satisfying.

Her song had enraptured the Mow as she'd looked inside its mind. In some way the Tracer was linked to the ancient gateway magic that decided the worthiness of the travellers. For those who passed her testing, she couldn't make them become "gateway chosen", but, with Taz's help, she took care of those who were harmless, summarily dispelling the ones whose hearts were not pure.

Although he'd made it clear it was a onetime assist, Sean was interested to see how she managed demons from the warrior clans. For one who hadn't become "gateway chosen", it was nothing short of miraculous that she'd been gifted with the ability to "communicate" with the old magic.

Siren had also lied about something so inconsequential that it now troubled him. Did she owe some allegiance to Miranda Levy? And more worryingly, why defer to Taz? How did an insect like Taz gain the clout necessary for his operation? Her knowledge would enable them to avoid running into an organisation that would enslave them, but there was more to it than that.

Not wishing to alarm the girl unnecessarily, he had neglected to tell Siren about the mage he'd found at his arrival, perched outside on the bedroom window sill. He had easily cut through Judy's mind, recognising envy as her driving force, not any real need for information. Clearly not one for voyeurism, he'd learnt that Judy's concern was the threat she saw in Siren. Not that *she* cared for the Agency, no; the former enforcer wanted to exact everything she could from the organisation. If Siren knew the contents of Judy's thoughts, she would have a right to be afraid.

It had only taken a moment for Siren's innocence to be impressed upon Judy.

Taz's operation interested Sean now more than ever and he resolved to investigate further.

CHAPTER 10

Mario

"You missed breakfast," Mario announced as he breezed into Carolyn's room, glad to see her sensibly dressed and ready to go.

"Katie sent me something up."

"So I see," said Mario, taking a slice of cooled bacon from the trolley. "Still good," he muttered.

"I don't know why I was so tired," Carolyn confessed. "Did I miss anything?"

"No, your aunt Sylvia was there, but she told me that Arthur had left already with Ethan and Lawrence." Carolyn's aunt and uncle had arrived at the fortress the previous day and she had seemed weirdly pleased to see them. The conversation had been kept light, deliberately ignoring the undercurrents. Lawrence and Ethan had surprisingly found common interests, and not just their appreciation for the tobacco and alcohol produced in the realm.

"Council day, remember?"

"I know," said Carolyn, suddenly animated. "We should go."

Mario choked on his second piece of bacon. "Dusty old men talking politics and such." There was no point in trying to understand her reasoning, and Arthur wanted her there, but Mario simply didn't trust it. "You'd really like to go?"

"Not when you put it like that," she said, smirking, "but yes, don't you think I should see how he is with his people … and make sure Ethan's okay."

"You want to check he keeps his promise." She was predictable in her worry for the enforcer. "Fair enough." Mario couldn't fathom Arthur's motives in this. There was no way the chief would be happy publicly endorsing his daughter's human connections, but who was he to speculate on the chief's plans.

"Okay, I'm on board," he said, relenting. "As you know, it's a relatively informal afternoon once a month where people air concerns and attend to the business in the realm." She nodded agreeably as he went to the door and arranged with the guards to have their horses readied for the short ride. "Where's Beni?" he asked, realising the hound was not about.

"Oh, Katie took him away for some leftover cuts of … of venison." She paused, looking guiltily away. "I know. Bambi, right? But if it's there—" Mario chuckled at her justification. She was a cute combination of girly horror and a matter-of-fact acceptance of Bambi's demise.

"You spoil him, Carolyn."

"Hey, it was Katie."

"Knowing that it pleases you to see him well looked after."

"I hadn't thought of it that way."

"Right then. Let's see to your tattoo first." She seemed genuinely confused for a moment, unwittingly increasing Mario's resolve.

"You know, Mario, I just totally forget it's there now."

"Mmm." He nodded grimly. "I've been over-spelling it, and there's an accumulation of layers that I think are responsible for rather a lot with you."

"Whatever you say." She sat on a fireside chair and presented her arm. "I wish Ethan had waited for us."

Mario felt differently, thinking it would have been a bother to explain his actions. The last thing he needed was the smug enforcer giving him more grief about the damned tattoo. "We'll join him soon," he said, soothingly. Taking Carolyn's hand in his, he prepared to set the spell. "You know, it's good to let the guy get away from us for a bit."

How could he find the best excuse for what he was about to do? Dampening Note's claim had been beneficial to Arthur, but it was creating problems that the chief clearly hadn't thought through. Arthur failed to understand that, for whatever reason, Ethan seemed to be the next best choice for Carolyn. Mario had control over so little, but this? He could do something about the tattoo while Arthur was distracted by court business.

Maybe he was worrying about nothing. If he explained properly, who was to say that Arthur wouldn't agree to loosen his control and allow him to work the protective magic. Or perhaps not. Mario was naturally more concerned about protecting her against making an idiot out of herself with Ethan. The sexual tension between the pair had only increased during their time in Empustat. Mario tried to comfort himself with his justifications, but how could he avoid contact with the powerful chief who could so easily expose his thoughts.

Sweat quickly beaded on his upper lip as he got to work. It was freaky how magic could smother nearly as well as assist in life's endeavours. With Carolyn's pale arm before him he began to strip the layers that had accumulated day by day, all the while waiting for Arthur's magic to ratchet around him. It was almost a disappointment that he worked without interference. Mario stripped and tweaked until all that remained was a single layer that would merely take the edge off the anchoring and claiming.

"It seems to take longer every time." Carolyn rubbed a hand over the tattoo. "Oh, I can actually see it again," she added, and sure enough the colourful braided design on her wrist was now clearly present. "This is like my signature," she said wistfully, using her forefinger to trace a figure of eight in the design.

"Is it?" He tried to keep his sense of satisfaction at bay. They had worked with energy signatures and he knew exactly what Carolyn's looked like. In the main, they'd toiled with her over various samples without focussing too much on her own. The similarity to Arthur's own stretched out repeating infinity design was striking. That the braided tattoo contained the shape was in itself interesting, and he wondered if Morgan had chosen the original bracelet by accident or intention.

Did the red-head still wear her hair the same as he remembered. Had she found what she was looking for?

Carolyn nudged him out of his wanderings. "Is everything okay?"

"Of course. I think leaving the tattoo like this will help build up your tolerance." *And keep you from pestering me about Ethan.*

"Thanks, Mario," she said softly. "That's not a bad thing."

"It *has* been known for me to come up with a good idea once in a while." He forced a smile as she met his gaze. Trustful, damn it. She ought to know better. Then he remembered that he wasn't the one controlling her. He was just a convenient tool for Arthur to use. The chief hopefully wouldn't notice Mario's deviation from the agreed spell, but he was betting that Ethan would work it out.

Carolyn's anchor had been chosen by the powers that be, and Mario believed they'd made the right choice with Note. And if Ethan was reminded of his place, then so much the better.

Now time for the finishing touch, he showed her the pale leather cuff he'd made for her. The neutral colour Ethan had suggested was just too boring for their girl so he'd imbued it with a charm that would alter the design to match her choice of clothes.

He strapped and tightened it on her wrist. Testing the stretch on it, he answered her questioning gaze. "It has a pocket for a knife, or in your case, that screwdriver. The enchantment on it will prevent any accidents, and because you're a girl I've added a vanity charm, so it matches anything you wear. Complementum," he whispered into her ear and she beamed as the cuff rippled to mirror the shiny leather of her grey boots. Silver and blue etchings appeared on the upper rim. He smiled winningly as Carolyn fished the tool from her trousers and slid it into the inside wrist pocket.

"You're the best," she said, snatching him into a quick hug. "I love it."

"Would you like to practise with fire when we finish with the council today?"

Carolyn's pleased expression melted to something a little more hesitant before it vanished altogether. She'd spent too long away from the bond, shoring up her defences, and Mario would need to watch her carefully during the next few days.

"Defensive magic?"

He scoffed lightly, thinking it was best just to see how she fared without alerting her to the sizeable change in her "protection". "All that you do is defensive, Carolyn. It's merely that some defences are more aggressive than others. We've learned that you can do all sorts of magic, and I believe it's in your interest to learn to use everything at your disposal." She didn't look convinced, so he added, "Learning control is an important step in any mage's training."

"I understand that, Mario, and I remember how it was when we came here." She looked thoughtful, perhaps weakening, before adding, "You know what I want most?" Her cobalt eyes met his almost defiantly. "I need you to help me resist the *persuasion* of the Lilim."

Mario flashed a brilliant smile. This was perfect. Carolyn had given him the best reason ever for easing up on her restrictions.

"You managed before we came to Empustat," he said, remembering.

She swallowed, uncomfortably. "That was with Sadi's help." The Lilim kept his expression carefully blank as she explained how the parasite had been helping her since her anchoring to Note. Mario had already heard from Ethan the basics of what had happened to her parasite. It would do her little good to learn that Note had lost the stupid thing in Skean.

"You are whole again," he answered eventually. "And you are powerful."

"Powerful, huh?" Her eyebrows raised in surprise. "I don't feel very strong."

"Well, your father is the greater power."

"Of course he is," she huffed, as though it was a no-brainer, "but I should be able to resist Patrick and Peter without relying on my connection to Note," a link that Mario had been instrumental in all but severing. The motivation behind Arthur's instructions was becoming clearer by the minute. The chief clearly knew that Note had been helping Carolyn remotely and wanted to eliminate the hold of their link.

When had life become so difficult? In many ways Mario's existence had been simpler when he'd been kept in the cage. An involuntary shudder rippled through him. Carolyn offered an awkwardly sympathetic appraisal, mistakenly seeing it as fear of her father. Oh, he was terrified of Arthur all right, but return to the cage would be Mario's ticket to utter insanity.

What the hell had he just done?

Carolyn

Carolyn left Mario at the entrance to the building, stabling their horses at the rear. Zelda whinnied loudly as Carolyn fed each horse an apple from the barrel outside the wooden stalls. Sounds of a disturbance took her by surprise until she turned to find a grumbling groomsman trying to corner Beni with an ugly looking pitch fork.

"Whoa, stop that," she admonished. "He won't hurt you." *I think.* "Sorry. I'll get him out." If it weren't for the concerned whinnying of strange horses, she would have stuck around to give the man a piece of her mind. She couldn't, however, argue with someone who was only protecting his charges. "Where've you been, Beni? You're not allowed in here, and I doubt if I can take you in to the council meeting."

Mario approached, looking slightly out of breath. "Correct, pretty lady. He should be fine in the porch if you tell him to 'stay'." The wicked gleam in his eye didn't reassure her at all.

"You won't upset anyone else, will you, boy." Her hand sank into the longer hair of Beni's neck and he chuffed, as though agreeing with her.

When she and Mario returned to the front of the stone building, and slipped into its cool interior, they passed through a large, high ceilinged glass porch before coming into an eccentrically designed old style courtroom.

A few people sat on its curved, tiered benches that reached half way up its wall. The chamber's rounded central region was clearly where the action took place. Some observers stood in groups chatting, and another of about a dozen was seated together on a raised platform of benches on the side furthest from the entrance. Jurors?

Mario saw where she was looking. "Representatives of Arthur's districts," he informed her. "Wait a moment." He took off into the room while Carolyn hovered near the doorway, fussing with Beni.

"You can see everything from here, boy, so be good and stay, will you?" Baleful eyes stared back at her. "That's not going to work, I'm afraid."

"Peter's returned after having his hand slapped," Mario announced, Carolyn looking up at him, surprised at his quick return. He took her arm, and almost trance-like, she was led into the room.

Sure enough, Peter sat at one of three desks near one sidewall. He was leafing through the pages of what appeared to be an accounts book when he must have sensed her. When he looked up, Carolyn couldn't help but flush in embarrassment. This man had fooled her into thinking she loved him. She wanted to jump across the desk and wipe off the half smile that lit his picture perfect features.

A glance at Ethan beside him revealed his thoughts to be a little more murderous than hers. Had Father brought him here to see if he would break his part of their bargain? That would have been very naughty. She swallowed the laugh that had tried to bubble up, glad that Ethan had been able to restrain himself so far.

Mario chose exactly the right time to command Ethan's attention. "There's a nice surprise for you after this," he said with a grin, steering both the mage and Carolyn to their seats. Peter merely offered a mildly quizzical glance at them. "Keep it together, both of you."

Carolyn had been too distracted by Peter to notice another man at a central desk. A magic user, definitely, the Lilim was cloaked in a power akin but not equal to Arthur's. He was an older, frailer version of the chief, and he scanned the room periodically, seemingly bored. When he began the introduction, it reminded Carolyn of nails scraping down a chalkboard.

"Come on, we don't need to sit close to the front," urged Mario and directed them to a bench near to but not directly across from a desk occupied by Arthur. He'd elected to lean back on a bureau behind, striking a relaxed but professional pose, declaring he had no need of a barrier between himself and his people.

"That's Campbell." At Carolyn's side, Mario pointed out the older male at the centre of the chamber. "Arthur's uncle," he explained, "and former chief of the realm." Carolyn's eyes widened, seeing the resemblance that had initially escaped her. "I'm to introduce you later. He chairs these meetings and makes sure that the few rules are adhered to."

"But why when Arthur's here."

"Fair point. You might have noticed that all Arthur's guards are outside." She hadn't, and clearly Peter didn't count as he was here in some sort of clerical capacity. That had to hurt. "He thinks it sets the wrong tone for folks coming here." Carolyn got it: he wanted to show that he was a benevolent figure but also a formidable force, one that could hold its own without the repressive need of guards.

The chamber took their seats at Campbell's introduction. He explained that they only had news of a couple of items, as on the agenda, but that anyone was welcome to raise further issues after business was concluded.

The first person called to speak was a Lolilim by the name of Adair who trembled slightly as he spoke. "Sir," he began, "I paid my taxes this year as ever. Unfortunately, my crops have been so poor that I need to petition for help with next year's seeds and planting." He mumbled about having to lay off workers due to the way things were.

Peter rose and talked briefly to Arthur before returning to his papers.

"Yes, Adair." It might have been Carolyn's imagination but her father's tone had chilled. "What do you grow?"

"Potatoes and grain, my lord."

"Right. If you leave your details with my aid at the end of the session, someone from the agricultural contingent will advise on how best to proceed with your problem."

"Thank you, my lord, it's been a terrible worry," Adair finished, before returning to his seat and offering a charming smile to the woman beside him. The rest of the business was conducted along similar lines. Carolyn learned that there was a rudimentary health care system for registered workers in the cities, as well as crèche provisions. A healer petitioned for an upgrade of nursery facilities and Arthur agreed in principle but said his aide would have to investigate the matter before apportioning funds.

Carolyn enjoyed the way her father interacted with his people. He had no need for devices or visible tricks to make himself heard in the large space. When he spoke, everyone gave their full attention – except for Mario who continued to explain the nuances of the proceedings in Carolyn's ear.

Before long, the building had virtually emptied, and the man named Adair was with Peter, presumably passing on his details as Arthur had requested.

"There is no need for us to stay any longer," Mario said to Carolyn, and they stood in time to catch sight of Arthur moving to a rear exit with Lawrence and two of his men.

"Fine," said Ethan, "I was just about asleep anyway."

The three were almost at the door when Adair's elevated pitch made Carolyn stop. "I don't understand it. If my accounts are wrong then it's been a genuine mistake."

"You two go ahead, I'll catch up," Carolyn told them, her attention having been grabbed.

"No, it's okay, we can all st–"

"You don't have to cluck around me," and Carolyn glared at her companions. Did they need to watch her constantly? "I'll not interfere."

"But I'd like to stay too," said Ethan with a twisted smile, and slid on to the end of a bench. He raised his eyes, as though in challenge to Mario, and the Lilim huffed, his gaze lifting to Carolyn before he sat beside Ethan. She shrugged resignedly and pushed in beside the Lilim. "And I never cluck," Ethan stage-whispered over the back of Mario's head.

"A mistake?" came Peter's mellow voice; Carolyn hated the fact he sounded so confident. He hadn't caught her eye, but he had to know they were watching him at work. "Not unless keeping an expensive mistress and your miserable attempt to deceive the chief are your idea of a mistake."

"Oh, no," shrieked the woman now beside him. "All those times you said you were on business, I should have known." She was openly weeping and Patrick appeared from the side lines to offer the woman a handkerchief. "Why didn't I see," she wailed, and Adair's face contorted in anger.

"I can turn the fortunes of the farm around if you'd only give me a chance," Adair pleaded.

"This, coming from one bold enough to seek additional funds and assistance from the public purse," Peter coldly noted.

"My wife demanded it. I had no choice." The woman had dissolved into hiccoughing sobs. "I didn't know, honest, I didn't." Adair shot a look of utter contempt at his wife, and Carolyn's flesh chilled. "Be still, woman. I need to think."

"The time for thinking has passed," Peter told him, clearly enjoying the spectacle. "You have forfeited your property and have until sunset tomorrow to vacate the premises."

The woman gasped. "A day?"

Peter frowned in her direction before returning to Adair. "The decision is final. Be glad it's the only punishment. If members of your family wish to remain at the holdings as hired labour, provisions may be made for that. As per the chief's long standing directions on fraudulent activity, a more worthy tenant is to be selected. In this case, one Barnabas Finn —who you removed from the payroll – may take your place. The main house is to be occupied by his family as of tomorrow at sunset."

Realisation dawned on Adair's flushed face. "That little weasel spoke to you before all this, didn't he?" Peter didn't credit him with an answer. "Finn is untrained; he is not a manager."

"Neither were you when we set up the farm," Peter easily answered. "Your banishment is a leniency that can be revoked in favour of a more permanent punishment." The ruined farmer stumbled back to land on one of the benches. "Finn will make use of the resources you repeatedly declined through the past four years despite the gradual deterioration of the business."

Carolyn stood, and Mario followed suit. "Nothing damning to be found here," he said to Ethan, and Carolyn couldn't help but agree. It seemed that her father was part of a system that didn't suffer fools gladly, and justice was dispensed without fuss. "There will be troops allocated to ensure cooperation," Mario added, as though reading her thoughts.

CHAPTER 11

Edward

"Do you know if the people are revolting?"

Edward's eyes flashed with sudden humour. "I don't know, Krisp, but *you're* certainly a bit ripe."

The young men were shaded from the glare of the Skean sun as they walked through the leafy canopy between the north castle gates and the courtyard.

"Ha, ha." Krisp slapped Edward's shoulder with an open palm. Humour aside, it had been irritating that Lucas had effectively grounded him after his mother's abduction. The enforcers had either known of his allegiance or he wasn't worth trying to get back.

"Have faith," said Edward blithely. "We will succeed."

"I hope so," Krisp nodded vehemently. "There's a run planned to the Outlands but I expect we'll need to stay here." Hence the question about revolt, thought Edward, now uncomfortable. The outlanders could take advantage of a weak chief.

Even before his grounding, Lucas had made it plain that Edward would have to master his Kistatus form before being allowed far from the castle. Unless they were secretly growing military grade troops out there from the barren earth – and regular conscriptions for the chief's forces reduced the risk – then he had nothing to concern himself over.

"It's not all about the combat" Lucas would say. According to Hecaton, Edward would gain access to his inner demon if he shape-shifted. He had respect for what he saw of the unquantifiable force but didn't trust it. He trusted the muscles and skills of his human body and brain. Magic altered perception and reality. It was enough that Hecaton, his few mages and the

Chief stank of it; Edward was fine without the taint.

"Let's do some target practise later." He could always think more clearly when he was shooting.

"Oh, right, you wouldn't have heard," Krisp faltered slightly, piquing Edward's interest. The big Kistatus was never rattled. Edward motioned for him to continue. "Thomas has suspended practise with live ammo." His voice lowered conspiratorially as he put a hand on Edward's shoulder. "You know what I think?"

"Do I want to?" Edward braced himself for the joke he was sure was coming but Krisp kept a straight face. "That last shipment they brought through the gateway disappeared."

"What? Did it get snatched?" This was stupid. Edward didn't intend verbally sparring over a potentially serious matter. He wished Krisp would just get to the point.

Krisp shrugged but held Edward's gaze. "I'm worried that Lucas is failing in his ability to keep anything we get from other realms." Seeing Edward's lack of expression, he hurried on. "I mean … what are we going to do if our humans start to go missing?" *That* was more than enough for Edward. He launched at his friend and smacked him hard against the stone wall, drawing his sword.

"It doesn't work like that," he hissed. "You must not breathe this to anyone."

"But, I–"

"Not a single word. This is under control. I can't have you panicking the people."

"I've not… I wouldn't. I swear." Krisp stared at him as though he was possessed, which Edward would have found funny in different circumstances. "For the chief's sake, Edward, I'm only sharing this now to make *you* aware of it. I realise now I shouldn't have taken such a casual approach."

With a grunt, Edward released Krisp who'd refrained from defending himself by taking his Kistatus form. Clearly he was shaken by his friend's reaction, but how should Krisp have expected the chief's son to take the news that – magic aside – Lucas was on the way out?

Krisp could be loud but he wasn't a liar, nor was he a troublemaker. Edward had dismissed the dysfunction of the hot springs beneath the castle as a transient glitch, but this couldn't be ignored. Were there any other signs he'd missed that the castle was failing?

Edward sheathed his sword and hung his head. "Krisp, I–"

"No. Look, man. It was my fault." Edward wasn't about to argue the point, but instead, strode off.

"Where are you going?"

"Skipping practise." He walked purposefully through the portcullis and into the hot gardens beyond. His thoughts raced. If he didn't articulate this properly, he'd come off looking like a fool in Hecaton's eyes. If the high mage would stop treating him as an errant schoolboy, they might get along much better.

It's all I've behaved like. The answer was distressingly clear. Only an idiot would leave the kingdom in Edward's hands but there was no-one else. Hecaton liked his freedom, so he wouldn't take up the mantle. *Think, Eddie, think.*

He used to have a brain, something he'd not bothered developing given they'd had Carolyn to provide this for the family. What did he have to offer the Kistatus people? The mere thought of becoming something *other* brought him out in a cold sweat — useful now to stave off the garden's oppressive heat.

He knew the chief's magic worked to keep certain supplies coming in through the gateways. He had a history of large successes that none of the other chiefs could match. Edward should have been more vigilant. Really, he'd known the springs were failing as Lucas grew weaker.

Following his thoughts to their natural conclusion, the castle could indeed be at risk. How would his old friends react to the entire structure showing up again in Ayrshire, from where it had originally come?

Returning to his birth place as a teenager had been a horrendous shock, and Edward had believed his captors to be feeding him lie upon lie about his origin. There was no way he could have belonged to the Kistatus race, not with their terrible serpentine physiques and poisonous abilities. In those early days, Edward had vowed to free Amanda from her dreadful claim and return to his sister on Earth.

A fine plan if he'd had help or guidance but he'd been alone, indisputably on his own with a race that could eat him for breakfast. Edward didn't like to remember the chaos of his and Amanda's abduction from Earth.

After a week of being locked up, he'd got to see his mother again. Much good that had done him. She was clearly smitten with Lucas and begged Edward to stop fighting the guards. She explained their history in a way that proved the truth in what he'd heard.

Amanda and Lucas had been together long enough for Edward to have been born in Skean. They had apparently lived in the realm for less than a year before Protectorate forces overwhelmed the guard, at a time when Lucas and Hecaton had been out networking through the realms.

Enforcers had taken custody of Amanda and himself along with several servants. Something, though, had gone awry with their plans. The humans returned home alright but Amanda and her babe in arms had been misdirected somehow, and landed in the realm of Empustat where Arthur had taken them in charge.

A couple of years later and another Protectorate venture had led to the liberation of a young Edward, and Carolyn as the new baby in Amanda's appallingly repetitive history. It had been pretty much a miracle that they'd stayed hidden in plain sight on Earth, spending fifteen unmolested years there.

As a survivor, Edward had learned to justify doing whatever it took to gain Lucas's trust. He never expected that in so doing he would find approval and purpose, something that had been sadly lacking in his life. Like an addict, he'd soon craved it, and both Lucas and his mother had nurtured his abilities as he grew stronger and more skilled – becoming a favourite with his father's court, the guard and with the humans who served them. It hadn't taken long for Edward to realise he was exactly where he was meant to be.

Admittedly, Lucas hadn't been the best husband to his mother, but she had been *happy* after Hecaton had brought them home – well, after the claiming ceremony, certainly. He chose to ignore the times, especially during the weeks leading up to a renewal, when he would catch an air of confusion about her. Sometimes, more disturbingly, she reminded him of some of the humans when they first arrived at the castle, before they realised what a wonderful place it was.

They had only lost one human during the time Edward had been in Skean. With any luck, the new girl wouldn't end up the same way. *Stop it, Edward. Rhona is nothing like Sarah!*

The sweat was now pouring off him when a cart stopped at his side. "You're going to die out here," came a voice from its canopied driver's bench. Edward looked up to find the object of his thoughts scowling down at him.

"Rhona," he said, and scanned the cart, mystified. "Where are you going?"

"I'm dropping off stuff at the first village," she said impatiently. Edward hadn't been heading anywhere in particular, but the settlement would do for starters, while he worked out how to handle Hecaton. Being with someone else who hated him would be good practise.

"That'll do fine, Rhona." He flashed a brilliant smile from which she visibly recoiled. "It was good of you to stop."

"I'd get in trouble if I didn't offer you a lift," she grumbled.

"What have they got you doing, transporting goods?" He peered beneath the tarpaulin stretched over the bed of the cart. The girl was seriously trying to work a regular job?

"Yes, it was *my* idea. The pay's crap, and it's doing my back in something awful." She leaned forward and arched a brow at him before squinting up at the sun. "Why aren't you in training at this hour?"

"Keeping track of my schedule, eh? I didn't think you cared." He climbed up and sat beside her on the bleached bench of the cart, shrugging an arm over the backrest. She adjusted the reins, and he saw that her delicate hands had reddened in the sun.

"Girl's gotta know where to avoid." Edwards's lips twitched. Rhona was not, he suspected, as unmoved as she liked to suggest.

"Right." The girl was going to get a permanent line between her eyebrows if she kept scowling at him like that. The peasant garb seemed to accentuate the fact that she was a beauty – like a rare orchid found in a field of daisies. He ridiculed himself for such a romantic notion. This heat was making him fanciful.

"Where can I drop you? Barracks for a shower?"

Unable to resist, his smile returned. "Do I offend you, my lady?"

"Can't imagine it's just me you offend."

Oh, she was a smart one all right, and Edward was a fool to be so attracted to her.

"About that kiss…"

"Uh, oh." She waved a finger at him. "Really, Ed…ward. Let's pretend it didn't happen." He didn't miss the hesitation over his name and his eyes raised heavenwards at a half formed realisation.

His smile widened, salty residue stinging his cracked lips. Hadn't Rhona called him by the abbreviated version of his name when he'd kissed her? Even the closest of his friends, everyone apart from his mother, called him Edward. That she'd called him "Eddie" must mean she liked him.

"Fine. Let's not think on it."

"What?" Rhona looked surprised by his easy agreement. Did he imagine it, or did she seem a little disappointed?

"I said 'fine', Rhona. We can start again." It was odd how her quarrelsome presence had chased away his concerns about Lucas. Perhaps he could detour her for a while longer.

Hecaton could wait.

CHAPTER 12

Sean

Sean arrived at the Glasgow flat with the Veloces to find Jonah and Mel engrossed on the X-box. Mace appeared to be watching a movie on a laptop.

"Hey, Sean," said Mel, her eyes lighting at the sight of the demon beside him. "Speedy, you okay?" Mel's attention had apparently flagged long enough to lose a life. She groaned loudly and berated the Faery for taking advantage. "Want a shot after me? Jonah's killing me here."

"Perhaps later," intercepted Sean. "I thought you might accompany Note on the little mission he has planned." Jonah abandoned his game and stood to give Sean his full attention.

"I could also…"

"Thank you, Jonah, but I need you here at the moment." His tone left no room for argument, and he ignored the pouting demon. It was better to limit the numbers of enforcers who came in contact with Hecaton. "Mace, are you fine with this?"

"Absolutely." Mace being the epitome of physical strength and perfection, Hecaton would view his presence in a positive light, acknowledging that his involvement with the team, if not altogether welcome, had been appreciated. Sean filled the tea kettle while listening to the idle chatter of his crew. He was carrying the tray into the room when Note arrived at the flat.

"Sorry, I got held up." The young Kistatus offered a carrier bag to Jonah whose frown was literally turned upside down when he spotted the contents. Smart boy.

"Let's do this, then." Mel accepted a fruit chew from Jonah and planted

94

a quick kiss on his cheek. "Catch you later, Faery boy." Jonah rolled his eyes, feigning disdain, but Sean could see the importance he attributed to even the most casual of advances from the irascible mage. He would have to talk to her about it.

"Where's my kiss," interrupted Speedy, offering a comically exaggerated sad face. "I don't know what your boss has in store for me when you're gone."

"You'll live," she replied with a cheeky grin, and swaggered off with Note and Mace into the hallway.

"I don't usually drink tea," Speedy said, eyeing the tray on the table. A glance towards Jonah was all it took to send the Faery to the kitchen to fetch a soft drink for him.

Not being a member of the team, keeping quiet about Protectorate matters around Speedy was causing an unhelpful strain on the others.

"We're expecting another tea drinker." The Veloces sounded a little out of sorts when he popped open his can of lemonade. Having explained the requirements, Sean thought the demon remained unconvinced.

Jonah gave no sign of interest in the conversation, apparently content to stand beside the closed door of the room and demolish his chocolate stash. If only the others were as quiet.

"Just sounds all about control to me." Speedy returned to the matter that concerned him most.

"The precators are not 'about control'." The Veloces was getting to be as irksome as Melanie. "They are 'about' balance to the realms."

"Really sorry," continued Speedy, concern causing his voice to spike unnaturally high, "but I've just got away from that controlling bitch at the Agency…" The demon missed the sudden drop in temperature but Sean observed Jonah's reaction from his peripheral vision.

Still creatures, whatever their abilities, often "saw" things so much more easily than their hyperactive counterparts. He thought that perhaps Mel could learn a little from her demon admirer. Speedy was still rambling on. "So, there's got to be some way your bosses can use me and help me stay the hell out of—"

Sean's eyes flicked upwards before settling on the new arrival. He spared a second of concern for what was about to happen before drawing his shield tightly under control. Speedy physically jumped and rubbed at his arms. "He's right behind me isn't he?"

"She," murmured Sean before saying, "Nothing will happen to you without your permission. I had a duty to present my findings to the council. And you, my dear Speedy, are a 'find'."

The precator had formed more quickly than was usual. Sean repressed a smile, remembering the last time she had visited, wearing biker leathers, no less. Her work led to various situations for which she was always well equipped. No matter what she wore, the woman was a dazzling dark beauty. Clothed in a formal trouser suit, her heels made no noise on the hardwood floor as she moved around the Veloces towards Sean.

She acknowledged Jonah's presence with a tiny inclination of her head, and the shadow-Faery dropped his gaze, resuming his impersonation of a statue.

Speedy showed no such decorum, openly staring at the precator as she passed. He did, however, rise from his chair in a barely conscious acknowledgment of the power swelling within the room. Her attention belonged to Sean at that moment and she viewed him – apparently without *seeing* – from beneath lashes that framed her dark and striking eyes. There was no softness, no hint of their relationship, merely business.

The Veloces, suddenly catching up, eyed the mage with rebuke before emulating Jonah's quiet demeanour. A nerve ticked beneath his eye, and Sean thought it was right for the demon to be seriously unnerved. He wondered if the Veloces's heroics in the Agency fight had stemmed mainly from fear rather than his natural inclinations.

"Tea, Sean? How lovely." Michelle lowered herself to the chair next to Speedy and waited as Sean poured the brew carefully into a small china cup. He added a lump of sugar which sank with a satisfying plunk to the bottom of the cup. It was all about the ritual. A brief stir completed the process.

"You are fitting well into your new role," said the precator, taking a quiet sip from her cup.

"A temporary situation, mother." An eyebrow rose slightly with his acknowledgment of their relationship. He had clearly pleased her with the reception although she would be well aware of his duty to remove the knowledge from the minds of their companions.

Michelle turned pointedly to Speedy. "Had you come through the gateway, I would have been able to measure your worth, young demon, but as it is, we will work through less conventional channels."

Of course, the difficulty was not just Speedy's association with the Agency. He had no inclination to join Protectorate forces. "You are linked to another," Michelle said with no discernible change of tone.

The blood seemed to drain from Speedy's thin face.

"Your …" Michelle's head tipped to the side as she chose her word carefully. "Brother?"

"Of sorts. He's a little different from me," offered Speedy, and Sean felt an unwelcome swell of pride at his mother's effortless control. Powerless to resist, Speedy looked pained as he rapidly said, "I was created from his blood in the lab."

Michelle smiled, as though this was as she had expected, but Sean had *heard* a lie and shot a look of reproach at Speedy, although he was too focussed on the precator to notice. Sean slanted a look at Jonah who showed no reaction to anything other than unwrapping another chocolate bar. *He* was former Agency, but without knowledge of any details unless directly pertinent to his missions.

If Sean hadn't been in Judy's head recently, he might not have made the connection. Speedy had been less than honest with them but Sean sensed no ill will towards Protectorate forces. *A truth protection charm?* Still, he was *not* the Veloces he had led them to believe.

With such capacity to create, Sean would have thought that by producing hybrids like Jonah and their cloning of Veloces, the Agency would have had a greater sense of responsibility to their creations.

Jonah had been captive all his life, but the team had allowed him to exercise a measure of autonomy. The organisation valued Jonah's skills much more than the Veloces's. Suddenly it was important to Sean that Speedy not be reminded of his perceived lack of worth. He frowned slightly in thought, remembering a tinge of familiarly styled magic coating the blade that Speedy had used during his fight. A blade with which the previously undefeated Mow had been shredded.

Hush, my darling. You think too loudly. His mother's eyes sought his. *Allow me to sum it up.*

The Veloces is "unable" to speak the truth about this. His charm guards against persuasion and protects his brother.

Always a high risk prisoner, your Speedy killed two employees who were involved in his "reconditioning". The images Sean received equated that term with the worst kinds of torture. Speedy's reactions had been desperate and justifiable in any right-minded individual's view. No wonder he had no interest in enforcing with the others. The demon had been damaged in every conceivable way.

The Veloces was scheduled for termination during the Agency "fight club" event that you attended with Notechis. He promised his pledge if they sent his brother — a clone — to fight in his stead. When the time came, he pretended to make the switch, allowing the low risk subject to pass on a weapon which gave him a chance of defeating his opponent.

The clone is pretending to be the original and reporting to us.

A demon pledge? Sean couldn't begin to imagine the hideous repercussions that could come from that. Wait. The clone now owed a pledge to Miranda?

Enough, Sean. This is not your concern. You must rest assured that we will be monitoring.

Monitoring, Mother. How can you bear to use such aggressive tactics?

Don't be so dramatic, dear, and sarcasm doesn't become you at all.

It most certainly did, and her words served only to illustrate the fact that she really didn't know him at all. He shut her out, now mindful that he didn't want her rifling through his thoughts. She still could but her sense of propriety would normally keep her out unless invited. Oddly, she seemed relieved. Perhaps Sean should have been scouring *her* mind.

There was a detail about the pledge business that hovered on the brink of discovery. It slid from his reach before he could grasp it. There was another relevant point that deserved attention.

Your spy, the clone at the Agency, is working closely with Judy and Miranda.

Michelle absorbed the news with no visible reaction. *Good work with the defector, my dear. I see why we've not been informed of recent developments.*

In Judy's mind, Sean had seen the restrictions on the substituted demon. "I think I know of somewhere you could go, Speedy," he said to the Veloces who blinked away the effects of his precatorial induced stupor. Michelle only looked mildly surprised at Sean's switch in tactics. Given her talents, surprise was rare.

Her eyes met his, and he felt suddenly caught, as though she were *seeing* him without use of the usual tricks that accompanied it. Her strengths had grown immeasurably. Her inhumanness, always strong — even whilst cloaked — was now overwhelming. Why was she allowing him to see the change in her when he didn't want to reciprocate and show that the reverse had happened to him? Dear God. Was he ashamed?

Michelle blinked, reinstating her widely acceptable guise of being almost human. Having spent so many years as *other*, she couldn't manage more. He didn't sense that she saw *everything* in him, but she *saw* just the same.

"Yes, that would be agreeable, Sean."

Could she not pretend that his thoughts weren't hers for the plucking? Would she return to investigate and discuss the fact that he'd been — humanised? He had bonded to the team in a manner that had set him back in many respects but pushed him forward in another rather challenging yet compelling direction.

"So… do I have a say in whatever the plan is?" Anyone would have thought Speedy would be annoyed by the lack of control he had over his life but the demon was curious rather than bothered. He had just been validated by the Protectorate.

Note

"Wow," exclaimed Mel. "This is really something." Mace and Mel flanked the Kistatus as they emerged from the gateway. Both kept one hand on the hilt of the short swords strapped to their waists.

"I called, and you answered." Hecaton's mocking voice came clearly as the heat dissipated from the opening. Mel jumped as it sizzled shut at their backs. They had landed in the great hall of Skean castle, directly beside a set fireplace that was as tall as Mace, and more than twice the size across. Hecaton's icy human eyes glittered in amusement as he observed his visitors.

From Note's perspective, his father looked as though he'd stepped out of a "Merlin" set. The room seemed much smaller than the Kistatus remembered. Many celebrations had been held here. With recent events, Note suspected that festivities had halted.

A wave of sadness and remorse came over him and he tried to remember that he'd done nothing wrong. It was, of course, a matter of opinion. He had expected to be directed straight to Hecaton's oasis, but shouldn't have been surprised by his father's methods.

The youthful looking high mage gestured imperiously with a long staff in his right hand. "You are my guest for an hour or two and I believe your friends will find these accommodations much more pleasing than the last you shared." His voice sounded pleasant, but Note and the others – by their advance at his side – also distinguished the barely disguised threat.

"Ever the faithful," soothed Hecaton, his eyes resting on Mace. "It's not that I don't want you *helping* my son with the small task I have planned– "

"Father, I didn't agree to you screwing around with my friends."

Hecaton tsked lightly. "Notechis. I wouldn't dream of, ah – 'screwing around' with your delightful friends. As I understand it, and please correct me if I'm wrong, but you return humans to this world that you've adopted."

"You're saying you have–"

"A gift, a token, if you will. Should you find some unsuitable for transportation, I'll dispose of them by other means."

"But … but the chief can't be dead." Could he?

"No, just think on it as trimming resources." Mel's mouth dropped open at the realisation.

"There are humans you want to return, like unwanted parcels?"

"Recycling would be a more accurate term." He turned from her, oblivious or uncaring of her horror. "I assure you, Notechis, there is no trickery here. Both this room and the one adjacent are sealed against intruders, but your gateway access is free and unblocked. You and your friends may leave at any time."

Mel and Mace flanked Note as he approached and stood before his father. Hecaton shocked him by tugging him into an embrace that Note was helpless to resist. Not borne of affection, he felt the sweep of the high mage's mind against his like a wire brush against soap. He suffered the inspection and waited for the intrusion to stop. "You learn quickly, my son."

"I didn't have much choice."

"We may be some time, so your friends will remain here at the castle while you and I take care of business."

"No." Both enforcers stepped forward and Note raised his hands.

"I have been unclear?" Hecaton said in a way that suggested the opposite. "I assure you this will be a civilised visit, complete with refreshments and entertainment if so desired." He waved a finger at Mel.

"Some of us enjoy our entertainment more than others," he accused, causing Mel to stutter before Hecaton turned his attention to Mace. "And you, my dear Mow, are quite the work of art. No unfortunate side effects, I see."

"I am grateful for this form," Mace managed through gritted teeth and Hecaton smiled benevolently.

"It was the least I could do for such a fine friend of my son's."

Mel and Mace both coloured under Hecaton's scrutiny, but for entirely different reasons.

"I thought your friends could lay the groundwork before you see Edward again. I believe his ego suffered a considerable blow after defeat at your hand." His eyes caught Note's, meaningfully. "I would also imagine that, with Carolyn almost within your grasp, you would like to meet your future brother-in-law; kill two birds with one stone, as it were."

Hecaton had swung his net, and Note had no wish to cut through it. He was willing to stay and follow through with the consequences of his actions but his friends didn't have to. "I want you to return home," he said, eyes pleading for their agreement.

Mace looked apologetic while Mel appeared royally pissed off. "You heard the man. Can't resist a good party, me." She glared at Hecaton while Mace quietly said, "Not leaving the realm without you, buddy."

Note cursed his lack of foresight. He'd forgotten how much it irked him to be at the mercy of his father's whim. "Your assurances remains, Hecaton?"

"How very formal, my son." He brought a hand to his chest. "May the forces strike me down if I should dishonour my vow?"

Note couldn't help but catch Mel's "*Like we'd be so lucky*" through their link.

There was no disorientation when Hecaton reached out again for Note, but in the instant before they travelled, the scent of rich vegetation tickled his senses. It was as though Hecaton's oasis had reached out to snatch them in.

Note welcomed the softness of the new terrain beneath his feet. His father's were already bare as he took to the water, clothes melting away to reveal shiny Kistatus skin that cut through the lake in graceful motions.

Note took a deep breath of clean air and wondered if his change would be as flawless as Hecaton's. Compared to the practise with Mel's cat form, this should be nothing. Hecaton's triangular face broke the water's surface at a distance and a smile tugged his lips as Note leaped into the shimmering lake. Like Hecaton, he didn't need the touch of the water to accelerate his change; it rippled over him instantly.

The process of healing and repair had similarities across the realms and races. The same principles extended to the life of Hecaton's beloved oasis.

He approached his father at the centre of the lake, where the sun barely reached to reflect from the iridescent scales that covered and protected him.

You stayed here when I came for Amanda, Note ventured.

I did.

The unanswered "Why" lay between them as they began circling each other, slowly at first, keeping a fixed distance between them at all times. Magic liked symmetry, and both he and his father started to light up the water in equal measure, silvery green brightness radiating from them each. Note had done no spelling in his true form, and though he'd gained a lot of power to use for the Protectorate, his human usage paled in comparison to this.

Why didn't his father routinely take Kistatus form? Because of Lucas and his close association with humans?

Sanare receptui, sanare receptui… The healing phrase repeated as a chant, musical, mystical and undeniably pure. It was totally unlike anything Note would have thought possible from Hecaton. Note's eagerness swelled even as he despised himself for enjoying the time spent with the high mage. Readily, he followed Hecaton's lead in their ever widening circles of restorative dance through the lake.

CHAPTER 13

Sean

The lower level of Feeding Frenzy was busy with patrons appreciating a late lunch. Under partial cover, customers enjoyed drinks on the new decking area that made the most of the available sunlight. Sean discerned that there were two new demons in the building, suitably attired and *veneered* to allow for their work detail. Taz *had* been kept busy.

Sean and Speedy dealt easily with security and crept up to Taz's office like professional thieves. It had been only when opening the office door that the alarm sounded and Taz leaped from his chair, letting loose with a crossbow.

Speedy, true to his name, ducked from its path like lightening and Sean deflected the bolt back to Taz with a snap of transforming energy. *Unusually creative.* Sean watched as Taz caught the returned object – a fairly decent paper aeroplane – which the demon frowned at. "What the devil do you think you're doing," panted Taz.

"Caught you at a bad time?" said Speedy, taking the attack completely in his stride.

The normally well-groomed Motus looked exasperated, circles beneath his eyes and the beginnings of a beard. Sean couldn't help but agree with Speedy's assessment. "No, it's all good." Taz recovered remarkably well. "You might have called first."

"Were you expecting visitors with fangs?" queried Sean. Taking the crossbow that Taz had set down on his desk, he examined the item with interest. "Strike first and ask questions later. Not a terrible policy in your line of work." Perhaps it wasn't such a great idea to entrust Speedy to the fellow. Taz's office had changed since Sean had last visited. The previous bar section had been replaced with a screened off area from which he could hear the muted sounds of computer gaming.

"You bring your son to work, now?" The child's head peeked above the back of a sofa that faced away from them and waved.

"Josh," said Taz wearily, "these are just friends."

"I know that, daddy," returned the boy with a large smile.

"Hey, what's the system you've got there, little guy," said Speedy who raised a quizzical eyebrow at Taz.

"I can't imagine you're an axe murderer or Sean wouldn't have brought you here. Sure, go ahead, take a look," Taz allowed.

Speedy had merely killed – not murdered, Sean absently justified. Taz waited until Josh's excited voice was engaged with their visitor.

"You know I want to say 'No'. In fact, I've never wanted to say it so much in my entire life."

"He won't be any trouble," said Sean evenly. He had scoured and found no pledge on Speedy. He was confident of Taz's help as this was what the Motus demon did: found places for the displaced demons that were brought to him.

"If I had a pound for every time someone told me that." Taz was making too much out of the placement issue. The expression on Sean's face was obviously not one the Motus enjoyed seeing but it was useful.

Taz's hand reached up to scratch his chin, jerking a little when he found it coarse with stubble. The unkempt look was clearly new. "He's another one of *theirs*, isn't he?" Sean followed his line of sight to Speedy who was being happily – and noisily – instructed by the five year old. Shouldn't the child be in school? It was none of his business. He imagined that otherworldly children, hybrid or not, may be unsuitable for certain education systems.

Sean strode to look through the office's large one way windows. He believed there to be times when Taz would look out onto all the floors and feel like a god. Looking back to the somewhat haggard version before him, he gathered that now was *not* one of those times.

"The Siren turned out well for you."

Sean thought that the skilled emotion enhancer could sense a lot from someone like Speedy. Taz's eyes tracked to the demon, continually. "That's no bloody Tracer," he mumbled, but Sean could tell the demon was curious. "Veloces are rare but the stink of desperation hit me before your almighty cloaked darkness did."

Sean didn't know whether to be proud or mildly affronted at the demons insights. "About Speedy?"

"You don't have to sell me on his skills; I know exactly the things in which his kind excel."

"I don't mean to hawk you anything, Taz. It's a favour." The demon scratched his arm, likely where his mark from the destroyer had been. Sean was not talking about *that* but rather providing occasional back up to Taz's little outfit.

"Sean, I know you're interested in Siren and her motives. You don't understand why she would cleave to me, being as I am." Little more than an insect, thought Sean, realising and not caring that the demon could sense his emotions. His opinion of the Motus had actually improved over time. "I understand," he continued, "or more precisely: I don't think it's sexual with you, and she's enjoyed for once not having to shield who she is from someone."

The mage wasn't sure how he felt about her having discussed him. He hadn't set out to make a lasting impression but hadn't she done exactly that with him? "You see her for more than the virtues of her race and perhaps for more than her Tracer ability."

With the Motus, whose interests lay solely with his wife, Sean knew that the Siren's company could cause him to sweat. Before she took up with Miranda of the Agency, he'd suspected her preferences were for women. He couldn't say he blamed her, the fairer sex were all soft skin and silky lips. *Stop right there!* It was disconcerting how a Siren could bring out the worst in *any* man, apparently. If Taz noticed a change in Sean, he wasn't about to mention it. By the looks of him, he had enough on his plate without overthinking his perceptions about a magic user, albeit a talented mage like Sean.

Taz returned his attention to Speedy, jumping up on the sofa with Josh in some sort of victory dance. He shook his head, a glint of humour showing in the quirk of his mouth.

"If you propose a swap, Levy's never going to replace a Siren with a Veloces."

"I can't imagine why."

Judy

"Get your own," Judy snarled at the Faery hybrid as she grabbed a handful of peanuts from the bowl in her lap. Ella promptly spat a peanut that ricocheted off the mage's cheek.

Judy jumped to her feet, scattering the nuts all across the institution's polished floor. "You little bitch. Look what you made me–" The mage's magic rose up within her, begging release, but she had to remember that Ella was an unstable Faery hybrid. Well, her mental rather than the Faery status was unbalanced. Perhaps she'd feel better if she simply punched Ella on her pretty little nose… But, no.

"Vasch!" she called, but the other mage was already emerging from the tiny kitchen area.

"Now, now, Ladies," he called as he approached. Ella hovered so her face was level with Judy's; black wings had sprouted from her shoulders, creating a wind that threatened to knock Vasch back into the kitchen door. "I was only gone a minute," he fumed. Ella twisted around, her angry expression melting to fear as the mage pointed a hand-held device towards the ceiling.

"No, don't," Ella pleaded, her huge eyes widening further. Judy felt a rush of satisfaction as the circle dropped from above and Ella crouched, furling into a ball within its confines.

The mage turned his frustrated glare on Judy. "You might want to start calling me by my first name." Seriously, *this* was what annoyed him most.

Between the pair of them, they manoeuvred the Faery to her room and sealed the door, which did a great job of blocking out the dramatic sobs.

Their regular babysitting duties were a bore, and Judy suspected that Miranda sent her here especially because she hated the facility with a passion. Ella wouldn't even hint at what her Agency work with the boss and Loci entailed but they sure as hell weren't playing tiddlywinks. The lack of trust was galling after everything Judy had done.

Miranda kept a tight rein on her team and it was insufferable that Vasch was the only one who provided any answers for Judy. He, of course, thought she was making a big deal about nothing. Vasch was happy to carry out orders without question, and as a result Miranda was less wary of him.

Judy and Vasch were supposed to be "bonding" with Ella. To Judy, the whole idea was preposterous. Prisoners could not be forced into friendship. It was of little consolation that Ella's value would drop as soon as the gateway tear was repaired.

"There has to be another way to keep her in line."

"What would you suggest, Judy? She's the only one of her kind since we lost Jonah." Why did he have to sound so calm and reasonable?

"She can turn to shadow. Why isn't she escaping that thing?"

"It's been modified," Vasch returned with a frown.

Interesting he'd not wanted to share that. The big mage was clearly unhappy that she was annoyed with him. She was, but he responded better to sweetness.

"That's amazing, Aiden," she offered, and leaned into him, as though he were directly responsible for the technology.

It worked.

"Miranda's working on a portable device to ensure Ella's cooperation. It will also come in handy for when we find Jonah." Judy had met the male version of Ella, and understood that Jonah was the better option. Ella's early genetic modifications had produced additional side-effects that were difficult to work around.

"This didn't exactly turn out as expected, Judy. The boss expects her to function effectively with the team."

"Psycho Faery as part of our merry band?"

"That's not helpful, Jude. If she wasn't so jealous of you, I think it would go better." He scratched his chin, exasperated, and Judy's mind began to work overtime. Perhaps she'd been too quick to dismiss a closer association with the Faery.

She stooped to pick up an item from the floor; one of Ella's too large boots had fallen off during her strop. "She's not so hard to figure out," Judy said to Vasch, a sly smile forming on her face.

"You think?"

"Let me in to see her – alone."

"Last time didn't go so well, Jude."

"That was before I appreciated the need to 'befriend' her, Aiden." She almost laughed at the softening of his features in response to her tone. Judy was well aware of her shortcomings in certain situations, but she *was* inventive *and* a survivor.

"What do you want? Where's Aiden?" Ella tried to look behind the mage when Judy entered her cell, but Vasch was already out of sight. The Faery paced the floor of the small area as Judy dropped onto the only chair, one beside the door and bolted to the wall. Ella's thin shoulders were hunched protectively, and she appeared to be wringing something in her hands. Realisation dawned.

"Oh, is that your pretty slip?"

"You made me so angry," Ella accused, stopping only to glare at the mage.

"About that. I think I can help, if you want."

Ella made a loud scoffing noise and her gaze narrowed. "I can come back out? That would 'help' tremendously." Judy swallowed the grin that threatened to surface.

"I shouldn't have reacted the way I did before." It was as close to an apology as she could muster. Would it be enough?

"I … I shouldn't have spat the nut," returned the Faery.

Judy's idea was working. Whatever she thought about Ella, the being had developed some attachment to her already, and simply by letting her out for periods to indulge in fast food and to watch films in the lounge while the other subjects were locked up.

Judy began to tap on her computer tablet. "I think you'll enjoy this … activity." Ella's eyes gleamed with interest.

"What activity?"

"Have you heard people talking about online shopping?" The word "shopping" elicited the desired response from the Faery. She threw her damaged slip onto her pillow, wiped her hands on her leggings and crouched beside Judy. "Online shopping is one of my favourite activities."

"I don't know how?" and Judy angled the tablet towards the Faery.

"Watch what I do on this site. You need a slip, right?" A webpage appeared, full of advertisements, and Ella's face shone.

"That one." She pointed, unsurprisingly at the most inappropriate item on the page.

"Oh, that's a costume, it's not..." Ella's wide eyes filled up almost immediately. "Oh, keep your knickers on," the mage relented. "You actually want it?" Ella was jumping up and down beside her now.

"Yes, please."

"Let me check if they have it in your size." The Faery was tiny so Judy clicked on the "8-10" option, and feeling generous, added next day delivery. "There you go, Ella, it's due tomorrow afternoon."

Ella slid over to her bed and perched on the edge, her eyes not leaving Judy for an instant. "Why would you do this for me?"

"That's what friends do." Now for the piece de la resistance. "You want me to do a little magic and make your boots fit you?"

Judy's good humour lasted about five minutes after she'd left the happy Faery.

Vasch had snuggled up against her on the sofa and she was figuring out how to take off when he leaned in and whispered, "Didn't I tell you that you were wasting time with the Siren."

Judy stilled. "What do you mean?"

"Well, you've given up watching her place for starters, haven't you? I mean," he looked confused at her reaction, "with the security they've already got at the flats, it's mad for you to persist."

It took all Judy's control to keep her temper leashed. Vasch was a fool to think she'd give up so easily on something she'd set her mind on doing, he had, however, given her the prompt she needed. Having been wiped by the Protectorate, one of the first things Judy had done was to safeguard her mind. Her enhancement had cost a fortune, and it wasn't perfect as it couldn't prevent tampering, but she could retrieve data if she had a decent inkling of what she was missing. She activated it now, cursing the flash of pain behind her eyes.

Crap, she was probably frying brain cells with the effort. *Remember*, she thought. A tiny purple tab appeared in her mind and she mentally tore it off. Got you! Disappointingly, it was only her concerns about Siren that returned.

"I was only taking a break," she muttered, recognising that the spell had worked without any trace of its caster. Had Miranda noticed her interest and used someone to stop her? Not Vasch obviously, she would have recognised his sloppy signature all over it. Miranda had at least one powerful mage at her disposal, but would she waste resources with this rather than simply tell Judy to back off with her investigations?

Her thoughts were interrupted by the regular warden's return and so, with the Faery no longer their concern, they left the site via the lab. The samples for Siren were usually kept well stocked but Judy frowned to see that only a few vials remained. The labels marked them as mouth swabs. That would do fine.

"The boss is not going to be pleased about this." Judy only half listened to Vasch's complaints as he drove them through the city's nighttime darkness. Miranda certainly hadn't picked this team because of their cognitive abilities, which made the mage just a little worried about her plans. It wasn't out of the realm of possibility that the Protectorate mages had stopped her, but if they had, why allow her to continue? Why not dispose of her? When it came to keeping their secrets safe, they could be ruthless. At least, that's what she'd come to believe.

"You didn't have to come," Judy said, folding her arms sulkily. Her gaze slid to Vasch beside her, his big hands gripping the steering wheel.

"There is definitely something about that girl."

"She's a Siren, for God's sake. Of course there is."

Colouring slightly, he caught her eye, undoubtedly assessing what he should disclose. "It's not just that, Jude. I remember her when she arrived." It was certain that he would have. Vasch had spent years working full time at the beta site which housed a good portion of the Agency specimens. Ella was one thing, but the Siren would have been a very exciting addition to their dregs of demon kind.

Judy felt a surge of jealousy. Not of Vasch, he was a man and therefore predisposed to a Siren's charm, but she had become a huge part of their boss's life, and it wasn't just business. Yes, Miranda used the Siren to charm an Investor or two, but that was nothing. When Siren wasn't driving around in her top of the range car, she was lazing around at the spa and preening for nights out at the best restaurants and clubs in the city.

Judy had been following her for a couple of days, having discovered unaccounted absences in Siren's loose schedule. As yet, she'd found nothing damning, but it stood to reason that Siren was up to something. An affair could be enough to knock her out of favour, and that was all Judy wanted.

"In here." Judy tapped the dashboard.

"The multi- story?" Judy had captured his interest with the possibility of a flight.

"We should have brought Ella with us," said Vasch, and Judy smiled in the darkness. Their little demon would make the perfect spy.

"Yes, but unless *you* want to perch your feathery butt on her window sill for a few hours, we'll try a remote view. Just to check it out." Like Judy, Vasch could transfigure into a bird, which sounded fine, but there were distinct limitations as his form was an owl. Judy had never loved her crow form, but she could easily go out any time she liked. Flying regularly with

Vasch, they knew how to be careful.

"You can be a bit mean sometimes." Vasch's face glowed in the interior light of the car park.

"But that's how you like me," she said, pouting, and placed a conciliatory hand on his knee.

They had climbed three levels when Judy pulled out Siren's sample from her pocket.

"For God's sake, Judy. Wait until we're secure." Vasch's voice was seriously starting to grate on her nerves.

"Oh, just relax and park up at the top."

He sped quickly up the ramps, but with his tightly set features, Judy would have to throw him a crumb to keep him sweet. The mage opened her wallet to reveal what appeared to be a nail set, from which she withdrew a short slide. Using the swab, she dabbed the cells and sealed the slip with a short invocation.

Vasch parked on the open air top level, grumbling when she directed him to a better spot, closer to the edge. Even so, Judy could tell he was excited as well as a little scared. His breathing had all but stopped, and Judy took in his expectation with a smile.

She passed the prepared slide to Vasch. "We need to get you a reader of your own," he said, fumbling the device from his pocket. He placed the sample into its top slot. "Activate," he said.

"Welcome, Aiden Vasch" flashed on the screen.

"Right first time," murmured Judy wryly.

"If they do a spot check, they'll know I've been watching Miranda and Siren."

Judy snorted. "Like that doesn't ever happen."

Vasch looked guiltily away. Many of the magic users *looked* at Siren. They wouldn't be the first to sneak a peek in the hope they'd catch something interesting.

"We can explain." She knew they'd both rather not, but Judy's confidence had risen.

As Miranda described it, Judy had slipped up in some way from the Protectorate holier-than-thou obligations, and as a result they'd kicked her to the curb with nothing other than a vague sense of having been a part of something important. Her boss suspected they had altered her magical ability. Of course, she was still superior to her Agency peers, but she'd been messed up in that any spells she'd learned prior to and including her gateway experience had been forgotten.

Judy motioned to the displayed image of Siren's window and frowned at the drawn blinds. For some reason, she didn't trust the magic that showed the real-time image on Vasch's device. That now showed the scene beyond the blinds, and Siren looked to be safely tucked up in Miranda's embrace.

It was of no matter. Even if Miranda did stay most nights, Judy was now sure the Siren wouldn't simply be having an affair. That would be too easy, too predictable. It frustrated her that she didn't know exactly, but Judy was going to prove that the demon was doing *something* in her spare time that would cause Miranda concern.

"Remind me again why we're doing this here," Vasch said, interrupting her musings, and she wondered why she'd bothered to bring him along. Judy could have borrowed his device and activated it alone, but perhaps fear of being caught may have motivated her to share the blame.

"Remember when you were a teenager and would go 'parking' with your girlfriends." Judy ran her fingers lightly up the inside of his thigh. As he shifted uncomfortably in his seat, she felt only mildly disgusted by the lewd smile that spread over Vasch's face.

Siren

Siren felt the familiar magic-tech blend that informed her of watchers. Roused from her sleep, it was a nuisance rather than anything more sinister – usually.

Without opening her eyes, she turned towards Miranda, pressing her lips to the woman's bare shoulder. Her feelings were complicated about the Agency head. Miranda had many admirable skills but her commitment and dedication to her job came at a terrible price.

Siren knew that Miranda had once been an ordinary untainted girl, filled with extraordinary vision, passion and a desire to learn and create. Surely something of that remained; otherwise, Miranda couldn't be the tender and considerate partner she was.

No-one in the organisation had any idea of Siren's tracing abilities, and as far as she was aware, Miranda didn't concern herself about the magic users who would sometimes get their kicks by watching her. Occasionally, she would give them a show, and, if anything, it cemented their opinion of her.

Only once had a user "viewed" while she'd been "tracing". The underground mage with whom she'd been partnered at the time had intercepted it, so it would display as a failed attempt.

For the foreseeable future, it benefited Siren that the Agency and its minions saw her merely as a coveted specimen under Miranda's control.

CHAPTER 14

Edward

Rhona seemed impervious to the stench of rotting garbage from somewhere farther down the street. Late afternoon was the worst possible time to be on the main thoroughfare from which the many lanes bisected. Disposal crews didn't venture out until dusk, which brought about an entirely different set of problems.

"You didn't need to help me?" she said, clearly noticing Edward's distaste. She wiped her hands down the coarse smock she wore and proceeded to fasten the final strap over the provisions cart.

"You're welcome," he said, trying to hide his smirk. Her brows lifted in reproach.

"I wasn't–"

"No, no," he placated. "I wouldn't want you to feel beholden." The lie tripped easily from his tongue, and Rhona made a weird choking sound, unable to control the laugh that erupted.

"Right. You think I don't know exactly what you're up to."

"Why did you come to the realm," he asked.

Sobering up, her mouth thinned to a line. "Some bitch told me I'd find what I was looking for on this God forsaken world."

"That you could use your magic." He remembered what Cassandra had said to her.

"Yeah, well. I didn't even know I had any until they tested me and called me a latent. All I needed was an O.W.E. and a trip through the gateways to get me started."

"Why would someone help you like that?"

"I know, I'm stupid," she said angrily, "but why the hell wouldn't I take them at their word." Edward suspected she was mainly annoyed with herself for falling for a scam. He blinked when she added, "It was my career's advisor, Edward. Maybe she was getting backhanders for delivering fresh meat or something. I don't know."

Edward frowned. He'd heard of the O.W.E. permits, scorned by Hecaton as an attempt by Earth forces to spy on the realms. Without more information, he didn't know whether the high mage was right to err on the side of caution. Rhona was a poor choice for any organisation. She was way too conspicuous to be a plant.

"With the O.W.E. not activated, there's no failsafe for you here." He realised that reminding her of her vulnerability may not have been his best move for she rounded on him.

"Why are you bothering with this?" she said, pointing back and forth between them. "You and me? It's not going to happen." Her eyes sparkled and something clenched in his gut. The girl wanted to be independent, and he understood, but it could never be allowed.

She just didn't realise how much she depended on him already. Her safekeeping was assured only by her loose association with Cassandra and himself. Rhona had shown that she wasn't above using it, but there was a line she wouldn't cross. How long before that line blurred or even vanished? Part of him – a tiny part – wanted her to succeed, but there was a bigger part that waited greedily to pick up the pieces when it all fell apart – as it would.

Physically, she was no match for the job she'd taken. If he didn't get her away, the girl would either get herself killed or be taken by marauders on the passes.

The past two days had brought about a couple of rejections and still he returned for more. He'd been too serious about the first offer: that he subsidise her life while she rented a room from Cassandra. She had politely declined. The next – more of a suggestion and made partly in jest – she'd not so civilly refused.

"You don't belong here either?" she muttered and picked up the slate attached to the cart, to begin marking off the contents. Edward wasn't given much to thinking about his Earth life, but for a minute, he thought of the long summer days he'd spent hanging about the beach at Saltcoats with his school friends. "You hate the streets," she added with a surreptitious glance through her lashes.

"I *wanted* to see you," he said, the phrase sounding needier than he would have liked. Rhona's expression softened slightly, and he filed the knowledge away for future use.

"I can talk to you," she said, letting the now marked up slate fall to the side. "You helped me gain a few minutes with loading up." Holding his gaze, she leaned towards him until the street noise seemed to disappear and it was just him and her. "I mean, is everything okay with your dad and all?"

It was crap that everyone knew who he was – sometimes. Edward smoothed his hair to give him something to do with his hands. Rhona frowned, seeming vaguely puzzled at the change in him. "It's all just the same," he said tetchily.

"Well, you should get back to work before someone reports you."

"It would be a brave man to do that."

"Or woman," she said, dropping a wink and hoisting herself up to the front of the cart.

As far as distractions went, Rhona deserved top marks for everything except her refusals of his advances. It was bizarre that he could let her treat him and speak to him the way she did. He knew it would change in the days, weeks or months to come, but he would be patient and enjoy it before she broke.

***

The sun was low in the sky by the time Edward had been made presentable for his first – informal – ministerial task. He marched down the main castle hall, still trying to take in the fact that his father's attacker was in the realm. There was no justice to be had. Well, to be reasonable, they were going to use the Kistatus to heal their world, but it was the least the demon could do having messed it all up in the first place. Edward could see the logic of nurturing Notechis's power, but he didn't *want* to admit that the realm needed him.

Hecaton's plan relied on clever manipulation rather than force, and Lucas agreed. No-one knew the boy better than his father – but how had Notechis tapped into his realm-fuelled high mage power whilst on Earth? He was a child gifted with a force from the home he had abandoned. Where was the justice in that?

He disliked Hecaton's plan to induct Notechis back into the realm. It didn't seem to matter to Lucas or the high mage that he'd stolen from and incapacitated the chief. The Kistatus should have been strung up in the courtyard for the vultures; a clear warning to dissidents everywhere.

Notechis's new powers provided a loophole that not only forgave his actions but deemed them to be within the parameters of Kistatus law. The boy was smart, from what Edward had heard, but was he shrewd enough to outwit Hecaton and Lucas who had centuries of practise in the art of influencing others. He doubted it.

Perhaps Edward could learn from the masters.

As part of their good will, two humans – near their expiry – had been released to Hecaton for disposal. Edward didn't want to know what happened to those who grew too sick, old or ugly for service. The pair were to be gifted for return to Earth. Edward hadn't even tried to explain to them, but it was clear that his father and Hecaton didn't know humans very well if they thought it would be received as the benevolent deed they'd intended.

While the Kistatus was being tested, it was Edward's job to entertain the Earth enforcers. Was it awful that he hoped for failure when the future of the realm was at stake? He expected similar types to his father's guard and was confident he would know how to deal with them. Warriors were the same whatever their race.

When he entered the warded room, the sight differed from what he'd imagined.

The two servants stood at the edges of the room, as was expected of them, but the visiting enforcers chose to stand in the middle of the floor, as though waiting for a fight to begin.

As advised, Edward carried no visible weaponry. Introduced as Mace and Mel, the male was robust and impressive but clearly not in charge, deferring to the witch-like female who looked light and skilled, her discrete weapons only showing when she moved.

While the guests stood, the servants wouldn't approach. It was a protocol that usually worked quite well. In demonstration, Edward sat on a chair, accepting a small goblet of wine from one of the servants. He gestured to the unoccupied plush furnishings set around a glass and marble table. There was a tempting assortment of delicacies from Earth and Skean on offer.

He was amused by Mel's expression when her gaze rested on the caviar. Not overly fond of the stuff himself, it was one of the treats that Kistatus and humans could enjoy together.

"Why don't you sit down and have some refreshment," he offered. "You're stuck here until Hecaton returns with Notechis."

"Note," said Mel. "He goes by the name Note."

"Whatever," replied Edward, and proceeded to accept a dish from the server. It didn't matter if the pretty mage thought he was a bit of a dick, there would be no casting with Hecaton's wards in place. Mel clearly ignored her companion's non-verbal cues to relax, opting instead to take a phone out of her pocket to occupy her hands. She was in for a shock if she expected to catch up on Facebook here.

"They said we were free to go whenever we liked." Edward tensed, now realising the device was probably not a phone. She pointed it at an area beside the door. A man sized gateway shimmered into focus and the servants gasped. Edward relaxed back in his chair. He hadn't been lying when he'd said they could leave at any time, but Hecaton wouldn't allow anyone to enter.

"It's too early, my lady. We're to serve one last time," the servant nearest Mel informed her.

"So now you speak," Mel said. The tall, greying man bowed but his eyes shifted to his companion in confusion.

"They're servants, girl. You're embarrassing them." Edward rose from his chair and started to inform the servants that they would leave at whatever time the enforcers chose.

"Well excuse me," the mage interrupted. "They were quick enough to speak up when they thought they were going home early." Then: "Do you have a retention problem? My name is Mel, not 'girl'." Edward returned to his seat, goblet still in hand. He raised it and the servants hurried to refill it, each getting in the other's way. Twice in one day, Edward had been accused of being slow; he was starting to see some truth to it.

"Mel, then," he said at last, and the enforcer reddened. At least she knew her behaviour had been out of order. "The servants know you're taking them back to Earth. It's just not nice to tease them now when you don't plan to leave until later." He didn't miss the nudge the big enforcer at her side gave her.

"I didn't mean to offend," she said through gritted teeth and Edward sank further into the depths of his chair. The mere sight of his relaxed demeanour seemed to annoy her further. "My intention wasn't to … to tease the servants." She glanced briefly at her colleague, as though in apology. "The servers don't want to go home anyway, so what's the point?"

His smile was mocking. "I expect you'll offer them a nice retirement plan."

Edward watched as realisation dawned on her face. "I should've known that," she grumbled. "It's not my first or even my second time in Skean." She directed the next to the servants, pointing the device to shut off the gateway before pocketing it. "Just trying it out, folks."

Edward thought her power to be weak that she'd been issued with such a thing. Couldn't mages travel the realms by drawing runes like Hecaton? Lucas was fond of saying that Skean was spoiled by having a high mage who excelled over any the realms produced.

"So you're the destroyer's brother," said the big enforcer, and he sat down, quickly accepting some food.

Edward didn't want to be drawn into anything about his sister. She hadn't been so special three years before when Hecaton had left her to die on Earth. Yes, it was a surprise to hear what had happened to her in the interim but it was none of Edward's concern. Was she even a sister when they weren't the same species? He tried to ignore the nagging part of his brain that told him to grow up and accept the facts, wherever they led.

"And you're Dolf Lungren," he said brightly, eyeing the weapons and the impressively sized harness the enforcer wore.

"I'm a Mow," said Mace, and Edward stared in surprise. That was a hell of a magic to produce such a convincing form. He'd seen transfigurations and veneers aplenty with the visitors to Lucas's court, but this was something else.

"May I?" Edward asked and Mace held out his arm for his host to grip, almost missing Mel's exaggerated eye roll. Edward had to ask, "When you bleed—"

"Red, like yours … or any other human." Edward resented the pause even though he had mentally denounced his humanity moments before. He closed his mouth before saying something he might have regretted. The enforcer seemed nice enough but there was something about the way he regarded Edward. In a flash of inspiration, he knew exactly whose magic was responsible.

"Hecaton" he guessed, and judging by the uneasy look on Mel's face, he supposed he wouldn't be getting the full story any time soon.

CHAPTER 15

Mario

Mario led Carolyn to the east side of the house, towards the guards' wing. The intensity of fortress magic was at its most focussed here. He felt her anxiety mount as she stayed close, understanding that her unease wouldn't be due entirely to his work on her tattoo. Ethan had wandered off with Lawrence and the hound had disappeared – she was always happier with the dog around. Most importantly, there was the Lilim skills practise they were headed towards.

Keeping an eye on both Carolyn and Ethan had proved impossible, but the destroyer came first. The mage was fond of saying he could look after himself, and Mario couldn't split in two.

"I've never seen this part of the building before," she said, and Mario attempted to view it as if for the first time. Magically crafted, the fortress held many square miles within its walls, yet from the outside it appeared to be not much more than a huge Venetian star fort.

From the guards' wing of the residence, the fortress wall – which should have been miles away, could be reached within a few well-placed steps. He realised with a jolt that he now had access to the perfect distraction for Carolyn. Checking in with Arthur would just ruin the spontaneity. He flashed his widest smile, and she stared back at him, suspicion narrowing her eyes. She was about to see the fortress as never before.

He didn't stop to think for fear he'd lose his nerve. "Ostendite mihi vertice mundi." He pulled Carolyn toward a stretch of dividing wall where silver strands of magic had appeared. They crackled and sparked, running circuitously around the area in front of them.

"What *is* that?" Rather than explain, he grabbed Carolyn's waist and

117

scooped her up the two steps onto the line of the divider.

There was the sensation of stretching, like he was about to change forms and fly. Carolyn squealed in what he presumed to be part terror, part joy. Then she was trying to scramble away, but he caught her quickly and laughed. They wouldn't want to fall off the ledge.

Carolyn gasped in renewed shock as the wind whipped around them, and Mario took a moment to enjoy the effects of the lighter gravity as she took in their surroundings. They were on a ledge at the top of the world, or that's what it felt like.

"I'm showing you the city, pretty lady."

The shelf appeared to run around the inner length of the fortress retaining wall, close to the very top. A brisk, sea breeze stirred the air around them and Carolyn gripped on to his arm for dear life. The feeling of weightlessness would give her the impression they could drift away if she didn't hold on.

"Oh, my God, Mario. I hear what you say, but how is this possible?" With a man stationed on the ledge at every point of the fort, each clearly visible, they nodded deferentially when Carolyn's gaze swept past them as she scanned the fortress top.

Within the star, the entire city lay below them. Impossibly condensed, buildings, people and livestock were specks that swirled and moved in its density. The spectacle made Mario feel like a child at the fairground.

It was the jewel in the crown, a wonder of Lilim creation that defied the laws of recognised physics.

"As you can see," he said, raising his voice to be heard above the wind. "The complete fortress, the entire city is effectively watched over and protected by these few." He put his mouth to her ear to add, "In the event of an attack, however, we'd do need a few more men … or just one of your father, I expect."

Carolyn was rapidly breathing as Mario guided her to the nearest point of the star, incongruously west of their eastern access. He suspected she'd prefer the sea-view.

The watchman there moved aside to allow her into the farthest edge, cornered by a waist height granite wall. Mario leaned over with her, to look out from the dizzying height, expecting to watch the sea crashing in onto the rocks far below.

The rocks, though, couldn't be seen today, the sea spray rising so high it obscured them. The effect was surreal: the fortress appeared to float on a cloud in the sky. Too high to see individual waves, the ocean shimmered beyond the churning puff of white mist skirting the foot of the edifice.

Carolyn's bright hair freed from its braid and flew back like a golden flag. "It smells wonderful," she panted, her cheeks positively glowing, and Mario understood. The air had to be the purest and most potent of all the realms.

"I think you're becoming over oxygenated," he said, tilting his head in amusement.

"Is that why I feel a bit tipsy." It was nice to see her so joyful and carefree, but for an instant Mario wished it was someone else standing here, seeing him as the king of the world. His smile faltered only slightly when she said, "I suppose you're going to tell me that the creator of Dr Who was a Lilim."

Mario shook his head, chuckling. "Who knows, Carolyn. This fortress was created over a thousand years ago. It's a testament to the strength of a few that it remains intact." Though suitably impressed, she was still giggling helplessly when he eased her back down the steps and once more into normality.

Night had completely fallen by the time Carolyn caught her breath. The cloud had cleared to reveal a sky bright with stars, throwing the angles and turrets above their heads into sharp relief. Candlelight flickered from rooms behind the long roughly glazed windows that faced into the courtyard. Her mind was already stretched to the limits by what he'd shown her. He wondered if her Lilim practise would be best carried out at another time.

Beni had been waiting for them in the courtyard, but there was no sign of Ethan, and Mario wasn't about to drag him to their destination. He looked up at Ethan's chamber; the enforcer had been allocated the room next to Mario's.

Resisting Lilim persuasion was a tremendous skill and Mario knew that Carolyn had fared not at all badly in her dealings with Peter. A little guidance in her practise and Mario was sure she'd be working other Lilim like a pro. She'd been too tentative from what he had heard.

"The mind is a delicate thing, especially with Lolilim," she had said, causing Mario to laugh until tears leaked from the corners of his eyes.

"Why would you practise on *them*?" he'd dismissed then, but now said, "I've cleared it with your father; you are to practise on Peter and Patrick as part of their punishment."

"What?" said Carolyn, stopping abruptly. He turned to take her hand, the self-congratulatory smile vanishing from his face. She shuffled her feet on the hard packed earth serving as a path through the enclosure. Clearly uncomfortable, he thought it was more, almost like the repulsion she'd displayed before their capture. Was it too much to hope that Note's brand had started to exert its power? "You really want this?" she said, drawing away and wrapping her arms about herself.

"Hell, yes, Carolyn. Are you forgetting that Peter rid you of any defences by making you believe you were fit for nothing other than breeding?" His eyebrows waggled suggestively to help lighten her mood. Perhaps he should have changed the venue to the top of the fortress for this training.

"Well, it seems only fair that Peter gets some of that right back." Catching Mario's eye, she added, "But we're not getting them to act like monkeys or anything."

"See, you are already getting into my head, and *without* the use of special powers." He watched her reach to find Beni beside her. The beast had become an important part of Carolyn's life, but Arthur's indulgence served a purpose. When the time came, she wouldn't want to leave the hound.

"Do you think Father will leave him alone?" The glint in her eye showed that she wasn't talking about the dog. She was worried for Ethan?

"Less than a week to go, Carolyn. Your father's word is good. We can take each day as it comes and wait it out."

"Are *you* looking forward to getting back?"

"Of course I am." He spun around to take both her hands in his and thought he must have imagined the repelling force from earlier. She needed assurance – comfort, and Note wasn't here. "This is illusion; I don't forget how I was when you found me." The words cost him dear and he let her see it.

"I saw how fair he was at the council meeting, Mario. I've seen inside his mind. He's not all bad."

Mario had no doubt that the powerful Lilim had allowed Carolyn to view pretty much what he wanted her to see, but he wasn't about to shatter her illusions. Well, not too badly. Perhaps he hadn't recovered from the fortress top high, but he was determined to run with his thoughts. "People rarely are. You think wicked men don't love and care for their families. I'm sure they do, but they're still evil."

Carolyn blinked but Mario thought it promising that she hadn't puked at the suggestion of Arthur's "wickedness". "I don't understand how he could treat you so badly. With your connection to me, he should have treated you better; he could have exploited your worth." *Like he does now?*

"As I said before, pure bred Lilim have *too* much value here."

"It's the fact that he injured you that's helped me to remember *what* he is." She gave Mario a curious appraisal. "Strange how *that* seems to hurt more than anything done to *me*."

"One of the anchored destroyer's best qualities is supposed to be selflessness, Carolyn."

"One?"

"I'm not going to stroke your ego."

She chuckled, her face flushing at his turn of phrase, as he had hoped it would. Damn, but she was pretty. *Not the one for you.* "Right, no stroking," she said and pulled her hands gently away.

Beni nudged between them, earning a good-natured swipe from Mario. They quickened their pace, and the Lilim felt his defences shudder when the familiar form of Peter stepped into the lighted doorway ahead.

Carolyn

Still buzzing from their adventure, Carolyn thought that it may have lent her a false sense of security. Stationed at the entrance to the training room, Peter looked impressive. The Lilim guards were all in good shape. His eyes narrowed as they rested on Mario and she was reminded that her companion wasn't popular. Though wearing the chief's colours, as part of the guard, the men didn't willingly interact with him.

On her approach, she wondered if her former fiancé would try to talk to her. It became apparent that he was going to let her pass with only a respectful nod of his head. She quashed the words that threatened, and chose to catch Peter's eye. It told her absolutely nothing. If she hadn't recognised his face, the expression it wore could belong to any of her father's men.

"Remember, Carolyn. They won't speak to you unless you address them first." This was a basic rule for the troops who worked in and around the fortress, and Carolyn replied by taking Mario's hand and giving it a squeeze. The action, though not planned for effect, elicited a response that her mere presence failed to do. She felt the satisfaction of watching Peter's perfect face darken with outrage. Without true feelings for her, the Lilim, at the very least, was jealous of Mario's position in her life.

Taking the few steps down into the room, the temperature dropped perceptively. Ideal for physical training, but for mental? – not so much. The space consisted of stone walls and dark, scarred flooring. "I don't know about this," she whispered to Mario. The single figure in the room was seated; no, she amended, tied to a chair and blindfolded. If she hadn't known already, the blond hair revealed it to be Patrick. "Does he have to be–?" Noting the show of teeth from her companion, she wavered.

"Part of the punishment, I'm afraid." Carolyn gave herself a mental slap. Who was she to deny Mario the enjoyment of Patrick's predicament? Like Peter, he had returned from a day's work patrolling the fortress outskirts. If the blond Lilim was similar to Peter at all, then carrying out such a lowly task would in itself be a nasty penance.

Carolyn uttered a basic warming enchantment, feeling Mario adjust it by setting a time limit. The changes to her spell felt weird, but she liked it.

"I didn't know it could be changed like that. Thanks."

"We work well together, pretty lady. Keeping parameters means that even if you forget to cancel the spell, it's not draining you until it spends itself naturally."

"Let's just get this over with." She offered a small smile to soften her words.

"I'll start from the absolute basics. With your full Lilim skills and shield, this will be easy." Carolyn didn't like his eagerness at the prospect of a guided tour through someone's mind, but at the same time, it was weirdly thrilling to be exploring this particular set of talents.

On her first "soul surfing" attempt, she'd adopted Mario's term easily; she'd used it on her maid, Katie. At that time, Carolyn had been desperately seeking information. Looking at the powerful and beautiful Lilim now quietly waiting for her to do her worst, she had to remind herself that he and Peter would have killed Ethan without qualm.

There were two empty chairs in front of Patrick, and Mario motioned for her to sit with him before their subject. He cut her off from casting a secrecy spell. "No. Let me guess. It is part of the punishment for passers-by to bear witness to their humiliation." At Mario's nod, she sighed. "I didn't agree to that."

Mario sat forward, clearly intrigued at what he saw in her expression.

"Block extra oculos hominum auresque," she whispered.

"That's a… Oh, clever girl."

"We don't really want spying eyes. Right?"

"Makes it worse for Peter, not knowing what to anticipate."

Not exactly the purpose, but Carolyn could live with that. "I know it's not a secrecy spell," Mario said, "but the block will probably bring Arthur so I can't reinforce your work … not that it needs it." Carolyn spared an uncomfortable thought for what Arthur required of Mario.

Had they spoken about curbing her natural talents? Mario's words pointed to that fact, but she didn't want him to lose his position of trust. Weren't parents all about allowing their children to reach their potential? And yet, before she'd found Mario, the chief and his people had turned her into a mere shadow of herself.

Mario took her away from her meanderings by setting up a basic secure link with her. It was akin to what mages in the human world could manage but Mario was advanced enough to keep his involvement at a minimum whilst guiding her through the procedure. He was sort of like an invisible driving instructor.

"Remove your blindfold," said Carolyn, before erupting into a fit of giggles as Patrick squirmed in his seat. "Whoops, sorry." She took Mario's proffered knife and cut Patrick's bonds. The Lilim wriggled his wrists and fingers before raising his mask from his face. In the dim light, she could see the struggle on his features as his natural inclination was to resist.

"Can't you even look at me, Patrick?" His averted chin was suddenly in her hand and there wasn't the faintest resistance as she brought his blue-grey eyes to hers. In that instant, she fell right into his mind.

No, Carolyn, and Mario drew her back. *A little finesse, please. Like this.* He showed her how to narrow her focus and divide it so she was entirely aware of her surroundings as well as in Patrick's thoughts.

The effect was disorientating at first. Carolyn was sitting on her chair beside Mario but was also in a corridor – Patrick's mind. Every door was open and beckoned her.

Come in, look around. This was not right. Katie's mind hadn't been like this. Crap. Suddenly she recognised the mental voice, it was Patrick. *Please forgive. I want you here. Be with me.* She drew away, horrified, just as Mario yanked her out.

Right, two things. His instruction was different from usual, more brisk and professional, compelling her to listen. *You need to shield your thoughts from his, and you must dial everything down a bit.*

What do you mean? I don't remember needing to do that before.

Patrick and Peter are full-blood Lilim. They can't help reacting to your presence, either positively or negatively depending on how they feel about you. Once you're in there, it's outside their conscious control.

Okay. She flashed back to when she'd been in her father's mind. He had been passive by choice and hadn't shared everything willingly.

"And there's that." Carolyn couldn't understand his exasperation until she followed his gaze to Patrick, gaping at her as though she were the centre of the universe. "Don't get me wrong, Carolyn, it's useful in that you'll find all you need from them, but you'll muck up their normal thought processes and have to wade through all that sickly adoration."

Like what you did to me when we first met.

I apologised for that, Carolyn could feel his irritation and a tiny amount of guilt through their connection, *but look at him: times what you felt by ten.*

She remembered being affected by the beautiful soul-surfer, but had broken his pull enough to run to Note.

Note – bright eyes! A flood of emotion rose up and Carolyn's eyes widened in horror. Mario stretched out a wave of calm from his mind.

Trust me, it's good that you have that reaction again, but there's no time for that now – file it.

How am I supposed to– He showed her, revealing his surprise that she'd known exactly how to do it. She was the file queen, for heaven's sake.

God, this mucking about with the chief's plan is going to get me killed. Then: *Shit, Carolyn!* Mario's disbelief rang like a bell through the link. *I'm out of practise. You need to forget that slip. Look sharp, your dad's coming.*

Mario's thoughts had surprised her but she quickly agreed. Her ability to section off the feelings for Note was a relief. If she forced herself to look at them every so often, she thought it might be possible to desensitise a little.

Arthur stood at the foot of the steps, his expression conveying only mild interest. She allowed her annoyance to show in her face. Patrick's cooperation now made sense. She threw a furious glance at Mario, who merely blinked innocently.

"You've done something to make him more amenable," she directed at her father.

"I can assure you, my daughter, they were instructed to submit to testing, not to allow *this*." He cast a disdainful look towards Patrick who had stood to attention at the chief's announcement, but his eyes remained firmly on Carolyn. Arthur's gaze rested for a moment on Beni. The hound whined softly and Carolyn sighed.

"You're here now, Father. You may as well come right in." He hadn't exactly knocked on the door, but he *had* waited while allowing the pair to work within Carolyn's construct.

"Thank you," he said, and Carolyn felt his magic brush over them, impersonal and assessing. "This is a really good effort." The power of his approval relaxed and thawed the negative emotion in her. She tried to shake it off, glaring at Mario. He simply shrugged, his eyes cutting to Arthur before returning to her. She followed the prompt.

"I think you're forgetting that I need practise, Father. I'm not like other Lilim women. I *want* to explore the Lilim part of me and test its limits." She'd felt another surge of approval from him as she'd spoken of her heritage, and hoped it would predispose him to letting her have some freedom. "I'm not some– " She struggled for the correct analogy. "I'm not some baby bird that needs to be fed in the safety of the nest."

Mario snorted, trying unsuccessfully to control his laughter.

An odd smile reached Arthur's lips. "I didn't think on it that way, Carolyn."

"Well."

"I understand how you feel and I apologise for my lack of foresight. I have, yet again underestimated you, and for that I have no excuse other than my wish to protect you."

Protect her? Didn't he know what she was, what she had been before her arrival in Empustat? Carolyn felt the thickening of his magic and braced herself. "May I?" She nodded, not knowing what he had planned. The link with her teacher dissolved, replaced with a connection only to Arthur. Perhaps he'd caught Mario's visualisation of a nesting bird with Arthur's head on it.

"Due entirely to me," he said softly, "you were incapacitated for a long time. In my defence, it would have been foolhardy of me to expect your recovery to be so full and complete."

Carolyn struggled to remember that her recovery had not been the all-encompassing miracle he suggested, but she *filed* that one away for another day. "Okay, that's fine. I appreciate *why*, but I'll not work with this." She indicated the gaping Lilim beside them.

Arthur approached and took her hand, to lay it on Patrick's head. The Lilim fell to his knees, the chief keeping her arm in place, a warm grip so the skin remained in contact. She *had* to pay attention to what her father was giving her.

Aware now of standing with Arthur before Patrick, she saw how to create the separation needed so that, on entering the corridor of Patrick's mind, it gave her the short time needed to put her shield in place. Arthur's was already steady. The doors of Patrick's mind were not open wide this time, although some were slightly ajar, so there was still the promise of interesting findings.

You wish to see what happened with your horse on the night of the hunt? Arthur asked.

Why not? she responded easily enough.

Which door should you pick?

Carolyn could feel Arthur bolstering Patrick's will to refuse her. That was good, yes? Her inquisitiveness, she knew – because of Arthur? – would lead her astray, and she would never retrieve the desired information. Further along the corridor, there were more doors and arches of various forms, rapidly appearing, an assortment of magical signatures on or above them. Her father's distinctive mark appeared often.

Most acquired during early training or from service. None of these were open.

She halted from examining the accesses. *I'm approaching this wrongly. I can't narrow it down to a room, not in this mind.* She felt Arthur's approval, and it gave her confidence. *I need to see it as a single room, Patrick.* Then quickly added: *Nothing preceding my return to Empustat.*

The corridor flickered; she could see the room, but the busy passage kept trying to reappear. Instinct took hold, and she issued a mental push. *Show me what I want.* There was a faint cracking sound. *Oops!*

Nothing to worry about. Continue, my dear.

Fine. A single chamber had already reappeared, without all the flickering nonsense, and it was empty, save for a very ordinary looking lone cardboard box. She reached down to it, her fingers hesitating over its flaps.

Did she need to take out the memory and examine it? Carolyn had already accomplished what she'd set out to do. There was no remorse for what had happened with Ethan but she could feel Patrick's despair at his own failure. Strongly underscoring this, there was also a strong sense of his dedication and commitment to the realm, with a special emphasis on his attachment to Arthur, Peter and the peoples of Empustat.

It was enough. *Found it. Let's leave now.*

Don't you want to read the contents?

What's done is done. It's sufficient to know that if I search, I can find.

Arthur was surprisingly quiet as she withdrew from Patrick's mind and the guard stood to attention, his features clenched tight.

"Thank you, Patrick," said Arthur stiffly. "You may continue about your business. We have no need of Peter tonight."

"Yes, your majesties." Kneeling before Arthur and Carolyn, he drew his right hand to his chest before rising to leave with the waiting Peter.

"In this one night, I have seen you practise a fine skill with maturity, insight, and compassion." Carolyn thought she caught the faintest twitch of his lips as he added, "It's the last that concerns me."

She rolled her eyes. Her father was still a Lilim with skewed sensibilities. Carolyn didn't miss the pointed look he gave Mario before leaving. Great. What would he have in store for her friend, now?

CHAPTER 16

Siren

"This is all so unexpected but I trust you," Ella mimicked Siren during her earlier conversation with Miranda. Siren didn't care much for the weird falsetto the faery adopted as she scoffed from the passenger seat of the new purple Audi.

"I *do* trust her," muttered Siren, "It's just that this is all so unexpected."

"We're two of a kind," said Ella, stretching her arms up to catch the wind. Her dandelion fluff hair had been tamed and secured by what resembled a Christmas bauble fixed to the top of her head.

"Two of a kind?" On which planet or realm would that be? Ella's enthusiasm was becoming weirdly infectious.

"Imagine what it'll be like, Siren. You were restricted when you were staying in that flat, and neither of us was free at the beta site. This is our reward! You don't want to be away from the Agency?"

Siren didn't think they were being rewarded for anything. Miranda was tucking them away for her own reasons. Just this morning, her spa treatment had been interrupted by Miranda's visit.

At first Siren had thought Miranda had escaped work to spend a few hours with her, but no, she had wasted no time before dropping her bombshell. Leading her to the car park, Miranda had taken Siren's smart phone, and if that hadn't been intriguing or disturbing enough, the shadow Faery waiting outside raised her angst to frantic levels.

She and Ella were to be sent up to Scotland for an indeterminate period. Only Miranda could get away with such high handedness, commissioning coven services to work a spell on their new residence. Siren was smart enough to accept the instruction without rancour.

Miranda planned to shield them from all eyes, not just Agency ones. What she referred to as "The feral Coven of thirteen" was flying in from the islands and scheduled to arrive in a few hours. With any luck, Siren would have time to scout the surroundings, make whatever enquiries she – discretely – could, and prepare for their arrival.

Her new phone's sat-nav had been pre-programmed and set to skirt the shore-line once they'd crossed the border. Ella had slept fitfully for a while, waking only to declare the need for a bathroom break near the Lake District.

She and the Faery had a history stemming from when Siren had started out on Earth as a captive in the beta site. Despite the quirks and mood swings, Ella could be good company, however, *that* wouldn't be the reasoning behind Miranda's action. The information they'd been given, though specific, had been without any great detail. Siren and Ella were to stay at the house, the hybrid to be taken out for planned activities by Miranda. Once the witches had done their work, both Ella and Siren would be "safe".

Safe from what?

Having never spoken of her arrangement with the mages and the Veloces of the Agency, Siren had happened on the relevant information. Was Miranda getting her out of their way while she confirmed her allegiances?

What good was Siren to the underground or the Protectorate – Taz liaised well with them – whilst hidden away?

The Motus would find the positive in this. He wanted Siren out, and perhaps the time was upon her. It would have been easier to make a break for it if Miranda hadn't entrusted her with Ella.

Ella had been quick to boast that she'd been re-categorised as "terminated". It was as though she hadn't a clue as to the meaning, and Siren wasn't going to enlighten her.

She hoped this wasn't Miranda's elaborate method of getting rid of the little hybrid. Siren had been used to eliminate Agency enemies on occasion. It had made her sick, but she had performed her duties as required – on the surface at least. With the help of Taz's mages, she had been able to save two innocents from Miranda's wrath. In regard to the less fortunate of Miranda's foes… Siren had become accomplished at switching off her self-loathing.

The Agency head clearly had someone else to step in and carry out the distasteful tasks. Probably the Veloces, Siren thought. As she eyed the clueless Faery at her side, she hoped Miranda hadn't used Ella for the same. The delicate girl didn't need much more to mess with her mental state.

Adamant about avoiding gateway use for their relocation, Miranda had implied that her actions had been approved by the Investors, but what had she given them that could be worth such privileges? Pulling a fast one under their noses was more likely.

Unwilling to do too many rest stops, they passed into North Ayrshire in the late afternoon. Unused to the physical travel, she was stiff and tired but the latter part of the drive had been therapeutic. Siren stifled a shudder as she passed the Irvine junction which would have taken her to "Feeding Frenzy". She hoped it was only coincidence that placed her new base so close to the underground hub. If only John would tune in so she could update Taz. The Mow assistant was silent to her tentative "calls".

Ella began to get really excited when they reached the stretch of road at Seamill. It seemed just too good to be true that Miranda had secured them a property in the delightful village they were now entering. She had been apologetic about the location, thinking that Siren preferred the city, but it wasn't exactly correct. A Siren – any Siren – was called to the water. In an eerie way, it felt almost like coming home.

"Take a left," shrieked Ella, as if the sat-nav's prompt hadn't been loud enough. Then almost immediately: "Right, now. Right!"

The private road was not in great condition and they were almost instantly met with a set of ten foot high gates. Ella jumped out to open them. "You'd think they'd be automatic," she grumped, returning to the car once Siren had driven through. When the house came into sight through the tree lined drive, Siren and Ella gasped in surprise.

Ella's head whipped around fast enough to make Siren flinch. "Naked witch on the lawn alert!"

"Nothing I haven't seen before, little girl," said Siren smoothly, but her eyes widened at the unexpected sight. "They must have got an earlier flight into Prestwick."

The long driveway continued to the side of the house and she turned in sharply to an open doored triple garage.

When they returned to the front of the house, there was a total of thirteen white bodies of various ages, from a girl who looked to be about sixteen to an elderly man whose only accessory was a cane.

"Do I need to take off my pretty dress?" Siren noticed for the first time that Ella wore some sort of pirate wench's Halloween costume. It was of the all-in-one-piece, thin lycra variety that people tended to wear over their usual clothes. Ella, of course was wearing the get-up with little or nothing underneath.

"Nudity will be entirely optional," Siren assured her. The coven members were strangely normal looking. Ordinary and covered in goose bumps, she would imagine.

"Welcome," said the girl who appeared to be the youngest of the coven. "Please stand in the centre of our circle."

"I've got a bad feeling about this," whined Ella, gripping on to Siren's arm.

"It'll be okay, just don't freak out at anything they do." However commonplace the witches appeared, Miranda wouldn't be hiring fools.

"Can I–?" said Ella, her limbs beginning to dissolve.

"Oh, wow. No, I'm guessing you shouldn't," Siren cautioned. "These are wild magic users and it's best not to risk being stuck like that." Ella's face registered shock and she restored rapidly to solid form.

"Didn't think about that." The faery's wide eyes appeared glittery – almost fevered as she made a point of not looking at the coven. Fear was appropriate, but Siren hoped the girl would keep it together for a while yet. Feral witches harnessed magic that was not always predictable.

"Jings, get a move on," the eldest witch said, and Siren was sure he was swearing crudely under his breath.

"We just stand here?" Siren ventured.

"Stand, sit, lie down, it doesn't matter as long as you don't leave the circle."

Ella trembled at Siren's side. "Is it okay if I just look at you," she said, placing her two small hands in Siren's. It was hard to tell if the Faery had a thing about nudity, or whether she was simply overwhelmed by the coven. Now dead centre of the circle, a quiet had descended and Siren felt something akin to the static before an electrical storm. She squeezed Ella's fingers in an unexpected surge of protectiveness. The shadow-Faery smiled sweetly, like a trusting if somewhat dangerous child. "You'll not let anyone hurt me, will you?"

"I guess I won't."

The witches had already set up their chant which began to the steady beat of a drum which couldn't be seen. *The heartbeat of the earth?* Siren didn't know if she was being fanciful or that her thoughts were accurate.

After a moment, it was hard to stop herself from joining in with her own Siren harmony chant. As it was, she knew that, despite her lips being pressed together, her song was still leaking out.

The voice of the youngest witch rose, the language like nothing Siren had ever heard.

Another witch screamed, the ground rising beneath her to create a pillar that lifted her up. Earth, thought Siren. From the witch's mouth, a ribbon of bright green magic spiralled out, becoming silver as it wound around the next to her right and before it poured directly into the open mouth of the next one along in the circle who accepted it with her head thrown back.

No sooner had this occurred than debris began to swirl around them as a localised wind whipped up. Small gashes appeared on the witch's skin from the grit and stones drawn into the resultant funnel. By the rapturous expression on her face, though, she clearly felt no pain. Siren suspected the collective were absorbing it somehow.

A flash of light appeared from behind Siren and she turned to see the southernmost witch cup a flame in his hands, and the whirlwind from the Air witch sketched a path around the two, between Air and Fire, gradually reducing in strength. When it reached the Fire witch, the male was engulfed in flame. His face wore the same expression as Earth and Air.

Water next, thought Siren. A trail of fire broke off, weaving through to the water witch, past another two bodies before it encircled the one on Siren's right.

Siren recognised that the witches between the elementals were instrumental in controlling the strength of the forces they wielded.

The Water witch's skin was now wreathed in ribbons of fire and it glowed from beneath before she appeared to disappear.

No, I'm wrong, Siren thought, she hadn't vanished, but she was translucent, and the trails of fire were being quenched by the watery manifestation she had become. Stretching out, the woman on the pillar of earth called incomprehensibly and a stream of the water spouted up and disappeared into her hand.

The ground swelled and pulsed at their feet. The circle was closed, living and vital with each of the four elements supported by the others. They were waiting, writhing, lost to the music and the forces of the components. Siren heard her own personal plea, along with Ella's jumbled thoughts, find their elemental voices as they were ripped from their throats to join those of the coven. Their intent, their wishes were sealed to become one in a giant wave of power.

The force spun completely around the circle of elements, teasing, playing and welcoming its servers. Then it gathered above their heads and shot high into the sky like a rocket before reversing, rushing back down. Siren wished she'd closed her eyes, as Ella had done. The entirety of the enchantment had been drawn into a fiery spiral, containing every colour of the rainbow, beautiful but looking deadly, and it was gathering speed.

Is this what Miranda had paid for?

Siren wrapped herself around Ella, forcing them both to the ground which rose up to catch them. When the spell struck, she screamed, or thought she did as she imagined her flesh char and strip from her body.

Silence descended with a tangible weight before it vanished, leaving only Siren and Ella in a now damp and slightly charred garden. The Faery sprang up from Siren's grasp, taking in the sparse signs of disruption about them.

"I thought protection spells were simple," she gasped.

Miranda

It had been with great reluctance that Miranda had left Siren with Ella, but keeping them together at a secure location had been the right choice. Miranda's meeting with Croft was too important.

So easy to forget that her lover wasn't human, she had no such difficulty with the Investor. She fought her revulsion, feeling his small sharp eyes rake the length of her. The arrangements to cross the gateway with the Investor were being finalised and she could hardly wait for them to take their trip.

Loci caught her cue, and the gateway sprang into existence in the centre of the room. The red and gold shimmer cast a bright glow that temporarily robbed Croft of his features.

"Why did you suggest we do this alone?" he asked, his eyes resting pointedly on Loci at the control panel. He didn't trust the demon as had been expected; more likely he'd hoped to see Judy at the controls. It was he who had stipulated that no extra staff be present. That Miranda had chosen the Veloces over the mage had been no accident. Judy was still to prove her worth.

"I must have misunderstood; this way, no-one important knows about our trip and you get to demonstrate the elixir effects to the board." If the Veloces heard the slight, he didn't let on.

"Yes, yes. Under proper precaution." His eyes strayed again to Loci who merely looked on, inoffensively.

"Of course," said Miranda patiently, "and we're doing this now, deliberately without staffing. On entering an unpopulated world, we will receive all the benefits minus any risk to us."

"We have our devices, but he," she indicated the Veloces with a flick of her fingers, "is here to record our findings and retain the gateway from this side." Miranda struggled with referring to her killer pet as gender specific, but he performed better if thrown a bone on occasion.

"Your device is programmed using the best bio technology to keep you safe."

The last of the destroyer's blood had proved to be of distinct use. Vasch had, under instruction, sealed a spelled drop to Miranda's especially prepared carrying medium. They'd watched each other steadily as the thimbleful of contents had been administered. Croft fingered his gateway device, a flush rising to his pallid cheeks. "Where is yours?"

"Right here." She removed the object from her jacket pocket, curving her fingers around the slightly yielding protective coating. "It is identical to yours." Her eyes hardened. "It's a daunting thought to use the gateways at first."

Croft shook his head, frowning. He had overseen the creation of the elixir, and Miranda had been annoyed at using the last of the blood for him, but the end result would make it worth her while. He was right to distrust but not for the reasons he believed. Having seen the unbelievable results with Bob, he wanted this desperately, but not greatly enough for any leap of faith.

Miranda moved towards the open gateway. "Tell you what, I'll step in for only a few seconds and when I return, we can use it together." She turned from him and stepped into the opening without a backward glance.

The lack of trust rankled. She stood dead centre, her outline shadowy for a moment before stepping back into the room.

Croft's features relaxed. "Thank you for the demonstration. May I see your device?"

Miranda gritted her teeth and passed it to him. She had expected as much.

"Holding secure?" she asked Veloces, unnecessarily.

"Yes, Ma'am."

"Then let's do this." On entering, Miranda gave the ring on her forefinger a discrete quarter turn to the right. There were still too many unanswered questions about the gateway wrought changes for her to risk it all just yet.

Croft strode confidently into the opening and it sizzled shut behind them. He sprung around, his confidence vanishing. "You were supposed to leave it open," he spat.

"It's only precautionary." He wasn't fooled by her soft words. Miranda smiled, genuinely amused as he used both their devices, trying to reopen the gateway without success. "It's not broken," she added, thoroughly enjoying his rage as it flowed from him.

Miranda surveyed the land before her. She and Croft were standing in tall, seeded grasses that swept to above knee height. Amid the grasses, impossibly red and yellow blooms made the area appear like the inspiration for Kiril Stanchev's "Sea Of Blossom". Mature trees and shrubs surrounded them far into the distance and Miranda could not see what lay beyond their sunlit grove.

"You got me here. What do you want?" Croft leaned forward and retched. So soon, thought Miranda as she observed his changes. "Wh…what's happening to me?"

"I didn't lie to you. You're getting what you wished for," she told him. "The spell has been modified to act more quickly than you saw with dear Bob. You should lose a few of your years right about —" His knees buckled completely. "Now," she finished.

"You crossed me, you bitch." His voice was hoarse, and he was certainly angry, but the Investor didn't refuse the compact mirror Miranda offered.

Croft took another breath, seemingly now over the nausea, and leaned back to face the sun. The years were melting away from him as she'd promised; his skin appeared to thicken and brighten. He tipped his head, the better to see his refection, but dropped the mirror on the grass when his arm muscles twitched. He ran a hand over a bicep that became more defined under his fingertips, and blinked several times, as though unable to see. Standing up, he removed his spectacles, discarding them to land with

Miranda's mirror.

"Why haven't you changed," he asked tartly.

Her lips curled in a self-satisfied smile. The ring had protected her from irreversible changes that could damage her focus. "You'll never be handsome, but in your new condition, I would say you're a worthy offering."

"Offering?" In fresh alarm, his gaze strayed to where Miranda had caught some movement only a moment before. "You plan to leave me here? Don't you think I'll be missed?" He wasn't happy, but she'd expected him to have been hysterical by now. Perhaps his improved appearance had dulled his sense of self-preservation.

"Oh, I forgot to mention," said Miranda, suavely. "Only this morning, you were so kind as to sell all your interests in the Agency to me." Croft seemed to have trouble digesting the words, and Miranda drew the last out as much as she could. "You boarded a private jet about an hour ago, to celebrate with your mistress in Marbella. The aircraft suffered unfortunate engine trouble leading to an accident over the sea. As I understand it, your estranged family are unlikely to shed any tears. Your lady friend will shortly be celebrating her new freedom with her long term boy toy, enjoying the fine package you've provided."

Croft's attention kept returning to a point in the trees beyond.

"Ah, yes. I'm hoping the sisters will at least enjoy your company for a time. You might even like it here, given your proclivities."

"What sisters," he forced through gritted teeth. Miranda watched as two beings emerged from the tree line. "You may want to straighten up … and perhaps practise a charming smile."

"You've gone mad," he said, and there it was, thought Miranda to her increasing satisfaction, a high chuckle coming from his throat. "You think that giving me to sex creatures is going to stop me getting back to Earth and ruining you?" His expression changed, those small eyes holding a calculated, acquisitive gleam as the figures approached. Swathed in sheer white fabric that clung to inhumanly perfect curves, there was a blond and a brunette.

"*My* Siren is the only one of her kind you'll have met," she whispered. "You may find these a bit … different."

The women glided towards them. It was clear they weren't walking, though they kept close to the ground. The blond slid right up to the Investor, batting her lovely baby blues at him. The brunette came to Miranda's side and tilted her head in assessment. "A gift? How kind." Miranda's face shone gleefully as Croft blustered and tried to back away from the beauties.

"Now, just wait here. Let me tell you what I want?" Croft said.

"I can already *see* what you want," trilled the blond, and she pursed her lips and blew air in his face. Croft's alarmed expression grew as he froze, screaming and cursing now. It was music to Miranda's ears.

She didn't miss the brunette's tightened lips as her gaze landed on Miranda's ring. "You don't trust yet," she murmured, as though disappointed. Then, "Hush, human," and with a flick of her finger, Croft's now shouting voice became inaudible.

"You have word of our wandering sister?" None that Miranda was about to share. She would stick to her usual assurances. The Sirens would be able to tell, at least in a broad sense, if she were being honest. More importantly, she wanted to see more of their reaction to Croft. Miranda would feel short changed if they just carted him off without sharing any of the details.

"She remains very happy in her life."

"Show us." The girls did like to torture themselves, thought Miranda as she withdrew the tablet from her bag and retrieved this morning's footage. The women both sighed at the sight of Siren coming out of the apartment and crossing the parking area to reach her car.

"As I said, all is well – for now." Miranda couldn't help the implied threat.

The brunette began to circle around Croft, still frozen in place. The blond remained focussed on Miranda, though, her lips drawing tight against her teeth, showing a glimpse of white. *Show no fear.* "Our sister will die if she stays in your world for much longer without full access to her powers."

Miranda wasn't stupid; she knew the danger the sisters represented and was desperately glad that Earth-Siren was different. She resisted the impulse to step back and cringe as Croft had done. When Siren had first arrived on Earth, it had been a huge disappointment that the demon had been stripped of her – more useful – powers, but now, Miranda wouldn't have it any other way. It was said that demons who crossed, powers intact, were referred to as "Pure hearts". It would seem that *her* Siren hadn't qualified.

"Don't play with our gift just yet," trilled the blond, seemingly annoyed with her sister. Miranda saw the other Siren trail her tongue from Croft's neck to his ear but the Investor was not basking in the attention, as Miranda would have expected. There must be quite a difference shifting from predator to prey. Sweat had already darkened his clothing. The fact that the Siren was fearless had clearly reduced the erotic appeal for him. She bent her long legs at the knee and floated in and around to surround him, her white garments whispering across his skin and clothes.

"This is indeed a gift, sister." She drifted behind Croft, her head resting on his shoulder before slowly spinning around to face him. Her eyes darkened perceptively, and she whispered, "You have a weakness for the fairer sex?" Miranda could see the Investor was trying to nod. The blond Siren reached for her sister's hand, Miranda forgotten as the pair spiralled around the man's frozen form.

"You held her down while you satisfied your desires," they said to him in concert.

The blond continued, "You are going to learn the difference between a Siren, incapacitated by your world, and one who is in full control of her powers." The sisters simultaneously struck. The sound of flesh tearing seemed loud in the stillness, one at the nape of his neck, the other at his chest. The terror and pain on Croft's face brought such a strong feeling of euphoria that Miranda almost wished she could join them. The blond stopped when Croft crumpled to the ground. "Stop sister, it would be unfitting to allow a quick death with this one. Take him to the caves."

The brunette spat on the ground and grabbed the unconscious Croft by his hair, a beautiful melody spilling from her lips, absurdly lovely in the gruesome circumstances, which seemed to make his body weightless, like hers. No stranger to torture, Miranda recognised that the wounds, though numerous, were not deep. No major vessels had been severed by the Siren fangs. He trailed limply behind, blood oozing from him and spilling on the earth. Miranda watched, transfixed, as new blooms erupted where it fell.

"A killing field like no other," said Miranda, wowed at the concept. "How long do you expect to keep him alive?"

"His infusion to our land is only part recompense for what you have allowed our sister to endure. He is unlikely to last more than a year and we will deny him death by his own hand." Miranda couldn't have hoped for better. Her gateway device buzzed in warning. The Veloces would give Miranda a further five minutes before calling on a mage to assist.

The Siren looked distant… and hungry. "You didn't feed on him." Miranda knew instantly that she'd disrespected the demon and apologised immediately. The words felt alien on her tongue but these ladies were worthy of some regard.

"Would you eat the rats that crawl in the sewers of your own world?" The Siren stepped close to Miranda. A remembered flash of sharp teeth caused Miranda to check that her ring was still in place. "That bauble protects you now," said the demon, "and though not averse to carrying out your dirty work… this time, I expect to see my sister when you visit again."

"But I don't—"

"Spare me the lies. She is with you." The Siren slowly circled as her sister had done with Croft. "I feel it, human. I also detect your feelings for her. Perhaps she returns those; I have no way of telling."

Miranda found her voice in the midst of the Siren spell. "She felt she was wasting her life and so *chose* me."

"And you repay the favour by sharing her *skills* with such as that?" the Siren challenged, pointing towards where Croft's body had last been seen. "Whore her out again, and I promise I will find out. Then expect me to cross the gateway armed with forces that will overwhelm your silly bauble."

Miranda could feel sweat trickle down the small of her back. "I must go now, lady Siren. I thank you for your caution and promise that at this very moment I'm doing all I can to assure your sister's happiness and safety." The Siren studied her face but Miranda was confident she would see no deception.

"A visit then," hissed the beautiful creature before her. "Show your love by bringing her to us."

"I'll see what I can do." Miranda's smile was strained as she left to return through the gateway. The satisfaction at ridding herself of Croft was quickly waning.

Loci sealed the gateway and Miranda collapsed into the swivel chair beside the Veloces. She was grateful of the dim lighting for a headache had sprung up behind her eyes. Loci proceeded to summarise their arrangements to cover the Investor's disappearance.

"Yes," Miranda agreed. "I'll finalise it and you can get on with finding Harris." Of all the Investors, Harris was the most difficult to locate. If luck was on her side then he'd be dead already from his extreme sports pursuits.

The visit to the Sirens on Anthemusa hadn't gone exactly to plan. She'd wanted to feed them tiny bits of information and use them for a while yet. Their psychic skills were a problem that she needed to learn to work around *if* she ever had to deal with the sisters again.

Remembering her ring, she turned it back to neutral and her headache eased. All magic came at a price and Miranda was happy to pay for her acquisitions. The Veloces looked at her expectantly. "I can never let Siren see her sisters again." Then: "What...?"

Ella misted from her hiding place in Miranda's shadow, rising up to appear before the woman in wide eyed fright. "I can't believe she's related to them!"

"*You* are supposed to be with *our* Siren." Miranda's hand passed straight through the Ella shadow that had taken form. "How do you still have a voice?"

"Damned if I know," said the Faery, "but I bet even Jonah can't separate his Faery and shadow parts like this." Miranda could feel her headache returning, stronger than before.

"Why are you here?"

"Ooh, I was dreaming and showed up here when you were going through the gateway?"

"How long have you had this skill?"

"Honestly?" Her wide eyes seemed to take up the entirety of her face and Miranda wished for the hundredth time that they hadn't tampered so vigorously with her DNA. "I don't know. This hasn't happened before. Wait..." Excitement raised her voice to crystal shattering levels. "If I'm still sleeping, can I do anything I like?"

"No!" Loci's voice joined Miranda's.

"I understand about Siren. You don't want her to become a monster."

Miranda turned the gem on her finger a full circle to ensure compliance and secrecy. The stone hummed its disapproval, but she dismissed its censure. Her will encompassed the Veloces as well as Ella. "This stays between us." The Faery was now simply staring into space. "Ella?" With a blink, her focus trained on Miranda. "You must always let me know before you accompany me anywhere. We can work out a code if you like. Do you understand?" Ella nodded eagerly and Miranda bestowed an indulgent smile.

Her decision to place Ella with Siren had been deliberate, taking advantage of their history at the beta site. Their instincts would compel each to care for the other and Miranda could use that to her advantage. "I'm trusting you with the most important person in the world to me, dear. If she was to hear about this thing with her sisters, Siren wouldn't get over it."

"What do you think she would do?" asked Ella, her eyes tracking things that Miranda couldn't see.

"She would leave."

CHAPTER 17

Arthur

With Sylvia and Lawrence visiting, meal times were much more animated than usual. Arthur watched his sister gush over Ethan as though he were royalty. The boy was polite enough but seemed uncomfortable with her attention.

"I'm so glad everything's out in the open, now. None of us, Arthur included, was happy to keep my beautiful niece restrained." Arthur's eyebrows lifted, and he set his teacup carefully on its saucer. *Sylvia had cared for Carolyn for almost an entire year without your input. She means well.* He had been perfectly content for Carolyn to be made safe by whatever means necessary. He was not used to being adaptable – it was rarely required – but so much had changed over the past months, it was clear his daughter could not be expected to live like a Lilim lady. She had proved to be more worthy of using her talents than any of his men, his second included.

The boy caught his eye briefly before turning back to Sylvia's attention. "She understands why you thought the measures necessary," the mage said, "but I'm sure we can all agree that she belongs on Earth." Arthur smiled at his forwardness. Though he believed Ethan's courage to be admirable, Carolyn *belonged* on Empustat. "Once the gateways are accessible again, I'm sure she'll enjoy visiting you all." Sylvia's laugh was a little too shrill, undoubtedly sensing danger

Arthur had risen from his seat while Ethan had been talking. "Of course I'll visit," said Carolyn, entering the room like a beacon of light. Arthur's heart swelled, and he wondered briefly if she'd absorbed more than just the chatter as a kiss was planted on his cheek. She seemed to have forgiven Sylvia. Did her clemency stretch to *him* for all that had occurred in the past year – all that *would* happen in the time to come? The thought was preposterous, yet wouldn't he forgive her anything? No being held that kind of sway with him, not since Amanda.

Both Lawrence and Sylvia greeted her warmly and Carolyn allowed them to overwhelm her for a moment before turning to reassure him. "Everything's going to work out fine." Arthur felt another, less welcome twinge of emotion. The compassion on her face told him that she was sorry to leave, but not for the reasons that he would have preferred. Arthur had studied the mechanics of her relationship with Ethan and Mario and it had been interesting to peruse Ethan's mind as he'd slept. The boy was entirely unsuitable but there was no doubt that he loved his daughter. Mario, a marginally more suitable – and Lilim – candidate, loved her also, but it was the love of a sibling which, *if* it remained untouched, wasn't good enough.

Ethan, he noticed, had dampened Carolyn's effect on him by using outside magic. No stranger to the unorthodox, Arthur had respect for the boy's strategy. His daughter still benefited for he continued to provide a distraction from the Kistatus that Arthur had gone to considerable effort to repel. The chief couldn't bring himself to believe that her fate lay there. Ethan's "casual" comment about the gateways made Arthur uneasy. With reinstatement of realm activity, Carolyn would again be susceptive to the primitive laws.

In any event, if she left the realm, and all that he'd done came to light, Ethan and his team of enforcers would never allow her to return. That much he'd seen in the enforcer's head.

CHAPTER 18

Mel

Mel had been dreaming of class – in that horrible way where logic was entirely suspended and she was still her grandfather's golden girl who could do no wrong. The dream had stemmed from a memory of her school days where she'd been educated in various realms with an assortment of otherworlders.

She'd been messing around in class while the human teacher had been explaining about Skean realm law, such as it was. There had been mention of the chief being succeeded by his heir, and a trial that the chosen had to complete after which he was gloriously accepted to take his rightful place.

At that time, Skean had been through a punishment phase whereby few Kistatus could adopt their true forms. Lucas had frozen many in human – translate "weaker" – forms following a pathetic attempt by the people to overthrow his rule. Conversely, Note, as the High mage's son, had been fixed to his Kistatus form, and with it, they hoped to distance his connection with the rebel outlanders. Politics having no interest for Mel, she had never discussed it with Note.

History was boring, and if it weren't for her friend, she would have skipped the class. Mel considered herself to be smart, well, clever enough to ask Note to help her with the assignment sure to follow Dickie's lecture. She didn't understand the whys and wherefores but she knew that the history she learned about was slanted. It made no difference to her, but Note cared.

Note, in human form, had been gorgeous. In fact, looking at him, as she often did, she didn't see the large reptilian form hunched over a too small desk. She *did* see that he struggled to take notes with the end of a tentacle wrapped around his pen. Loathing his punishment as she did, she *mostly* saw his quiet strength and determination. When he turned his bright expressive eyes on her, it never failed to make her heart stutter. She loved *him*.

In her boredom and fuelled by her dislike of Dickie, Mel doodled a fairly decent caricature of the teacher, detailing his hair rising into something vulgar and, by her own estimation, wickedly appropriate.

Note didn't look at it right away and her annoyance rose enough for her to consider a spell. She'd been learning magic but her infrequent twice weekly classes weren't sufficient. Note tried to slide the paper discretely under his folder and that was when the teacher smacked a ruler in front of his face, landing with a thwack on his desk.

Shit. Dickie had been watching *her* during his monologue. The offending article was duly snatched from beneath the Kistatus's folder. The teacher's face contorted as the entire thing then flared up and turned to ash before his very eyes. Dickie's attention flicked in the direction of the smoke detector amulet that hung in the middle of the classroom before rounding on the perpetrator of the arson attack.

Crap! Emma Vint, their resident Lustro, or fire demon, was the only other student with more demerits than Mel.

"What is your plan now, Miss Vint," Dickie rasped, choking slightly on the ash surrounding him. Emma was already stripping off her t-shirt as Dickie blustered, "I told you that if the fire alarm was set off one more time–" Emma's top flew to the smoking remnants and the collective breath of the class held as it absorbed the charred remains. A few silent seconds followed when the students watched a wisp of smoke hover near the detector. The five schoolchildren eyed each other before cheers arose.

"Looks like that expulsion will have to wait, Sir." Emma's eyes watered with mirth but Mel wasn't fooled. There would be consequences regardless of whether the alarm had gone off or not. The fire demon sniffed her shirt and grimaced before shrugging into it again.

As pleased as I am that you've gained a portion of control over your abilities, young lady, you have destroyed what I gather to be the only piece of work done by Melanie in quite some time. Mel frowned as the boy in front snickered.

The similarity to real events ended for Mel at this point. Note pushed his chair away in disgust and his form filled out to become larger than any grown Kistatus Mel had ever seen. Layers and waves of gold, purple and green magic clung to him. Everyone, including the teacher, prostrated themselves on the floor.

What were they doing? This was Note! Mel's somehow unblemished picture of Dickie was now back in her hand and she turned the image to Note.

"You would have got a laugh out of this if you hadn't *changed*," she said brightly. Only now did Mel begin to feel the effects of his power. Note's bright eyes burned with a fever irreconcilable with the boy she'd accepted, yet it was him. It was still *her* Note.

"I have no interessst in gamesss." He reached out to touch her, and she knew – the way one sometimes "knows" what's about to happen in dreams, that he was going to kill her. She also "knew" that this was how it *had* to end – no, *more* than that – that it would be a fitting finish. If someone were to off her, and she was forced to admit that chances were good that she deserved it, then Note would be her method of choice.

The classroom melted from existence, and she moved eagerly towards her would-be killer, rising onto her toes until his limbs wrapped around her and he lifted her to a more accessible height.

Mel felt no fear, only fascination as his fangs extended to an extraordinary length, silver venom glistening from the drops dangling at their tips. Anticipation made her quiver as he leaned in. Note pierced the skin beneath her ear and, incredibly, there was no pain. Surely there should be agony. A feeling of well-being and hope swept through her, slowly increasing as she gripped him tightly. There was not a chance in hell she was letting him change his mind now and … beep … beep … BEEP!

Mel's eyes flew open and she jumped out of bed, alert, heart racing. That dream – Oh God – a dream? The anti-climax brought tears of frustration coursing down her cheeks. God! She needed therapy.

Hastily donning her work clothes that lay under her night stand, Mel forced her breathing to become normal. While fastening her boots, Sean, Rake and Note winked into existence before her. "Were you all awake at this hour?" She glanced at her phone, now wishing she'd kept her mouth shut. She couldn't believe it was already nine-thirty in the morning.

Great. A rude awakening and no breakfast. She'd be brilliant company today.

"Sorry, Mel. You deserve a lie-in, and here we are tearing you away," Note said as he moved forward and helped slide a weapons harness over her arms. Rake secured it at her back as she grabbed a pack of chewing gum from her dresser. "Stop jumping about, little mage," he scolded, and Mel forced herself to stay still for the second it took to finish.

Avoiding Note's slightly puzzled gaze, she made a conscious effort *not* to broadcast her thoughts. The link was inconvenient at the best of times, but flushed with sleep and the wayward considerations of her dream, it required all her strength to keep a lid on things. "Always happy to get to a call," she said aloud. And it was true. Who needed sleep when you could be adventuring through the realms with the only people in the world who gave a shit about you? Life didn't get any better. "You know how I hate to be left out."

Her heart ached a little with Note's proximity. The strain the past weeks had placed upon him wasn't fair. She could almost forget the changes he'd undergone recently, but the fact was, with the powers he'd had to accept and with rescuing Amanda, Note was even less attainable than ever.

"Where to?"

"Arranan," said Sean, and Mel could've sworn that, just for an instant, his irises sparked gold. Her eyes widened as she digested the name.

"Really?" The Faery realm was currently about as accessible as Empustat. She *had* paid attention to race studies in class and remembered it had been rumoured that the Faeries had helped create the gateway foci of the realms.

"No, probably not," said Sean, straight faced.

"You are such a sh—" She stood in wide-eyed but familiar frustration as Sean's magic removed the rest of what she'd intended saying. Unlike Ethan, Sean could somehow get away with his non-Protectorate sanctioned brand of discipline.

"Now, Melanie. Such words should never be uttered by a lady."

Rake grinned widely. "Little mage shouldn't rise to the bait."

"B…but," she spluttered as the power of speech returned. "You are *so* infuriating." Any of the others, she would have continued berating, but with Sean, it really wasn't an option. Mel had only been talking to Jonah the day before about investigating the halves of his origin. Jonah had neither walked in the Faery nor the Shadow world, genetic star that he was.

"Has something's come out of the Faery realm, then?"

"We won't know 'til we arrive," answered Note. "Might still be a trip to Arranan on the cards."

Mel warmed at Note's appeasing tone, feeling ridiculous as usual when colour rose to her cheeks. *Get a grip, Mel.* She smoothed her messy locks into a ponytail as best she could while Note retrieved another pack from her closet and slipped it over his shoulder.

Sean pulled them through the web to London before opening a gateway to the locus of their call. The travel constraints were continually giving Mel's constitution a work out she could do without. Taking a circuitous route, they stuck to the strict protocol that had been put in place following Amanda's rescue. Mel's recent visit to Skean hadn't erased the memory of the castle dungeon she'd visited before.

"Urgh." Mel's nose wrinkled as she scanned her new surroundings: they were in a barn, several cows staring balefully from the stalls beside her. "Hi there." Mel stepped over a fresh cow pat, then a few more before they left the massive byre in which they'd arrived.

"Did you mean to land us in there?" she quizzed Sean, but the mage was paying no attention as he led them towards a nearby farmhouse.

"What is it about this place?" Note said before he turned from the farmhouse and looked dreamily into the distance. Rake stopped beside him as Note then said, "Over the crest of that hill is where I came into this world."

"Your birthplace? How nice." Mel regretted her sharp words as soon as she'd uttered them, but Note caught her eye. Icy blue rather than the gold he reverted to in private, she felt the weight of understanding within them. Why did he have to be like that?

"In a manner of speaking, I guess it was," he said without changing his tone.

"You know who lives here?" she asked hopefully before turning her attention to Sean. "Is this where the gateway opened? I can't believe we had to go to London when this place is only a few miles from our base."

"It's no big deal," shrugged Note. "Can't return to normal until the Skean problem's settled."

"I wish Edward had hung about long enough to see you, yesterday. It was weird him being called away when Hecaton really seemed to want you two to meet." Mel recognised his worry that the chief had died or something but he was crazy to concern himself about that. The chief could blame no-one but himself. There was also the perk that Amanda's troubles could soon be over. Note was too damned sensitive, and Mel knew she wouldn't change him for the world.

"Perhaps for the best," he said, and Mel didn't have to wonder what he meant. He would have worried about Carolyn's brother picking a fight, and if rumours were correct about his skill, the pair could do a lot of damage to each other.

"This shouldn't need more than two of us," Sean said, giving Mel the distinct impression he knew exactly what they were walking into. She would have to pre-empt the notion of his sending them away. Rake wouldn't mind as he was accepting of all his orders, unlike Mel who lived for all the experience she could get.

"We've got used to the stench now," she offered, still intrigued as to why a gateway would have opened here. "What's the harm in sticking around?"

"Very well, but let's not dilly-dally," said Sean.

Sean and Note tried the front door while she and Rake headed to the rear of the property. "Rake, do you recognise that green hatchback." The big demon shrugged but looked in at the windows with her. "I'm pretty sure this was parked at Feeding Frenzy the other day."

She then peeked in through the farmhouse's kitchen window, but nothing could have prepared her for what she saw. Her expression was reflected on Note's face, unsurprisingly, from where he too stood looking in but from the doorway across the other side of the kitchen.

"Well, I'll be damned!" Mel gasped.

"Is that a true Faery, little mage?" Rake asked.

"Yes, but not just any Faery, Rake. See what it's wearing. That looks like—" Mel halted, textbook illustrations flicking through her head. "Never mind." How was she going to get closer?

Stay back.

"Stay back," echoed Mel in response to Sean's command through the link as she watched him and Note engage with the Faery.

"Sorry," she blurted out, "but I'm going to leave you here, Rake, to keep watch. I'll go round the front." Rake nodded resignedly. He would guess that curiosity would kill her otherwise. She could "stay back" and still catch what was happening. Mel helped Rake activate the basic concealment charm from his tattoo before activating her own. His shadowy presence was visible to her, but only because she knew what to look for. Next, she set a temporary ward of the house, extending it to twice the size with a quick motion of the blackthorn rod on her key ring.

With all in place, she hurried around to the front, went in and stood by the kitchen doorway. Sean didn't look her way, but his approval surged in their link. It would be fine for her to stay as long as she kept her mouth shut and let Note and Sean handle things.

Mel noticed other occupants who had been previously obscured from her line of sight. The Faery reclined at one end of a huge sofa. He was taller than Jonah and his eyes were even larger, the bright hair on his head long, baby fine, and tethered to hang down his back.

There was no sign of any wings, but she suspected his garments were cut to allow them to break free whenever he chose. Mel couldn't sense his magic but knew he could use it and shield well. His wings would be stunning, not at all like Jonah and the other shadow demon's. For the first time, she wondered if the genetics from another magical creature had been used in the creation of their almost bat-like appendages.

Mel tore her gaze to the sleeping figure on the opposite end of the sofa, then to a child, sitting on a rug in front of an old style fireplace, an array of assorted objects – toys? – around him. Was the sleeping woman his mother or a babysitter? Mel couldn't tell. The child's features didn't look at all like the woman's, but for the sandy hair, the shape of his face. Not wanting to leap to conclusions, Mel finally felt there was a familiarity. Perhaps his being a magic user was the draw. There was a glow surrounding the little boy, of a shade she'd never before encountered.

"Yes," the child was saying to Note, "but you mustn't be sad." His eyes grew round in earnest. "The other one's with her."

Mel's heart lurched. Holy hell, forget the Faery, this little one was a seer.

The Faery continued to sit, his large eyes taking in everything around him with an almost bored expression. That Jonah shared genetic material with this being was almost laughable. However comfortable the creature appeared, he didn't *belong*. Mel thought of Note, Rake and Mace – what was it that made *them* fit and the Faery not? She felt the cool scrutiny of his gaze for an instant before his focus returned to Sean.

When the Faery spoke, all misconceptions were washed away. This was not some unfeeling, manipulative creature. The voice was hauntingly beautiful – *he* was beautiful, and Mel only wanted to listen forever to the amazing creature. This was– Anger surged through her when Note shot her a jolt of power. She now really wanted to *hurt* her friend.

And *that* broke the spell. She could never feel that way about Note, not by natural means – any of the others, yes – possibly – likely, even, but not with the Kistatus. Still out of sorts, Mel gritted her teeth and ground her palm into the rough brick wall beside the doorway and her senses instantly snapped back into focus. Note's alarm and an apology buzzed through their link. He remotely activated a charm in her tattoo. She hadn't known he could do *that*, but then had to focus on what the Faery was saying.

"The child called *me*, high mage. I would never interfere with Protectorate business."

"And yet here you are, Ankou." Ankou? Thankfully, not the Faery king, but close.

The little boy gave the mage a hard stare, a comical effect. "Don't get Ankou into trouble. He's helping me."

"With what, may I ask?" If Sean was surprised by the child's attitude, he didn't show it. He picked up a pencil sketch which was clearly Josh's. "Art?" The mage really needed to get some people skills. The child's lip trembled a little, but he stood firm before the mage.

"He's just worried about you," soothed Note, coming to the rescue. "We're actually the good guys, but you know that, right?"

Ankou's lovely voice sounded again. "You think I'm the only Faery the child has attracted?" His gleaming eyes slid momentarily to Josh, "I'm not some bodach come to slide down the chimney and carry him off while he sleeps." Was Ankou casting himself as some sort of protector? The Faery winked at Josh and the boy giggled.

"Remember, Ankou? He was *so* funny."

"Yes, Josh, but you don't want to live with us." Mel could just imagine the "yet" that belonged at the end of that statement. Ankou pouted slightly, and the child rushed on to try make amends with his Faery friend.

"I'd miss mum and dad too much. But it was nice to visit." Mel pitied the poor woman who had clearly been put to sleep for Josh to continue his adventures.

"You've been to a lot of places, little guy, haven't you," said Note lightly. "May I see this?"

The boy's expression changed to something resembling guilt. "That's my dad there." He pointed to the picture, clearly not feeling he had to identify his mother, also in the photograph.

"Thank you," said Note as he looked at the image. Sean grumbled slightly through the link that they shouldn't discuss anything in front of the Faery. *He already knew.* There was no doubt in Mel's mind that Josh's father was their underground contact, Taz. Smiling brown eyes seemed to reach out from the happy family photograph. It would be easy to forget that Taz was a Motus. Not especially dangerous but such an emotion manipulating demon could do a lot of damage in a crowd. Mel wondered if the woman on the sofa really loved the man or whether he was kept busy reinforcing the love by less than noble means. Morgan was the expert on emotions, she would know if the female had been manipulated.

And what then? Mel's thoughts ran to a natural conclusion, using what she'd learned through her enforcing experience. Rescue the human? Remove her half-demon and clearly gifted son as well as his father from her life?

Way too complicated for Mel to continue *that* train of thought.

The Faery's interest in Josh made complete sense. Faeries, she understood, were acquisitive and greedy creatures. When they moved between worlds, they always had a motive, even if it was just boredom – though generally their intentions were not morally sound. Mel almost laughed at her thoughts. She believed in giving people a fair chance, didn't she?

"Gateway's closed," said Note.

"Yes," Ankou agreed, then addressed Sean. "This is not what it looks like." He clearly recognised the powerful mage as their boss, and it irked her that he appeared not to consider any of the rest of them as a threat.

Sean steepled his fingers beneath his chin. "It looks like the child drew you here and you're keeping him amused until you figure out how to get home." A casual observer might have thought Sean was sincere. Mel knew better, and she was curious of the Faery's response.

She was suddenly glad it was Sean and not her that was the object of Ankou's stare. The Faery waited a little too long before answering, "Right you are. Not that we baulk at taking a willing specimen or two, as you will know, enforcer, but this little one—"

"Wouldn't last at his stage of development," Sean finished for him. "Not to mention the trouble an untrained child with his talents could cause."

"What did you do with *her*?" Sean motioned to the sleeping figure beside him.

"Ah," and Mel thought the Faery's regretful tone almost convincing. "I'm afraid I had to use 'Faery *forgetfulness* dust' on the child's mother. She became rather hysterical at my appearance." Curious, thought Mel. He should have been able to captivate the woman by merely saying "Hello".

"You were telling me about the princess," said Note, displaying amazing calm. Mel had forgotten Josh's earlier remark. The boy squinted at Note, clearly *seeing* more than he should.

"Oh," he said apologetically. "She's got her friends."

Sean's eyes narrowed, like Mel, clearly trying to fit the pieces together. Unlike her, he had probably organised them perfectly. The child looked human but was clearly more than that: a seer who could call beings from the gateways. Where exactly had it opened up anyway?

Note had gone pale under the child's intense regard. *I think Carolyn rescued this one from the Mow.* Mel didn't know if he'd meant to send the message through his link to them all, and Sean made no show of hearing it, but Mel felt the team's acknowledgement.

It might have been her imagination but Mel thought Sean looked tired. Sure, he was all model perfect, superior and infuriating, but she had noticed at times, more especially now, that the strain of Ethan's role – in addition to his own – was beginning to show on him.

CHAPTER 19

Hecaton

Hecaton felt satisfied with the way everything was progressing. He was confident his son would have prevailed whether Edward challenged him or not. Disappointingly, the boy had left before Notechis had fetched his friends from the castle.

When the seer had given Hecaton the means to double his power, he had been circumspect, but having witnessed his son's magic first hand, any shred of doubt was burned away. He would soon be spending a lot more time in his beautifully restored paradise, but all good things had to wait. Lucas needed him and Hecaton planned to allay the chief's fears as best he could.

Finding a girl so close to his quarters wouldn't have been a problem ordinarily, but the castle staff knew how to behave around him. Usually, they skittered out of his path and this one was no exception. When she looked up, however, he recognised her as the human who had captured Edward's interest. If she was aware of his own history, she would be right to keep away. It was not particularly suspicious that she seek out Edward at the castle if only to berate him for having her watched.

Her treatment of him – from what Hecaton had witnessed – was, in the high mage's opinion, an orthodox way to ensnare him. Whatever her intention, she *had* gained Edward's attention, and it hadn't gone unnoticed.

Her expression when she met his eyes was more than mere surprise. Reflexively, and more from curiosity than suspicion, his mind brushed against hers. Concern blossomed when he couldn't read her at all.

He had heard of the budding witch who had been sent with an O.W.E. certificate to learn magic in his realm. Hecaton had paid it no heed, not least because she was clearly substandard. The marauders had captured and traded her with no great tales of magical involvement so it had been easy to dismiss her presence. He *should* have realised when she hadn't appeared at the castle events that she wasn't their usual type of immigrant.

"Explain your presence, girl. You work on the lower levels, the streets, don't you?"

"Ah, yes. I make do," she said, backing away slowly. "Actually, I'm on my way there right now." He couldn't read her thoughts but the girl's heart raced like a bird's, and though she should be afraid, there was more to her reaction than the circumstances merited. Perhaps he was being paranoid, but then his power *had* suddenly seemed to diminish, unable to access this simpleminded human?

"Not so fast." The girl yelped when he dragged her by the arm and led her to the staff room adjoining the chief's chambers.

A few nurses and servers looked up in alarm at their entrance. Hecaton's charge shrugged insolently at the curious eyes upon her. The humans were speechless but, when he reached for their minds, he was assaulted by the racket.

The vivid and petty meanderings of their race had not diminished. He sifted through for good measure: fear and greed for starters, envy and lust most prevalent. Lust? His eyes tracked to a pretty nurse who blushed. Maybe later.

Hecaton heaved an inward sigh of relief; Notechis hadn't acted against him; His talent hadn't waned. Before him, all the humans were laid bare – *forget the nurse*, all, it would seem, except the untrained witch at his side.

"Thalamis meis," he incanted abruptly, not that he'd needed to speak it aloud, but the spectators were due a show. His cloak billowed out to encompass the girl, and they vanished, transported to his rooms. She would be more concerned over being in such a personal space than if he'd taken her to the dungeon.

"You are here from the Earth's Agency to spy on us, aren't you?"

"What? No," answered the girl belligerently. She hadn't even shown surprise at the transportation. "I have an O.W.E. These are accepted in all realms except here on Skean." It looked as though she'd wanted to add more but had hesitated at Hecaton's dark expression. In a swift motion, she reached into a pocket of her robe and withdrew a scroll. "If you want to see it, it's right here, with the appropriate seal and everything."

The high mage seized the document and unravelled it. "You bring me a seal from some ridiculous human." He passed the document beneath his nose. "This is from a lesser magic user who ought to know that we do not accept these here... Rhona Deborah Barbour," he read from the document. The name sounded as ordinary as he thought her to be, until now.

"Too progressive for *you*," she mumbled, before saying loudly, "It would have been nice to have had that information before I came here."

His mirror chimed and both he and Rhona looked at it. "Don't mind me," she said, wide-eyed. "You should maybe get that."

"Sit," commanded Hecaton, amused by the girl's shock when her body collapsed into a chair against her wishes. She would remain there until he commanded her to do otherwise. He couldn't see into her thoughts but he could certainly take care of her actions. Hecaton saw her attention move to the arched entrance of his bedchamber. The high mage turned his back on her, allowing her to absorb as much as she liked of her surroundings. He could answer the annoying call from his mirror but already knew what it was about. When he resumed his questioning, the girl didn't appear nearly meek enough.

"Why don't you tell me of your interest in us? I am not blind. You've been gathering information, and I'd like to know to whom you are expected to report."

"I'm not 'expected to report'," she said with extravagant air quotes, "to anyone except the O.W.E. issuer after my year is out."

"You're loyalty is commendable, but in case you haven't realised, you have been left to fend for yourself without the valuable tuition promised. Furthermore, I understand you are merely being humoured with this freelance venture until Cassandra trades you to another realm where your distaste for certain work will not be such an issue."

He had stretched the truth a little and the girl's aggravated expression was a sweet reward. "That's inhuman," she hissed, and Hecaton allowed a visible slip of a fang. "She told me she would try—"

"I said no. What *are* they teaching youngsters these days?"

"Not 'PC rules through the realms' to be sure," answered Rhona, and the high mage wondered if he was enjoying the little human rather more than he ought.

"There may be a way of developing the latent skills you possess."

"I thought I was worthless."

"Untrained, yes. It is hardly worth the trouble for a magic user to spend valuable time training one of your limited merit for results that will be less than outstanding."

"I want to be the best I can."

Hecaton chuckled. "Unless you are royalty, then nothing other than exceptional is expected."

He turned abruptly to the mirror when it chimed again. "Speak."

"I'm very sorry, my lord," came a strained male voice from the mirror. Hecaton didn't need to activate the visual component to identify the guard. "The young prince is here to seek an audience." By the muffled curses in the background, news had travelled fast, and Edward had abandoned his duties to fly to the fair maiden's rescue. How times never change.

"Tell him she and I are discussing her job application and send him away, Aswan." The background noise came to an abrupt halt and Hecaton could just picture the scene. Time for the knight in shining armour to exit the building. Not only had the boy failed to challenge Notechis, the object of his unrequited love was about to receive a better offer.

Hecaton was having a remarkably good day.

CHAPTER 20

Carolyn

Mario lay on top of Carolyn's massive bed while she sat cross-legged on the rug in front of the fire. No matter how she concentrated on the pretty opal before her, the power she subjected it to kept pinging back at her. "It's not working," she grumbled, and, looking up to frown at where Mario lay, added, "And take your shoes off if you're going to be on my bed."

"Was that an invitation?" His eyes sparkled mischievously. "I wondered when you'd notice."

"I noticed, Mario. I'm just a little busy at the moment with this hopeless task." Carolyn put her hand up to stop him from removing his boot.

"On second thoughts, no, Mario." She returned to her task. "I must be missing something."

The Lilim flopped back on the bed. "You cleaned the gems in fresh water?"

"And salted; check."

"Rinsed?"

"Check."

"Dried with the cloth I gave you?" Understanding crept over his expression and he spun to the floor. "Sorry, Carolyn. That's the opal you've been working on?"

"I liked it better than the others," she now groaned, seeing there was plainly a problem. "You said I could use any of them."

"Yeah, well, discard it; opals are too porous for the spells we practised. I'll fix it tomorrow." Mario slid down to mirror Carolyn's position, and she laughed at his efforts to cross his long legs. "I keep forgetting the size

154

difference," he smirked, choosing to let his knees flop out widely to the side to give him access to the pile of gems on the floor.

Reaching into his breast pocket, he withdrew a single clear stone, no bigger than a little fingernail. He rolled it between his finger and thumb, the light reflecting from it. "What do you see?"

"A crystal?"

"Knowing me as you do–"

"A diamond, Mario?"

"Nothing but the best will do."

"For you, right. That's why I had to practise with river stones."

"In unskilled hands, this lovely stone could be shattered to tiny chips."

"It's impossible to wreck a diamond."

"That should be true, pretty lady." He pocketed the diamond and plucked another clear gem from the pile before Carolyn. "Diamond would be preferable, but this is well suited to our purpose. Remind me to introduce you to Sparkly Bill when we get home." Carolyn was sure he was kidding, but she quirked a brow.

"No-one's seen the fool for years," chuckled Mario. "Apparently he's holed up in the welsh mountains somewhere. His face is dotted with chips." Mario's fingers traced the left side of his face to illustrate their position. "I suspect it was quartz crystal like this. I've never given it much consideration, but this stuff is mined in Wales and Ireland, and it's easily available."

"So what's the big deal about that stone?"

"I thought you'd never ask, little apprentice." He held it up to the light. "A.K.A. witch's mirror or star stone. A gem used throughout the worlds by magic users since days of old; most notable for its projective *and* its receptive qualities. In modern times it is popular with new age healers as well as true users like us."

"True users?" Ever the elitist.

"As much as I love my new age friends, they are different."

"You're right," said Carolyn. "*They* might be nice to know."

Mario continued, unaffected by the barb. "The crystal is to be found naturally occurring in every recorded realm. If you look closely at Bill, it really is the strangest thing. The chips are part of his skin. There's no proper scarring and they won't come out."

The Lilim leaned forward conspiratorially. "Anyway, the point is that magic users underestimate the strength of what they're working with all the time. Ethan used a circle with you and gained a scar. Bill used a gem on a foreign destroyer." Oblivious to Carolyn's mounting alarm, he continued, "At least the scar you gave him is pretty cool, but could you imagine someone like him dealing with cute sparkly bits on his face."

Carolyn's mouth had dropped into a surprised "Oh" and Mario cursed.

"Hell, you didn't remember that, even before Arthur's meddling. I'm sorry, I should have realised. The chief couldn't return what he hadn't taken. Those first years are probably best forgotten."

"I can't believe I gave him that scar. How could I? He's Protectorate." Carolyn chose to focus on what troubled her the most.

"You're missing the point," said Mario, irritation spiking his words. "He should never have tried to capture you alone, with only a circle, and if I remember rightly, you were trying to answer a call at the time. Much the same as with sparkly Bill. He overestimated himself and underestimated the reaction a feral destroyer would have. You were a weapon then, Carolyn – an unguided missile, wielded by the powers that be."

"What am I now?"

He winked. "One fishing for compliments, pretty lady." Smiling wickedly at her glower, he tapped a finger to the end of her nose, as though she were a child. "The weapon part of you has been buried – don't get me wrong, you're obviously not defenceless, but ... well, you weren't far wrong. You've more or less been deactivated."

"Well, thanks a lot, Mario." She flicked an emerald from the gem pile which bounced off his knee. "You make me sound more like a neutered cat than anything else."

"Don't go worrying about Ethan's scar, Carolyn. He deserved it. He *knows* he deserved it and that's why he hasn't tried to reduce it with a spell or surgery. Sparkly Bill's the same. They wear their marks as a cautionary tale to others – well, until Bill became a hermit, and Ethan probably keeps his scar to impress the girls."

"A ladies' man," said Carolyn dourly.

"Anything with a skirt and a pulse from what I've seen."

It was stupid for Carolyn to think Ethan might have any special feelings for her. If Amanda had stayed around, she would have warned her daughter to stay clear of players. "You sort of like to gossip, Mario."

"Moi? Common knowledge, Carolyn. That's all it is."

"But–"

"Look, forget it. Ethan's got his own crap to deal with. Let's get back to the crystal. It's just another part of an arsenal at our fingertips. We need to protect you." He put his hands up. "Yes, I know I said you can take care of yourself, but I'm watching out for you all the same."

Weirdly, Carolyn let the subject go without difficulty, and it wasn't as a result of the sectioning off of her feelings for Note she'd managed to achieve. It was possible to admit to the feelings without falling apart. Unwilling to give it more thought, she moved closer to Mario, ready for him to start.

"Right." He seemed surprised. "First, I want you to check out my energy signature. Describe it to me as we progress with this."

Mario began to call his magic from within, and Carolyn concentrated on the shapes that formed across his skin and around his body. "It's sort of like the number five repeating, the top part – the flicky bits – of the fives are short. The accompanying sound is similar to rain falling on a hard surface."

"Well spotted. Not everyone has a dual signature as you will have noticed."

She had, *and* she'd worked out the connection between signature and personality. "Mario, could I influence you?"

"You already do," he answered, the familiar sly smile appearing for an instant. "Now, focus. If I'm under your thrall, I'll not be able to guide you through the process. We'll schedule something for tomorrow maybe?" He held the stone in the palm of his hand. "I'm going to deposit a store of magic into this gem and I'd like you to watch what happens to my signature."

Carolyn watched a trickle of lilac coloured magic weave from Mario's palm and into the gem. "Your signature is sort of contracting and it's – returned to normal."

"That's right. I've lost practically nothing," he explained. "Now, I want you to draw on my energy and try to channel it into the stone and tell me what happens. Use a lot."

"I don't know about this Mario. What if you end up like Sparkly Bill."

"Then I'll wear those sparkles with pride."

"Do I need to touch you?"

"Do you want to?"

She spluttered a laugh. "You should be more serious after telling me about underestimating magic."

"I trust you, but no, physical contact is not required. I can feel my energy drawing to you already." He was right. Carolyn focused on the bright lilac strands that were now escaping to converge between their bodies. Really concentrating, she could see Mario's signature in them.

"It's pretty," she said, drawing on the magic which streamed into her mouth and up her nose.

"That'll do," croaked Mario, and Carolyn shut off the flow, alarmed.

"You okay?"

"Yes, I wasn't expecting you to be quite as effective." Carolyn could no longer take offence at such statements. "Now pour it into the stone before it attaches fully to you." Those little fives were trying to flatten and mirror *her* own signature.

"I touch the crystal?"

"Please do."

Instead, Carolyn leaned in and breathed on the stone upon his upheld palm. He shivered.

"Or you could do that," he said with a sigh. The magic channelled to the stone still had Mario's signature, but hers was also entwined, creating a new, very intricate shape. Mario's signature had shortened slightly but was returning to normal as she watched.

"Relligo," he prompted, and Carolyn repeated the word to bind the energy to the stone. "Right, now I'm going to take the energy from the stone as I would if I needed a quick reserve. As demonstrated, it's not essential but usually advisable to touch the stone whilst working with it. When the magic within has part of you *in* it then it's possible to do this by simply picturing it in your mind. If someone else prepares the gem, you need to have physical contact with it."

Arthur's Lamia statue popped into Carolyn's mind. Mario had wanted to steal it but her father had woven himself into it. The potential for dark deeds made Mario's tutoring just a shade more sinister.

"Usually," he continued, "if you're using stones, then it's because you can't cast normally or you're depleted. It's an instant fix to throw a powerful spell or set of spells released through the stone, but you are acting like a catalyst to the process."

"So … what if you don't need all the stored magic? Do you hoard it in your body or send it back to the stone?"

"When your competency increases, you should be able to do either. I'm going to infuse the stone with a single disguise spell I've prepared. I want you to tell me what it does to my energy signature when I trigger it. *Ad suum dilectum.*"

"Now to activate it. Repeating the last two words of the original spell works best. So—"

"*Suum dilectum,*" Carolyn mouthed as Mario spoke it, and a wash of rainbow colours spiralled over him. "Now look at *my* signature." Sure enough, the little "five" shapes had become more condensed, but the tops had become longer, weaving around the upper stems of the shape in front. "That hurt more than it should have," panted Mario, before lifting a new bright yellow gaze to meet hers.

His appearance knocked the breath from Carolyn, now unable to speak … or think. She couldn't be expected to deal with her thoughts, not about the being now sitting before her.

"I can do better," said Mario, seeming oblivious to her upset. "Temperare." The crystal lightened slightly. Mario's form stretched a little and the bright eyed boy of Carolyn's dreams sat across from her, wearing an expression that didn't resemble what she remembered of the Kistatus at all. Of all the emotions coursing through her, she latched on to anger.

"Ethan's right. You *are* a little shit." She reached over and slapped Mario-as-Note soundly on the cheek.

"Hey, what did you do that for?"

"What the hell is wrong with you," she raged. "A warning would have been nice."

"I wanted to see what your reaction would be to the guy who risked everything for you just to have you panting over a scoundrel like Ethan." Carolyn blinked, her heart beating double-time.

"But there's nothing–" Nothing what? The chief had never discussed Note with her but she knew exactly how he would feel about her association with the Kistatus. Arthur was in the house. What would he say if he popped in on her training as he had done during practise with Patrick? "My father mustn't see you like this. You need to change back. Now!"

"We both know it's not just the chief. It's you," said Mario-as-Note, aggravatingly calm. "You're being a baby. Why are you so terrified of your anchoring to Note? Don't you *want* to go home?"

"I *do*." She wanted exactly that. Her eyes prickled with warmth. "This is unfair, Mario. Why can't you trust me to do what's right when the time comes."

"And what if it *doesn't* come?" She was now overwhelmed by the sight of him, even as she understood Note to be a world away. Mario was toying with her emotions, but she knew the Lilim thought he was helping her, and in his own warped way maybe he'd succeeded in forcing her to recognise an indisputable fact.

"The right time will–" A loud knock sounded on the door and Carolyn filed her budding revelations for a later date.

"My lady?"

Carolyn's eyes widened in fear. Oh, God. Her father wouldn't ask questions, he would likely kill Mario-as-Note first and then ask them. She knew it from the depths of her being and it terrified her. "Don't come in." Mario's brow furrowed, struggling with the change back. *Out of power?*

No, something else.

"I'm not decent," she called out, and reluctant humour spread across the face that so resembled Note's.

"The chief requests your presence immediately." Oh crap, the door was opening and Carolyn acted on impulse, leaned forward on her knees and slapped Mario-as-Note soundly with a force that snapped his head to one side. Energy crackled and spat in a stream of sparkling light. *Referro*, she thought. It *had* worked on the screwdriver.

"Apologies, my lady, but if you could come with me now?" She didn't recognise the guard. He'd been one of several who had arrived at the fortress with her aunt and uncle. The sentry quickly covered his surprise at the scene. Coming to with shocking professionalism, he asked stiffly, "Will your gentleman be remaining?"

"He's no gentleman," said Carolyn, relieved to see Mario-as-Mario, "but yes. He's with me." She pocketed the stone they'd been working with and offered him her hand. "What went wrong?"

He pulled up smoothly beside her. "I tried to reverse it with my own magic, instead of ours," he grumbled in her ear. "We've learned that if we store or cast using *your* magic, then it needs *you* to cancel or reverse it. And before you ask, I don't know how you get away with that Referro crap. I thought that just worked for inanimate objects."

Carolyn grinned, despite wanting to stay annoyed with him. He'd made his point, and she'd made hers. Time to move on.

Beni came rushing in past the impatiently waiting guard to join them and Carolyn realised he'd been gone a while … again. Hopefully, the dog wasn't trying to woo her uncle's huge French Poodle. There would be hell to pay for messing with *that* pedigree.

A bloodcurdling scream sounded from outside, and Carolyn leaped, almost tripping over Beni in her rush to follow the guard who was already out of the door. Mario skipped around her and out, but the dog grabbed at Carolyn's tunic with his teeth. She struggled to regain her balance, tearing away to leave the hound with a scrap of fabric in his mouth. He bounded forward only to stop her again. The fabric dropped from his mouth, and, tail tucked in, he whined softly. Beni was trying to protect her, but from what? She *had* to see what was happening.

"Stop that," she cried in frustration. "Don't make me use magic on you." He shook his big head but did then allow her to pass. Her boots pounded loudly in the silence that had rushed in on the tail of the scream. Her anxiety only deepened further when she saw that that guards had abandoned their posts in the main hallway.

What had happened to warrant all hands? The north, she thought.

The chief's wing.

Her breathing sounded harsh in her own ears as she rounded the corner at the end of the hallway and struck something solid: Mario. He grunted as he saved her a fall. "Something's happened?" Carolyn gasped but freed herself from Mario's hold, making towards the commotion.

"Not to the chief, Carolyn. He's fine." Taking her arm, he held her back, glancing surreptitiously at the guards now blocking access to the north wing. "We need to get back to your room."

Relieved, her head rested briefly on Mario's shoulder. The thought of her father being hurt had affected her much more than she could have imagined. Mario's rich brown eyes were assessing her, his lips tight.

"I want to see," she now said, and he released her, but reluctantly. Clearly, this went against his orders, but the guards stepped aside to allow them through. Carolyn caught the definite scent of incense and another earthier substance as they passed the guards and went in to the rear of the wing.

"It happened here in the conservatory," explained Mario as he led her through to it. Outside lighting flooded through the many windows and she was shocked to see Lena being raised by Patrick to a sitting position on the tiled floor, one arm cradled to her chest. A makeshift bandage covered her hand and Carolyn wondered, somewhat unkindly, if the woman was making a habit of touching things she shouldn't. "Minor crushing injury," whispered Mario.

The French windows were open to the garden, and fresh air swirled in. A pretty fountain could be seen directly outside, beyond a group of guards standing just inside the window, Peter amongst them. His hands were in motion; the Lilim was clearly issuing orders to the men as they scrambled to order, one hurrying to close the room against the chill night's air.

"What happened here?" Carolyn asked.

"A very good question, my dear," her father said, a look of reprimand crossing his face at the sight of her with Mario. Although she'd not noticed him here when she'd entered, now his commanding presence seemed to take up the entire room. He stood with his back to the guards, surveying the scene dispassionately.

Thankfully, all seemed to be in hand and Carolyn was simply relieved that Lena appeared okay-ish.

"I wanted to help." Carolyn said, meeting Arthur's gaze squarely. He was deceptively composed but she could *feel* the anger in him.

As if he'd just noticed his men, Arthur dismissed them all except Patrick.

"Bradley?" Carolyn got the attention of a guard who was normally stationed close to her. "Could you please check on Ethan?" The man looked to Arthur whose brows rose, but he nodded his assent and the guard began to leave.

"Confine him to quarters," Arthur added.

"That's not..." Carolyn blustered. "Ethan wouldn't harm anyone."

"I know – I'm merely assuring his safety, daughter."

Arthur crouched down at Lena's side, Carolyn finding it hard to be annoyed with him. Something unspoken passed between him and Patrick and the guard nodded before scooping Lena up, as though she weighed nothing. The woman moaned as her limbs folded and the Lilim apologised, setting her securely on the sofa.

Mario came forward but Arthur's eyes widened when he saw what he was about to do. "The court healer has been summoned," he said, and Carolyn cringed. Any of the Lilim could have helped Lena, but they hadn't. Why would her father let Lena suffer longer than necessary?

"But surely we could–"

"There may be evidence of the perpetrator of this attack." Arthur's mouth tightened in a grimace.

"I didn't get a chance to explain," Lena said, wincing from the pain, and

Carolyn's heart squeezed in sympathy. "There was no attack," and her eyes lowered, guiltily. "I was practising magic."

"I thought Lilim ladies didn't use their skills," said Mario warily.

"They don't." Arthur's attention didn't stray from Lena. "While you are indisposed, should we use the time to discuss this newfound desire of yours?"

"It's not new, my love," said Lena, sighing deeply. "I didn't realise you'd reset the anti-magic ward on the building to encompass everything. If I had, I never would have practised here."

Carolyn flinched at the suggestion that Lena's injuries were due to Arthur. She and Mario had been able to work magic within the walls. Were there additional wards on the north wing? And what sort of spell had Lena attempted that could hurt her? Uncomfortable, Carolyn cast her eyes towards Mario. Was it their fault for maxing out the ward's levels with *their* own practise? Mario crossed his arms and didn't have to catch her eye for the "Keep quiet" message to be received.

The chief stood still, looking out towards the garden. "I must not have been clear, Lena. I categorically forbid you to use magic in this house." He turned, casting his face into shadow. "If it hadn't been for Patrick–"

"No need to dwell on that, my lord. I owe him my life. If he hadn't found me when he did, I could have died."

Arthur turned his attention to Patrick. "May I ask what alerted you to the lady's plight?"

"I… I was investigating something at the tree line outside when I saw a flash of light from the house. I thought the wards had crashed from an irregularity within zone eleven, although the lights remained in the conservatory. I sounded the alarm and attended immediately. I assumed it would have been…" He offered Carolyn a look of apology. "I expected one of the guests to be in trouble. I didn't expect to find milady Lena."

"And why would you?" said Arthur dryly.

Lena's tone became almost wheedling, her words punctuated by winces. "Don't you see? That's exactly *why* I need to practise and gain control of my talents?" The little Lilim was trying to manipulate her father, and really, who could blame her? Carolyn was no different. Mario caught her eye, his expression serious and willing her once more *not* to get involved.

"A lady shouldn't have to," said Arthur, his tone clipped, authoritative. Lena pointedly looked at Carolyn. Damn, it *was* her fault.

"I know I don't have *her* gifts, but I need to control what I *do* have." There was nothing Carolyn could say. Lena was right and her father was being monstrous. She knew he wasn't a progressive but would it really be so difficult for him to lessen controls on the household? Could *she* help Lena gain a little independence or was Arthur going to crack down on all things magic. Carolyn was betting on the latter.

"I will not lift the barriers in my home."

"No, I wouldn't expect you to do that. It was silly of me to try this."

"Then why?"

"I simply needed to do something that would challenge me."

Arthur's brows raised a fraction, and Carolyn knew he had made a decision that someone was not going to like. "This can be discussed at a later date. In the morning, you will take the coach to the lodge and remain there for one week until I join you." Lena's eyes bulged in alarm.

"I'll miss Carolyn leaving." Her breathing hitched as though she was about to cry. "I can't believe you're punishing me this way?"

"What would you suggest I do?"

He was certainly not looking for a response. Lena should have known better than to challenge the chief in his own home, and in front of anyone. The full force of Lena's humiliation struck. Even without using a shred of his power, Arthur exerted an overwhelming authority that *had* to be recognised.

Lena's eyes glistened, her tone now penitent. "My lord, I forgot myself. It's the misaligned spell that's making me muddled. Of course I'll do whatever you think best." Carolyn wished she'd listened to Mario. Her place was not here.

A short rap on the door heralded the arrival of their healer and another officially dressed individual. Arthur took the opportunity to step out without acknowledging their grovelling greetings. Lena's face crumpled and Carolyn couldn't bear to watch. She hurried after Arthur, Mario following closely behind.

"Just go to bed, Mario," she hissed when he reached out for her. "I need to talk to him."

"You're crazy to speak to a chief who's *that* pissed off." The Lilim had raised his voice, causing one of the guards to lay a hand on him. Mario shrugged it off. "You know what, Carolyn?" She gave him a quick frustrated stare, and he turned away in disgust. "On your head be it."

"Don't be like that," she cajoled, but her eyes never left her father's receding figure.

"No really, I'm done."

Carolyn would deal with his wounded feelings later. It was obvious by Arthur's pace that he didn't want company. She eventually caught up with him, having to skip to match his long strides, but he didn't stop until they'd reached the entrance to his walled garden.

"Do you really think that sending Lena away is for the best—" Seeing the tightness of his jaw, she hesitated. "I mean, wouldn't Lena be better here where you can keep an eye on her." Arthur's angular features softened slightly before he turned his face up to the moonlit night.

"You don't understand, my dear. Things have been changing between us for quite some time."

Carolyn's startled "Oh" carried into the air. What was she to make of Arthur's statement? She spotted two guards approaching, stopping to observe from a respectful distance. "Lena made a mistake, Father, one I can relate to." At his narrowed glance, she pressed on. "Why should Lilim women *not* use their gifts? It's a waste."

"She should not have disobeyed me."

Carolyn willed herself to remain composed. He was a chief. The rules for the likes of Lena and herself were different than they were for ordinary people. But then again, why should they be?

"Maybe it's no wonder, seeing how you feel about it." So much for keeping calm. By Arthur's lack of response, it was clear she wasn't helping.

He considered her carefully for a moment. "Each member of the household has their duties and certain agreed expectations are not unreasonable."

"Well, I can't imagine I've fulfilled any of your hopes, Father. Perhaps I should go back to the lodge with her."

"By all means, daughter. I'll not stop you." His eyes gleamed and Carolyn realised she was behaving as though she had a vested interest in fortress affairs. Why was it sometimes so hard to remember that she was leaving? "This is between Lena and I, Carolyn." He stretched a hand to cup one side of her face and she leaned in to the touch. "I know you mean well, but it is not open to negotiation. I'll see you in the morning."

When Arthur's attention shifted to the waiting men, Carolyn couldn't shake the thought that he'd acted in everyone's best interests.

Had he just *influenced* her?

CHAPTER 21

Carolyn

Carolyn wasn't surprised by sounds from outside her room. She heard the deep tones of the guard trying to discourage a visitor. Perhaps Ethan, but more likely Mario here to scold her for challenging Arthur. To her astonishment, it was Lena, and Carolyn eagerly ushered her in. If the woman hoped to hear that Carolyn had swayed her father, she was in for a disappointment.

The Lilim walked purposefully towards the window and drew open the curtains.

"What are you doing," exclaimed Carolyn. "Wait, I'll get that." The woman obviously needed some air. "Are you all right?" Carolyn cracked open the sash.

"Yes, it's all going to plan," she said softly. "The healer fixed me up, but we don't have much time." Lena pointed to the door to indicate that the guard might be listening. Of course, her sentry would be waiting as well.

"We must get you out of here," she said earnestly, and tried to guide Carolyn towards the window.

"You're not making any sense." Carolyn drew back, her lips twisting as she remembered the last time someone had wanted her to leave by a window.

Lena put a finger to her lips. The woman appeared to have healed well but her colour was high and the thought struck Carolyn that Lena might have cracked from the strain of her earlier ordeal.

"Lena, I don't need to leave for a while yet and I'll miss you, but you've had an awful night. Maybe we should get some rest before you—"

"Before I'm sent away where I can do nothing to help?" Frustration

165

sharpened the Lilim's sweet voice, and she brought her hands together in earnest. "I *know* things that you don't, Carolyn. Trust me when I say he's *never* going to let you go. Can't you feel what he's done – what he's doing to you?"

Carolyn's brows drew together as Lena pressed on. "You don't really *want* to leave, and that's because of your father. It's Arthur who's keeping you from your team and it's not just to save you from the heartbreak he once suffered." Lena's expression hardened. "Once I get you away, you can be free to make your own choices without *his* interference."

"But Father promised!" Lena's mood was catching. Carolyn could feel the truth of what the Lilim was saying but everything within her wanted to deny it. "There has to be a better way than just disappearing into the night." *Cowardly*, she thought bleakly. "I could talk to him." *Like I did earlier?*

Lena folded her arms across her stomach. "Then he will remove your will entirely. It's not safe for you to stay. Not now." The intensity of her gaze had become almost hypnotic. "I didn't want to worry Arthur – or you – about what really happened today, so I lied. I wasn't just practising magic tonight. It was exactly as Patrick suspected. I was attacked in the garden and *fought* with something. I didn't see what *it* was, but I had my hair covered and it seemed to think I was you."

It? "But–"

"No, Carolyn. Someone, some *thing* was sent to kill you."

"Father needs to know," Carolyn mouthed weakly.

What sort of being could have crossed Father's wards? It didn't make sense unless the Agency had made improvements that the Protectorate couldn't match. It seemed unlikely, but it wouldn't be the first time the organisation had overcome a problem with their blend of technology, genetics and magic. Could they have sent Ella back?

"It's too late for that. We can't tell Arthur after that show I put on." The spectacle was to help Carolyn? "You might not have noticed, but with all the extra provisions he's been making lately, and the fact that Peter and Patrick are being punished, the chief has not been delegating responsibility to his best men."

"So he's weakened." *Because of me.* If Ethan hadn't come to save her, then Patrick and Peter wouldn't have tackled the threat of Ethan in the way they did. There was a lot more to it than that, but the crux of the matter was that Carolyn's presence *had* upset the natural order of the fortress and consequently the realm. Was Lena offering a means to sort it all out quickly? The Lilim appeared to be waiting for her to come to the proper conclusion.

"What about my friends."

Lena had started to widen the opening of the large bay window but paused to offer a sly smile that reminded Carolyn terrifyingly of Mario. "I saved the best part for last. They're headed there right now. We must catch up before Arthur realises."

"But, where are we meeting? There's no gateways allowed, and we can't use the tear."

Lena's brows lifted. "You know about that? Oh, such a terrible thing. There's a spot, not too far from it, where I've been practising. I can access a gateway without Arthur's knowledge but I'm going to need power from all of you to accomplish it."

Crap. Her father wouldn't just let Lena off with a trip to the lodge if he found out about this. Carolyn's respect for the pretty Lilim soared. "Won't you be in trouble for helping me?"

Lena hiked up her skirt and very sprightly swivelled her legs over the sill. "You heard your father; I'm in enough bother already. Don't worry about me." And with that, she dropped from sight.

Ethan

"She just doesn't get it," ranted Ethan as he paced his room. "Arthur's tightening his grip in such a way that Carolyn's never going to leave." He turned sharply to Mario who had somehow come to be lying on his bed, arms stretched up, hands behind his head. "Move the hell off my stuff," he added irritably. That was *not* an image he wished to carry to his dreams.

"I think the gentleman doth protest too much," said Mario in a flirtatious tone that made Ethan want to punch his pretty boy face. The Lilim swung his legs to the floor, clearly sensing the danger. "There's only one chair in here," he grumbled, but rose to take his place on it.

"I get that you're angry about being cooped up here when things are happening, but it was really no big deal." Ethan stared hard enough to make his eyes water, and Mario moderated his tone further. "Only a little more time, Ethan, and *then* we can leave whilst maintaining good relations with the realm. Whatever the personal difficulties we face, the Protectorate will be pleased with the result if all goes to plan."

"That's part of the problem, Mario. I'm not sure whose or which plan we're implementing."

Ethan had been livid when the guards escorted him back to his room following the incident. He'd overheard a bit about Arthur's consort being in trouble. He wouldn't have thought her capable of causing such a fuss, but then, Lilim women had similar skills to the men. Unfortunately, they were treated like silly princesses in this realm.

Something still didn't sit right with him about that. He couldn't dismiss it or the familiar tension that had tightened his gut, the type of strain he might have felt before answering a particularly hazardous call. He scrubbed both his hands over his head in frustration.

Who could tell *what* was real under Arthur's roof.

Mario had left Carolyn with her father – alone. Was that why he felt the tension? Some sort of referred pain? The destroyer would likely be upset by the night's events. She was very fond of Lena – not that it was any of his concern – but *that* wasn't it either.

"We need to go to her, right now."

"No, *I'll* go check," said Mario, seeing Ethan's intent. "You'll only set them off."

"The guards?" He reached down and grabbed Mario by the front of his shirt. "*You* still have power, so why don't you impress me – I know you want to – and get us to Carolyn's room." The Lilim gritted his teeth.

"You catch more flies with honey, you know."

Ethan released his grip, surprised at the boy's control. It would have been easy for him to repel with magic but he hadn't. Could the little shit have matured in spirit as well as body during his year away? "This could get us both locked up but I'll do it." Mario smoothed the front of his shirt and opened the door, ready to enthral the waiting guards.

Mario had *influenced* three more sentries before they arrived at Carolyn's chambers, finding Patrick and another Lilim stationed outside. It seemed unlikely he'd have enough juice to disable more than the five already down, but Ethan had come too far to give up now. As Mario handled the Lolilim, Patrick wasn't expecting Ethan to leap in with a physical assault.

The proud Lilim staggered from a jab to the face, an angry spell taking shape on his lips, but Ethan wedged an arm into his throat, pushing him against the wall.

"Uh, uh, uh," he cautioned. Patrick's mouth was already starting to swell with the initial blow, and his eyes glinted dangerously. "The punch was for setting the dogs on me," he said brusquely. "Call Arthur if you want, but don't use magic. Who knows what will happen with the wards being as they are? I just need to check on her." Then, with a flash of inspiration: "You're guarding Lena?" The Lilim nodded, his face turning blue at Ethan's hold.

Mario's exclamation from the open door drew them apart and Ethan cursed when they were met with empty space. He wildly pushed past the dazed guard that Mario had disabled. The curtains billowed out from the open window as if in fond farewell. It hadn't even occurred to Ethan that Lena would help Carolyn escape. Ordinarily, that would be a nuisance, but there was real danger with the pseudo gateway out there. Carolyn was only flesh and blood, she wouldn't survive a trip through the tear if it called to her.

Ethan felt suddenly cold. Surely to God he was wrong.

"How did you know something was up?" Mario said, staring incredulously at the window. Ethan spared a thought that maybe he should scratch the boy off his hit list. Even as Mario had thought him to be overreacting, he had helped regardless.

Mario's eyes narrowed, as if he'd read his thought. "Even without your powers, Ethan. You're still a scary bastard."

Ethan didn't pause for the predictable come-back but leapt for the open window, realising that nothing in the realm would keep him from getting to Carolyn as fast as was humanly possible.

Behind him, Ethan heard Mario's call to Arthur, and he almost winced at the power of it. He couldn't hang around to see if the chief would rush to Carolyn's rescue, not when everything within him screamed to get to her himself, to find her before she disappeared from all their lives. In the dark, he ran, stumbling when his vision failed him. He was cursing the loss of his talents when he felt their return in a dizzying blast of Arthur's power.

It was like every good feeling in the world wrapped tightly into an electrifying and breath-taking package.

Ethan's lifted his arms to release himself from the binds of the earth and soared into the night sky.

Halleluiah!

Sean

"The tear is swarming with Agency." Morgan smacked her device down on the table. A map of the area was displayed, logging movements around Saltcoats harbour. "There's something happening and we haven't a chance of getting near that circus, not with all that Levy's got going there."

"Yes," said Sean, turning his laptop so she could see the larger version on-screen. "I've been monitoring for the last few minutes."

"This must have been planned." Sean heard an unspoken accusation.

"Our people haven't caught a thing about it." In truth, they had been more concerned about the Investors who had all too conveniently disappeared or sold their interests in the Agency to a single "mystery" Investor. No prizes for guessing Miranda was responsible.

"We need to get someone down there."

"Just give me a moment; they've disabled regular communications, so I want to try something else. The worse that can happen is that they retrieve Carolyn and we intercept before they take her to the block."

"That's not the worst, and you know it, Sean." Morgan wrung her hands like a scared little girl. "They could open a gateway anywhere… They're not running with our restrictions. The entire area is floodlit on either side of the wall," Morgan now rapidly told him. "They have a dozen mages, at least that many vehicles *and* a helicopter. I can't get a read on the tear. Either they've scrambled it or… hell, I don't know." There was no need to speculate. The tear led to only one place and Miranda Levy had assumed full control of it. "They've got *so* many magic users."

Sean was strong enough to confuse a few mages. "I could go." He watched her hope rise and die in a breath.

"No, they'll suspect something. There's too many for you to influence." Her eyes narrowed as a denial rose to his lips and she pressed her forefingers to them. If she hadn't known before, she knew now. "Just save it, Sean. I've known for a while what you gave up." The obvious compassion irked him more than he thought possible. "If it makes you feel better, I could remind you that you're not helpless and still outclass any mage I know."

"Yes that would help," he muttered.

"You *never* work for them without an invite. We'll be picked off too easily if we try to get close."

"We *need* to get closer, Morgan. I can set up a remote view and put Jonah as our man on the ground." Her expression told him she hadn't thought of the Faery.

"Right, okay. That's a plan." She shrugged into her backpack.

"We'll call the others to 'Feeding Frenzy' and set a base from there."

Carolyn

The night air was uncomfortably cool, and Carolyn wished she'd brought a jacket. The night sky provided limited light, and she knew her vision was better than her friend's when Lena stumbled at her side. Carolyn caught the Lilim by the arm and rushed them away from the building.

"Halt," called a voice from the shadows ahead. An unhindered escape wasn't going to happen. Was it wrong for her to feel relieved?

"I'll handle it," whispered Lena, sweeping forward from Carolyn's grip. There were only two guards and Lena proved that her delicate form was no impediment to her Lilim talents. The Lolilim faces blanked readily, and the men moved to let them pass. Being a natural magic, Lena assured Carolyn that Arthur wouldn't be alerted, but the process left Carolyn's stomach churning. This was happening too fast. Her father's enchantment still felt thick in the air. Using a born skill was one thing but how did Lena expect to crack Arthur's wards enough to use the magic needed to break the gateway lockdown.

Carolyn wished she'd had the chance to speak again to Arthur – to convince him? But she had every reason to run. Lena had been telling the truth about Arthur's plan, but Carolyn still felt like a guilty runaway. In his eyes, he wanted simply to reclaim what was his. Having been inside his mind, she knew his pain, understood it, but how could she condone his methods?

It was the promise of finding Ethan and Mario that spurred her on. She needed to speak to them and ask if this was really the best course of action. Lena *had* to be given the chance to join them. The Lilim clearly loved Arthur, but after what her father had said about their relationship, and following Lena's deception, could the woman afford to stay and take the consequences?

"I really appreciate you helping us out like this, Lena." She had slowed her pace and Carolyn felt much warmer in the depths of the forest. The clouds had blown over to reveal an almost full moon, its soft glow filtering through the canopy.

"I know," Lena answered, and turned a bright Lilim smile upon her. "Can you feel it yet?" They stopped to listen in the silence, the pleasant scent of moss and fern surrounding them. It seemed as though their journey had been too short.

As Lena released her arm, Carolyn felt suddenly exhausted. Were the day's events only now catching up with her, or had Lena done something? She shook off the ungrateful thoughts – the Lilim had risked everything for Carolyn and her friends.

"Go forward, just a bit." Lena seemed to be speaking slower than usual, and Carolyn moved at her encouragement.

"No, wait, I–" Lena's smile widened as Carolyn puzzled it through. Yes, there was ... something. Carolyn stretched out her arms as though waiting for an embrace, her feet seeming to move of their own volition. She could hear as well as *feel* something that shouldn't be strange to her but was.

This was no *calling* like Carolyn remembered from her past. The strength of it increased as she stepped forward, homing in on its source. There was a brush of sadness and an undefinable quality, rancid almost – disease? – incorporated into the call. It gave Carolyn pause and she tilted her head to one side, focussing on it.

"Let me help you with that," said Lena, and Carolyn felt she should definitely be worried about the Lilim's tone.

A veil lifted from the forest about Carolyn, and now she could *see* the thing that called to her. Hideous as it was, Carolyn continued to move forward, her eyes widening in alarm. The opening was filled with a dark purple-red gateway matter. It shimmered and shifted but it was like no other gateway she'd ever seen.

Not circular, the opening was a ragged slash of energy, wider at its base; it appeared as though it had been hacked several times in an effort to increase its size. The edges looked like those of a festering sore. Black necrotic tissue seemed to weave spiderlike veins from its periphery. It oozed and dripped a viscous substance onto the ground below which held a mound of the same rotting, semi-solid matter. Carolyn at last found her voice.

"This is not a gateway," she panted. "I can't go through that. I can't." Her feet didn't act in concert with her feelings, though. "What is this, Lena?" Oh, God. Lena knew. Of course she did, and if Carolyn quit rationalising for even a moment, she had every chance of leaping into it.

"It is the tear, you foolish girl. Arthur's stopped access to the realm, so this is the best I could do. All my effort will finally be worthwhile."

How could Carolyn have been so stupid? It was all starting to fall horribly into place. With certainty, she knew that Lena wouldn't or couldn't open a true gateway. Ethan and Mario could have no idea of the Lilim's plan. "You were supposed to be my friend." Carolyn's voice cracked on the last word, but she took a breath and continued. Her tattoo itched strongly, and pausing to scratch it fiercely, the pain brought her back into focus.

The smell of the tear was stronger now, like decayed flesh rather than the decomposition of plants and flowers. Carolyn was not going without a fight but first she needed to slow Lena down. "At least tell me why," Carolyn pleaded. "I deserve to know why."

"You deserve? You are worthy of nothing," the Lilim spat, and the venom in Lena's voice was nothing short of horrific. Still, she'd got her attention and Carolyn's feet had stopped moving towards the tear.

"I want to understand."

Lena glanced back in the direction they'd come, and Carolyn kicked herself for allowing the guards to be influenced. How long would it be until the sentries posted at her door noticed they were missing? "Understand this," said the Lilim bitterly. "Before you arrived in the realm with your little friend everything was fine, better than fine." Lena's mouth twisted in a parody of humour. "Arthur and I were close. We had fun; we were *together*… and now? Do you have any idea of what you've done? That man has hardly looked at me since the night of your arrival." Lena's eyes narrowed on the tear before returning to Carolyn.

"At first, I was patient. I thought he just needed to get used to his daughter being here. But no. You brought much more than that. He has been disappearing for hours on end, and I know that when he's not attending to business or spending time with you, he's in the stores looking at that damned portrait of your whore of a mother."

He had a portrait? Whore of a mother? Carolyn couldn't even begin to tackle the issues. "Lately, though," continued Lena, "lately, he goes where no magic can trace him. Where do you suppose that is?"

Not skipping out for a pizza to be sure; Carolyn was grossly uncomfortable with the subject matter but she couldn't let Lena say such awful things about her mother, not without defending her. "I don't know, Lena. As I understand it, my mother had no choice in the match with Arthur. Breeders are stolen from their worlds to be used. How does that make her a whore?"

Lena laughed spitefully. Carolyn was desperate to scan for the help that *had* to be coming but didn't want to spur Lena on in her mission. "Oh, you are so deluded, little girl. Let me tell you the story. Arthur was *promised* to me and our wedding date had been set. The whore simply," and Lena snapped her fingers, "appeared in the realm one day and seduced him. By the time I realised what was happening, it was too late. He even took in the Kistatus brat as though it were his own."

Oh, God. Carolyn felt like she'd been punched. She had hardly thought about Eddie these past weeks and now she'd been thrown too much information to handle. "*I* was sent away," Lena now said with even more venom in her voice. "Can you imagine the humiliation of that? He wasn't supposed to *love* her; I could have coped if he'd just used her." Carolyn flinched at the concept. How dare she denigrate her *mother*.

Distaste clearly showed on *Lena's* face as her tirade went on. "You are the same as her, only less smart. Amanda would never have been taken in like you. The whore fooled Arthur into thinking she cared for him – and I'm not talking about the claiming nonsense. He never claimed her! She made him believe that she truly loved him before betraying him."

As Carolyn digested these nasty snippets, the tear looked increasingly attractive. "You think that killing me is going to get him back into your arms."

"If everything goes to plan, then you are expected." A sly smile crawled over Lena's face, illuminated by the sickly glow from the gateway tear. "The Protectorate have their hands full, I understand, but the Agency have resources to ensure you never see the light of day again."

"So where's the shadow Faery?"

"That's not my concern. I've brought you here, so my part in this is almost finished."

Goosebumps erupted on Carolyn's body. Lena was going to send her through the tear regardless of whether she was protected or not. Delusional, Lena had said, and she was right.

"Father will find out what you've done."

"Perhaps, but by that time I'll have produced an heir of my own." Her hand moved to her flat belly. Oh, no. Was she expecting?

"He won't think to question me about your disappearance. He believes I'm poorly skilled and untrained, not worthy of the mind tricks he uses on the men."

"The boys are not coming then."

Lena laughed. "Oh, they'll come eventually. They might even scour this tear. I'm not going to waste energy concealing it. But you'll be long gone by then."

Carolyn squeezed her eyes shut as a realisation hit her. She had been focussing so much on Arthur's restriction that she hadn't realised so little applied to her.

The Lilim didn't know everything about her and had relied on deception to get her here. Carolyn was capable of magic that Lena would never suspect. With focus, it would be possible to overwhelm her. But what about the baby? Carolyn now felt the pull of the tear in pulses. Sensing she only had control enough to run from it, fighting off the shadow demon would then be impossible in her weakened state.

Drained after practise, Lena had clearly interfered with Carolyn's rejuvenation. Some power remained. If she circled the Lilim, would it hold long enough for Carolyn to return to the others?

"You know you want to, destroyer," taunted Lena. With a glance behind her she'd obviously decided that now was the time to end it. "Do what you're supposed to do best." And with that, Lena dropped back. "I know you can't fight it," she shrilled. "You injured yourself at the Agency trying to answer their gateway calls. What are you waiting for?"

Lena kicked over a stone and produced something that resembled a gateway device. Its glow flared as Carolyn began to cast, the circle spell freezing on her lips. Lena's new toy worked like Mario's stones. Carolyn dropped, her arms thrown forward as her residual magic streamed from her fingertips to the device. "Ella was most informative when she brought me this. I can't pretend I could have controlled you without help. I was counting on your call but you seem to have lost that as well as your magic." Lena chortled. "It's interesting that they got that wrong. You learned to control the call."

Carolyn cursed her hesitancy, hands slapping back to her sides. The smack of something hard in her pocket was the sound of hope. She'd put Mario's crystal with their combined energy in her pocket. Could it hold enough for her to cast? The woman was too dangerous to be left behind if Carolyn chose to run.

Sliding the stone into her palm, she kept her face angled away from the Lilim, spelling as Mario had taught her. Reaching inside herself, she found her skill waiting, wanting to be released, to be directed by her. It was useless as anything other than the catalyst for her only chance.

"Circle," she called and sent the power through the stone to pick up the energy for the spell. A silver barrier pushed up to ensnare the Lilim.

Too slow, it missed its mark. Lena was small and fast, dodging the attempt with a growl. Animal-like, she advanced, showing Carolyn her teeth before taking an inhuman leap towards her.

Instinct drove Carolyn to duck and roll aside, but to her horror, the gateway tear was closer than expected, its tainted warmth a scant inch from her back.

Lena had no hope of stopping herself. An unholy scream shrieked from her, but although Carolyn reached out to grab her, it was too late, the Lilim had already vanished into the noxious mouth of the tear.

CHAPTER 22

Miranda

"Hush, Judy," hissed Miranda as she listened at the site of the tear. The device they'd sent through weeks ago had fed limited data to its twin she carried. "Where the hell is Ella?" The demon had returned with information that had allowed the forces to be placed. The area was as secure as they could make it. Protectorate enforcers would arrive at some point and she was ready for them. A helicopter buzzed overhead and the steady stream of reinforcements, magical and otherwise, were arriving by the minute.

"She's here," said Judy as Ella streamed into existence before her. "You've done great," she assured the Faery, turning from Miranda's harsh glare to look at her. "You must bring back the destroyer as planned." Miranda cursed when she heard a scream from her device, echoed within the tear.

"Now," she shouted, and Ella took a second to shrug her impudence before spilling into the opening.

"Something's wrong," Judy exclaimed as the shadowy mass streamed straight back out with a splatter of bright red blood. Miranda drew a finger across her forehead, seething at the dark fluid now on her hand. Destroyer's precious life force? The commodity that would ensure Miranda's place in modern history. The damned Faery had come too late.

The stream of particles reformed in a heap before Miranda. "What the hell are you doing," she muttered. Ella sprang away from the small captive and wailed, "I couldn't bring all of her. It was too fast. She was supposed to wait."

A harsh laugh erupted from the Agency head. "Not only that, my dear.

It appears you brought the wrong person."

Lena jumped to her feet, white faced, furious, and cradling the bloody stump of her right arm. "Are you suicidal, girl?" said Miranda threateningly. "This was not the agreement. Where is my destroyer?"

Note

Note's solitude had been brought to an abrupt halt by Sean's direction to wait for him at Feeding Frenzy. He'd caught Mace and Mel as they'd returned from a call, and the trio had piled into the car to drive to Irvine. Note was glad of the company, and Mel's driving would get them there fast.

"Why didn't we leave them there; tell me again?" Mace was annoyed with the girl they'd "rescued". "She called me a sick old man who liked touching young girls."

"The idiot was just ticked at you bodily removing her from the realm, Mace. It was nothing personal. We need to take them home because it upsets the powers or something, doesn't it."

Note murmured agreement from the back seat of the car. The conversation stopped him from dwelling too much on Carolyn.

"Seems to me the rules should be different for the ones who *want* to go."

"They should get an O.W.E. permit then," said Mel irritably, "and define 'want'. Who's saying they're in their own minds when they agree to take a walk on the dark side?"

"How dark can it be? She said it was no different than going to Paris on a year's work experience."

"Difference is that she's heard of the permits but didn't or couldn't get one. Also, she's not at the other end of a phone for her folks to check on her."

"We don't get to make the rules," offered Note, sympathetic to the big guy's frustration. They'd all answered calls where the victim was unwillingly saved from trade or from their own stupidity. "We just need to play by them."

Note's wrist itched, and he scratched the site of his tattoo. He had almost given up trying to reach Carolyn through their bond. He *needed* to be comforted by its presence and had spent significant time imagining the peace it would bring him, the gentle bitter sweetness of her subconscious as it reached for him.

Mel shot Mace a look before casting a curious glance at Note in the rear view mirror. "I hate to be crass, but did you just flash?"

"Don't be…" Note had thought they'd caught the headlights of an oncoming vehicle but that wasn't it. His tattoo *did* seem to be glowing faintly but he couldn't face the disappointment of thinking it could be a sign of something more. He didn't have much longer to wait on Carolyn.

Sean believed the bond had been subdued by Arthur's enchantment, but Note knew a lot about magic users – they wouldn't waste energy by retaining long and powerful spells indefinitely, especially if the recipient were unwilling – he pushed the thought away.

Arthur could have secured his will to a permanent source of power. If not, then surely he had to relax the constraints on occasion, especially when the Protectorate had agreed to his terms and the team were staying back – mostly. If Arthur had been aware of Jonah's sporadic visits, then he clearly *allowed* him to report on Carolyn's wellbeing.

"Well, the rules suck," Mace continued, oblivious to Note's internal struggle.

The tattoo flared again, this time burning white hot, and the car skidded. Mace had twisted around in his seat, trying to make a grab for him, but Note didn't even feel solid any more. Pain shot through his body as his mark illuminated the shock on his face. "What do we do," shrieked Mel. The wheels bumped over rough ground before they were thrown to an abrupt halt. "What do we do?"

Note's vision darkened, and a deluge of emotion lit through him: *Carolyn's.* Confusion and alarm merged with the distinct sting of betrayal. He *felt* her call, tainted with revulsion, fear and pity. In that instant, his life energy surged and responded in a new and bizarre manner.

"What the hell's happening, Note?" He certainly couldn't explain. Dimly, he was aware of Mel and Mace, their voices raised in panic. Something sizzled, Mace swore, and a half formed spell halted on Mel's lips. With a single thought, Note had stopped her.

He had to leave – now!

Mel was shrieking at him to stop but *that* wasn't an option. His form had become nothing but burning energy. He had to act before it expended.

At what seemed like a hundred miles an hour, he burst through the side window in an explosion of glass and molten car parts. Rising into the cool air did nothing to lower the temperature of his new form; he was on fire. Gathering speed into the night sky, he was nothing but sentient magic with a purpose.

Note was going to be whole again. Those who hurt his lady would be blasted from the face of Empustat. The focus granted him access to every particle of power at his fingertips. As the destination sprang up ahead, awareness brought him to another burst of speed which would propel him through the tear unharmed.

Note's form gathered into a spear of light and energy, streaming forward. Nothing could stand in his way.

CHAPTER 23

Ethan

Ethan dropped to the ground, running, in time to see the two figures before the tear become one. His heart thundered in his ears, imagining the worst. This had always been a threat. They should have repaired the thing already. The link it provided hadn't been worth the loss of a life. At least it hadn't been *her* life. Carolyn's red-gold hair shimmered as she stood before the sickly glow.

Safe for now, he had to ensure she stayed that way. *"Tuitio."* Magic shimmered and crackled over the site and Ethan thought he could hear its disappointed shriek. "I think you've had enough blood for today," he said wryly. Unsurprisingly, Carolyn looked stunned. He approached slowly, and she didn't move. Ethan hoped the tear was no longer calling her. "Hey, I knew the control I taught you would come in handy one day."

She nodded slightly, and the enforcer heaved a sigh of relief at the confirmation he sought. She drew her gaze to his, a small twist forming at her mouth; not the smile he'd been after.

"She wasn't what I thought."

"I know. She was a bitch," he said, all the while watching Carolyn's face. The hell with it!

He wrapped her rigid form into his arms, hoping the emotion would transfer somehow. "I'm sorry," he whispered. "If I'd been quicker, maybe we could have saved her." The words spilled easily, intending only to comfort. He thanked the powers that be for taking the Lilim rather than Carolyn. He felt her struggle back from his hold but he held on tightly, watching Mario and the chief approach from out of the shadows. How long had they been there? A silent line of guards could be seen at their backs.

The "cavalry" had been too late, leaving the "princess" to save herself.

"Daughter." With that one word, Arthur elicited the very response Ethan had sought. He fought his annoyance as she threw herself into the chief's arms.

"I'm sorry," she said. "You've lost so much." Ethan's eye twitched. If she thought Arthur was upset about the loss of Lena, then… Who was he kidding? Ethan wouldn't even try to put Carolyn right. In fact, if he had any sense at all, he'd get the hell away from the wretched realm at the first chance he got.

Arthur's words were for Carolyn but he met Ethan's gaze over her head. He was enjoying that she cared for him more than her friends. "Hush," Arthur whispered. "What Lena told you was a lie. She wasn't pregnant."

Carolyn tipped her head back and stared at the chief. "You heard that?"

"I don't know why she let you think it." Arthur's expression was tight and unforgiving.

If that was right, then Ethan knew exactly why she'd lied to Carolyn. The bitch was evening the odds for a fight, and she'd almost won in her attempt to push Carolyn into the tear. He felt as though the stench of the thing had seeped in to root itself in his brain. Carolyn's eyes returned to it, and he knew exactly what was going through her mind. She didn't disappoint.

"We need to fix that." Her gaze encompassed Ethan and Mario as she drew away from Arthur.

"That's not our responsibility," said Ethan with a pointed look at Arthur. "It was Lena's creation."

"It could have killed Carolyn," Mario added unhelpfully.

"I know that." Ethan raged inwardly. Arthur was going to get exactly what he wanted, and that was bad enough, but the enforcers were going to do the donkey work for him. The calculated gleam in Arthur's eyes didn't inspire confidence. He knew that the amount of energy they'd need to raise for a repair would be crippling.

Carolyn gave her father an apologetic look. "We must repair the tear and reinstate proper gateway access." Indirectly, she was blaming him for the tear. The thing would never have been created if Arthur hadn't blocked realm access. Of course, following that rationale, Carolyn could still have been coaxed to another realm on the Lilim's whim. *Regular gateways don't mutilate their users.*

Ethan understood that the monitoring system in Empustat was superior to all other realms. Carolyn had been true to her word, so why not reinstate them?

The answer came quickly. Ethan was not to be trusted. He stopped to examine Carolyn's face, smudged with dirt and tears. How could Arthur stand to say "No" to her?

"I know how upset you must be about Lena." Carolyn told Arthur, but he slowly shook his head.

"No, daughter. I am disappointed, and she is not dead. Death would have been her sentence if she had remained." Carolyn's eyes flicked to the dark sheen of blood splattered across the ground. She hadn't realised that the spray had caught her as well. Arthur wiped a blood spot from beneath her eye and examined it, rubbing the stain between thumb and forefinger. "I expect one of your shadow demons guided her out, but not without injury. The traitor is still alive."

Man, but that was cold. Ethan, who thought he'd seen everything, couldn't help but baulk at Arthur's calm dismissal of his longstanding partner.

"The blood used to create the tear can close it?" Carolyn's question gained weight as Ethan and Mario locked gazes. The creator's blood would lessen the cost of repair. Under the tear's glow, Ethan was the first to draw his blade. Whatever the lady wanted.

Arthur stepped towards the men. "My subject – my steel."

Fine. It irked Ethan to accept Arthur's small concession. Ethan nodded, passing his blade to Carolyn as he accepted Arthur's knife. His hands were steadier than they had any right to be. No stranger to blood rituals, he was the best choice. Carolyn guided him to a large spatter on a thick tree root. Arthur's weapon felt alien – in a good way, the hilt plain and a comfortable fit in his palm. He knew it had performed many rites though few conducted with pure intentions. The collected blood clung to the polished, minutely scarred metal.

He couldn't quite believe he was going to destroy their only method of escape. Perhaps Arthur would give points for trust. The chief hadn't agreed to reinstate gateway access before Saturday, but it had been *implied*. Not that Ethan trusted him but Carolyn wanted this, and he knew the realms *yearned* for the repair.

Ethan approached the ragged opening and tuned his energies for the ritual. Shoulders straight, he lifted the knife high and thrust the blooded blade into the centre of the tear. He would have to keep it there until the spell was activated. Carolyn and Mario took their positions at his side.

"Do you want *me* to activate it?" Her honeyed summer scent washed over him for a blessed moment, pushing back the diseased odour of the tear.

"No. I'll ... wait." Why had he given her his blade? His gaze shifted to Mario. He didn't want to ask for *Carolyn's* blood but *his* would do just fine.

Seeing his intent, Carolyn shook her head.

"You're right, of course," whispered Mario, his eyes fastening on Carolyn. "We need powerful blood and I don't see your dad offering."

"Not getting any younger, you two." Ethan momentarily pondered the stupidity of trusting the chief enough to use his blade. Not only the arm he held aloft but all the muscles throughout his body burned at carrying a higher user's magically infused blade. Perhaps Arthur had planned for him to collapse into the tear with the effort.

"I want to do this," said Carolyn, and Ethan caught her ghost of a smile. It wasn't fair that she could make his gut churn. "It was my idea after all."

"Just remember that," mumbled Mario, and Ethan felt the instant when the edge of his own blade crossed her palm. It was as though the scent of flowers and honey had exploded into the air. His pain lessened a fraction. Should he be worried at the sensory overload he was experiencing? Mario seemed curiously unaffected by Carolyn's blood sacrifice.

"Is this enough?" Carolyn said as she turned her palm over the blade. As with Lena's blood, it clung to the steel. Were they doing the right thing? Ever the gentleman, Mario tapped Carolyn's palm to heal it without invocation. The little shit had gained serious skills while in Empustat.

Carolyn flexed her hand and placed the blade above Ethan's, in the centre of the tear, all eyes watching as the blood from both blades gathered together. Ethan was happy to leave the invocation to Mario, the better showman.

"Benedic et cute integrum restituere": bless and restore the integrity of the skin. Nice.

In an instant of confusion, it felt as though Sean had reached through the opening and bolstered their spell.

"You only had to ask." Arthur sounded surprised and irritated — an unfortunate combination — and Ethan realised his own pain had vanished. Carolyn caught his eye meaningfully. It was high mage power that now wove strength through their ceremony. Kudos to their girl, she had tapped the chief's magic which now flowed through her and at her own direction.

"It just happened. Should I stop?" Her eyes remained closed, focussed as she was on the ritual.

"Sorry, my lord," said Mario, "but it's begun and the old magic may not take kindly to us leaving the job half done."

"Agreed." Arthur's power rose clearly during the process. As the tear filled with pure healing ether, the air flashed bright for an instant and the ground beneath them shuddered. "Interesting," Arthur said, and it seemed to Ethan that his irritation had given way to something else… a barely restrained sense of triumph perhaps.

In the light of it, Ethan's satisfaction waned. He caught Carolyn's eye, and she gave a telling smirk. He realised her tapping of Arthur hadn't been as accidental as she'd insinuated. Mario sported a half smile as well. At least the price for this would be paid by the one most able to afford it.

CHAPTER 24

Jonah

Jonah was aware that the team wanted him but he needed to collect enough data to give them a proper report. Mel liked him to be thorough. Perhaps today was the day she would look at him – even for a minute – the way she looked at Note. In fairness, the Kistatus would often receive that special regard for no reason Jonah could work out. The Agency helicopter was about to rise from the ground with its cargo when Mel's message arrived. He looked up in time to catch what appeared to be lightening or a meteor blaze crossing the sky towards him, where he now floated as a shadow beside the tear.

"Oh, Shit!" his lovely Mel would be saying about now. Jonah laughed in delight as two agents tried to get out of the lightening's path. They leapt into the water from the sea wall and everyone else scattered. The instant of the strike, the Faery realised that the tear had vanished. There was simply nothing there, the meteor impacting with a deafening crack, crumpling against the sea wall.

He recognised Note's power – how had the demon found such a form? – and considered his timing unlucky indeed. Screams continued as the earth below Jonah split and a large crack appeared in the stone wall close to where the tear had been. Flames shot from another crack that had appeared on the promenade. It spread out in a wide star shaped pattern. Even in shadow, Jonah could feel the scorching blast, though it did him no harm. People fled, choking.

A middle aged man jumped onto the top of an Agency vehicle, shouting insults at the armed officers as they fled to safer ground. "Power in the wrong hands..." began the fanatic, but his monologue was cut short as the earth tilted once more and the vehicle rolled forward to wedge itself front first in a fissure in the concrete surface.

Jonah thought the Agency softer than he remembered; not exactly weaker, but Jonah had become strong. Morgan didn't agree with that, not exactly. She said he would be on a learning curve until the day he died. Jonah had learned so much; he didn't know how many days he had left. He only knew he needed to win another kiss from Mel before that last day came.

Turning his attention back to Note, he saw that a female agent had almost reached the fallen demon. Jonah fell upon Note immediately; he could at least hide the Kistatus from view. Their forms became indistinguishable among the debris of the crash. With Note's integral abilities, it wasn't much of a challenge. For a moment, he considered if anyone – Mel – would find out if he chose to leave Note for the Agency to discover.

In a matter of minutes, the magic users on site were joined by many more. He was interested in the way they carried out their work with varying degrees of efficiency. It was almost an hour later when they'd finished with their machines, labels and little plastic bags. Jonah rarely thought back to his time in the Agency. It was a shock to realise he hadn't felt fear since he'd left their control. The Faery trembled when he at last regained his form to answer the insistently buzzing device in his pocket. Mel would be angry with him. In hindsight, his curiosity about the agents had been a mistake. He should have taken Note straight to the others without delay, something he now put to rights.

Once in the basement room in Feeding Frenzy, the Faery found out it was worse than he could have imagined. Mel sobbed at the sight of the broken Kistatus and Sean ordered everyone out. Jonah had hoped to comfort Mel in a quieter part of the building, but she was too busy shouting at Sean, telling him that Note needed to change into something without bones.

"Kistatus have bones," Mace said, and he told Sean that the group could share their animal mage forms. Jonah realised that if he'd bound properly to the group, they could all have changed to shadow. He experienced a brief, dizzying relief that he hadn't agreed and was consequently still special.

"I don't think he's breathing." Rake had his hand on Note's chest and Sean moved almost quicker than the Faery could catch. Jonah had stayed at the bathroom door for a full minute before he realised that usual rules didn't apply. He could barely see past Mace, Rake and Mel but felt and saw the edges of magic radiating from Sean. Water had rapidly filled the bath; it ran from the overhead shower and gushed from the taps. If Sam were here, he would chastise them for wasting so much water.

Jonah shadowed in to observe from high up on the wall and saw that

Sean and Note were in the bath together. Note was still clothed but the dark mage had taken off his shirt, now kneeling in the water, his hands pressed against Note's torso. Jonah imagined that the weight of the mage wouldn't help with the problem of the crushed bones. He focussed on the pair, trying to blot out the terrible hiccoughing sobs coming from Mel.

"Whatever the hell it is, Sean. You need to do it right now!" she implored.

Sean sent her an aggravated glare, making Jonah wish the dark mage had also been broken. His long hair was soaked and plastered to his face and shoulders. He didn't look comfortable. "Hush, girl, and turn off the bloody water." Mace and Rake beat her to it, and she slumped onto the tiled floor, almost at eye-level with Note.

"Don't you dare die without finding your girl," she whispered. Mace and Rake shared the type of expression that Jonah had often seen in the medical drama he liked to watch with Mel … and sometimes Morgan. It was how people looked at each other before someone expired. Jonah hoped that when the time came for *him* to die, Mel would be the only one present and there wouldn't be so much noise or liquid.

Sean's hands flared silver and then black over Note's chest. Eyes lifted, Sean's body then convulsed. Mel shrieked, grabbing Mace's hand and plunging it into the water. "I don't care where she is, I'm drawing Morgan's too." The bathwater bubbled and Note turned silver, along with Sean, Mace and Mel. Then Sean fell forward as Note was suddenly no longer there.

"We did it wrong," shouted Mace, and unbelievably, Mel laughed.

"Sean? Guys? I love you all, you know that, right?" Mel said.

"Not out of the woods yet, my dear. He needs to change back." Sean told her as Jonah watched with interest as a large river snake slid slowly to the surface.

Jonah knew he would never forget the horrific sound Note then made when his friends forced his change to a Kistatus form – Sean said it was a stronger one – and then back to human. Jonah wasn't sure, but believed Note was well enough to complete the final change without the others, but they continued to fuel him even as he complained. Mace called him a stubborn ass which Jonah thought to be about right.

Sean and Mel continued to work on the Kistatus for a time, checking all his vital functions before making him comfortable on the sofa. His limbs were as straight as anyone's and that alone seemed to be cause for celebration.

Worried about telling the team his story, Jonah was surprised at the reactions he got.

"You did great," Mace said, and Jonah was cheerfully high-fived by the Mow and Rake. Sean thanked him for his quick actions and Mel smiled. They understood he'd had to wait for the magic users to go from the site.

Sean thought the time he'd spent in shadow had probably helped save the demon's life.

Jonah experienced a very new emotion that made him feel full and sort of happy, though he hadn't eaten anything. Mel said he should be proud, so Jonah supposed that "pride" was a good name for the sensation he felt. Mel was the last to thank him and he thought his rapidly beating heart would burst from his chest. Her eyes were moist when she wrapped her arms around him and he basked in her attention, now content he'd done exactly the right thing at the site, if not for the reasons Mel would have preferred.

Driven on by his new feeling, the team's approval and Mel's excitement, he deliberately placed a hand at the back of her head. Having planned this moment too many times to count and uncaring of his audience, he swooped down to press his lips to hers. She had kissed him several times, always taking him by surprise. Now, it was his turn.

She gasped and clung to him, and when her mouth moved against his, he thought he might come apart from the fierce, possessive joy that overwhelmed him. He forced his body to remain solid; warm, compact and perfect for having Mel wrapped around him.

He felt the loss of her lips as she drew away, gaping for a long moment, blinking only when Sean mentioned something about the joy of having a room full of quiet enforcers.

"Um, wow," she said eventually, coming back on form. She encompassed the others in the sweep of her arm. "And that concludes our demonstration on how best to kiss your fellow enforcers."

"You want them all to kiss you?" Jonah's euphoria slipped away in the silence. Rake's grey eyes twinkled, and he thought Mace looked hopeful. Jonah felt a surge of dislike before laughter erupted. "I expect," said Mace, between guffaws, "that you are the only one brave enough to try that with the little mage."

Morgan burst into the room, taking in the scene with wild eyes. "Who needed the dra— Oh, thank God you're back, Jonah." Her eyes grew round when they saw Note, sprawled on the couch. "Crap, Sean. What the hell did you do to him?" Note raised a hand to show that the crisis was over. She scrambled over him to find the remote control for the television. "It's all over the news that the harbour's been hit by a meteor or something. It's a mess down there."

"You shouldn't have gone," scolded Sean angrily. "We are a team!" *And they needed her.*

"I knew you'd stop me," she mumbled. "I needed to see if I could do something."

"It was irresponsible, Morgan. You could have jeopardised our entire operation." The mage flinched at his own cold tone.

"It won't happen again."

"I could return and find what's happening now," said Jonah, relishing the tightening of Mel's hold on him.

"No, you can't go back," Morgan sighed. "I have no idea what magic they're using and Carolyn's not due until Saturday."

"Yes," agreed Sean, seeming to collect his thoughts. "We need to hope for the best, continue our watch remotely," he directed at Morgan, "and we will follow a plan."

"So, what do we do right now?"

Sean's satisfied gaze strayed to Note. "We celebrate," he whispered, relaxing back between Mace and Rake who now sat at Taz's table. Jonah waited for someone to produce the amber liquid that would normally accompany such statements but it didn't appear. On this occasion, everyone seemed content to "celebrate" by doing nothing. Feeling Mel's warmth resting at his side, Jonah felt he could die at this very moment, and be happy about it.

CHAPTER 25

Edward

"Great, I'll see you tomorrow," said Edward, grinning as Rhona danced out of his reach.

"Don't do me any favours", she returned, throwing him a nasty look. He would think she hated him if her words hadn't been tempered by the glint in her eyes. It was only a matter of time before her "couldn't give a damn" act crumbled under his charm.

"You have a taste for the most interesting women," said Hecaton from the shadows, and Edward bristled with annoyance. "Another tough nut to crack," he continued, and Edward's face whitened with the reminder. "There are so many better choices available," Hecaton taunted, "or do you simply enjoy women with a little fight in them."

Edward knew the High mage was testing him, and he struggled to gain control. "You might be under Lucas's command to keep an eye on me, Hecaton, but I don't have to like it."

"It's *your* likes that concern me. The relationships you cultivate do not tend to end well."

"You have no right to speak to me that way." Edward ground his teeth. He didn't trust that the high mage had taken an interest in Rhona. The man was pure poison. It could be no accident that Hecaton had stepped in when the girl had actually begun warming to Edward. She challenged him in a way that none of the others had managed.

Not challenging, Sarah had just been special.

I killed her.

Hecaton was quick to use anything to unsettle him but he wished that the Sarah incident could be forgotten. Edward couldn't even damn the high mage as he was nothing if not damned already.

Despite the obvious, Rhona was nothing like Sarah. They had both been selected for the castle, Sarah traded from a life of squalor, and Edward hadn't understood her problem. Positioned as a server to the court, her skillset had placed her where she would best fit in.

He had often wondered in hindsight if it had been that or the lustful thoughts of the acquisitions officer that had led to her placement. Sarah had been well looked after, provided with food and shelter. She'd known that many of the women who served performed a variety of services, and always willingly. After a few weeks, Edward had overheard the complaints – much like Cassandra's problem with Rhona – that she'd been misplaced.

He had been very young and really liked the girl. In those days, inexperience had kept him away from women. Sarah had been different. Her peers had taken advantage of her sweetness but she had never grumbled when he'd found her engaged in the most menial of tasks. He discovered later that she'd done extra work to compensate for being "unavailable" for entertainment purposes. He would seek her out and chat every day, if only for a few minutes, just to see her face. One day, she hesitantly confided that she was to be sent elsewhere. Edward couldn't allow that.

He hadn't wanted her sent away to work in a factory or a field somewhere distant. She had been the first girl to spark his interest in his second year in Skean. He'd intended asking Lucas if he could keep her. Edward had never asked for anything, but he knew the chief would make a gift of the girl if he asked. These were his thoughts when he'd led Sarah to the widow's walk on the south castle turret. He couldn't keep his eyes off her as he'd explained – as it had been explained to him – how things would work for them.

She'd refused to look at him during the entire time, explaining in a soft voice that she was happy to do menial tasks in her meaningless life. To ask for more was wrong and that it shamed those who enforced the traditions of the castle. It only made Edward angry. He had worked hard and spilled a lot of blood in an effort to fit in to the demands or exceed the ways of the castle.

This girl only had to appear beautiful and bat her lashes to be accepted. At the time, he knew he was oversimplifying, but his emotion had fuelled thoughts that his mother –pre-Lucas then – would have baulked at.

Looking back, he knew she had been dressed and prepared for him. Her hair had shone like black gold and her skin made soft with fragrant oils. She looked exotic and stunning and when she eventually turned her limpid gaze to his, he'd come alive with anticipation.

Edward had failed to listen, or maybe he'd been under a spell she'd unconsciously set on him. He remembered reaching out to kiss her – she wanted it, right? And at first, he thought she had thawed, her words uttered purely to alleviate the guilt of having ensnared the prince. Her lips were soft, yielding, but then he'd tasted the salt of her tears. Gentle hands had closed around his face, and he'd felt her warm breath at his ear.

"You are lost."

Lost indeed!

She'd had both legs over the railing, and Edward had laughed, as though she were playing a sick prank on him. He was still reeling from the excitement of having her fit so well in his arms. He should have known better. Reaching for her, she'd released one hand, her eyes imploring.

His confusion had burned away, sudden understanding bringing him to focus. "Please, Sarah. Let me help. We can work something out."

"I don't want to be lost, too," she'd said, and let go of the railing.

The expression she'd worn had been one he'd seen often on his mother's face. Not despair, that was the emotion that usually followed … resignation … a deep powerful acceptance of what she couldn't change. On more than one occasion he'd urged Lucas to bring forward her Claim renewal ceremony that would then grant her respite for months at a time.

Rhona was *not* Sarah.

What he felt for Rhona deserved exploration, and he would take care with her. Suspecting she loved herself too much to employ drastic measures, he planned to avoid the widow's walkway just the same. Sarah had been burned into his memory for a long time but Rhona's appearance had brought him to relive that earlier misfortune but minus the ache it usually brought. Without any doubt, Edward knew he belonged with the monster that was Lucas.

He couldn't properly explain his refusal to take Kistatus form. Could it be that he was monster enough himself without such physical manifestation? He felt it to be more than that. What if it prompted the magical change in him that his father longed for? As things stood, he was a skilled warrior. Tapping into latent skills would, he considered, ultimately prove him to be a demon and set him on a course from which there may be no hope of salvation.

CHAPTER 26

Siren

Siren wondered at the weirdness of her life as she slid her phone back into her bag. Miranda's call had been short and cryptic and she didn't know what to think. Ella bounced unhelpfully at her side in the kitchen. Having had little sleep the previous night — she had come home very late — it was unsettling to see the Faery bursting with energy. "Do you think we should get a dog?" she said.

"A cat or a dog might be nice," Siren agreed warily, pausing to tear open a bag of coffee grounds. She set the timer for later in the afternoon when they expected to return. It was silly, really, but the place was as close to a home as she could have imagined. The smell of fresh brewed coffee when she returned would just add a sweet torment. Self-torture with her wishes was one thing, but she didn't want Ella to get too comfortable with their arrangement. Both were still subject to Miranda's whims. "I don't believe we'll get to stay here for long," she said carefully. "Miranda seems to think that the witches made too good a job of concealing us."

And it was true. The Agency head hadn't been able to visit. When Siren had gone out to meet her only the previous day, she hadn't been able to lead her in, much to Miranda's frustration. It was only when Miranda left that Siren had been able to return to the house. It was nice security, but something over which Miranda had no control. She intended to put the matter to rights.

Siren was glad she'd insisted on jackets when they emerged onto the beach at Seamill. Her phone pinged several times, indicating that reception had returned after their walk through the village. It was a decent meeting place, if a bit open. Ella and Siren had an amazing view of countryside leading onto a sandy beach beyond which the Isle of Arran rose through a glittering expanse of water.

"You know she's just pissed that she can't locate the house." The Faery tapped a nail on Siren's phone. It wasn't simply that, though. Miranda had said that the property had literally fallen off the map after the coven's interference. "Those witches really knew their stuff."

Tap tap … tap tap. "They did at that, Ella." Siren opened the love heart nylon shopper she'd brought and handed it to the Faery. "Why don't you find some more of those pretty shells and we'll make a collage or something when we get home."

Ella sighed wearily and Siren was sure – although she said nothing – that the girl somehow knew of her communications.

John?

Where the hell have you been?

So nice to hear from you too.

The system's all screwed up. You're showing just a few miles away.

Ta da! So near yet so far, John. She explained the situation with Miranda, that she'd sent her to the safe house with Ella.

No more Tracing for you until we sort this out. His exasperation came through clearly on their link. *You need to pick up a disposable phone and – never mind. I'll have someone meet you at the hotel, there. Get your little friend to join you for a spa treatment or go for a swim.*

Way ahead of you, John. I called earlier, and they said to stop by. I'll arrange for a brochure and timetable from them. Signing out.

Me too. Loads happening but nothing you should be thinking about. Take care.

John?

No reply. *That* was just annoying. She was going to worry now. Her attention was drawn back to Ella. There was no doubt that the witches had done something to her. In all her time at the beta site she'd never seen the Faery as "normal" as she had been since their arrival. Sometimes Ella's behaviour would be a bit erratic but Siren thought she was trying to mask the changes, which meant the Faery had a good instinct for self-preservation.

"I could only find this one I liked." The girl pressed a perfect shell into Siren's palm.

"And uninhabited, too," she teased lightly. "You're learning." Siren admired the colours running through it. "We should take a walk every day and collect more of these." It would give her a regular time to chat with John and catch up on news.

"I know you're worried we won't get to stay," said Ella suddenly, "but as long as I do everything they ask, we can remain here for ever if we like." Siren watched Ella flick her hair over her shoulder with an air of confidence. Revising her thoughts on the Faery, she understood the need to believe, but Miranda never made frivolous promises with demons, herself being no exception.

"I don't know if I want to stay indefinitely. I have ... family."

Ella gripped Siren's jacket, her eyes showing another flash of the old Ella. "No, they're not like you. You can't see..." the Faery drew away, her hands pressed to her lips as if she could take back the words. Then she smiled, a big "I know something you don't know" smile. This could be bad. Siren warred with her thoughts. Her position with Miranda was secure-ish. If she found out that Ella could share secrets, though, then ... well, the woman wasn't famed for her kind and forgiving nature.

"It's okay, Ella. You don't need to tell me."

Ella made a frustrated noise. "I *want* to share it – and now I know I can – but you must promise, Siren."

"I promise I'll keep you out of harm's way as much as I can."

Ella giggled. "I liked Judy for a while, but I *see* that it's just to keep me compliant. She's not always nice, and talks about me behind my back." Siren frowned. It seemed like they were going the scenic route to find her answers.

"I don't know what to say about that, Ella. Sometimes people are really affected by what life throws at them, and between me and you, I don't think Judy's had much to be happy about."

Ella pointed at her, accusingly. "See. This is what I mean. I get that now. I *realise* you're sparing my feelings. I wouldn't have known that before the witches spell. Judy's not really my friend," she sighed. "None of them are."

"Okay," and Siren threw her hands up. "Okay, Ella." She was desperate to return to what they'd started talking about – her family – but she couldn't bring herself to stop the Faery in the middle of her discovery. "You need to hide the changes."

"But–"

"Not from me, but you have been trying to hide them a little, haven't you?" Ella nodded half-heartedly.

"The Agency can't find out because they'll want to do more–" About to say "Experiments" she settled for "Stuff". Siren's lips pursed in thought. Whatever her discoveries, Ella was still very much a child who needed reassurance, stability and so many other things that the list could go on for ever. It was sad that Agency life would never provide them. Ella had cast her in a position of responsibility and Siren hoped she wouldn't disappoint.

"I don't want to tell you what to do, Ella. I can give advice but you need to work out for yourself what's best. Would Miranda put you back at the beta site if she knew you were different?" They both knew the answer. "You're curious about what's happened to you. Me too, but Miranda is the most inquisitive person I've ever met." And she really wasn't above taking the Faery apart to gain an understanding and replicate the changes in other subjects.

"You're scared for me, aren't you?" Ella seemed delighted. "This is great, Siren. I've never had that before." Siren's heart squeezed at the sad observation.

"I'm here for you, Ella. Don't abuse it. Now … getting back to what you were saying."

Siren tried not to show how much she was affected by Ella's story, but her eyes prickled. She chose to think it was homesickness rather than the sharp sting of betrayal. Siren was a fool for caring about a woman for whom the concept of love didn't exist.

At first, she wanted to pass Ella's story off as the product of her imagination. The Faery had been asleep when she'd "dream walked" to Miranda and visited the Siren realm. But the details were so clear, and the Investor? If what Ella had said was true then Siren was a complete failure as a spy. How long had her sisters been used? It was inconceivable that Miranda had played them as the Faery seemed to think.

The doors of the hotel now loomed before them, and Ella moved to stand in front of her. "Miranda said you would leave if you knew." That was a fair point. Siren didn't doubt Ella's belief that the situation was as she saw it, but the woman could have set them up, feeding them the information. As a test?

"Why didn't she compel you to secrecy?"

"Haven't you worked it out?" Ella's straight face broke into a grin which was infectious, though Siren had yet to find cause to break out the champagne. "That ring gives her some protection and power over people and demons. I must become a … well, a 'nothing' when I leave my body."

Siren watched Ella with newly appraising eyes. "You are definitely not a 'nothing'," she said earnestly, and Ella snorted with laughter.

"I'll be exactly *that* whenever I like." Her gaze strayed to the hotel notices, and she lifted an eyebrow at Siren.

"Yes. Let's see if we can get you in for a manicure."

One thing was clear to Siren as she left Ella to her treatment. Their village retreat was the safest place in the world for them. For an instant, there was a brush against her awareness, as though someone were watching her. The feeling vanished as soon as it had appeared, and she suspected her chat with Ella had seriously unnerved her. It didn't, though, quite justify hauling Ella away from her manicure and cancelling the meeting that John had set up.

CHAPTER 27

Hecaton

Hecaton had awoken with searing agony in his chest. He knew it was referred from one of his closest. His first thought of the chief was quickly dismissed. He could feel Lucas's presence, unchanged since he'd left him that evening. Robing up, he walked through to his mirror and scryed for his son. The sight that greeted him was unexpected. The Earth high mage was with him, and Hecaton was reassured that his investment was in competent hands.

He pondered the value of the enforcers, each alone amounting to nothing special. As a team, and with Notechis a part of their sanctioned alliance, they were a force that was … unusually poignant, with the potential for all manner of applications.

Perhaps now the boy would learn to gain control of his instincts and show some restraint before acting on his urges. Prior to gifting Notechis his power, Hecaton could barely remember a time when he'd been fuelled – and crippled – by the passions of youth. If his son failed to tether his impulses, his love for the destroyer would kill him.

***

"I trust that all is well," said Lucas, his eyes opening as Hecaton drew near the chief's bed. The girl warming it slid out gracefully. Lucas held his gaze until they were alone.

"I wished only to check on *your* welfare," responded the high mage.

"You want to speak to me about Edward."

"Astute as ever, my liege, but we do not have to discuss it now." He didn't like the dark circles under Lucas's eyes. They had grown, and in the dim light, the skin of his human form appeared grey.

194

"No, we've put it off long enough. You feel that my son is not ready — may never be equipped to lead the realm, and I fear you are right." Hecaton smiled grimly. It had taken Lucas a while to reach his conclusion. "Even now, he clings to his humanity and I am partly to blame." Hecaton curbed his inclination to disagree as the chief's gaze sharpened. "I know about the munitions."

Hecaton could at least quickly allay *those* fears. "My liege, we have lost nothing else." Notchis's infusion had boosted the realm magic but the effects wouldn't last indefinitely. There were no plans to replenish stores until the future of the realm had been secured. Hecaton was surprised that Edward had told his father about the arms. He would rather spare his chief the worry and act tirelessly to that end. Whether Lucas connected the boost to the realm with Notechis's visit was less easily determined.

"What do you suggest, my chief?"

"We do the transfer." Lucas moved slowly to get up from his bed, allowing Hecaton to guide him to a fireside chair. His chief required careful handling but the time for denial had passed.

"And if he can't hold it, another will take it from him."

Hecaton sat across from Lucas, watching the flickering shadow play on his strong features. The high mage knew some of what the future held, but losing the powerful chief was going to be difficult. "It's not that the boy doesn't show some promise." He could tell Lucas *some* of what he wanted to hear.

"I know." The chief smiled, the action highlighting the ravages that Notechis's bite had wrought. "My son is a warrior, but he is not true to us. My mate did him no favours by keeping him away these many years." Lucas leaned forward to light a taper from the fire and placed it to the charge in his pipe. Inhaling deeply, he relaxed into his chair and allowed the vapour to work its magic. Hecaton had known him long enough to see that his chief had come to an important decision. He hoped it would be the right one.

Lucas's eyes flashed copper from the effects of the drug. "I feel it," he said with a throaty chuckle, "the power I've always used without much effort — it is slipping away. We must do the transfer before it's too late."

Hecaton stiffened with anticipation and met his chief's gaze squarely. "In your current state, you would not survive the exchange."

"Yes, I'll need a little help." He offered Hecaton the pipe which the mage set precisely on its stand. "I will miss you most."

"And I you, my chief," answered Hecaton, knowing it to be true.

"Change is sometimes good."

"Not usually for old men like us."

"You're not so old." Lucas barked a short laugh which turned into a retching cough. He caught his breath, continuing, "I will speak to my son in the morning.”

Note

“How can I trust you when you pull stunts like that?” Note knew he was being unreasonable but no-one really believed that Carolyn’s father would send her home on Saturday. The tear had been a travesty of a thing, but it had given him much needed peace of mind to have it there for his backup plan. Sam’s footfalls were heavy as he approached and placed a small drink in his hand. Note downed it and gasped, eyes tearing up unexpectedly.

“Scots whisky, my boy. That’ll put hairs on your chest.”

“He didn’t lose the hairs on his chest,” said Jonah helpfully. “He crushed the bones of his body.”

“That he did, boy,” said Sam seriously. He lay an arm around the Faery and ushered him through to the others waiting in the next room.

“That’s exactly why you can trust me.” Sean peered at him intently and Note shook his head. Making use of an existing tear was different from creating one. If things went as Note expected, he couldn’t ask Sean to help him create another one between the realms. Apart from the moral concerns, the Protectorate would never allow it. Morgan had said as much when she’d brought him his breakfast this morning.

Using Feeding Frenzy as a base had been a good idea but the basement section they occupied was separated by thin walls. The others were trying to give him and Sean some space but Note could hear their whispering so loudly it was as though they were in the room *with* him.

“Jonah kept you alive, Note. I can’t explain what happened, but you returned here in human form. Crushed, as Jonah said.” Note didn’t need reminding of his otherness but Sean pressed on. “It was Mel who suggested we force your change. Carolyn is fine and you are well. That’s a result in anyone’s book.”

“But now we have no access.” He had revisited the tear site with Jonah, Rake and Mel. There was nothing left of it. Fresh concrete had been poured everywhere, it seemed. Even the rocks had been bleached clean of possible evidence.

“Does this mean you don’t need me anymore?” The chiming of Jonah’s enquiry caused Note to get up from his seat. “Just come back in, guys. I can hear every word. And Jonah?” the hybrid appeared with Mel stuck to his side. “Don’t be ridiculous. You are *essential.*” Jonah now beamed.

Note suspected he would have offered similar assurances to any member of the team. He tried not to listen to the jeering voice in his head. He hadn’t a clue how he’d transformed and got to the tear the day before, but he was sure he would have made it through safely *if* it hadn’t been sealed. His chance of replicating the process, according to Sean, was nil. His plans were worthless without Jonah.

"The skin of the realms has been repaired." It didn't help for Sean to say the words aloud. Note sagged on his feet, not quite recovered from his collision. It was as though the Earth had released a breath it hadn't known it was holding. He could still feel it – relief at the tear's repair – but it made Carolyn's return seem like an impossible dream.

Note couldn't have cared less about the realms at that moment. He could only focus on Carolyn being kept from him. If she wasn't back by midnight on Saturday, then his contemplation of the unthinkable would become a reality.

Edward

Thoughts of Rhona and Sarah had plagued Edward into the morning. He couldn't be happy that she was training under Hecaton. He was certain the high mage had only taken her on so he could mess with his tactics.

The knowledge drove him to the arena where he could safely vent. That it didn't work to plan was a nuisance. In less than an hour he'd alienated all of his friends during practise by sparring like an animal in the pits. Both Krisp and Yanik required healers' services.

Lucas wanted him to accept a change that would effectively erase the man he'd become, leaving a Lucas substitute in his stead. If all went to plan with the transfer, and Lucas's power passed to him, he wouldn't be burdened by further negativity. At least, that's what he understood by it all – so why was he not comforted?

Emerging from the dusty heat of the training square, Edward knew he should clean up before seeing his father and Hecaton. Though wooden blades were used for practise, blue-grey splatters of Kistatus blood covered his skin and clothes. Wielded with determined strength, even wood could split skin and shatter egos.

"Taking out your frustrations on the men?" drew Edwards's eyes to lift, narrowing against the brightness of the high mage's full demonic gaze. At his side, Rhona's yellow robe sported a single red stripe on its hood, denoting her apprenticeship level. Aesthetically, they looked good together. Hecaton, imposing in full Kistatus form, his bright markings complemented by Rhona's colours. With her knee length robe, the clothes beneath were of the same dark red as her stripe.

Beautiful as ever, she didn't look pleased to see him. Belatedly, he remembered that working with the healers was one of the crappy jobs students did. She would think he was trying to impress her, or worse, that it was an attempt to put her off the work she'd chosen. He considered making a crack about it "helping to build character", but Rhona had more than enough "character" already. "Well, off you go, girl," said Hecaton, brusquely. "Time waitss for no-one." Rhona scowled and brushed past Edward towards the barracks.

"Tsk, tsk. You simply can't find good help these days. I trussst that you left her with a challenging mess today."

"What's done is done." How difficult could it be to work a healing charm or two? Eyes drawn to the impressive markings on Hecaton's Kistatus flesh, Edward felt his frustration return anew. His father believed that he could take his power and be guided by Hecaton. What Lucas failed to realise was that the high mage would never respect his leadership. After hundreds of years under strong rule, Edward knew he wasn't up to the job, and if *he* believed that, then the people were well aware of it too.

He wasn't naïve enough to think there wasn't a backup plan if they were unsuccessful but Edward hoped it was a good one, one he could survive.

CHAPTER 28

Note

“**S**am, are you sure you’re okay about this?” Note felt weirdly calm about meeting Amanda after her removal from Skean but he was worried about Sam. Just because she had asked after the caretaker, it didn’t mean she would welcome him with open arms.

“I don’t want to stop you, boy. You *should* be here.”

“Not that, Sam,” Morgan interjected from behind as they walked down the length of the corridor towards Amanda’s rooms. “He’s talking about *you*. She remembers you from before.”

“From before,” Sam repeated. “Yes, she does.” The difficulty was that Sam didn’t remember *her*. “She wanted to see me, Lad, and Sean thinks I might help to keep her calm...” The big man’s voice dropped off in thought. Sean was busy elsewhere, but he’d charged Note and Morgan with the task of supervising the visit. If Sam was offering support, then Note hoped it would take the edge off the effect Note might have on her. After his brush with the tear he had healed well ... better than ever, actually, and it didn’t upset him too much that it was due largely to Hecaton’s power gift.

“Well, just remember, Sam, no matter how impressed she is with you, you’re still ours.”

Sam’s smile was sad. “I’m different from who she remembers.”

Morgan tossed her bright locks back from her face and caught Note’s eye meaningfully. “That’s why we’ll be with you, Sam. Who knows *how* she’ll react. Amanda thought you had died when she came back to Earth after having Carolyn.”

“I wish I could remember more about those days.”

“Hey,” Morgan cajoled amiably. “For now you’re going to work your

199

own special magic with Amanda." Note was uncomfortable with them using him to remind Amanda of the evils the chiefs had perpetrated. No-one could underestimate the effects of the claiming bond, and she would be experiencing the dips and surges that came along with the separation.

Note suspected that with Carolyn's father Amanda must have shared a weaker connection which had helped her to avoid Protectorate control and raise Carolyn and Edward for fifteen uninterrupted years on Earth.

"Oh, hi Pierre." Morgan smiled at the enforcer who rose to greet them from his post in the corridor.

"How wonderful. You couldn't stay away from me." His words were teasing but his expression tightened at the sight of Sam. He threw both arms around the former enforcer before falling into the traditional warrior's greeting.

Note laughed at the big man's bemused expression. Sam was aware of much, but Pierre had left him stuck for words. "The lady, I expect, will be delighted to see you," Pierre said.

They found Amanda curled on a sofa, a book in her hand. She slowly closed it without marking her page and Note watched as Sam approached cautiously, his palms facing her. Amanda's eyes rested on Note briefly, a flicker of emotion before she favoured the man stepping towards her. Yes, thought Note, Sean was right when he'd suggested the visit. This was a good reaction, one reasonable to expect.

Disbelief – recognition – shock – and then there was a calculating gleam in her eye. Neither he nor Morgan reached them in time as she rushed to greet him with a kiss.

It was a brief, full-on-the-mouth affair. But more, somehow. The air crackled as Pierre bolstered the wards on the doors. Morgan cast a strand of power to join his and Note followed suit. If there was a problem, then Pierre could quickly draw from Note and Morgan. It was clear from the start that Amanda didn't intend to hurt Sam, but there was more going on than Note could fathom.

Pierre shrugged deceptively from his position near the door. Note could feel the energy they held in check, like a stretched elastic waiting for release. The Frenchman surprised him by sending a wave of calm over the gathering. Note would enjoy learning that trick, it was one his father had never valued.

Released for a short moment, Sam staggered back a step, his face red. Amanda licked her lips, the gleam in her eye shifting somehow. Her eyes strayed briefly again to Note and Morgan who were similarly dismissed before Amanda's attention settled on Pierre. He was deemed at least worthy of a soft scoffing noise.

Sam began to bluster, his voice rough. "I'm only needing to know how you are, Lass. It's not that I mind a kiss, but–" Sam didn't get a chance to explain further for Amanda tipped her head, as if to assess the perfect angle, and set her lips to his once more.

"Is he okay?" mouthed Morgan to Pierre.

"I'll say," Pierre replied aloud. "She's never allowed me her hand to peck, but for Sam…" His eyes, though, contradicted his levity, and so Note and Morgan took positions loosely around the pair. Sam's body remained upright in Amanda's embrace; his hands patted her shoulders as though in comfort. Was it time to break the kiss?

"We should separate them?" Pierre said, nodding, and Morgan moved to touch Amanda.

Not her, the mage's mental voice boomed, as he linked seamlessly with her and Note. His eyes widened in surprise as he clearly now recognised the sheer power Note held in check. *Try for Sam.* Morgan quickly got over the shock of Pierre's link. *I'm not deaf, Pierre.* God, she envied the old ones sometimes.

She placed her hands on Sam's sturdy shoulders. Though he seemed relaxed, Morgan couldn't budge him. A feral growl came from Amanda, but the mage reinforced her efforts.

She's not hurting him. Just stand back. "Let's maintain the field for now." Pierre didn't seem hugely concerned but Note could feel him monitoring everything, from the air currents to each nuance of their protective triangle.

Morgan shuddered slightly, and that's when Amanda's wild magic punched a hole straight through their construct and out into the ether.

CHAPTER 29

Siren

Siren loved the old world charm of the house. Everything looked too new and shiny, though, to be the original fittings but it had been sympathetically renovated. Having lived her whole life from a variety of perspectives, she took none of her privileges for granted. But this? It was as if she'd accidentally found where she needed to be.

Ella had chosen a corner room for Siren with a window on each of its outside walls. The Faery had wasted no time before moving her things into the adjacent suite. She clearly wanted the security. Siren thought they both did. There were ten bedrooms spread over the upper two levels – they had counted – and Siren didn't know if Miranda had bought it outright or whether it was leased. It had been well looked after and the gardens had yet to be explored. Siren planned to do exactly that when she returned from her meeting.

The dull thud of Ella's music became deafening when Siren opened the door to the Faery's room.

"That's it, girls. You are loo…king great. Let's turn it up." The huge flat screen displayed a perky blond in hot pink sweats. The Faery seemed absorbed in learning dance moves, ever so well demonstrated by the onscreen trainer.

Ella stopped jumping for a moment and spun around to face Siren, using a complicated move that made her look every bit as graceful and coordinated as the instructor. Ella was proving to be a fast learner. Siren clapped her hands together.

"You're a natural."

"You really think so?" Ella muted the sound and settled into a repeating side step. "You sure you don't want company?" Her cheeks were flushed from the exertion.

"No. It's okay, I just wanted to let you know I was popping out." She could do without the prearranged visit from Miranda's mage but at least she didn't have to bring anyone back to their new sanctuary. Siren fastened the middle buttons on her light jacket. "I'll bring some ice cream?"

"Sure," said Ella, turning back to her dance work out. "Ask for marshmallow sauce if they have any." Siren couldn't help but grin; the local ice cream was a novelty they could exploit. She closed Ella's door and moved through the house to leave at the front. Her stroll to the gates was pleasant, the previous night's rain having left the ground settled, revealing no hint of the witches' activity on the front lawn. Everything looked perfectly serene.

She came to the wrought iron gates but hesitated before opening them. *Don't be silly.* Miranda's mage was probably just coming to deliver the rest of her stuff. The sense of "wrongness", though, grew stronger as she hurried through and closed the entrance behind her. A tiny shimmer of colour passed beneath her fingers and she silently thanked the witches for their work. Siren stepped out along the short dirt track to the road.

"That's the damndest trick I've ever seen." Siren jumped as Judy's voice sounded from directly beside her. Of all the mages on the payroll why had Miranda sent this one? "I *know* the house is there," continued the Amazonian, and she stepped close to Siren. "I can't see the bloody thing; I can't even sense it."

"It's the witches that Miranda hired."

Judy laughed. The sound was harsh, and the mage wore an expression that conveyed she *knew* something. "Miranda made a mistake that's about to be rectified." Her tone suggested she was talking about more than a problem with the covens' magic. "We're taking you back to the beta site." *Taking you.* What about Ella. What about the illusion of choice or did Siren not merit *that*.

"Miranda didn't mention." As the sun appeared from behind a cloud, Siren slid her sunglasses over her eyes. It would be smart to gather as much information as possible before panicking.

"Ooh. Did she forget to discuss it with you? You should talk to her about that." Siren could have done without Judy's mockingly sympathetic appraisal. "That's what's wrong with relationships nowadays, dear. No trust." She held out her mobile to Siren. "Want to call her? Speed dial-one should get you through."

"No, it's fine." Siren didn't think the mage would bluff. "Whatever Miranda wants." Judy's disappointment was clear. Had she expected a fight? Siren's concern spiked, but she needed to hold it together. Even without the use of magic, Judy scared her, which was too weird as Sean — the more powerful and darker mage – just didn't. She *was* in awe of his magic, but he didn't mean her any harm. What had Siren missed that Miranda had sent Judy to threaten her?

"Let's move, girl. Vasch is waiting right up here." Siren followed Judy's gaze towards the main road. "I don't know what the boss was thinking, putting you up here so close to everything." Siren dutifully followed the mage, wondering what she meant by "everything". Did she have information about Taz's operation in Irvine or was she simply referring to Carolyn's home town of Saltcoats which was even closer? That they were going to a car was good. A drive would allow Siren valuable time.

Judy was quick to dash her hopes. "We'll take the car up to a nice country spot and open a gateway. You'll be having … tea with Miranda within the hour." With a sidelong glance to gauge her reaction, the mage chuckled.

This wasn't right. Their gateway travel would be monitored. It made no sense to do away with Miranda's plans for secrecy, unless… No, they *couldn't* know she was working for Taz or feeding information to the Protectorate. Could they?

"What about the car," said Siren stupidly? If Judy took them through a gateway then her options were going to be seriously limited.

"Like I said, we have agents everywhere in this area." *Agents everywhere?*

"You know, I *will* call Miranda," said Siren, stopping to fish the phone from her bag. Holding the device high in the air, there wasn't a single bar. Damn. Judy smiled widely.

"Morning, ladies." Now on the road, a man passed with an enormous black Labrador in tow. Siren mumbled a reply. The villagers were courteous and sweet. She would miss that. *You're not away already.*

Judy stepped quickly away from the dog that had stopped for a sniff at her. The owner scolded, indulgently ineffective before they moved on. "Wouldn't want to clean up after that," Judy said to Siren with a wink, and strode towards the main road. They passed a lot of people en route. Had the entire community decided to check out their visitors? Judy frowned at Siren, as though she was directly responsible for the influx of traffic and pedestrians. The street was busy with parked cars and groups of people chatting on the pavement.

"Summer fete at the Hydro," explained Siren, spotting a banner. It was clear she'd have to play along with Judy's plan for now, but the business of the village was a plus she could take advantage of. It would be madness to go anywhere with Judy and Vasch while she had the smallest chance of escape.

Timing was everything, she thought as they reached the curb. Aiden Vasch's blond head could be spotted further down the road. Remembering him from her time at the beta site, he hadn't been the most objectionable jailor.

Traffic roared beside them, way too fast for what had to be a thirty mile an hour speed limit. Siren started towards him, but then a noisy group of teenagers passed, separating Siren from Judy. This could be her only chance. Spotting a gap in the traffic, she sprinted across the street, unsure what to do next.

She might have made it all the way had Judy's magic not frozen her in a simple halt spell. The mage had to be really pissed off to use magic in front of the villagers. The wing mirror of a passing car clipped the bag on Siren's trailing arm. The force spun her and she struck the curb with bone jarring force.

A cry left her lips. She'd gambled that the mages wouldn't reveal themselves in public and they probably hadn't, but Siren knew she had lost. The pain of the accident was nothing compared to her frustration. If it hadn't been clear before, her actions had now shown that she had something to hide. Judy and Aiden were going to pick her up like trash at the road side and haul her off.

"Oh, my God, are you all right?" Siren heard the voice as if from a distance.

"I've phoned for an ambulance," called another. "Did you see that? She just stopped in the middle of the road."

Aiden and Judy were now beside her, traffic clogging the road as Siren sat up and vomited into the gutter. "This is a major fuck up. Were you trying to kill her?" Aiden's voice? Siren couldn't see well from one eye. There seemed to be something blocking it.

"Not so pretty now, you silly bitch," said Judy, and Siren could feel the mage hover over her. "That'll scar with human medicine." Siren collapsed on her side in the gutter, a surge of hope taking hold. They were going to leave her here?

"Shut the hell up and let's get away." Judy's voice.

Siren's vision darkened at the edges; she was about to pass out.

"We'll pick her up from the hospital."

Struggling to remain conscious, a persistent wailing noise sprang up in her head, destroying rational thought.

At some point the noise had stopped, replaced by a gentle lethargy that soothed and calmed Siren. All would be well. Slowly, her senses sharpened and she winced as she tried to turn her head. The room wasn't exactly quiet, not with the electronic beeping of the heart monitor beside her, but she was now aware of a presence that didn't register as health professional or even remotely human.

"Who *are* you?" Siren asked. A more appropriate question would have been "What are you?" but Siren thought it wiser to try for the basics. Her lips had cracked when she'd spoken and a whimper now escaped her lips.

"My apologies. I had to burn out the opiates from your body long enough to gain your attention." The voice was distinctly female, coming from a shadowy recess in the corner. The visitor exuded a strong and quite alien presence among the mundane trappings of her primitive hospital room.

"You have my attention," said Siren, trying to focus on the shape of her visitor. "This is a regular hospital." Her relief was palpable.

"Yes, Siren, though they expect to transfer you to a private facility later today."

"What do you want?" She may as well get straight to the point, she thought. It was unlikely the woman offered free assistance.

A throaty chuckle erupted from her guest. "I was thinking more along the lines of 'What do *you* want', my dear. That you don't wish to return to the Agency is patently clear. Also very clear is the fact that you cannot be harboured by your underground friends at this time. It is indeed a dilemma." The woman moved closer, and Siren imagined that a trail of frost formed in her wake. "What did you think of the house in West Kilbride?"

Ah, thought Siren bleakly, the place she would have liked to call "home". "It was too perfect, I suppose." Oh, no. Siren's eyes widened as she remembered, her hand reaching up to support the painful side of her face: Ella was waiting for her to return with ice cream. She needed to get back to the house before the Agency sent staff to fetch her. Maybe then they'd run. Siren's bank accounts would be useless now, but she had already stashed money behind the dresser in her new home. Would it be enough to give them a fresh start?

"Sh." The caller tapped a long finger to her chin in thought. "It would be a shame to waste the coven's good work."

Surprised, Siren wondered afresh. The woman spoke as though the witches' work had been *her* doing but it would be mad to trust her. Siren didn't even know *what* she was, but in contrast to the witches, her power seemed distinctly "unearthly".

"I see your dilemma, Siren," the visitor said, as though she'd read her mind. "I'm aware of your history with the Agency, the demon underground and with the Protectorate, but your unique situation has been compromised." Siren recognised Sean's phraseology tripping easily from the woman's tongue. The dark mage had been right. Siren should have left earlier, but if she'd done that then Ella might not have had a chance. "If I may propose," continued the woman, "I would like you to return to the house on the basis that you take care of some people I'll be sending to you from time to time."

"But?"

"Please don't interrupt. It's still secure, my dear." Siren accepted the rebuke, letting her visitor resume. "It would be short-term care that these people will require." Siren sat up, her head spinning. The tubes and wires attached to her stretched and nipped as she came to the obvious conclusion.

"I may be a Siren but I'm not running a—"

"Don't say it, my dear. The powers that be are easily upset."

"I'm so sorry." Siren was now affronted. She reached for her face, frowning at the drip line attached to her arm. "You're Protectorate?" She wondered if it was hope or fear that was making her stomach churn again.

"What did you think?" Her midnight eyes pierced Siren's. "Oh, I see how you might have thought as you did. My people skills are not well exercised. You have been used in ways that would make you expect the worst." It was odd to hear her position boiled down to bare facts by this impassive creature. "Now that the penny has dropped, as it were, you know that I propose nothing dishonourable."

"What about—" She was reluctant to mention Ella, so settled for: "I would be trapped?"

"No, Siren. This is a job offer for which you will receive a simple salary. What you choose to do on your days off is entirely up to you. I am talking about the running of a safe house. That's all." Her eyes raised heavenward before returning, softening somehow.

"You've been doing as much already as I understand it. Your Tracer abilities would still be used by the underground and on occasion by Protectorate forces. If the basic terms are agreeable, we can formalise everything later."

"Are you an angel?" Siren couldn't help the words escaping her and wondered if the woman had truth charmed her.

"What a strange and dangerous child you are. I can almost understand what my son sees in you."

"Your s…son?" The phrase had barely left her lips when comprehension dawned, and with it a measure of newfound trust.

"I am precator Michelle, whether angelic or otherwise is not for me to say." Large unblinking eyes focused on Siren and she didn't know what to think. Precators didn't run around glibly asking people to join their ranks. She personally didn't know anyone above the rank of enforcer. Were they all like this?

"Tick-tock, my dear. Yes or no."

"Yes," breathed Siren. The air popped with the weight of the promise. *Don't worry, Siren, it goes both ways.* Precator or not, angel or demon, one thing was clear. Sean's mother was a saviour.

"I'm so glad that's settled. You may rest now."

"You're going?" Disappointment swelled in Siren. Couldn't they leave now? The Agency could still grab her again. It wasn't as if they'd wish her well and organise a leaving do. There would be hell to pay if they knew she'd cut a Protectorate deal. Siren's eyelids grew heavy, though, and she saw that the steady drip of her medication had now resumed.

An icy touch brushed Siren's forehead. She heard words that urged her to forget something, and then her senses faded to nothing.

CHAPTER 30

Carolyn

"How're you doing?"

Carolyn watched Ethan wipe bacon grease from his face with the back of his hand. She should feel honoured the mage had joined her for breakfast. Almost midday when she'd surfaced, Katie had claimed that Carolyn needed the rest. Ethan grimaced under her scrutiny.

"We'll find out about Lena tomorrow," he said. Did he think she cared? Well, on awakening, she'd had a fleeting sense of panic regarding the Lilim and whatever the Agency had done with her. Laying in a warm and comfortable bed, Carolyn remembered the cages the organisation held for new otherworlders.

Lena had chosen to deal with them. If things had gone to her plan, then Carolyn would have been the one in a cage.

She wondered if Levy would call in Sean to help with the Lilim. But, no. Lena would provide all that they could ask for. Protectorate involvement, if any, would be limited to keeping *their* secrets.

"I'm not interested." She had waited too long to answer and the unscarred side of Ethan's face drew up in a half smile.

"Sure you're not." Damn him.

There was no warning: Carolyn's head snapped up in sudden pain and her eyes rolled back, a wail escaping from her clenched teeth. Ethan gripped her face in his hands, then a wash of searching magic swarmed over every inch of her. Callused fingers finally slid down to her neck.

"Shit, I don't recognise this." He said and *shook* her. Carolyn thought for an instant he was going to slap her like they did in the movies. She was

209

completely aware but somehow not in control, neither hysterical nor possessed; this was something completely different.

"What's happening? Talk to me."

Carolyn's eyes caught a flash. A spear of gold light burst from the empty space above them and she rose, knowing it was meant for her. She gasped when it struck the middle of her forehead. *What now?*

Robbed of speech, her features froze in horror. Ethan and Mario – where had *he* come from? – were now at her side.

"What the hell flew into her?"

"Just get it the fuck out!" Ethan's hands squeezed on her shoulders, a welcome relief from the pain in her head.

"Look at her eyes," said Mario. I can't interfere with that, and I don't know if I *should.* Flashing between witch green and Carolyn's cobalt, the question had been answered.

"How can the realms be pierced without a mark to show for it?" Ethan marvelled and then Carolyn's sight returned, her eyes still alternating colours. Ethan was right, however, it had happened, there was no tear, and no gateway essence.

The power renewed its surge through Carolyn, threatening to burn her synapses. Oh, God, it hurt. Her mind wide open, she had been incapable of preventing it. Feral – searching – and really familiar…

Mum?

Not the mother Carolyn knew or remembered, certainly, this one was single minded in her mission, searching. Confusion coursed through the link with Carolyn.

What trick is this? Give to me what was lost.

No trick, mum. Carolyn realised exactly what Amanda wanted, and it was hers for the taking. *It's me. I found it and Father let me take it.*

Oh! Her mother had clearly thought her connection to be with Arthur? No wonder she was confused. *Isn't it a bonus that you only have to come through me?*

My clever girl. Her mother's acceptance caused an abrupt change in her control, and Carolyn's pain vanished. *How did you manage to get Arthur to release the trapped soul?* Confusion still buzzed through Carolyn's mind, but this was her *mother* and Carolyn basked for a moment in the softer, approving presence. *Show me how.*

And that's when Carolyn found complete access to her mother's thoughts. Sure, she was carrying out advanced magic, but it was fuelled by exterior sources. Amanda was barely keeping *her* soul together after what had happened. Her life after Carolyn flashed before her in less than a heartbeat.

It seemed Eddie had suffered only briefly in Kistatus hands. He had embraced his heritage. *I lost him, baby. I'm so sorry, but I lost him.* Her mother was still agonising from the effects of the claiming and Carolyn's gut tightened at how similar it was to what she'd had with Note.

In that instant, she was in her mother's physical body. Sam – his mind open – in her arms, lips soft and… Carolyn forced her eyes to open, senses widening to find Morgan, the Frenchman – her mind accepted him simply as that – and, dear God, she'd found Notechis… Note. Amanda's thoughts were merging with hers, trying to guide her. The Frenchman halted the Kistatus boy. He had changed…

No. No. NO! How could that be? Strain, desperation, longing, she could see it all reflected in his pale, icy blue eyes.

Wrong. That was wrong. In a flash of recognition, his irises flashed to burning gold. A slow smile removed the tortured expression she'd imagined on his face. *Do what needs to be done. I don't know how much time you'll have.*

Yes, of course. Sam. Dear Sam. He had helped Amanda get away from Arthur, allowing her fifteen carefree years with her babies until her first love, the Kistatus chief, had reclaimed her.

Lena was right. Amanda had wanted Arthur regardless of the fact that no claim cemented their deal. Why leave if she loved the Lilim? Carolyn's head was fit to explode. *File it all.* There were too many questions for which the answers would only be unacceptable.

Carolyn wrenched the little box from her mind, the one where she had stored the remains of Sam. *Let's focus, mum. Fix him. Make him whole again. Some of us can be complete.*

Even as she'd said it she knew her mother was far from whole, and Carolyn wasn't much closer to such an ideal. The discordant twang of shared despair sounded through their link, replaced by something else for an instant, and Carolyn's blood sang.

Oh, mum.

Neither of us is whole, baby, and that's fine for now. Carolyn needed to take advantage of her lucidity.

I'm so glad you're okay. Amanda took charge of Sam's little black box.

You kept it safe.

Just recently, mum. Arthur had it. Remember him? The dad I didn't know about. Carolyn couldn't help the tiny bit of resentment that leaked out with it. Amanda's confusion returned through the link, and Carolyn cursed her insensitivity. *Sorry, mum, I know it's not easy for you to work like this and you need to get back to Sam.*

She allowed her sense of urgency to permeate the connection before Carolyn thrust her mother and the prize from her mind. Carolyn's body arced as a spear of gold light traced through her body and then flamed, piercing the air on its return to Earth. *I love you, mum.*

But there was nobody there. It was all over before it had barely begun; mere seconds, yet seemingly an eternity.

In the real world, Carolyn became aware that she was laying on something … someone. Her cheeks were wet and she trembled violently, but Carolyn didn't feel weak. There was a loss, though … a deep grievous loss.

Not yours.

The warmth behind her was Ethan, his arms wrapped tightly about her. She felt every breath he took, waiting for her to come to. Cool fingers rested on the top of her head – Arthur. The scream when it left her lips could have shattered a mirror, and Ethan expelled a whoosh of surprised breath as she elbowed him in the ribs whilst scrambling from her father's reach.

Arthur simply stood before her, his hand elevated as though examining it for the truth. Ethan fruitlessly reached for the comfort of his weapon's hilt – now no longer at his hip.

Note

Morgan incanted and dispensed with the clinical veneer of the report room to reveal a structure lined with runic arrangements of Baltic amber and black tourmaline, materials proven to repel attack and prompt memory. The beauty helped take the pain out of mundane tasks. With the veneer intact, it was an uninspiring space, conducive only to the speedy compilation of reports.

Note avoided eye contact with Morgan while they compiled and filed their findings with the precators. Morgan often joked that it was a miracle they could read each other's scrawl, but Note suspected it was a Protectorate benefit bestowed on them. It didn't lessen the fact that they worked well together.

"I expected them to come and quiz us personally," mused Morgan as Note finished dictating on the system. She scrunched up the handwritten records and Note opened the incinerator hatch; the remains of the previous contents tickled his nose. Morgan tossed the wad of paper into the receptacle which fired up as soon as he'd closed the flap.

"She hates me," said Note as they left the building. It probably hadn't helped that he'd kept staring at Amanda during their visit, willing that Carolyn's presence would return. He kept replaying the flash of Carolyn's blue eyes as she'd communed with her mother.

"Amanda was protecting you, Note. Didn't you see her fighting her instincts before trying to set Sam to rights in there? I'm betting that Pierre's babysitting duty is close to an end." The Frenchman was recouping somewhere while the replacements exchanged concerned glances in the corridor.

Note's blond brows arched. They had no idea if Sam was better or worse off after Amanda's stunt, but he intended to return. Note felt he and

Morgan had been rejected. The woman had displayed power that would concern the precators, but she'd used it only to heal Sam.

And then, in using Carolyn's energy signature to erase her breach of shields and realm travel, Amanda had ensured that no-one, neither Lucas nor Hecaton, could trace her to the facility. Note felt humbled by Amanda, imagining as he could the indescribable pain of her actions.

CHAPTER 31

Miranda

Miranda struck Judy with the back of her hand.

"Enough!" It was bad enough that the tear to Empustat had been repaired and all she had to show for it was a dour Lilim. Now, to deal with the circus Judy had brought about. Aiden Vasch was weak when it came to the Amazonian but she hadn't realised just *how* weak until now. His jaw clenched as he stood with the quiet Veloces, waiting for Miranda's instructions.

Sean had the appropriate skills to clean up the mess her team had made, but they'd failed yet again to contact the mage. At this point, she would have gladly offered a hundred thousand pounds for his services. There was no Agency mage who could even come close to what was required.

Her body shook with uncontrolled temper, and at the back of her mind she knew the problem had to be addressed. At the moment, it felt good to let loose with her rage. The footage that Judy had shown was damning, but not damning enough to warrant their actions with Siren. There could have been a variety of reasons why the Siren had met with the Investor.

"You knew I needed to ... to speak to Harris, and you lost him. If you hadn't been so busy recording their meeting, we could have taken them."

"I thought that if I could gather proof—"

"And you left the Faery where no-one can contact her until she decides to wander. I have people scouring that village right now, so you better hope she ventures out soon or I swear..." Miranda's entire face had become a mask of fury. "Remember those military personnel you turn your nose up at..." Judy could only nod, her eyes darting from Vasch to Loci, neither of whom could come to her aid. "If I don't get my Siren back, whole *and*

214

undamaged, I'm going to *gift* you to them." The tall mage blanched.

"I misjudged. Please, boss, just give me another chance." The mage indicated to Vasch. "We'll go and fetch her from the Kilmarnock hospital."

"Crosshouse," provided Miranda, disparagingly. It was ghastly news for the buildings there were protected from gateway use within their walls. Anyone who wished to travel would need to do so from the periphery. There was the added complication of having to arrange for records and memories to be wiped throughout the entire human based system.

"If we go via the web to transport up there, we can get an Agency ambulance from The Block to transfer her to the nearest focus."

Miranda drummed her fingers on her office desk. The Block in Glasgow would be the safest option for Siren, and despite what she'd said to Judy, their healing expertise would indeed be required.

In an ideal world, Sean would have come to the rescue, assuring absolute discretion with the hospital staff. And, as she'd witnessed once with the destroyer, the superior mage was also a very effective healer. He would have delivered the Siren fully healed and wrapped in a pretty pink bow if she had asked.

"Fine. Make it so." Even with extra support to help with the hospital staff, they would be kept busy for many hours with the clear up.

"Do you wish for me…?" The Veloces let the offer hang, his lean face betraying nothing.

"Hmm." She had no worries about his allegiance. He had already helped her remove two Investors, and she had planned to use him for Harris.

"Yes," she said decisively. "Judy, take Loci," Her eyes rested on him long enough to convey her point. The demon would report everything back to her.

"Thanks, boss. We'll not let you down." Aiden grabbed Judy, and they left as though the hounds of hell were after them. If they failed, Miranda would ship them to the very realm where such beasts existed.

CHAPTER 32

Sean

Precator Oscar had left Sean with a choice he couldn't make.

The mage's frustration turned to wondering disbelief when he felt a gateway open nearby. Stretching out his senses, he knew exactly which world had accessed them. He didn't move from his position, but waited the thirty seconds before the outer ward on the building was breached.

A further ten, and Sean couldn't hear but *felt* the intruder in the shared entryway, moving quickly on the stairs outside the flat. Twenty more ticks for the door enchantment to fall. Seventy, and the visitor circled the first bedroom. A clockwise search was predictable. Sean intercepted the prowler while he dallied in Morgan's room.

"The lady doesn't like anyone in her underwear drawer," he directed into the room.

"No change there. You haven't lost your touch, I see." The intruder stuffed the dresser contents back in place and turned slowly to face Sean.

"Haven't you forgotten something?" Sean had hardly taken a step inside before the man approached, arms thrown wide.

"Do you know how long it took for me to find you?" Sean could have sworn the words were choked with emotion.

"More than a minute. You're slipping."

"That's what I thought," said Mario, breaking off to look at his old teacher. "You've changed." At Sean's raised eyebrow, he added, "I hate to break it to you, man, but you know you're warm, right?" Sean knew the charm kept his flesh as cool as ever, but the Lilim had easily seen through it.

"Very droll," Sean said as he moved to the doorway to flick on the light.

216

"The others suspect but I have not shared it with all. It's been a long year."

"Don't I know it."

"I'm not the only one who's transformed," and Mario spun on the spot and gave a deep bow. "When are you expected back?"

"ASAP. I'd like to take Note with me, but I wanted to clear it with you first."

"You don't trust Arthur."

"Well, as you can see, he's lifted the block on gateway access but who knows how long it'll last." Sean looked at the man, still *seeing* the boy he'd trained. "Don't let my appearance fool you. Arthur only reversed the curse a few weeks ago. I fucking hate him." He dodged the half-hearted swipe Sean directed at him.

"You've been spending too much time with Ethan, I see." His apprentice may still have hated the chief, but he also feared and respected him. Sean could also discern a remaining magical attachment. Mario's appearance had come at a very convenient time, thought Sean, unable to resist taking advantage. "Another hour or so wouldn't be a problem for you, would it?"

Mario grinned. "What *have* you got for us?"

"I've been given a choice, it would seem. Precator Oscar decided to test me. Unfortunately, it would seem that lives may hang in the balance."

"Typical Friday, huh?" The boy flashed a brilliant smile before asking, "What are the choices?"

"I have to decide whether to rescue a Siren or attend the initiation of the new Kistatus king." Disappointingly, Mario showed no surprise at the latter. Perhaps Arthur was in attendance. "The Siren is a Tracer whose been helping us from within the Agency."

"You are in such demand. How can you stand it?"

"I know." Sean smiled grimly.

"So call the team and split us up to manage both."

"Oscar stipulated that I should answer these alone." Even as the words passed his lips, Sean knew he would cover both jobs as best he could. The precator could not expect him to attend them simultaneously.

"*Should...* That's not definitive, Sean. It implies suggestion. Deploy me. Set it up however you like." Mario smoothed a hand over his dark waves; his hair had grown long. "You need me," he said, his smug smile warming to a full-on grin. "Maybe involving the whole team is pushing it, but I'm not formally back. I don't count. The shadow Faery might not either."

"He *is* in training," Sean mused, Mario's enthusiasm being infectious.

"I'm here to collect Note," said Mario, and Sean caught the hidden warning flash sent with Note's mention. Sean thanked the powers that be for Mario's strength. The boy continued as though his task was innocent enough. "So where's the harm in us deciding to check out one of your jobs en route.”

“Jonah and Note.” Sean tested the names on his tongue. It felt right.

“Arthur and Carolyn are attending the ceremony.” More good news. Part of Oscar’s test was clearly to see if Sean would take advantage of having their destroyer within easy reach? “My instruction is to have Note waiting in Empustat for their return.”

Sean understood why Arthur would want the young Kistatus off-world while Carolyn witnessed her brother’s date with destiny.

As luck would have it, both enforcers were available. Note was wary about returning to Skean, but the promise of seeing Carolyn swayed his decision to follow Sean’s plan, and Jonah was very interested in the job of fetching the Siren. In the end, it was decided that Mario and Note would go to the inauguration while Sean and Jonah dealt with the Agency on Earth.

Note

Mario kept sneaking glances at Note as they waited in the grand hall of the castle. Slipping a hand into the vest beneath his charcoal jacket, he found Sean’s pocket watch. It was a stylish enhancement to the guise, a perfect copy, just like Note and his clothes. He noticed the hands of the timepiece had frozen in place at the time of their gateway entry. Slightly unsettled, he doubted the original would have done that, so he stuffed it back into his vest.

He wondered if Edward would make a worthy chief. The realm deserved proper direction, but the chances were too good that Hecaton would rule in all but name. The high mage had mellowed with age and there could be a bright future for the realm under decent leadership. In Note’s head, he could imagine liaising with the outlanders if his father would allow it, and recent events suggested definite possibilities.

The seating arrangements had been staggered in groupings throughout the room. The attendants smoothly wove around the tables, busily taking orders for refreshments and seating individuals and groups from the realms. There was a raised dais at the centre, and although Mario and himself hadn’t been seated with the dignitaries close to the platform, they hadn’t been shunted to the outskirts either.

“Quit grinning. It’s creepy.” Mario’s elbow connected with Note who straightened his face as best he could. “Keep in character.” Apparently *Mario’s* character hadn’t changed as much as his appearance. What had it cost the Lilim, other than the obvious? He had recovered fairly well after Note had taken Sean’s form. “I would have preferred you as Morgan,” Mario said with a smirk.

“Right, because that’s not at all creepy.”

Mario’s eyes widened in mock horror. In fact, the pretty mage would have been ecstatic to have had him back. Mario had been excited about the group tattoo and knew that Sean had made provisions for the new pledges.

"Look who just came in?" Mario said, and Note's stomach lurched, but when he only saw Roland, high mage of Rask, he slumped back in his chair. "Okay, so I haven't been out much … or at all lately. Cut me some slack, Note."

Hecaton entered directly after the Rakshasas, in a wave of comparable energy. Note forced his body to relax. The high mage would have a lot more on his mind than watching his son play dress-up – if he even noticed. An attendant ushered Roland to a ringside seat where refreshments were already flowing freely. All the ranking representatives were vying for attention. Note wondered why Hecaton hadn't carried out the chief's transfer in private. The high mage had to be very sure of success even to consider such a gathering.

Note felt a prickling sensation in his foot. The favour he owed East? He turned, as if to speak to Mario, daring to scan behind him. Right at the back of the room, he saw the resistance leader in her full Kistatus form, robed and as regal as ever. Catching her eye, he nodded deferentially, as Sean would have done.

Note's father had a lot of explaining to do when they next met. Pre-resistance, East had been part of the established regime. A powerful mage of noble descent, she had moved against Lucas, spending the last decade in exile with the outlanders.

Knowing his father, this had to be the product of a conciliatory pact that allowed him to keep his enemies close. Perhaps East expected a better ruler in Edward. East's presence *had* to be a good thing. Until the transfer was finished she would want to blend into the background at this event where best behaviour was anticipated, but there was no magic to enforce the rule. Unclaimed knives could still appear in guests' backs. Maybe her position at the rear had been deliberate.

"Don't look now but your father's on his way."

"Wh–"

"High mage, Sean," said Hecaton smoothly, and Note rose to bow in greeting. Sean was taller than Note so it was strange to be looking down at his father. If Hecaton saw it was Note beneath the guise, he didn't let on.

"High mage, Hecaton," he answered stiffly.

"I must insist that you sit up front with us." Hecaton had already turned, robbing him of the "Thanks, but no thanks" option.

"You're really too kind." He shot a quizzical look at Mario who shrugged indifferently. *Adapt.*

"He just wants to keep an eye on the other high mages," said Mario into his ear as they followed Hecaton out to the more comfortable, Kistatus friendly arrangements at the front. There were six groupings around the dais, each separated wider than the others for the number of realm heads expected to attend. "I think he's hoping you all challenge each other."

Note grimaced. He didn't intend daring anyone in the gathering, however tempting it might be, to have a shot at Roland. The Rakshasas was eyeing him with interest and Note raised a brow before finding a place in the adjacent seating group to his.

The Motus high mage across from him grinned at Note's decision to sit close to the greater threat. The Motus were a race of power but they liked to work – interpret: *interfere* – with others; a trait they shared with the Faeries.

As though they'd answered him directly, a gateway appeared at the edge of the room and Ankou arrived with his mate, Anita. Both wore silk robes of green and silver. Remarkably, they were followed closely by the Siren novice. The title was deceptive. The novice was training to succeed the current Grand Siren of the realm. Hecaton spoke with her for a moment and Note could have sworn his father had not remained unaffected.

That's what he got for sharing power with his unwilling son. That said, Hecaton's rejuvenation had been remarkable and any residual weakness negligible. Surprisingly, the Siren joined the Motus delegates. Note had to stop himself from laughing at Roland's clear disappointment. Alliances could be forged at these events where the attending races would observe and then make their assumptions.

"It's not that unusual, Note. There's only six places at the front and a dozen races. She's doubling up with them to pre-empt the possibility of being seated with less agreeables."

"I wouldn't have thought this number would attend."

"I think they've been expressly invited," muttered Mario. "Look at their faces. It's going to be a show and they're like kids on their first visit to Disneyland."

Note wasn't convinced, but it *was* a big event, the level of excitement heightening by the minute.

CHAPTER 33

Carolyn

Carolyn awoke with a start, her head buzzing with the unmistakable sensation of a gateway opening nearby. Beni whined from the foot of her bed as she jumped over him. Her body clock told her it was barely dawn. The first thought as she pulled clothes on over her wrist cuff was that a threat had been posed to the realm. This was something else, though, for there was no shouting, screaming or call to arms that could reasonably have been expected.

Her next thought was even more preposterous: that Arthur had opened the access channels in preparation for her departure. She wasn't due to leave until the following night. Why now? She burst through her door, armed only with the screwdriver from her dresser. The guard at his post outside looked alarmed.

"My lady?" His hands reached out to stop her – as though he could. He clearly knew nothing of the gateway that sang to her blood. She raced to it, old instincts taking over even as she knew this was not a "call" like she'd had whilst on Earth. It felt clean and unspoiled, unlike the tear they'd repaired. There was no-one needing rescue … at least, she thought not.

The guards outside Arthur's chambers crossed their weapons over the door. "The chief does not wish to be disturbed, for any reason, my lady."

Beni growled at her side, and Carolyn set a hand on top of his head. "It's all right, boy. I've got this." She stepped forward, as though to remove the spears the men held, but they withdrew them from harm's way. "You will let me pass." She hadn't meant to use Lilim persuasion, but the tiniest leakage of power had occurred, almost as though her will had preceded her.

Stepping into her father's antechamber, she came before three wide arches that led to separate rooms. The white noise of the gateway came from the one directly ahead, and she rushed through, excitedly, to find the chief's bedchamber. It was empty. Slowly, she spun around before looking down at her feet. Beni's entire body had lowered in submission as the section of floor where they now stood, dropped from beneath them. Carolyn sank to her haunches for stability, an arm around the hound.

Now beneath the chamber, her senses lit up at the presence of the gateway behind her. Opened correctly, it was huge, stretching at least two meters in circumference, a rich oxblood red which shimmered and separated as the dark figure of her father paced out.

"Beautiful, is it not." Carolyn jumped to her feet, sharing a guilty look with Beni, well and truly caught in the act.

"Mmm. Aren't you going to seal it up until tomorrow?"

Arthur tipped his head slightly. "Do I need to?"

"What?" said Carolyn stupidly. "No. I gave my word." Something like humour glinted in his eyes as he stepped closer.

"I have just received notification of an important realm event." He motioned toward the gateway. "Your request to open the access has nothing to do with this." He could have pretended, thought Carolyn. "As there's been no recent contact, I have opened a channel."

At her incomprehension, he explained, "It's a tunnel, if you like, and it's currently re-burning the routes to the realms. As with your Earth gateways, once this is done, all focus points in Empustat will again be active." Meaning that Ethan, Mario or anyone could go home whenever they wished. Would they stick to the agreement she'd made on their behalf? Did it matter when they were due to leave the realm the next day? Carolyn watched him study her reaction, waiting for her to come to a conclusion.

"You'll still be able to monitor and … and alter things?" she said.

"Like stripping unwelcome parasites from visitors. Then yes. Exactly." Carolyn remembered Sadi with conflicting emotion. If she'd been able to stay, then everything could have gone quite differently.

"Why now?"

"Ah!" He withdrew an envelope from behind his back and Carolyn felt an unwilling grin appear on her face.

"You knew I was coming, even while you were there."

"Perhaps because of it." His lip quirked. "I *always* have contact with my realm no matter where I am. I have, however, encountered … not a problem as such in regard to our agreement, but we need to revisit the terms."

"I'm definitely going home – to Earth," she said, as though it needed clarifying. "Tomorrow." The tightening of her father's jaw conveyed what he thought of her lack of faith. She had to stop herself from being penitent. *He's a monster; remember what he did to Mario – to you.*

Then, in a surprisingly boyish manner, he moved to put the envelope in his pocket. Curiosity roused, she reached for it but Arthur caught her fingers as they closed over the embossed paper. He really believed this was going to please her?

"Before you open this, remember that I truly regret any suffering you have endured at my hands." Carolyn was fairly sure the "you" was singular rather than inclusive of her friends, but somehow that was okay. "Also, in regard to this," and his gaze slid to the envelope, "I'm aware your knowledge of the realms is somewhat lacking, so we should try to remedy that – or at the very least make a start on correcting the gaps in your knowledge."

Carolyn's curiosity had ratcheted up only to plummet now.

"The races were once closely aligned," he said. A history lesson? She hoped Arthur didn't catch her lack of enthusiasm. "Unsurprisingly, *all* are affiliated with humanity. Earth is the first and largest of the realms, a source of – many things, as you know. Physically, some of us appear human which has always engendered trust."

Carolyn nodded to show she was keeping up, and her father continued: "Our people were once aligned with Arranan, Peruro and Skean, amongst others. Each of those associated with their favourites, and so on and so forth." He clearly wasn't comfortable with the topic which did wonders to raise Carolyn's flagging interest. She already knew the realms he mentioned were home to the Faery, Fire and Kistatus races.

"The importance of humanity is understated. The worlds would fail without the system which was set in place by the Earth Protectorate. It is, in part, the reason for the shape shifter races adopting human-like forms as easily as their own. It is also why each *traveller* hears his native language throughout the realms, though the feature can be disabled by certain magic users for reasons of their own."

Knowledge was power. Right? Arthur allowed her to take the envelope. She rubbed her finger across its wax seal which depicted the image of a Kistatus face. The chief's? "Is this an invitation?" Hesitantly, she offered it back to Arthur, but he folded his arms.

"Open it." It was almost a pity to break the seal and remove the green-gold card from within.

"To, the most honourable and distinguished Lilim crown and lady Carolyn," she read. Arthur smiled indulgently as she rolled her eyes at the formal titles. "You are cordially invited to attend the inauguration of the new Kistatus king." Hmm. If as boring as she suspected, then her father was welcome to go without her. "There's no date."

"It's for today, Carolyn. Invitations of such importance are sent out on the actual date of the event." He continued to eye her expectantly. What was she missing?

Her jaw dropped in realisation.

She *really* was a self-centred, self-serving brat who seemed to take after her father too well. He wanted to discuss *terms* when her brother Eddie was about to go through a life altering event? Poor Eddie – was he alone now? Had Lucas died? He needed to have at least someone from his family to make sure he was all right.

She stilled that part of her that blamed her brother for giving in to his Kistatus half, but then look at *her*. Carolyn was blithely using Lilim guile whenever the opportunity struck.

In truth, she'd parcelled off Eddie, to deal with at a more convenient time. Yes, *she* had been through a lot, but Eddie? *He* had become a man during his time in Skean. But to imagine him as chief? She had witnessed some of the power the Kistatus high mage and their chief wielded. The Eddie she remembered would have baulked at all they represented. Carolyn knew he had overcompensated and worked hard to become accepted in the chief's personal guard… But this?

"Eddie?" she no more than whispered, the gravity of the situation having descended. She was now very afraid for him.

"Yes." Her father seemed uncaring of her evident inner turmoil. She looked at him blankly. "The terms I wanted to clear with you are simple. You could be tempted to use the opportunity to return to Earth. I ask only that you come back here for your final night in the realm."

Carolyn blinked rapidly. He wasn't bargaining for any more time than they had already agreed. Not only a brat, she'd done Arthur a disservice for *he* was at least showing some sort of consideration to her *and* Eddie.

Could she push her luck and request that Mario and Ethan go to Skean as well?

***

Ethan's tense gaze stayed with Carolyn as she stepped through the first gateway she'd accessed in over a year. The formalwear had been a prerequisite, and uncle Lawrence had called her a burnished goddess when she'd appeared in her tailored frothy, coppery ensemble.

Carolyn didn't feel at all comfortable, reconciled as she had been to remaining in the realm until her time was done. Now, with so little time until the end of their agreement, they were en route to Skean.

Excitement churned her stomach. *This is not a rescue. Calm down.* Her brother wasn't held against his will and her father thought she should be happy for him. How could that be when Eddie and his mother had been so horribly removed from Earth? How could he be Lucas's heir? Ethan and Mario had explained what they knew of it, but there was still a lot to get her head around.

Eddie had become a fearful warrior among the Kistatus race. Believing herself to be adaptable, not only had Eddie also adapted but he had embraced everything about the realm as his own. Did Arthur think he could expect the same of Carolyn in Empustat? That Eddie could serve as a role model?

If her mother was in her right mind, she'd be upset, but would she stop it? Could she? It appeared there was no saving Lucas, and the realms welcomed a change.

Having been warned by Ethan, she was almost disappointed by her reaction to Hecaton who greeted them on arrival. The physical similarity to Note *was* striking enough for her to stare a little. The high mage didn't touch her, merely offering a stiff bow as he delivered an odd compliment about her gown. She could tell he was keen to speak to Arthur, and he sent her off with an attendant while he and Arthur got busy with whatever high mages and chiefs did together.

If she hadn't been so nervous about meeting Eddie, or if she'd still been working with the Protectorate, their friendship may have concerned her. When the servant raised her hand and opened a door, it revealed a yellow robed mage who looked upset. Recognition surged between them. "Debbie?"

The girl snorted. "I should have known *you* would remember. I've been going by 'Rhona' here." At Carolyn's confused expression, she added, "Debbie's my middle name. I thought it would make me less homesick." She wiped a tear from her cheek as her other hand clamped around Carolyn's arm. "If you visit again after all this madness, I'd like to catch up?"

"Absol…utely." Debbie reddened and let her go. Carolyn wanted to find out more, but her old friend was already sweeping down the corridor.

A deep voice rumbled from within the room. "I should have known who she was."

"Damn right you should've. Debbie's only been in love with you since we were five." Carolyn strode into an opulent space. A server took a position against the wall, apparently awaiting instruction while Eddie continued as if they were alone and nothing out of the ordinary had occurred.

"You know me, sis. I could barely stand *you* when you were young never mind your screeching wee pals." His words were tough but Carolyn saw the way his eyes followed after Debbie as he closed the door behind her.

Eddie wore only a pair of shorts and Carolyn's eyes flicked to the door before returning accusingly to her brother. His laugh sounded brittle. "No, it's actually *not* what you think." She didn't quite know what to think. They were both adults. But still.

"You really didn't recognise her?" Carolyn couldn't ignore what was happening to Eddie though her mind screamed that she should. Surveying the dressing room, tension gnawed at her gut.

"To be fair, I only met … Rhona quite recently, but I never was one to follow clues." He ran a finger down one of the two robes that hung on a wide dressing screen. His back was rippled with muscle, the kind Carolyn had only ever seen on the most seasoned of warriors. Eddie turned his suntanned face to her. It was older; three years older than the version she remembered. Youthful slenderness had filled out to Ethan-like proportions. A lot could happen in three years, as Carolyn knew. His expression was cold … resigned? "She's Hecaton's now," he finally said.

He opened his arms but Carolyn felt weirdly numb. Who was this man? "What? No hug?" He swaggered back with a mocking sneer, and Carolyn pushed aside any regret at refusing to play *her* part in a game for which her brother's part was plainly unwillingly played. Taking a step closer, she searched his angry green eyes for the truth. "I always planned to rescue you."

"What were you waiting for – the next Ice Age?" Nice comeback. It had the desired effect of both making her feel guilty and irritating her.

"I was *lost*," she said, her voice little more than a whisper. Eddie's expression closed. She'd hit a nerve. He turned from her, thumping his fist into the dressing table. It shattered on contact, spraying oils and accessories onto the floor. What was *that* about? They were about to perform a dangerous ceremony for which her brother was clearly far from ready. What the hell was Hecaton playing at?

Eddie took a deep breath and returned to looking at her, his arms crossed in front of him. "We are all lost." Carolyn looked into her brother's face. Did his thinking mirror hers? She'd let him and her mother down in the worst way. What could she say that didn't seem trite and inadequate?

He seemed to become aware of the closed position he'd taken and shook out his limbs, scrubbing a hand against the back of his neck. "It's fine, I'm just a bit off, Carolyn. It's a big day for me."

And mum isn't here to see it, stop it, or even check the safety of the procedure.

If Carolyn voiced her thoughts, would it anger or upset him enough to change his mind about the transfer … or would it weaken him so it would fail and kill him instead? What was Arthur thinking when he'd sent her to him? Did he want her to sabotage her brother for some evil purpose? It seemed increasingly unlikely that he simply wanted her to make peace with him. Nervously, she cleared her throat. "How are you going to manage it?"

"Same as everything is managed now." At her silence, he added bitterly, "Hecaton. I don't have a choice, Sis. The system is fucked. When I take it on, the power will bind, or I'll die. Either way, I'm not going to be worrying about it once it's over."

"What do you mean, you'll die?"

"I've always done very well here as a human, sis. I've not needed to change before." Carolyn hadn't thought about *that*. The Kistatus form was physically stronger than most. If he had embraced this life as well as everyone believed, then why hadn't he accepted the boon of his change. God knows, Carolyn had begun to enjoy changing her form. "I *never* expected this, but your little boyfriend put an end to Lucas, so now I'm the salvation of the realm – and I *want* to save it."

Carolyn was disappointed that he hated Note so vehemently but it was to be expected. It followed that her brother wasn't too keen on *her* either, so why bother going through the farce of a welcome? Someone else's idea? "I *want* this," he reiterated, and Carolyn was taken aback by the resolve that shone in his eyes.

"Okay. I'm not saying anything. It's just–"

"Lucas will die during the transfer – if he lasts that long." He sounded so upset about it that Carolyn was appalled.

"I don't care–"

"But *I* do. Why am I even talking to you? You are so selfish." Carolyn flinched but couldn't disagree. "Your boyfriend's a coward who struck at the worst possible time for our realm." Carolyn couldn't believe her ears. He spoke as though the realm owned him… Perhaps it did. Who owned *her*? Yes, selfish again. Earth and the Protectorate had a right to her, didn't they? Did she belong to each of the realms too when she was wearing her "destroyer" role? *Enough!*

"Note is *not* a coward." Carolyn could admit to being selfish, but Note? He'd only done what Carolyn hadn't been able to do. Note had saved her from a very short and violent life by his mere appearance. The Kistatus had made sacrifices and had always put *her* needs, *everyone's* wants, before his. Note was *good*. "He rescued our mother."

Eddie dropped onto a chaise, looking like he'd fallen into the set of "Anthony and Cleopatra". He leaned forward, resting his elbows on his knees. "From what, Carolyn?" He gestured to the pleasant surroundings. "From this? From being loved and cherished her whole life?"

Unbelievable. "You are deluded if you believe that's what this is." Carolyn began to pace, annoyed she could see where he was coming from. She *recognised* that terrible willingness to do whatever it took.

"After the transfer, that's exactly what I'll think, Carolyn. Any doubts will disappear and I'll continue where Lucas left off. Anyway, enough about me. Who brought you here?"

Carolyn turned to his deceptively casual tone. "Arthur."

"Have you been home?"

"That wasn't part of the arrangement."

"You make me laugh. You're the one dancing to a demon's tune yet you look at me like I'm the devil for making the best of the crappy deal I got stuck with." He was right. God help him, but this realm was not Empustat. Look at what had happened to Debbie – and Carolyn knew that Debbie had struck lucky. Was she magically gifted from before, or had the gateway changed her when she'd travelled to Skean?

"Debbie came looking for you?"

"Subject change, princess?" His brows furrowed. "I wouldn't know. Nobody tells me anything." He stretched up to the robes hanging beside him. "What do you suggest, purple or orange?"

"Are you for real?"

"I'll just go for the pur–"

"Eddie… This isn't like you." She tossed the purple robe over the screen and slapped the orange one on its hanger to his chest. His hand rose to close over hers.

"No, sis. It's been Edward for a long time. I know you managed fine without us, but it's not been quite so straightforward here." The edge in his voice contradicted his gentleness.

"You think it's been 'fine' since you left – that it's been easy?"

"You're some sort of gateway queen, Carolyn. We could all be together for this day. You could go right now and bring her home in a matter of minutes."

Carolyn snatched her hand away. "She *is* home." This was bad. The team had got their mother to safety, and Eddie wanted Carolyn to get her back? Her voice was shrill and there was no dampening it. "It's not what she would want. You *know* that."

"She wanted us to be happy," he countered reasonably, adding fuel to Carolyn's angst. "We grew up without fathers. How can you condemn kids to that?" He went behind the screen with the robe she'd chosen.

The kids – wow. Ethan had glossed over that part. Carolyn had yet to meet her new brother and sister, but she was now desperate to see them. *He's playing you, Carolyn. Just stop.* "They will understand when they're old enough. *I* do."

"That's not what I heard." Eddie's tone had harshened. "I heard that you and Notechis have *exactly* that going for you, but you would condemn our mother to a lifetime of misery." Carolyn had an answer, thankfully.

"*I've* got support and I'm *fighting* the anchoring and the claiming, Eddie. I can't pretend I know you anymore. I don't know all that's happened to you during these past years but I'm really sorry I wasn't there for you."

He now looked small when he emerged from behind the screen in his orange robe. Supposing she could get him home, suffering from Stockholm syndrome or whatever, he was an adult. Carolyn knew he would have a plan. He would grab the first chance to bring their mother back with him, willing or not. Staying in Skean, he could get himself killed by his sheer bloody-mindedness. *Think Carolyn. Think.* Suddenly, with purpose, she moved towards him.

"Whoa … little sis. You didn't want a hug, remember?" He eyed her with a new wariness. Eddie hadn't lost the ability to read her pretty well, and it made Carolyn smile for the first time since she'd seen him again. Tomorrow would take care of itself, today, her job was clear. She had to help him survive the transfer.

"I changed my mind," she said. "Did you mean it when you said you wanted to change to Kistatus form?"

"I *never* wanted it, sis, but the extra strength would come in handy for the ceremony." He was playing it down, but she was right. His form could be the difference between life and death. Was that why Debbie had cried? Had she failed to help him with magic?

He stepped forward. "I'm okay with it." She let him pull her into a hug where she smelled the scented lotions on his skin beneath the silk of the robe. Under it, though ... she imagined she could discern the faint scent of home. "I've shape-shifted many times," she murmured.

"Into what, you little smarty pants? Care to impart any helpful tips?" Carolyn suspected he'd been waiting for the crisis to pass rather than take on the new responsibility, but she could have been wrong.

"If you want to try one more time," she said, "I think I know how to trigger it. Remember the day you and mum were taken?"

He tried to step away. "No, Carolyn. That's not a great idea."

She gripped him. "I'll not try to force it with magic. Just do what I ask. No harm done if it doesn't work."

"Fine." The agreement meant little. He didn't trust her and it was a big ask. Why hadn't Hecaton helped with this? Or, had Eddie's dislike of him pushed the mage away. If Eddie had resisted that sort of magic, then Carolyn's idea needed tweaking. "On Earth, I remember you were the type of boy who baulked at all things fantastical. You wouldn't have anything to do with Harry Potter when everyone else was mad keen on it."

"Is this a long story?" She could tell he was listening.

"I think that if you had accepted that magic existed when you were first taken, then you would have changed immediately."

"Maybe so, but I landed here thinking it was a nightmare, that my real body was probably in a coma somewhere." Carolyn wasn't about to ask when it had become real for him. They had wasted enough time, so she pressed on.

"I want you to remember the fear and the frustration of those first days. You must've wanted to rip their heads off. All that rage ... they didn't explain ... you probably thought they'd killed mum ... or worse." Along with her words, she'd pushed the tiniest bit of searching energy into her brother. She could see his ability, tightly wrapped in grey magic at his core. "It's right there, Eddie. I'm not using magic on you for anything except to take a look. If you could just imagine unwrapping your power, it'll take you over."

"But I—"

"Do you trust me?"

"No," he said, but his eyes glimmered with dark humour and she felt him draw on his negative emotions in a way that threatened to overwhelm her.

"Good, now don't—"

"I won't."

Carolyn froze in shock as Eddie unwrapped his gift, making Carolyn think of old television magicians who smoothly pulled bunches of flowers from their sleeves. He just glided into his new form, filling the robe with the physique it had been made to enhance.

A gasp drew their attention to the forgotten servant who now sidled along the wall to the door. Eddie's triangular head tipped forward as his hair receded to reveal an intricate pattern of black and gold over the light-reflecting amber of his new skin.

From bright gilded eyes, elliptical pupils threatened to dazzle her, and he turned his seven, no, eight-foot frame — not counting the tail — to the mirror. Carolyn could only gape in appreciation. Her — oh, so complicated — feelings didn't matter now. This was her brother in his natural form, huge for a Kistatus, and completely stunning. Catching her eye in the mirror, he seemed to enjoy her reaction. "How do I look?"

She felt her lips twist in reluctant humour. "Like you have a chance."

CHAPTER 34

Sean

Sean felt remarkably unconcerned by the precator's demands of him. He had no doubt that his actions were justified. Jonah was *very* interested in the human hospital. That curious nature of his had led him to the gift shop, and Sean allowed him to purchase a variety of items, not all of which could be for Siren. Impulsively, Sean handed him a "Get well soon" bear that had caught his eye. He palmed the hybrid a few notes to take to the check-out. When the Faery joined him again, he carried an electric blue carrier and had opened a pack of chocolate caramels. Sean refused when the Faery offered him one. As usual, it was the right response.

The Agency ambulance had already arrived – Sean had sensed the presence of the former enforcer as the vehicle crossed the boundaries – but the Siren had apparently stalled for lunch. Sean hadn't risked seeing her before the trip. Did she know that help was on the way? He owed her an "I told you so," but gentleman that he was, he would refrain.

In search of decent coffee, he led Jonah to the staff canteen. His nose hadn't been wrong. There were three machines on the back wall with only one out of order while a girl filled the top compartment with fresh coffee beans. A push-button later and he held a steaming cup of the brew in his hand.

He wasn't surprised to find Jonah had moved, but he wasn't at the cake display. Sean checked the corridor, seeing a covered trolley, a porter at either end, which in itself was not particularly suspicious; it was a hospital after all, and as such, death visited often. He saw a life-force trail from the body it carried, straight through the oblivious porter. The deceased couldn't have been much older than Sean appeared. Chronic illness of some sort?

Cancer?

The weird part, though, was the sight of Jonah, partially changed in appearance, who seemed to be engaged in conversation with the spirit of the recently departed. Sean followed them in the direction of the mortuary, knowing that when the warding broke, the soul would be assessed, judged and shipped off to its destination in a matter of a few quick seconds. Sometimes the process took longer – but most souls weighed heavily for good or bad, and were dispatched accordingly. It shouldn't matter to him, but he hoped the Faery would be lucky with the one he'd chosen to see to the edge. Could he spare Jonah those few moments?

***

The garden beside the mortuary was sparse as far as its green areas went, but Sean cautiously approached the bench from where large Faery eyes now looked up at him. He listened as Jonah told him what had happened. The spirit had obviously made a lasting impression.

"I wouldn't have brought you here if I'd realised, Jonah. Humans learn very quickly that death is a part of life and that the one you spoke to would have found it hard to leave. That is one realm we can't travel. You may be different from the rest of us, with your shadow demon blood, but the souls around you are not bound for the shadow realm. They're going somewhere else entirely."

"I don't come from up there." His eyes went heavenward. Sean cursed inwardly at whoever it was who had caused the boy to doubt his own validity.

"People throughout the realms have all sorts of beliefs and lots of shared ideas. You are a miracle of science, produced by merging the elements of the realms, and I have no doubt you possess a soul that's no different from anyone else's."

"I wanted to see where he went." Jonah cast his eyes up again.

"Yet you didn't try."

"I was … worried."

"You shouldn't ever follow the dead, Jonah. They don't always go to a good place."

"What about young ones?" Jonah's wide Faery eyes, though child-like themselves, had witnessed too much already.

"Oh, they're guaranteed paradise," said Sean solemnly. "I'm assured it's the fairest place imaginable, where the races exist in harmony."

"And they call you 'the dark mage'."

"Yes," said Sean, feeling oddly defensive of his title.

"Hmm."

"Try not to spread the word, Jonah." Sean couldn't help the smile that threatened to surface. Although Jonah was skilled, the Agency had done him no favours by limiting his education. Sean would speak to the precators and see if they could make proper provisions. In the meantime, the boy shouldn't be preoccupied with death. "You should expect three score years and ten at the very least."

Jonah's surprised expression took Sean aback. Perhaps he'd spoken too soon. He didn't know enough about the hybrid to dismiss the possibility of an early expiration date. Jonah looked up as the mortuary van passed and another soul separated from its body and streamed up into a cloudless sky.

"Where these spirits are going is strictly one way. Death can be staved off for a while with healers and hospitals playing their part, but nobody defeats it."

"It would be impossible."

"Right, Jonah." Sean stood and flicked a tiny piece of lint from his jacket. He could feel the unappealing presence of Judy drawing near. It was time for action.

With a little prompting, Jonah streamed them into the ambulance where they hovered in shadow form on the underside of its roof. The minutes stretched out before Siren was carried in and her trolley clipped into place.

The space became quickly crowded. Though dressed as ambulance crew, the mages were inept caregivers, making a poor job of strapping Siren in. An arm dangled off and Sean had to stop himself from putting it to rights and blasting the crew off the vehicle. The driver he recognised as the other Veloces – Speedy's brother.

Miranda Levy would have an aneurism if she lost both Siren and the Veloces on the one job. Siren's lovely face was distorted, heavy bruising over one eye. The vehicle smoothly left the hospital grounds but went too quickly around the first roundabout, causing Judy to curse loudly.

"Should I just pull in here?" The Veloces indicated a lay-by ahead.

Judy leaned into the front of the vehicle. "No, Loci. Hang right at the second junction and you'll see a cookery school further down the road. Park as far from the building as you can and I'll open a gateway."

"But we need to heal the Siren," said Loci, squinting in concentration at the road ahead. They were soon in the car park, the demon bringing them to a halt, pulling heavily on the parking brake. "Her face—"

"Is not your concern," grumbled the male mage with Judy. He stretched out his hand to perform a healing spell, but Judy slapped it away.

"I'll do it."

"I really must insist on taking over."

Almost comically, the three froze when Sean did a cast himself, his face forming from the shadows above them. "Adhuc." Partially formed, he squeezed past Vasch to reach over and undo Siren's upper restraint. Jonah had already got to work on the lower fastenings as Sean began to scoop up the Siren. "You're sure you can manage three?"

"Yes, it's only a short distance," and Jonah's eyes slid to the mages and settled on the Veloces. "You want me to take *him* somewhere first?" Sean sighed and set Siren down. He placed a hand on Loci's head, searching for a good reason that would allow him to leave with his companions. As far as he could see, there was no active pledge on him. It would do no harm, though, to have him assessed.

"You know the safe house on Brodick?" The trip across the water wasn't perfect for Jonah, but the rarely used property was the ideal drop off.

"I do." Jonah's eyes had lit with enthusiasm. Perhaps he'd spent time climbing Goat Fell with Melanie.

"Good. Take him there and I'll get someone out to him later."

"What about this?" Jonah said, indicating the ambulance.

The Faery was right, time could be an issue. He scanned the car park and sighed. Adapting to reduced skills hadn't been all negative; he'd found the use of minor human traits like "improvisation" strangely satisfying. "I have it," he said. "The spell will take another ten minutes to wear off."

Sean covered his tracks, cloaking the high visibility ambulance until the occupants could awaken. He *borrowed* a van from the cookery school, enjoying the lingering scents of fruit cake and pastries. Siren stirred at his side.

"Oh, it's you?" she said, her soft voice sounding as sweet as the recent contents of the van. Interesting that her first words were not "What the hell happened?" or "Where are we going?" as Sean would have expected.

"Very perceptive, my dear. We're bypassing the three towns' area and heading to your safe house." She reached up to touch her face and Sean felt the sudden need to explain himself. "I took the liberty of healing your minor injuries."

"Minor, huh?" She smiled and flexed her jaw. "Thanks. I didn't know how the spirit lady was going to manage this." Her widening smile tugged at him to return it. He cleared his throat instead.

"Spirit?"

"Yes, well," but when she then blinked a few times, Sean was sure she could have won a place in the Guinness book of records for the length of her eyelashes, "I may have been out of it. I don't know *what* they gave me in that hospital but the lady who came to me said I was to run the place in West Kilbride as a safe house."

"For?"

"I didn't ask. I thought maybe for supernaturals like us."

Sean deliberately ignored the way she'd said "like us." More specifically, he ignored the desire to take the words to mean far more than she'd intended. With a quick mental spell he muted the flush rising to his cheeks. He needed to equalise with Note sooner than he'd expected. Was it the Siren effect?

She didn't seem to notice. "You don't think that's a good idea?" he asked.

"It's a great idea," she enthused. "Ella can quit the Agency." It was interesting to hear the warmth in her voice in reference to Jonah's counterpart. "I'll be like Taz, except I'll be under a lot less pressure than he is." Sean forced his expression to be still. It still irked that she thought so highly of the demon.

"You'll be taking some of his burden, I imagine."

It took longer than expected for Siren to find the property in the village. Sean wondered if she was still suffering the effects of her head injury, but he was in no rush now, not with the job's end in sight. Sean admired the intricacies of the coven's spell when he eventually closed the gates behind the van. He hoped they'd charged Miranda a fortune for the job.

Ella dashed out of the house to meet them as he parked in the driveway. "That's just brilliant," the Faery railed at Siren. "I've got all sorts of people showing up, and you go to a cookery class. Did you even stop to think I'd be worried?" She stopped to sniff the air like a wild animal before asking, "Did you bring me anything?"

"Cookery… What?" Siren held her stomach as she read the logo on the van. Her laugh bubbled up like music. "No, Ella. I was in an accident."

"Shit. Are you okay?" The Faery glanced back to the house as a child's voice called out.

"Mum, mum. Here she is." Sean now had a compelling new reason to leave. The woman approaching was clearly Taz's wife who he'd last seen incapacitated in her own home while her son chatted and played with the Faery Ankou.

"Siren?" Josh's mother seemed very pleased to see her. That they were friends shouldn't be surprising, but it was. She and the child put their arms around Siren who hugged them back unreservedly.

"Oh, Jean," gasped Siren. "Does Taz know you're here?"

"Long story, I'm afraid." Another person appeared in the doorway and Sean shook his head, eyes flitting from the new visitor to Siren. She had agreed to this?

"Good to see you, Sean."

"You too, Harris."

"Staying here will be good for my health, right?" With his unfortunate inheritance, Sean had called on him a number of times for his assistance with Agency matters. Those days were apparently now over.

He answered the surfer boy smile with a slight nod. Avoiding Miranda's hit team would surely benefit the one remaining Agency Investor.

.

CHAPTER 35

Carolyn

Arthur tucked Carolyn's hand under his arm and led her into the busy hall. Never had she seen so many of the races in one place, and they were all dressed impeccably in an overwhelming display of wealth, style and colour. Even the guards, she noticed, wore sashes over their ornate dress uniforms. She didn't feel overly conspicuous in her rich gold clothing with its own embellishments. Most males were dressed fairly conservatively, like her father, but many of the others were as decorated as she, the Kistatus race among the most adventurous. Carolyn was absurdly glad she'd chosen the bright robe for her brother.

"The meeting with Edward went well?" Arthur asked.

"Yes, thank you."

"He wouldn't remember me," said her father, grimacing. "Yes, I cared about the child. How could I not when your mother loved him so. Amanda refused the nanny services that were provided." Carolyn grimaced, disliking that she now so easily recognised her mother in his assessment.

His mouth twisted in recollection. Amusement, tempered with regret or sadness? "It was easy to forget the boy's origins." Did he even know what was wrong with that declaration? Carolyn would have liked to hear more about life pre-Earth, but she couldn't shake the feeling that Arthur's openness was meant to lull her into a false sense of security. That said, he *could* have used magic to put her at ease and hadn't.

He offered no more and Carolyn clamped her lips tightly shut, convincing herself that she didn't want to hear anything Arthur had to say. Would he tell her if she'd screwed up his and Hecaton's plan? Had she performed as expected, or merely robbed Hecaton of the chance to step in and save the day?

There was nothing to be done but watch the entire farce play out to its conclusion. "This will be interesting," said Arthur, and Carolyn's mood lifted as she saw Mario approach.

"My liege, please forgive my detour but I agreed to accompany the Earth mage to this event."

"High mage Sean, I presume." Arthur graciously took the development in his stride. "I have yet to make his acquaintance. May we share your table?"

"Of course, sire," said Mario smoothly, "but they are preparing for you at the first table." As distracted as Carolyn was, she saw that Mario seemed unusually tense. Sean had obviously needed him and Mario hadn't refused. He had practically been raised by the mage. Arthur, by his agreement, was showing himself to be decent.

"It should be fine," the chief dismissed. "As you are part of the human contingent, we do not want to give others the wrong impression. Do we?"

Sean rose from his seat as they passed his table, his features set in little more than professional interest. He and the team had been coping without her and Mario for a year, but Carolyn didn't want reminding of that. Could they really be a part of the Protectorate machine again? She resolved to prove her worth to them when she was free.

As one of the few Earth mages who held the capacity for light and dark enchantment, Sean cut a dashing figure amongst his peers. Other than her father and perhaps Hecaton, she hadn't met a more powerful mage. A surge of power had arisen at their passing. Sean's shield? Pique threatened her, but she couldn't blame the mage for protecting himself. In response, her father – and several others – had drawn up their own protections in a tense wave of power.

A frisson of fear crept up her spine. Whether it was for Arthur or for Sean was debatable.

Carolyn didn't know how she could have missed the Rakshasas high mage who leered expectantly from his table. He too had risen so Carolyn forced a nod in his direction. Her father's companionship became a lot more welcome at this point.

A sudden hush sucked the air from the hall and everyone stood up as the chief entered with Hecaton. It made the display by the dignitaries seem like a pale imitation of real power. Carolyn's first impression was of magnitude, a strength beyond imagining, and everything within her wanted to collapse and perform some sort of … what, Carolyn? Homage?

Who *was* this? All about her, bodies fell to the floor doing exactly as she'd felt compelled to do herself. Her father raised an enquiring brow. This was clearly of limited concern to him. She followed his lead, keeping her head bowed respectfully. Oddly, Sean seemed to be experiencing the same trouble that she and Roland were evidently having with the assault on their senses. The sound of individual and heartfelt cries rose and echoed around the large space in an eerie lament.

The chief and Hecaton took their places on the dais. Lucas cast his benevolent golden gaze over the crowd. How could this powerful creature be dying? He radiated such health and vitality, like nothing Carolyn had ever seen before.

Illusion?

And then she *saw* the shadow thread of dark magic that spun from Lucas to Hecaton. Wrong. It whirled to Lucas *from* his high mage. Seemingly oblivious, there were many people in the crowd who it now encircled – everyone who had fallen to their knees ... or their faces. Mario groaned as a wisp of the magic wove around him and Carolyn took his arm, nodding thanks to Sean who'd taken a hold at his opposite side. Between them, they held Mario straight, and the draining tendril slid from him. She deliberately didn't link to Mario for an explanation – she *felt* what was happening, but the physical contact with Mario and Sean helped them all.

Carolyn met her father's inquiring expression with a frown. The lines of magic were actively feeding energy to Hecaton who directed it to the chief. Almost everyone in the company was contributing to Lucas's show. The force of it called to Carolyn, and she had to dig her nails into her palms to keep control.

In a room filled with predators and prey, it wasn't *that* comforting to find out to which group she belonged. The energy pulsed as it gathered and passed a few scant inches in front of her. It hadn't been so close before, and she wanted very much to touch ... to *take* it.

The line was *bowing* towards her.

Arthur's fingers curled around her free wrist and she felt her control return. She allowed his mental voice to fill her thoughts. *It's all part of the torture, my dear. If you had been weaker, you would have dropped like those about us, and been oblivious to the drain of your power. That you can stand amongst the most powerful in the realms is an enormous achievement, though it comes at a price. In regard to the ceremony, if you were to give in to your instincts and disrupt the flow, it would not be ... mannerly. In fact, as my daughter, it would be an unforgiveable sign of aggression.*

Great. Whatever this was, she shared it with her father, Sean and all the others left standing near the dais. Why hadn't he prepared her for this? In her right mind, she would never have tried to take the energy meant for her brother. She wanted to *help* him, damn it.

You are very young and so new to your powers. I think your control is outstanding and I cannot begin to express my pride in you. Carolyn nodded and drew her shield around her thoughts. Arthur returned her hand to the crook of his arm and she let go of Mario's. Sean had also withdrawn and didn't catch her eye. She found no comfort to be had with Arthur's assurances. She needed

Mario and the Protectorate more than ever to train and help her with just about everything.

Hecaton's silken sibilant voice sounded as though it came from a great distance and Carolyn breathed in a calming breath of air laden with the fragrance of rich oils and wine, and through it she thought she caught a lighter, lemongrass scent. The entire mix wrapped around and soothed her.

"Friendss, family and otherworlders, I welcome you to Skean castle where, today, we witness history in the making. As high mage, I would take the opportunity to remind all of the neutrality of this event. Provisions are set to ensure standardss."

The crowd rose to their feet, some looking dazed but most gazing worshipfully at the sight of Hecaton and Lucas. Edward had also appeared on the dais, his form remaining true – thank God. The trace of lemongrass wafted to her more strongly now, diverting her. Her heartbeat raced, and she made no effort to disguise her searching gaze. *Calm down, Carolyn,* she thought. *It's Note's realm. The scent will be particular to the race, not the boy.*

She tried to catch her brother's eye, but he was scanning the crowd for someone other than her. Debbie? Anyone else would be concentrating fully on their life-changing ceremony but her brother was chasing after a girl's attention and Carolyn was imagining Note's presence. They both deserved a good slap. Eventually, Edward's burning eyes found Carolyn's, and she opted for an encouraging smile. *You can do this.*

Lucas laid his right upper limb on Eddie's bowed head, snaking around her brother's shoulders. She couldn't hear the murmured incantation at first but Hecaton repeated, "The Kistatus regime continues with the chosen." *Who decided on the chosen?* The old magic wielded by Hecaton and the chief was something separate. The feeling intensified as the hall filled with the response from the gathering.

"Let the chosen be blessed." Carolyn followed suit, murmuring the responses with the others. Though all attention was on the dais, she saw that the top tier of guests were slightly on edge. While the magic moved and swirled around them, they all seemed to be on high alert, their powers tightly reigned.

A beautiful couple looked towards her with large unblinking eyes. They both smiled simultaneously and Carolyn returned it, dreamily. These were true Faeries, she realised as the male, seeing her distraction, winked and turned sideways to her. Inviting her to admire his silvery sheer wings? Impatience flickering in his expression, he clearly expected something from her. Resisting an eye roll, she simply mouthed, "Gorgeous," and, as the creature's smile widened, Carolyn forced her concentration back to the ceremony.

Arthur stiffened in outrage. "That impudent Faery is attracted to your power. The fact you have not bound to any of the realms makes you desirable, but to do that in my presence…?"

Carolyn soothed him as best she could, thinking the Faery would have anticipated her father's reaction. "My fault, dad. He knows you can't do anything about it here. I shouldn't have caught his eye. It's just something else for me to bear in mind."

His tension fled, replaced by something much more heart-warming. "Dad?" he said. "I think I like that term." Had she really called him that? A slip up rather than anything conscious, she wasn't about to dampen his restored humour.

Hecaton continued to incant, emptying a vial of what looked to be a light dusty substance which puffed in a cloud over Edward and Lucas. It whipped around the occupants of the dais before dissipating.

"What was that?" she whispered, stifling a cough.

Arthur grimaced and her eyes grew round. "Different customs are followed by each of the realms. This is one of the nicer observances."

The previous chief's ashes? As Hecaton continued the ritual, she understood that the residue had been created from the former ruler's heart. She found herself wondering bizarrely where the rest of his remains were kept. Her eyes were drawn to two urns on the step leading up to the platform. They were going to cremate Lucas as part of the ceremony?

Arthur shifted at her side and she caught him frowning, his blue eyes darkening with some new knowledge that obviously concerned him. She followed his gaze to her brother who was no longer looking so good. His large form shuddered before his father on the dais. Lucas continued to look at Hecaton, energy swirling and embracing their every inch.

"What's wrong?" Carolyn murmured. "This isn't usual, is it?" Why did her brother's power seem to be feeding Hecaton and consequently Lucas? "Tell me."

"There's nothing we can do. The process has begun."

"What?" Carolyn felt her gut tighten as she watched the flow of magical currents in the room. Almost everybody fed Hecaton and Lucas but the power from her brother appeared to be pulling away from him. He seemed smaller … lessened. "This is supposed to be transference, but it looks like…" Arthur laid a hand on her shoulder as though in sympathy. He too could see that Edward was failing, and that Lucas was bursting with power.

Something passed between Hecaton and Lucas when a surge of power was drawn from the crowd. The chief looked in command but he reached under Edward as though to assist him in standing up. He held him close and Edward's bright eyes slipped shut. "Oh, my God," Mario gasped. "This isn't a transfer, it's a sacrifice!"

Carolyn's lips froze before she could utter a word, Arthur's power wrapping around and stilling her before she could jump to her brother's aid. Tears stung her eyes as she struggled to remove herself from her father who seemed genuinely perturbed. Edward was clinging on to Lucas, his Kistatus skin now significantly paled, but he wasn't dead yet.

I'm so sorry, Carolyn. Edward hasn't been strong enough. I swear I didn't know this would happen. Lucas was ready to hand over the realm … I'm sure of it. His words had taken on an odd quality and Carolyn realised he had suspected this might happen.

A blurred form swept on to the dais and the crowd gasped in horror as Sean appeared before Lucas and Edward. The sound of tearing and hissing drowned out everything else, but Hecaton barely paused during his incantation. His proud features gave nothing away, but Carolyn had the distinct feeling that Sean's actions were expected. It was only when she caught the Earth mage's transformed face that she realised it was Note – and there was no doubting that this was *her* Note.

His eyes burned into hers as he approached Lucas and Edward. Oh, no! What was he planning? It seemed to take a great deal of effort for him to tear his gaze from her, and Carolyn wrenched against her father with renewed intensity. Her head moved slowly from side to side, unable to form the words she needed to say.

Whatever game they had been playing, not everyone was following the plan, and by the glimmer of rage in Lucas's eyes, *he* had not expected this. Someone was about to die on the platform. *Oh, God. Please let it not be Note.*

The disruptive demon stepped forward, all his attention on the chief. "I challenge for the crown," Note boomed.

Lucas scoffed, a loud whisper that grated through any semblance of calm Carolyn possessed. "You would test a half dead boy."

"No, my liege," Note replied, still managing to sound respectful. What was he doing up there? "I challenge that you choose life for your son and accept me as the chosen." Even as he spoke, Carolyn watched the magic bow towards Note before returning to Hecaton. Lucas's eyes dimmed to copper as he very gently laid her brother on the edge of the dais and there kissed him.

Carolyn's heart flipped when she saw that her brother still breathed.

Note was still speaking to Lucas. "Edward was never the chosen. He *is* a powerful warrior but not the *chosen one*. I don't believe you want to use him as a source of power. He would give you no more than twenty more years on the throne." Lucas's irises flickered in contrast to the steady gold of Note's. The chief was clearly angry, but listening. Note's bright eyes met Carolyn's for an instant and her throat constricted in panic. *Whatever it is, don't do it,* she broadcast.

Carolyn felt Arthur's spell release her, and she sputtered, "W…what are you doing?" Her feet took her to her brother's side. Note's face was almost serene as his gaze swept past her to take in the crowd. She wasn't fooled. She knew, damn it, but she couldn't beg that he *not* interfere. She couldn't belittle *his* sacrifice. A hush descended as Hecaton's soft chant created a bespelled background against which Lucas spoke to the gathering. His magic demanded and compelled his audience to hang upon his every word.

"My son is indeed a fine warrior and perhaps one day he will be worthy of the Kistatus crown, but here the true chosen has returned to us." Lucas swept his limbs out towards Note and the crowd appeared to turn their adoration towards the challenger. Though standing firm, Carolyn could tell he was uncomfortable under such attention. "My faithful, behold your king!" Arms outstretched, he stepped in to embrace Note whose burning gold eyes met hers as she felt restricting hands on her shoulders.

I do this for you, those eyes seemed to say.

Carolyn could only watch in utter helplessness as Note struck like lightening to fasten onto the chief's neck, the pair engulfed in fiery, destructive magic. Carolyn's scream was drowned out by the cries of a frenzied crowd from which ribbons of sizzling energy poured out in streams towards the fiery mass of light now at the centre of the dais. Silent tears tracked down her cheeks as Edward's form returned to its human shape before her.

His eyes opened, revealing surprise, and pride swelled within her for what he had accomplished. Her brother would see it as an epic fail, but he had tried and survived. That was better than being dead. Right? Eddie's gaze slid from her to the spectacle of the chief's light spreading towards them. Almost as one, Arthur and Mario drew them from the platform where they'd stood, entranced.

Carolyn's thoughts filled with Note: he had saved her from a feral existence, leaving behind all he had known. She had soon become a challenging and demanding partner, though, but he'd never become frustrated or angry with her, even as she'd cursed his restraint and manipulated him, using their bond as her tool of choice.

Unable to distinguish between the forms on the dais, Carolyn burned with shame at her treatment of him. There was only so much she could blame on forces outside her control. Without the separation of worlds, she could never have stuck to her resolve to keep away from him. How ironic then that she was now losing him to another calling.

Her wrist tingled, and, for an instant, Carolyn could feel *his* bond with the team, a group which appeared to have evolved beyond all recognition.

How much of their and her boy would remain when he became king?

How could they and she let him go?

"I choose you," he'd said – and proved his devotion to her– over and over.

Note

Note felt like he was dying when Lucas came to him. On the surface, the chief had been all bravado but Note experienced the pain of his sovereign. Yes, Lucas would have drained his son and gained another few years, but the sacrifice of his family would have made for an unsatisfying victory.

Events had conspired to lead them to this. There was no point in wondering how things would have turned out if any of the variables had been different. East had once told him to embrace his destiny and forget the girl. Never would he have imagined choosing the chiefdom to save Carolyn's brother.

Hecaton's involvement was clearly suspect. Had he *foreseen* the problem with Edward's inauguration? If Note hadn't been present, would his father have stepped up to the task or would he have continued to drain Edward and fuel Lucas. The possibilities had been many and yet, here he was, fulfilling the fate against which he had been warned.

If Hecaton believed that Note's rule would resemble Lucas's, then he would be in for a shock.

Note's blood bubbled and burned as the magic sought to complete his allegiance to Skean.

The realm cannot have it all!

As he watched Carolyn through the fire that changed and removed Lucas from the world, he accepted *most* of the changes needed to fulfil his obligations. How could he possibly keep away from Carolyn now after everything he'd done to get her back?

Her tears caused him pain but his lady was resilient. Her life would be full and complete with her family accessible. The team would guide and protect Carolyn in her duties.

She had *never* belonged to Note. Hecaton had even taken *that* from him, but once he explained it to Carolyn, she would find comfort in Ethan – her true chosen.

Ethan would love her in the way Note had given up at the very instant he'd challenged the crown.

CHAPTER 36

Carolyn

Carolyn had felt dazed well into the next day after having returned to Empustat with Mario and her father. She had slowly sifted through the facts and had come to the conclusion that she should be thankful for the way things had worked out. Knowing that and *feeling* it, though, were two different things.

"It'll take a few days for it all to sink in," Mario had said. Ethan, on the other hand, seemed annoyed with her.

"He didn't save your brother so you could be a miserable bitch," he'd said, but Carolyn couldn't bring herself to rise to the bait.

At their last meal together, Carolyn had worn a new dress and prettied herself up, making an effort for the sake of the others. If they saw that her smile was strained and forced, nobody said. Everyone appeared to be having a nice time despite the oppressiveness in the air. It wasn't only Carolyn's doing, her father radiated the same sense of dissatisfaction.

Dinner tasted like sawdust, and she toyed with her food, responding appropriately as her aunt tried to inject life into the conversation. Uncle Lawrence had also lost his usual bluster, and Ethan and Mario made their best efforts by her side. Arthur had resumed his usual stoic persona since their return, and Carolyn wanted to hate him for his aloofness. She didn't, choosing to believe he'd been as affected as the rest of them by the events in Skean, if perhaps for different reasons.

He *should* be happy, she thought. Note, by his terrible selfless action, had removed himself from her future. *What about you, Carolyn? Note's made your life a lot easier in more ways than one.* She wanted to tell her inner nagging voice to shut up, but it wasn't that easy to deny the truth. Note wasn't a threat to her serenity any more.

At the end of the evening, they changed into serviceable clothes, and Carolyn strapped on the knives that had appeared in her room. Her father obviously thought that returning Note's gift to her was a good idea – and it had been. *Oh, Note!* Now wasn't the time for tears. She strapped on the knives, fastening their sheaths as tight as she could, and shrugged into a soft leather vest which kept the weapons discretely hidden. Returning to the others waiting in the library, she felt lighter and more focussed.

While they were saying their goodbyes, Ethan opened a gateway in the courtyard. Arthur didn't look pleased when the mage returned to the gathering and announced its presence. Trailing outside, the air smelled sweetly of roses and damp night air. Lawrence fussed over Sylvia who dabbed her cheeks delicately.

Having played a large part in her "rehabilitation" under Arthur's orders, the lady had gone as gently as she'd dared with Carolyn. With the subsequent heavy-handed techniques of her father and Peter, Carolyn couldn't dredge up a single negative thought about her.

"Aunt Silvia, you know I'll visit, and when I'm all set up, perhaps you and Lawrence can come see *me*. I'll even book a show if you like. An opera?" Sylvia's eyes lit up.

"I'd love that." Carolyn kissed the couple and turned to her father who stood rigidly beside the gateway.

"You know this isn't for ever." Moving forward, she stepped in for a hug. "Do I need to leave something with you as collateral? One of my friends, perhaps?" A rumble sounded from Arthur's chest. Drawing back, she saw that his humour had been reluctant.

"Like you could," said Ethan, taking his place at Carolyn's side.

"After what transpired in the realms yesterday," her father said, "you know my thoughts on the matter. It would be wiser for you to stay awhile longer. I don't want you doing anything hasty."

Having languished a year already in the realm, Carolyn assured him they weren't acting in haste. Seeing her resolve, Arthur asked for a moment alone, and Carolyn nodded to Ethan and Mario. When they'd withdrawn, he took both her hands in his, and surprisingly, it wasn't too hard for her to guard against softening.

"You need to listen, Father, because I'm done with repeating, reinforcing, and practically begging for your approval." Her brow lifted at his wounded expression. It wasn't real. "This," and she glanced down at her serviceable clothes, "is what I am. I *understand* that it's some sort of embarrassment to you." He couldn't reasonably deny it. "I'm *happy* when I'm called to the gateways." Arthur's brows rose at that, and she shook her head slightly. "What I do, what the team does … matters." Her gaze slid to the door behind which the boys waited.

"I know how it sounds and I'm not so arrogant as to think it's all about me, either. Ethan, Mario, even Note from a distance, they're all a part of it – the bigger picture. I'm proud to be numbered amongst them." Her eyes searched his for some sort of understanding. "I'm ashamed that I lost my way."

Arthur's jaw ticked with some sort of emotion, and his grip tightened on her hands as he said, "You have nothing to be ashamed of. I tried to tame that which could not be tamed, and now I pay the price. I believe we would have reached this point with or without your friends."

He thought they were slaves to fate? Carolyn couldn't bring herself to believe in *that*.

"I'll miss you." She embraced the Lilim, blinking back her tears. Backing away, he remained with his arms outstretched, as if expecting her to return to their safety. She didn't have to feel the gathering of energy from him to know he could *do* something. "You believe this makes me weak," she said as he dropped his arms, shaking his head in swift denial. "I *love* you, Father, but I'm not blind to what you've been doing. If you try to stop me now then you'd better be prepared to kill me because death would be preferable to a lifetime of illusion, pathetic tricks and nothing special."

Arthur remained still as he watched her. Carolyn didn't want to hurt him but she resolved that, no matter what, she'd be back on Earth with her mother before the day was out.

"I hear you, daughter." Carolyn wondered, uncomfortably, if he was referring to her inner thoughts. "I can only hope that you will one day forgive my attempts, pathetic as they may have been." The latter part he delivered with a twitch of his lips.

"No, I didn't mean…" She suddenly thought of Peter, sent to charm her, and just grinned, despairingly. "You know what? Yes, some of the tricks *were* pretty pathetic." His eyes widened and a genuine chuckle escaped him.

"You are truly your mother's daughter." He hesitated for a moment. "I don't like to ask," *sure you do*, her suspicious brain supplied, but she tried to remember that they didn't have much time left, "but could you do something for me?"

"Of course."

"Amanda should know this already, but I would be grateful if you could remind your mother that I'm still not entirely a monster." Carolyn's brow furrowed. He was right, he was only "sometimes" a monster, but Arthur's wording was vaguely prettier. "She is in my thoughts every day. I am a patient man and hope we will one day meet again."

"Hmm." Carolyn could feel the subtext behind his carefully rehearsed words, and it sounded a little like a stalker. "I need to tell you that—"

"Yes, I know the tactics I've employed in the past didn't work out well. I try not to repeat my mistakes." Carolyn bit back everything else she could have said about that. Could she help doubting his sincerity.

"Same here, Father. Compromise isn't weakness." She saw his gaze slide to Beni.

"He's better with you," he said, and Carolyn had the feeling that Beni would have tried to join her whether Arthur had agreed or not. He was hers.

Arthur wasted no more time before calling Ethan and Mario back, to accompany Carolyn on her short trip home. She motioned for them to step into the opening first. Ethan cursed under his breath but did as he was asked. In the next instant, she and Beni entered and, unable to help it, she glanced back at the proud figure on the gateway's edge.

Her heart ached at the new loss but she didn't have time to ponder it. Her stomach lurched and Beni gave an excited yelp as the gateway tunnelled before them. She felt Ethan reach for her but Carolyn could only concentrate on keeping hold of Beni.

The exit then split before them and Ethan and Mario slipped to the right as she and Beni were catapulted through a much smaller but powerfully pulling branch to the left. They were squeezed so tightly the air was crushed from their bodies. Then, like a bottle cork, the pair were spat out in a tangle of paws and limbs on a hard slippery surface.

"Oomph, get off." She blinked in bright artificial light. It would have been nice to have had some time for orientation before the gateways messed with her, but she'd chosen this, hadn't she? Beni lifted his soulful eyes to her as Carolyn scrambled to her feet. Though wearing knives, it was her screwdriver that sprang to her hand as she readied herself to face the new threat.

"You came!" a child shrieked from a few feet in front of her and Carolyn hurriedly tucked the screwdriver into its cuff as the little boy jumped up and down. She glanced at Beni, suspiciously. Neither looked like Santa Claus, so why was the child so happy?

"Where are we?" she asked.

"You're home, of course," said the child who then turned to the hound, his eyes shining merrily. "Hi, Henry. I've missed you." Beni rolled over and presented his belly, submitting to a thorough hugging. "You've been watching out for the princess, haven't you, boy? I've been really good," he said proudly, casting a shy look towards Carolyn. "I didn't call until I saw it was okay."

"Okay with whom, Josh? Not me, for sure." A fraught looking woman had appeared in the hall doorway leading from the kitchen Carolyn now saw she was in. This couldn't be good.

Why was Taz's wife and son pulling her through a gateway? Which realm was she in?

"Where are we?" she repeated, unable to see much of the dark landscape through the brightly lit kitchen window. It looked like Earth: the surrounding appliances were as any she'd see in a human kitchen or as sold by their local stores. The feeling from the house was what confused her. The vibes she felt weren't *bad* exactly, but they were definitely otherworldly.

"I'm so sorry," said the woman. "I didn't know he could do that here. This is a safe house – well, it's meant to be – in the village of West Kilbride." That was all Carolyn needed to bring a sigh of relief. She was very close to her home town – could probably run to her old house if she wanted to. *There's no-one there for you now?* "If it's any help, I don't believe he was trying to get you. He's just missed Henry, that's all."

Carolyn had the distinct impression the beast was avoiding her gaze. "I've been calling him Beni."

"No. *That's* the seers' watcher," said the woman decisively. "I've only heard about him from Josh and Taz and I don't know if I believed he existed until now, but Josh called him through that," and her brows gathered into a frown as she stared at the small opening now hovering near the floor. "And it's not even a proper gateway." Leaning hesitantly towards the red glow, she explained, "It's a branch or something."

"Whoops," said Josh. "I better close it then."

"No, dear. Let someone else do it. Please?" She turned her head to the door and called, "Siren, Ella? Could you come down here?" and footfalls approached too quickly.

Carolyn stifled a shudder. If Ella was the one she suspected, then hanging about couldn't be a good idea.

The hybrid was first in the doorway and she looked just like Carolyn remembered, except that she wore pyjama shorts and a hoodie.

"What's with all the–" Then: "Crap!" The glare the child's mother gave Ella was almost comical. "Sorry... Um – Oh my?" she said, inoffensively.

"I've got it. It's fine." Another woman slipped through the doorway, looking like she'd just stepped off a lingerie photo shoot. A silky kimono didn't hide much of the girl at all. She aimed a device at the tiny gateway and it sizzled shut. Her eyes found Carolyn's, and she offered a wide smile of perfect white teeth. "You must be Carolyn. I've heard so much about you. I didn't think you were home yet."

"I'm not, officially. I was on my way when I was brought here ... by mistake?"

The beautiful girl shook her head, losing only a little wattage of her smile. "No mistake, I'm afraid. Josh managed a misdirect of some sort, to catch Henry I expect, and you ... you were holding on to him?" Carolyn's face must have shown her guilt because she nodded. "That's why he caught you too."

"But–" Carolyn's eyes returned to the hound, who'd lifted his paws to cover his face. She knew he wasn't a regular beast, but they'd called him the seers' watcher? What exactly was he watching out for with Carolyn?

"Josh is a seer," said the girl with the device as she moved to put an arm around the child's mother. The poor woman's face was wet with tears. Carolyn couldn't begin to imagine the damage that such a gifted child could wreak. Her memory tracked back to the Mow realm where Taz had traded his son. What were the chances that this was the freaky result of her rescuing him?

Carolyn still had the tiny silvery mark caused by the favour the Motus had bestowed. Maybe she'd have the team check on all the documented rescues. "Oh, where are my manners," the girl in the kimono now said . "Can I get you a drink ... something to eat?" She began to fill a kettle, introducing herself as Siren, Josh's mum as Jean, and Carolyn remembered Ella just fine.

"Henry's not mine," said Josh, sadly. "He belongs to the lady with all the faces. She lets him visit me."

Ella shrugged widely and pulled out chairs from the kitchen table so they could sit down. "That's a new one on us," she directed at Carolyn. "Trust me."

"You seem different," said Carolyn, thinking it to be more than the muted zeal of the Faery.

"Shush, it's a secret." She grinned broadly at Carolyn. "We're just one big happy family here. I'm surprised *everyone* wasn't woken up by all this."

Jean took a seat at the table, nursing an empty cup in both hands. She definitely seemed to need the support this place appeared to give. "Taz saw the signs and was promised a cure when he traded him through the gateway." Her features seemed hollowed out as she stared at Carolyn. "It turned out to be a horrible scam. Thank God for your intervention. But Taz—" Her eyes flicked to Josh and she sniffed miserably. "Things got worse with Josh as you might imagine, and the precators offered us sanctuary here."

Not quite what Carolyn had envisaged. "I'm glad you're safe," she said. Knowing only a few details from Mario about the Protector's top men, they sounded like a scary bunch. If they couldn't protect them then no-one could. Carolyn turned to Josh who was starting to give long blinks as he curled up on the floor with Ben ... Henry. "Do you sneak down here a lot to open gateways?"

Josh giggled. "No, I came down for some milk but when I felt that Henry was free, I just brought him here."

"You've spoken to him ... not as a dog. As a human?" Catching the hound's gaze, she wondered if somewhere deep down, she'd known from the start. With everything that had happened, she hadn't thought to ask about Arthur's missing guard, the dog had been welcomed into her life like an old friend.

If he wasn't her father's, then who did Henry work for that Arthur had agreed to his presence? *That* ruled out Protectorate involvement.

"Not human," said Josh, "but you wouldn't be able to tell the difference."

"Great. He's probably seen me naked a dozen times."

"Oh no," said Josh, sniggering. "See? He's shaking his head."

"That makes me feel so reassured," said Carolyn. Henry had watched over her in Empustat, but now she didn't know whose side he was on. A deep breath did nothing to steady her. "I really need to get going." She stood up from the table. "It's been nice meeting you all and I hope to see you again, but I should get back to the others."

"It's all sorted," said Siren, peering out of the kitchen window. "I put out an alert earlier. Someone will be here–" a loud rapping noise sounded on the door. "Right about now. That'll be Sean."

"Knocking?" said Carolyn, incredulous. "Why didn't he just do his usual?"

"The wards prevent anyone zapping in or out," said Jean tiredly before focussing on the hound. "Usually."

Ella tapped the boy on his head and he gave her a sleepy yawn. "Josh here is apparently the only one who can open a gateway on this site."

"That's really something," said Carolyn. She sympathised with him. Even as an adult, it was tough being far from "normal". By the look of things, he was in good company.

"Isn't it, though." Ella scooped Josh into her arms. "Back to bed for you, babe. Think you can sleep for the rest of the night and give your poor mum a break?" He was already snoring lightly when Ella turned in the doorway to watch Sean enter the house.

Carolyn found herself wrapped in the mage's unexpected embrace. She savoured the coolness of his cheek as it brushed against hers. His magic comforted and drew her in. "Thanks for coming to get me."

"No problem, my dear, but there's been a slight change of plan." Sean then acknowledged the other occupants of the room, and by Siren and Ella's response, he was clearly welcome to stick around.

"Aren't you forgetting something?" Jean didn't sound tired any more. Her expression sharpened as she pointed to the hound.

"He's a Seer's dog, not mine," Carolyn said. "I didn't even name him right."

Josh turned in Ella's arms. "Hey, you little fraud," she mock complained. "I thought you were sleeping. You just wanted the cuddle, didn't you?"

Fixing bleary eyes on Carolyn, the child quietly said, "He likes the name you gave him better. If he could change back, he'd tell you himself, but the lady stuck him like that for being bad."

"Really?" Carolyn gave the beast a surprised look, and he whined.

"You need to keep him 'til she calls for him again."

"Right, the lady with all the faces." Yes, Carolyn was really looking forward to meeting her. "All right then." She loved Beni already but now she knew there was a man in that furry body, it changed things a lot. Were the seers good guys? What was going to happen when the scary mystic called for him?

Sean clasped her hand. "I need to tell you—"

"I know you're all very busy in there," a familiar, rather frazzled sounding voice called from outside, "but I'd appreciate some help with this pram. Mack makes a terrible fuss if his sleep gets disturbed."

"Sean?"

Carolyn's vision darkened at the edges. She'd imagined that voice a million times, and it didn't matter that they'd communicated mentally while her mother had fixed Sam, nothing could have prepared her for hearing it again, not here on Earth where she belonged. Sean supported her weight as the long awaited event crashed into her consciousness.

Her mother was home.

CHAPTER 37

Carolyn   (One Month Later)

Carolyn's sister squealed at the interruption to her play.

"Sorry, Tess, but mum wants you back for your nap." The child struggled for an instant before realising that Carolyn had an apple in her hand. The threatened tantrum drained away as she reached for the fruit. Pretty amber eyes turned to Carolyn, and she marvelled yet again at how Tess and her baby brother had so quickly stolen her heart. A month after Note's inauguration and, surrounded by loved ones, she had coped remarkably well with the transition.

Carolyn had been delighted to have her mother join the team at their mountain retreat in Glencoe.

"Where's Beni?" asked Tess, through a mouthful of apple.

"He'll be back for dinner, I expect." Carolyn tried not to worry about the hound and the fact he could be called back to the seer at any time.

"Maio, maio!" called Tess, bouncing on Carolyn's hip as the mage appeared with a flourish from between the trees in the glen.

"I swear that child is gifted. I can't sneak up on anyone when she's around." Tess put her little arms out, and Mario scooped her away, gently admonishing, "You sound like a cat, little one. Let me hear you say 'Mario'." He accentuated the "r", more growl than speech, and Tess giggled.

"Maio funny," she burbled, but Carolyn's smile had already thinned. Her mother wanted a normal life for the children but it wouldn't happen any time soon. When either child became too excited, Tess would spontaneously change to her Kistatus form, and as adorable as she was, it ruled out an entirely human setting, at least for the meantime. Carolyn had passed on Arthur's message to her mother, surprised by the reaction it had evoked.

As she'd eagerly returned her mother's hug, Carolyn had known she'd never go back to being the careless teen who shrugged off such attention with embarrassment.

"My first *real* love," Amanda had said, her forest green eyes glinting in remembrance. "I just didn't trust it." Her response had been followed by a long and adoring look towards Tess and baby Mack. Carolyn understood that her mother would never criticize Lucas's contribution to her life.

Without further gateway use, Amanda would be expected to age normally from now on, which was what her mother wanted. As far as the public were aware, they were sisters, and with Protectorate help, they'd soon have the documentation to prove it.

Eddie had outright refused to return home. They planned to visit him soon, and with so much changing in the realm and Note in a position of authority, their safety could be reasonably assured.

Carolyn chased Mario and Tess back to the garden where Morgan approached to pick up the toddler and show her a magic trick with flower petals. Mario, show off that he was, took control of them, and they changed to an arrow shape that tagged each of them as it chased them through the shrubbery. Spotting Amanda's watchful eye from the kitchen window, Carolyn was glad she hadn't put an end to their fun.

"Tess's nap time?" she scolded when Carolyn entered the kitchen, but she was smiling. Sam looked up from his task of rocking Mack to sleep in his pram. The enforcers would take care of the children with their lives though Carolyn wouldn't put it past Mario to *induce* a nap if Tess got cantankerous.

The baby cooed at the sound of Carolyn's arrival and she dropped a kiss on his soft cheek. Mack was very accepting of all the new faces in his life, and Tess, though less trusting, had them all wrapped around her tiny pinkie finger.

Amanda's gaze flicked to Sam. "We're going to set up outside for the barbecue."

"Sounds great," Carolyn enthused. "Need any help?"

"No, lass," said Sam. "Your mother and I have got it all under control."

With about an hour to pass before dinner, Carolyn felt only a tiny bit guilty for excusing herself to hike up to the middle of the Etive range. It was a joy marred by her thoughts of Miranda Levy and the worrying development of O.W.E. permits. Her friend Debbie, like others, had entered the realms on work experience passes that the Protectorate had stepped up their measures to monitor. Carolyn knew that, if she came across unhappy humans who had signed up for OWE's, she was likely to bring them home regardless of the consequences. Fortunately, as yet, she'd not crossed her seniors, but it was only a matter of time.

At a good height on the range, Carolyn found a decent crevasse in which to practise with the knives she now unwrapped from the harness in her backpack. The sun had begun its descent, casting half the lower valley in shadow. The play of light and shade lent an otherworldly beauty to the brush and heather filled slopes. She was content to meander through, wondering if a rabbit or a pheasant would be easy to barbecue. She couldn't bring herself to think about culling any of the adorable deer that scrambled to find purchase on the surrounding slopes.

Note was *always* at the back of her mind. Of late, she'd been too busy to dwell on everything that had happened, but spent a little time each day examining her thoughts like some sort of bizarre cognitive therapy course.

As she'd learned to do with the others, she sensed Ethan before he came into view. He still had an effect on her like none of the others, but it was contained. *She* was more controlled, she amended. With her tattoo modified to connect with the entire team, Ethan believed she'd gained a stability that was superior to the anchoring and kept Note's claim from posing a problem.

Why was she still avoiding him when her friends – both old and new – visited him in Skean as often as they liked? *Because it's different for you*, her brain supplied. *You let him down, and you can't face his disappointment or rejection.*

"I'm glad you got the knives back," said Ethan, softly mocking, "but you're going to be forever sharpening them." Carolyn looked down at the knife in her hand and tossed it to spin in the air before deftly catching it.

"It's not the same with the practise blades." Returning the knife to the harness now strapped around her waist, she couldn't remember having put it on. Ethan placed a finger under the leather and Carolyn's breath hitched.

"It's softened enough now." Irritation flickered briefly in his eyes, giving way to a strained concern. "Are you doing okay? I know it's been tough, adjusting." She nodded, watching his mouth form the words. With a step back, the enforcer scowled. "You think I can't see how things have changed between us?"

The thought of discussing it gave her palpitations, but she was an adult, damn it. "You know, I can't thank you enough for trying to save me in Empustat."

"Very true." His eyes conveyed that she could try harder to be grateful, and he folded his arms, drawing attention to the beautifully defined muscles of his upper body. Not fair. *He's just pushing your buttons*. No. It was more than that, she realised now. He was protecting himself from her, almost exactly as she would protect herself from Note.

She and Ethan were alike, and having avoided the conversation for so long, she was sickened with herself. If truly honest, Carolyn *wanted* to have

Ethan as her safety net but there was too much respect between them to allow that.

Neither she nor Ethan was brave enough to allow their vulnerabilities to show, and it wasn't necessarily a bad thing. Ethan would never refuse any advance she made, but he knew better than to initiate it. He was as proud as her, and even more scared of rejection. She owed him honesty.

"That kiss on the riverbank—"

"Forgotten." He'd clearly expected this. That was good – it made things easier. He surveyed her with narrowed eyes but Carolyn sighed in relief, latching on to the words gratefully.

"Thanks. I'm sorry about that." She caught a glimmer of his pain before his gaze shifted from her.

Oh! – Carolyn didn't want to see that, but it was his right. He wanted her to know she'd hurt him. She didn't deserve to be let off too easily. He was clearly doing his best and Carolyn appreciated it. Ethan wasn't blind, he would have noticed she was doing fine without the angst that anchoring brought. Her main worry in regard to Ethan was simply her overactive hormones, and she was subject to those in the same way as every other teen on the planet.

"Hey, it was a confusing time, but that kiss was pretty much the highlight of the trip for me." His tone was light and mocking, but she wished his expression hadn't betrayed more. "If you need some practise 'til the right guy comes along, or maybe some tips, I'm at your disposal."

"I'm in need of tips, am I?"

Ethan's eyes gleamed from beneath his dark brows and she stifled a shiver. He was aware he wasn't "the right guy", but he wanted to be. "You should go see him."

"What?" *Him* – Note obviously.

"Much as I hate to say it, you owe him." Ethan scrubbed a hand over his recently shorn hair, and Carolyn noticed his stubble was about the same length. With his scar slightly covered, he looked less like a thug.

She supposed it best not to share that fact though her feelings about the scar were mixed. Was he hiding it to let her know he didn't want or need to wear her mark? Mario had made it sound undeliberate but Carolyn couldn't be sure. There was a darkness in her that craved the wild irresponsibility that her unanchored self had enjoyed.

"You need to see if he still affects you," Ethan grumbled, and Carolyn tried to follow the thread of his thoughts.

"You think he's a threat now he's chief?"

"No… Yes, maybe, Carolyn. I don't know, but it's something the team need to know so we can—"

"Control it?" She couldn't help the edge that crept into her tone.

He shook his head. "I was about to say 'so we can move on, or take measures'. If it's any consolation, I don't think you're anchored to anyone anymore."

"Except to the others," she said with the beginnings of a smile. The connection to Ethan's enforcers felt right. There was no overwhelming dependency from her or from any of them. They all contributed, even Note. Although he'd walled himself from them, he had still been drawn upon by the team. She eyed Ethan thoughtfully. "We need to see if the claiming has a pull after Hecaton's involvement with Note."

"His dad's a manipulative bastard, still. But Note…?" he struggled with the words. "Note's got real power now, and he'll never abuse it." The admission clearly hurt him. Carolyn was amazed that Ethan's opinion of Note had changed so much – but he'd spent a year working with the Kistatus, and they'd grown to know each other pretty well.

Arthur hadn't abused his power with Amanda either but their relationship hadn't had great results. Could she avoid repeating at least some of her mother's mistakes?

"You know you're still demon mate bait."

It always came back to that indisputable fact. Did Ethan want her to go or not? He could read her too easily, and Carolyn saw through his tone to the man beneath. "I'll always be that, Ethan. The claim gave a false sense of security."

He nodded approval at her admission. She could see he was torn about her going to Note but it wasn't right for her to let him think they stood a chance together. Ethan *loved* her, she felt it in the link, and he would sense her feelings in return. She loved him too, but couldn't *say* so. With a little nurturing, it could grow into something powerful and epic. To end the possibility… hurt. But it pained her more to think she'd cut off Note – in whatever capacity he'd have her.

Note had stayed away while he'd dealt with his new responsibilities. There was the potential for him to return to the team in a limited capacity; the situation had been left entirely in his own hands. She knew in her heart that if she and Ethan became closer, it would lock Note out of the team dynamic completely.

Love defied explanation, much like magic. It could be spun, shaped and moulded to take on a wonderfully beautiful shape … or the exact opposite. The emotion itself was not complicated, and Carolyn was surrounded by the sentiment in so many forms. Even with the new members of the team who she'd been getting to know fairly well, there was love in their friendship. The only bit of awkwardness that remained was with Mel, but Carolyn understood it.

Ethan squinted into the setting sun, patiently waiting. His honest, questioning gaze seemed to see right through her barriers.

"I don't need to worry about being unclaimed when I've got the team to keep me out of trouble." He gave her a grudging smile at her show of faith after all that had happened.

It was true, though, Carolyn had changed from that girl who, only a year ago, had suffered deep paralysing fear that had made her force Note to claim her. Not only that, but she'd left Note to deal with the fall-out. She'd caused him indescribable pain, not to mention what he'd endured with Sadi binding to him. And for what? His claim had only provided an illusion of security. It hadn't stopped her from being taken. Arthur had just monitored and waited it out while Note grieved a realm away.

Ultimately, her father had proven he wasn't a monster. He'd let her go as he'd done with her mother.

"Let's get back," said Ethan at last, his eyes glinting in sudden mischief. "Don't want to miss the entertainment." At Carolyn's confused expression, he explained, "Barbecue?"

"No time to waste, then." In the spirit of mutual benefit, she added, "Let's take *your* form." Ethan couldn't hide his surprise. "You know how to…" Carolyn tapped her wrist tattoo, where Sean had applied the team's enchantments.

"Race?"

Ethan pointed to the edge of the crevasse. "It's only a couple hundred feet drop from there," he said casually.

Well, *that* was a challenge! Carolyn didn't over-think it as she pivoted slowly into position. Ethan cursed when she bolted into a run for the edge. Ooh, but it was going to be close. Her heart thudded with the adrenalin rush.

In hot pursuit, Ethan's curses faded. The mage radiated reprimand, but more importantly, she could feel he was as thrilled as she was by the delight of the chase. The earth seemed to propel her forward through her toes. Ethan's change began first, his footsteps stopping before Carolyn alighted from the edge.

Without practise, Carolyn's change wouldn't be fast, but she had faith which seemed to power extra air under her leap. Quickly overtaken by Ethan, his form streamed before her. Carolyn's stomach lurched in the free fall, but her focus sharpened and the updraft of air met with extra resistance as the clothes melted from her body.

Shifting, shortening and ultimately feathering in an all over ripple of energy, she became the seabird image of Ethan. Her companion's reproach quickly faded to approval as they soon swirled, glided and drifted in the intoxicating lift of the updrafts.

CHAPTER 38

Miranda

"**S**he is *not* to be disturbed." Sonia's soft voice had an unusual edge but Miranda knew the cause of it. Her gaze strayed to the moving door handle of her office.

Miranda's ring gave a warning pulse from her finger but she ignored it. "I'm sorry for intruding, Miss Levy." Judy had the appearance of a woman on a mission.

"She wouldn't listen—" began Sonia, looking tiny and prim beside the mage.

"That's all right," dismissed Miranda. "You may leave us." Sonia threw the mage a seething look before leaving the room. The door slammed shut, leaving the two women alone.

Miranda knew she looked like hell as Judy sauntered towards her, taking in everything.

"Medela." A ripple of violet darted out to encompass Miranda in a wash of healing magic. She curbed the need to berate the mage for being so presumptuous. The Agency head was intrigued for the cameras had revealed that Judy hadn't come alone.

Waiting outside stood Aiden Vasch, Bob Wentworth and their recent acquisition, Lena. Nobody trusted the Lilim but Judy had found a way to protect herself and the others against her persuasion. Lena had the required skills and the flexible moral compass to make for an interesting and valuable ally.

Though taking a break of sorts from her duties, Miranda had been kept informed of relevant news, notably Lena's numerous escape attempts, each one bringing her closer to her goal. It was Judy who realised that the Lilim had nowhere to go and needs to be met. A few conversations had led to a new understanding and certain concessions.

Life without Siren had been tough for Miranda and she had a few regrets. Perhaps, if they'd got rid of Croft earlier, Siren would have stayed within reach. Every effort to contact the coven had been stonewalled and Miranda suspected their involvement in her lover's disappearance.

The rage had turned to apathy.

Judy set a cup of coffee directly before her, and Miranda simply stared at it as the mage said, "Seventy percent of the company belongs to you, but *all* of it is under your control, boss. If you don't want the government faction moving in, we need to show them you're on top of your game. You've worked too hard to allow some eleventh hour take over." Judy fiddled with her weapons harness before straightening again.

Miranda smiled thinly, wondering what Judy thought she'd benefit from in their exchange. Some sort of leadership role, obviously. After having lost Siren and Loci, Miranda baulked at the prospect.

"You should start by delegating and take the supervisory role you deserve. Harris was never a serious player as an Investor and there's none of the others left. You're *it*, boss."

Judy had gained the cooperation of Lena, and their faithful guinea-pig was still alive and eager to prove his mettle. What more could Miranda lose by allowing the former enforcer the illusion of power. First, she wanted to clear up the matter of her stone recognising a similar magic.

"Where did you get the stones?"

Judy's gaze flicked to Miranda's hand, and she collapsed into the chair in front of her desk. "One stone, and it was small to begin with."

Miranda's eyes widened. She could hardly believe the mage had got a hold of a powerful magical artefact and broken it up for the team. Such an act would be completely unthinkable to any respectable mage.

"It belonged to Vasch's father," said Judy, defiance tightening her features.

Miranda immediately understood. It explained why Judy hadn't taken the gem for herself. "So where do you wear the—"

"Chips. They're inserted beneath the skin and have been configured to our commands."

Vasch's idea, no doubt. Miranda experienced a small surge of something close to pride in her little team which had been so busy while she recuperated. Bob's blood continued to yield promising results for further study, and there were other angles she could explore with a team capable of realm travel.

"Right then," said Judy, seeing the change in her. "Or should I say 'Game's afoot', or something."

Miranda bit back the suitably scathing reply on her lips. Miranda was many things, but above all else, she was a scientist. All great men and women suffered setbacks, but how many in their efforts had reached the heights Miranda had ascended? Perhaps it was time she streamlined her projects, not least of which was the matter of her abandoned O.W.E. permit holders.

Miranda had been too single minded in her pursuit of Carolyn McInally. Though the destroyer of choice, she wasn't the only one of her kind on the planet.

CHAPTER 39

Note

"**M**an, that is one scary lady," said Mel as they looked through the window at East and her guards in the castle gardens.

Note spent a good portion of every morning with East and the new makeshift parliament he'd created. His enforcer friends visited often, catching up with news. "Your dad likes *her*, I bet," Mel said snapping a length of cord against Mace, he caught it on the second pass.

Stretching out a long arm, Mace snapped it back, landing her ungracefully on the floor. Jonah's brow furrowed as Mel leapt up to berate him. The Lady East turned to look in through the window and Note felt ridiculously caught. An unwilling smile tugged the corners of his lips. He was free of his debt to her.

Note turned and perched on the end of one of the chief's giant sofas. He hadn't wanted the rooms but both Hecaton and then East had declined. East's new position in the hierarchy was meant to come without *obvious* perks. Needless to say, Hecaton had provided her with an exceptional on site suite anyway. "She already thinks I have too many dodgy contacts in the realms."

"Seems like you can't have too many of those." Mel said and Mace nudged Jonah, as though her words had been intended to include the Faery as one. He nudged ineffectually back. Mel and Jonah had become close during Note's absence, though the Faery had learned *not* to watch her every move as he had before. Then again, the illusion of distance would be more likely to attract the contrary beauty.

She sidled towards Note, coyly. "It's part of what makes you so special, my liege." Giggling, Mel flicked the tasselled end of the curtain cord at him.

It was always easier just to let her continue; she'd get bored and stop harassing them eventually. "I still can't get over you being the chief, Note."

True to his prediction, she wrapped up the tether and fixed it around the tie back handle for the window curtains.

"Me neither." Note's gaze slid down to the tattoo on his arm. "You know I can feel when any of you answer a call." He could actually sense a lot more than that. Mace's sharp look made him grimace.

"It's been intense at times with everyone together … without you."

"I can imagine," returned Note. That was part of the problem. He could visualise so much happening with the team – Carolyn in particular – that it didn't help him sleep at night.

"When is one of you going to swallow your pride, or deal with whatever is keeping you two apart."

"Hey, Mace," snapped Mel. "You're not being reasonable. It's complicated."

"Always is," injected Jonah with a tartness that didn't surprise.

"I am a bit sick of watching Ethan think he's got a chance." Mel watched Note as though his face would answer for him.

"No. He knows that Carolyn needs her space," said Mace definitively.

"That's exactly what I'm trying to give her." A little of Note's frustration seeped through and he ignored the sympathetic looks from his friends. "It's just that this job, the setting up of the new regime, is making that part easier."

"Is it?" said Jonah, curiosity making his large eyes extra reflective. "If you two have … sparks, they shouldn't be ignored." His gaze darted briefly to Mel. "Sparks are important."

"Okay," Mel shrugged in practised indifference. "Sparks aside, if you don't tell her you're still in love with her then maybe someone else should."

"She knows it, Mel."

"Then what's stopping her." Note couldn't hope to explain it to Mel. She didn't hide from herself the way others did. For better or worse, everything was laid out clearly, and at that moment, Note envied her directness.

"We both have responsibilities and she is taking her calling very seriously I hear."

"Ah, yes. Sean and Ethan have been great with her." Note's jaw clenched involuntarily. "I don't know how she's managed it," continued Jonah, oblivious to the Kistatus's discomfort. "She's not replaced you and there's no sign of her going feral."

Note's pride in Carolyn was tainted by the unreasonable hurt he felt. She could do her job perfectly well without an anchor or a mate – without *him*?

"At least nobody's caught her leaving *Ethan's* room in the morning." Mel could always lower the tone, thought Note, despairingly. Her eyebrows waggled suggestively as he covered his face. Some enforcers couldn't be trusted to keep their mouths shut. At one time, Carolyn had needed him physically close at all times, though not quite in the way Mel suggested. Note ignored Jonah's sudden interest in the conversation.

"I'll tell you exactly what you're going to do," said Mel, her eyes flashing with an idea. Note groaned inwardly. "You're just about done with the changes to Skean rule." She stepped over to the fireside and examined an ornate shisha pipe in the hearth. "Do you?" Note shook his head, it had been one of the chief's things he'd kept unchanged.

It seemed Mel had lost her place in regard to what she thought he should do. He didn't quite know how to feel about that. Mel could be flaky but she'd always tried to look out for his best interests.

"It's empty, Note. What usually goes into it?" Mel unravelled the hose and fixed the mouthpiece on its stand. "You've got people who would set it up for you." She sounded quite envious but there was no point in telling her that he avoided using the servers as much as possible. Mel slid a few pieces of charcoal onto her palm, and Jonah huffed.

"He's not going to fill it just so you can play with it." Usually, it was Jonah getting into trouble for his inquisitiveness.

"Besides," moderated Mace when he saw Mel's annoyance with the Faery. "The chief's blend will likely be potent."

"It was here when I moved in," explained Note, taking the charcoal from Mel and replacing the pieces in their box.

Mel wiped her hands on her trousers, a look of fresh disgust on her pretty features. "Ew, it'll have dead guy's germs!"

Note pulled a face. "He wasn't dead when he used it."

Mace chuckled and Jonah simply looked perplexed. Note often missed the weirdly comforting "dysfunctional family" antics of the group. "Right — fine," said Mel. "So now we know you're not spacing out under the weight of your responsibilities, what's stopping you from working with us when you've got nothing else to do here?"

It was a good question. He *had* considered the possibility, and with Hecaton keeping an eye on Edward and working with East, real changes had been felt already across the realm. Edward had even sworn allegiance under Note and the temporary parliament. Note's position would eventually be advisory, which was ridiculous, as he knew so little about running the realm. It was, however, the only way he could abdicate from full responsibility. Carolyn's brother still harboured a grudge but Hecaton's apprentice had been helpful in dealing with Edward.

Note's heart was split. He was privy to every tug, twitch and alteration that occurred with the team and his link to them. He had felt the inclusion of Ethan, Mario and Carolyn in his absence. Rake and Sam had followed suit by pledging to the group. They numbered ten plus one, with Jonah maintaining his provisional partnership.

Having never officially left the Protectorate, he suspected that Hecaton wouldn't complain as long as he saw to Skean matters first. When Carolyn was ready, he intended to discuss some sort of proposal.

Note felt the usual pangs of loss when the visitors prepared to leave. He wasn't sure Mel was even aware that she held Jonah's hand whilst urging Note to join them for dinner.

How long could he keep away from Carolyn without completely cracking up? Everything he'd heard suggested she still cared for him and that she hadn't been tempted away by Ethan. What if he too was giving her time to adapt before making a move? Lucas's pipe was starting to look good to Note in his current mood. The gateway had only just closed when he felt it open up again behind him.

"What did you forget?" His smile was automatic when he turned, expecting to see Mel or Mace. He blinked several times, as if the portal had somehow reached into his mind to play a cruel trick on him. Carolyn's expression was unreadable as she stood before the fiery portal.

"Your eyes look weird," she said slowly.

"I can change them," he muttered, but Carolyn looked away as they flashed to the gold she'd always known him by.

"Don't do that for me. I know how long I've been gone and everything you've been through." She moved around the edge of the room. Graceful and beautiful as ever, his eyes followed, hungrily drinking in every detail. Without his enhanced senses, he'd be struggling to catch her words. "I haven't been avoiding you... Well, that's a lie. I have, but not for the reasons you think."

"You know how I think," he said stupidly.

"I should." Note hadn't realised the sheer size of the room before, not until now as she kept evading him. Why was she behaving this way? Carolyn paused at the shisha on the hearth.

"I've not taken up the habit." He failed to make her smile. A crease formed on her brow and she rubbed absently at it.

"Do you know that I ask the others for every little detail when they come back from seeing you?" She caught his gaze at last and held it. "I realised I was being an idiot."

Never, thought Note as she paced to the window, distancing herself even further. He couldn't seem to move, or think properly as her sweet perfume teased at the edges of his senses.

"So much has happened, Note. We've been trying to chip away at the Agency. Levy's livid at losing Siren, Ella and the Veloces Loci. Turns out he's a gateway sanctioned demon, which is weird as the Agency created him. The US team have requested that he join them."

"That's good news," murmured Note, a new anxiety taking a hold of him. He had thought her arrival meant she'd made her decision, *choosing* him. Why wasn't she in his arms?

"Mum and the kids are doing great." Carolyn's face smoothed in an instant of utter peace and Note cursed his thoughtlessness. Her mission to save her family was finally complete … as much as it could be without Edward. Lucas's death had ended Amanda's suffering. "Did you know she was never claimed by my father?" Note's eyes widened in surprise. He understood the levels of control needed for that. Was that why Arthur had wanted to see him before Carolyn came home – to assess his intentions, or for more sinister reasons?

Carolyn shook her head thoughtfully before brightening again. "There's this lovely little safe house in West Kilbride run by a Siren who seems to get on really well with Sean. It's a pity she likes girls, because I think they'd be a match in every other way."

Note's lips lifted slightly. Carolyn was adorable when she rambled. He had never wanted to take her in his arms so badly, but the visit was clearly difficult for her, not made any the easier by the barriers she'd put up. He focussed on the sound of her voice as it wrapped around him. It was sweet torture to have her so close.

"Oh, and you need to see Sam. He came on a call with us a few days ago and stepped back to Earth looking like a male model from the eighties." She continued to pace, stopping only to pick up and examine some of the former chief's articles. He sensed no real interest; she was only busying her hands. Note hadn't moved his own things into the suite – couldn't make up his mind if he needed them here. With Carolyn, there was no such dilemma. He was starved of the sight of her.

"I'm going to Empustat this weekend, and I thought that maybe, if you didn't have anything better to do, you could come with me."

"Arthur still wants to see me?" Note would eagerly have attended but for Mario having talked him into the Skean job on Sean's behalf, the rest being history. If Note was a suspicious man, he could have made something out of Mario's request, but such things were fated. Seeing his hesitancy, Carolyn scolded him with a look.

"Don't be like that," he soothed. "It's just that I haven't seen you for such a long time and now you act as if you'd rather be anywhere else than here with me."

"Oh, Note. That's totally not true." She made as if to step towards him but he saw her check herself.

"Arthur's not a modern man," he said, wondering if he'd guessed the reason for her concern. "I'm thinking he'd want to kill me or have our intentions properly outlined."

Her eyes sparked in outrage. "Killing you is off limits," she declared. Then: "Our intentions?" and her lovely brow furrowed in confusion. Surely she knew Arthur would see him as a threat.

Note felt foolish as realisation dawned. "You mean to introduce me as a friend?"

She inhaled sharply and looked up at him, the tiniest trace of a smile on her lips. "You *are* a friend, Note, but yes, I see what you mean." She swayed lightly on her feet, her eyes still not meeting his directly.

"I could tell him that I love you, and I'd follow you to the ends of the earth and beyond." Her manner was light and Note's lips twitched in response. "But that's very dramatic, and you already did that for me." Carolyn seemed to force herself to move a few steps closer.

Had she really said she loved him? He felt almost dizzy with relief but still too much space existed between them. *The weight of unsaid truths?*

The blue of her eyes had turned deep, gleaming in the dim light.

"I could explain that I can't imagine life without you, but again, that would be a lie. I *have* lived my life far apart from you … long enough to make very bad decisions."

Note opened his mouth to speak but Carolyn raised a hand to stall him. "I've learned sufficient to know that I can let you go if that's what you want."

How had she come to the conclusion that he wanted to be free of her? "But you need to know that I love you, and that it's not all about forces conspiring to put us together." Her voice cracked a little and Note could stand it no longer. He stepped towards her, words of comfort brimming at his lips.

"No!" He felt the force of it as a physical blow before it softened. "Shush, now. There's more you need to know. Although I'm not proud of myself, here it is." Note stood transfixed. It was *he* who needed to confess, although her next words stole the breath from his body. "I kissed Ethan in Empustat…"

What? He'd allowed hope to bloom without even realising it. Why would his friends lie? Carolyn looked miserable as she continued, "I can't say it meant nothing because at the time it did."

Conflicting emotions washed over him as he tried to make sense of it. He had known there was something between the pair, and with Hecaton's involvement, how could Note deny the enforcer his chance.

Was any of it important? His eyes burned to copper as he watched her struggle with her thoughts.

"It is over," Carolyn said earnestly. "I don't expect you to fall into my arms or anything like that. You need to know that nothing can compare with what I feel for you. If you're not able to get over that, I will understand, but I wanted to be totally honest with you." Her eyes begged for understanding and Note simply couldn't respond. "I don't want to make excuses for what I did, but at that time I think I needed to have some *reminder* of the connection, and I'm ashamed to admit I used Ethan for that." She averted her gaze. "He knows we're never going to be together."

"You don't think you'll need to be reminded again?" Note said, but could've ripped out his tongue when her pale face contorted with pain.

Her laugh was self-derisory. "You *know* I'm not like you. I was scared of what we had ... so scared. Even now, I remember the effects of the anchoring and the claiming and it gives me chills, but I'm not in their thrall any more. What I feel now is real, and it's even worse in a way because I can't *blame* anything for it. No, actually, Note, I blame you for just being you." Note's lips twisted. It wasn't good that she thought badly of herself, and he had only reinforced those feelings.

"You're not the chief by accident," she now said passionately. "You are the type of person who others aspire to be ... but me?" she scoffed lightly. "I like to take the easiest route to everything and I'm ... I'm humbled by you. You literally lit up my life, and I did all that I could to erase that. I don't need Mel or anyone to tell me I don't deserve you – I *know* it. But my life needs *you* in it – in any capacity you can manage. I'm not going to ask for your ... everything – I haven't earned it."

During her speech she'd glided to be directly before him, and he knew that nothing but the love she'd confessed really mattered. He could see his reflection in the depths of her eyes, see his own coppery irises, inhuman and gleaming in the fading light. Her lashes dropped and Note's gaze drifted along the curves and hollows of her face. She appeared very calm, but the pulse fluttering beneath the skin of her neck betrayed her.

"Look here," she said, and Note's throat tightened as she again tried to lighten the mood, "I can be close to you like this without adverse effects from anchor or claim." Her head bent slightly, her eyes seeming to focus on his jaw. "In other words, I don't feel the raging need to tear your clothes off." His blond brows rose at that, and she groaned. "Okay, you got me, Note. I do. But it's not tearing me up like it did with the claiming. You feel that too?"

She drew her hands up to either side of his head, their gazes locked, and he couldn't begin to describe the emotions he saw reflected in the depths of her eyes. This glorious girl had told him *everything*, and he loved her all the more for it.

It was time for him to repay the favour. "You say you're not good enough," he whispered, "but nothing could be further from the truth." Her eyes closed, and he saw that her lashes glistened with unshed tears. He couldn't help but draw his mouth across them. She trembled, and he felt her fingers curl into his hair. "Sadi died while I was keeping her for you."

"I heard what happened, Note. There was nothing you could have done." He saw clearly that she blamed herself for losing Sadi, but Arthur would have been no more likely than Hecaton to suffer the thing to live.

Note steeled himself for the next:

"The anchoring was split by Hecaton," he said, and her eyes snapped open, rounded in horror. "You could have been *meant* for Ethan." He forced the words out, despairing of what it would mean. If she wanted to blame her kissing of Ethan on something, then *that* was a perfectly viable option. Note didn't have any reasonable excuses for his failures. He took her hands, drawing them between their now closer bodies.

Had her confession brought her the same wretched relief he now experienced? "If you choose him—"

Her eyes flashed in determination. "It doesn't matter, I've already—"

"I can't ever be just a friend," and he pressed his forehead against hers, feeling it as almost more intimate than a kiss. He needed to be totally clear with her. "There's no-one else for me, Carolyn. You are the centre of my universe, and there's nothing — not love of my people, my realm ... not *anything* that comes close to how I feel about you."

"Oh, Note! That's the most insane and beautiful thing I've ever heard." Her lips brushed against his with the lightest touch he could ever have imagined. His senses scattered as her breath fanned his lips and her hands slid from his face and up inside his shirt, leaving a fiery trail of sensation. Gently, ever so gently, she trailed her fingers over his lean muscles and around to his back. He groaned and drew her tightly to him.

His face was in her hair, and he was surrounded by her fragrance. The primitive urge to claim rose but then settled as he willed it. Note would do nothing to influence them beyond what their hearts dictated. He drew back enough to look into eyes that had darkened with desire, but there was something else in those windows to her soul, something perfect and faultless.

He captured her hands as they slid towards his stomach. Some things never changed, he realised.

His tattoo now hummed with outside interference.

"It's just Sean checking up on us," she said lightly.

All's well. Thanks, Sean. Note was keen to dismiss him.

Wow, this works great through the realms – Morgan?

Note shut the connection down with a quick apology.

"I know you're busy with being a chief," said Carolyn, now thoughtful, "but I don't suppose you'd like to—"

Her mouth dropped open in a surprised "Oh" as he covered her lips with his in a short, hard kiss that left her not only breathless but promised of so much more to come. He flicked his fingers into the air, sketching the runes he'd memorised.

"Do you trust me?" he said.

"You never need to ask." Her fingers rose to her lips, and he felt the brand of their new unwritten pact.

He took her hand and kissed it as they stood before the newly opened gateway. Their fingers entwined, and he wondered if she saw the simple connection as he did: a symbol of their unity with the potential to thrive and survive without either losing any part of themselves. Together, they reached their free hands into the liquid heat of the new gateway.

The air was cold where they landed, and Carolyn's first breath was accompanied by a small noise of pure delight. "You brought me to my beach?" Beneath the glow of a half moon, the constellation of Orion straining above, she *was* once again the feral beauty that had changed his life for ever. Their lives held no guarantees, each carrying responsibilities that would test them, but together there was nothing they couldn't face. Fated or not, supported or not, they were a force with which to be reckoned.

The beach itself was wilder than during her previous visits. It seemed fitting somehow. The dimly lit promenade stretched into the distance at their backs, the dark sand and rocks leading out to the expanse of sea before them. She needed no encouragement when Note moved towards it. Soon out in front, she laughed with carefree abandon. The warmth from their bodies rose and merged together to counter the expected chill of the water ahead. They barely slowed for the rocks and then, quite abruptly, there was nothing before them but the drop to the churning waters. Note could feel the force of her love, as wild and pure as the crashing waves.

I choose you, Note! and the Kistatus felt as though his heart would explode when she wrapped herself around him, when they leaped together into the first adventure of the rest of their lives.

The end.

ABOUT THE AUTHOR

Louise White has had a variety of jobs, including waitress, library assistant, nurse, and police officer. She holds a BSc in Health Studies and a Post-graduate certificate in primary and religious education. She currently resides on the scenic west coast of Scotland with her family.

Louise's assorted life experiences were not strictly by design. Fortunate enough to come across some of the most amazing real-life characters, there's been good, bad, and downright ugly at times. She has been passionate about all the jobs she has taken, soaking in the experiences, and blanking out the worst ones for the good of her mental health. But they are all there, happily bubbling, or festering away, to be recalled when she needs them.

Louise didn't set out to write fantasy, but when she began writing it became apparent that she still believed in the bogeyman, the monster in the cupboard, and, of course, the fairies at the bottom of her garden. Suddenly, she found that she was writing stories of perhaps less than willing but more than able heroes who could be found both on our doorsteps and in the realms that lie beyond

A PERSONAL NOTE FROM LOUISE

A huge thanks to all you amazing and supportive readers who have followed the series. As a new author, I was terrified about sharing my work with the world but your reviews have sustained me. I have laughed and cried at the things you say, always grateful for the feedback.
I hope that you enjoyed reading and unravelling the mysteries of Carolyn's world as much as I enjoyed creating it. If you enjoyed this book, please leave feedback at your retailer or goodreads.

Please find me at:
www.louisewhitebooks.com
https://twitter.com/LGWhiteAuthor
www.facebook.com/louisewhitethecalling

I love connecting with readers to discuss my books – and others!
https://www.goodreads.com/author/show/7438156.Louise_G_White

GLOSSARY

Agency: A government organisation that is served by scientists (white-coats) and agents (suits).

Anchor: An individual with whom the destroyer* bonds.

Anthemusa: Siren* realm.

Arranan: Faery* realm.

Breeder: A rare magical female (demon*) who is able to produce enhanced offspring with the demon Chief* or the High mage* after Claiming*.

Chief: A long-lived leader of the demon* race.

Claiming: The process by which a breeder* is bound to a particular Chief* or High mage*.

Demon/Otherworlder*: Beings of otherworldly origin.

Demon mark: A symbol on the flesh that indicates a favour owed by or to a demon*.

Demon realms: The territories that are accessed through the gateways*.

Destroyer: A magical being who is empowered with varying abilities to fight evildoers through the demon realms*.

Empustat: The demon realm* of Lilim* and Lolilim*.

Enforcer: A member of a Protectorate* team.

Faery: A human-sized winged demon*.

Gateway: Any opening, usually occurring within a 3-mile radius of Gateway focus*, which allows controlled access to and from demon realms*.

Gateway focus: The central point of the area where gateways* may be accessed between the realms. Access may only be gained by High magic users, Protectorate* teams (including the destroyer*), and by technological means that have been patented by the Agency*.

High mage: A long-lived and powerful mage* who is ordinarily associated with demon Chiefs*.

Kistatus: A race of snake-demons* from the realm of Skean*.

Lilim: A magical race of soul-surfing demons*.

Lustro: Fire demon*.

Lolilim: A lower class of Lilim* without any magical powers.

Mage: A magic user. A mage may be "born" or "gateway created" for the Protectorate*.

Motus: A human-like demon* with the ability to manipulate emotion.

Mow: One of the race of jelly-like demons* who work under Mow of Mow Chief*.

Mow Chief: The demon Chief* of the Mow* race.

O.W.E. Permit: Otherworldly Work Experience certificate. (Term: One year)

Peruro: Demon realm* of Lustro*.

Precator: A member of the Protectorate* council.

Protector: A powerful individual under whom the Protectorate* operate.

Protectorate: The organisation that facilitates the function of enforcers*, including the destroyer* and mages*, in organised pockets throughout the world.

Rakshasas: A demon-goblin warrior race.

Rask: The demon realm* of Rakshasas*.

Sedert: The demon realm* of Mow*.

Seer: Psychic

Shadow: A demon* with the ability to become shadow.

Siren: A human-like demon* to whom individuals are irresistibly drawn.

Skean: The demon realm* of the Kistatus*.

Transfigure: The ability of a mage* to change into another "typically animal" form.

Veloces: A quick-witted demon* with skills of speed and strength.

ACKNOWLEDGEMENTS

As always, my heartfelt thanks and appreciation to all my readers. Your comments and reviews inspire me to work ever harder in the creation of my stories. Special thanks are due to the exceptional Clive Johnson of Daisy Bank Editing Services, and to Clarissa Yeo of Yocla designs for another amazing cover image. For my wonderful family – To Lorna, first reader and fan of the series, your support has been invaluable. Thanks to Michael for keeping me grounded and very special thanks to Matthew, Meredith, Nathan and Adam for being such wonderful inspiration.

Again, thanks to my dear mother and father who taught me to follow my dreams – where practical – and showed me that love is the strongest force on all the worlds.

Love to you all!

ALSO BY THIS AUTHOR

The Calling
(Gateway Series: Book 1)
Louise G. White

Chasing The Demon
(Gateway Series: Book Two)
Louise G. White
Find out more and sign up for updates at
www.louisewhitebooks.com

Made in the USA
Charleston, SC
10 March 2017